PRAISE FOR **THE COST OF CRUDE**

"An original and compelling read from beginning to end…Goss clearly demonstrates her master of the mystery/suspense genre and is very highly recommended..." —*Midwest Book Review*

"*The Cost of Crude* is a work of fiction--a modern-day murder mystery, set against the backdrop of a two large-scale oil companies dueling for maximum profits. It is a page-turning thriller that continuously challenges the reader's assumptions about what will happen next." —*The Portsmouth Review*

"The plot is well-developed and the reader is swiftly thrown into action from the very first page. .. *The Cost of Crude* is also filled with political intrigue…" —*Readers Favorite Reviewer*

"Page turning, seat gripping suspense"—*Undercover Book Reviews*

"A slick and well-crafted petro-thriller...Goss delivers a tightly written narrative with smartly rendered back drops from the start, where action comes quick and intrigue is sure to keep the pages turning." —*Book Viral*

"*The Cost of Crude* is a hard-to-put-down thriller. It won me over quickly, and every one of the many sticky situations Gwynn Reznick gets into has me reading as fast as I can to see if she can win free." —*Book Ideas*

The Cost of Crude

A Gwynn Reznick Mystery

Inge-Lise Goss

Olivebranch Press

Copyright © 2014 Inge-Lise Goss

Olivebranch Press

ISBN-10: 0-6923060-2-1
ISBN-13: 978-0-6923060-2-4

DEDICATION

To my brother, Arly, who died too young as a result of the Vietnam War, but he'll never be forgotten.

ACKNOWLEDGMENTS

My gratitude goes out to all the people who taught me so much about the oil and gas industry while I worked as an auditor. That knowledge laid the ground work for this novel. My deep appreciation goes to Julian Seymour whose comments and suggestions helped me improve the story. I am also grateful to the Las Vegas Writers' Group and the Borders Writers' Group for their critiques. In addition I want to thank Nicole Varela and my husband, Peter, who managed to read every word of very rough drafts. Without my husband's continued words of encouragement, my writing never would have come to fruition. I owe additional thanks to Lisa Binion and Nancy Buford for editing the novel.

PROLOGUE

"You won't get off this platform!" Kirk yelled as his attackers dragged him by his feet across the rough steel mat. The ridges dug into his flesh.

"You are wrong, sir; we will," the attacker replied in a heavy Slavic accent.

Kirk breathed heavily, almost heaving. Searing pain rippled through his torso from the blows he had endured. He felt blood gushing from his nose. He tried to raise his arms in protest but couldn't summon the strength.

"What's going on out here?" a male voice asked.

Something struck Kirk in the head. Everything went black.

Twenty minutes later, Kirk groaned, opening his swollen eyes. Through foggy vision he saw a gray tarp covering his body. He felt its coarseness against the bruised skin on his face as he turned, gasping for air.

"They don't want us to do anything about him?" he heard his Slavic attacker say. The scarred-faced man Kirk feared the most. He gave the orders. He delivered the first blow.

Kirk assumed they were talking about him. He briefly closed his eyes just as a sharp pain erupted in his leg. He clamped his teeth together in a determined effort not to make a sound.

"No," another male voice replied. "He'll leave the oil platform tomorrow. He knows what will happen if he says anything. Luke's been embedded with the workers for over a week. He'll let us know if the man talks."

"Why take that risk?" the Slavic attacker replied.

"They don't want any more casualties on the platform or at any work sites. It might draw too much attention. And the guy doesn't know what we accomplished here."

Chills swept up Kirk's spine as he realized they weren't talking about him. With all the strength he could muster, Kirk pulled the edge of the tarp away from his eyes. His heart hammered against his ribs. Every beat sent surging pain through his chest.

"Be still," whispered another man, dangerously close.

Kirk saw a dark silhouette lurking amongst the shadows. He wondered if the man came to help him or if he was another enemy. Fearful, Kirk remained silent while he waited for the man to reveal himself. He heard heavy footsteps pounding toward him from another direction. Kirk swallowed hard and his hands trembled. The dark figure lingered in the shadows, immobile.

The tarp flew from his body, yanked off by two of his attackers. Kirk's hopes of surviving vanished as they grabbed his arms.

"It's time," the Slavic attacker said.

Kirk was thrown over the side. He took a deep breath, held it, and felt the cold water splash around him. Sinking into what seemed like the depths of hell, he raised his head and forced his legs to kick. Spasms shot through his bruised muscles. His throat burned. Slowly, he rose to the surface. He inhaled, savoring the fresh air. Kirk attempted to swim to the platform. His damaged limbs were no match to the rough waves engulfing his body, sucking him under. The last bubble escaped from his lungs. He belonged to the sea.

CHAPTER 1

When the glare of Houston's morning sun hit Julie's windshield, she flinched and blindly lowered the visor. She breathed deeply to relax her nerves, blinked to clear her sight, and felt her stomach churning. This would be the first time she had ever showed up at work so early. It would also be the first time she had spied. Her oversized purse held the necessary equipment: three microphone bugs and one receiver, borrowed from a friend.

Today, John McIntyre, Wilton Oil's CEO, was having a meeting with some executives from CT Oil and Gas Company, Wilton's chief rival. Julie only knew about it because she was covering for Pam, McIntyre's secretary. She had asked her boss, Steve Hadley, vice president of Public Affairs, what the meeting was about. He didn't have a clue, and he was visibly irritated since he hadn't been invited. That was when she thought it might be the beginning of merger talks. There had been several in the oil industry recently and Wilton's stockholders were up in arms over the meager size of last year's dividends and demanding changes. Julie also suspected there was something unusual about this meeting since McIntyre didn't want it documented.

She knew merger talks started behind closed doors with only the key players in attendance, and only those in attendance knew what was discussed. Julie had been through a particularly brutal one at her last job that dragged on for over a year. Every day people wondered who was going to get the axe next. Some of her friends were laid off. A few lost their homes. Her boss had a heart attack and died. One guy committed suicide. No one talked about anything else. In the end, the company moved its headquarters to Denver, and she found herself unemployed. She never wanted to go through that again.

****

Stepping out of the elevator, she ran into Neil, a six-foot-six, brawny security guard in his mid-thirties.

"What are you doing here this early?" he asked as he quickly scanned her — twenty-nine, five-foot-eight, a slender, curvy body, big pale blue eyes, rosy cheeks, full lips, and wavy blonde hair that flowed down over her shoulders. He thought about her often and wished she'd dump her boyfriend.

"McIntyre's having a meeting this morning, and I just wanted to make sure everything was set up." She smiled at him. Then she felt uneasy when she noticed his eyebrows slant, giving her a suspicious look.

"Pam's not coming in today?"

"No. She's dealing with a family problem."

"So you'll be up here all day?"

"Yes," she said, walking away. She glanced over her shoulder and saw Neil still standing in the middle of the aisle, watching her.

Reaching Pam's desk, Julie's eyes darted around searching for other employees. She didn't spot anyone. Feeling a queasy sensation in the pit of her stomach, she took the bugs out of her purse. She held them securely hidden in her hands, tucked a steno pad under her arm, and then proceeded to the conference room. A large oak, oval-shaped table stood in the center surrounded by fourteen office chairs. On one side of the room was a long counter with cabinets above and below it. Colorful maps of oil fields hung on the other walls.

After Julie had two bugs in place, she began attaching the third. It slid out of her palm, tumbled to the floor, and rolled under the table. Pushing a chair out of her way, she heard heavy footsteps behind her.

"Is something wrong with the chair?" McIntyre asked. He was a tall, handsome man in his early forties, who appeared to be in great shape, with chestnut brown hair, graying at the temples. He had been married four times with the last marriage ending a few months prior.

Several of the secretaries had joked about wanting to be wife number five.

Julie flinched, eased down into the chair, and hid the bug under her foot. "No, Mr. McIntyre," she said, pushing the words out past the lump in her throat. "It just seemed a little stiff so I wanted to make sure the rollers worked."

McIntyre glimpsed at the steno pad lying in front of her. "Julie, I've already told you that you won't be taking minutes during the meeting."

She swallowed hard. "I know. I just want to make sure everything is set up okay." As she rose to her feet, she carefully kicked the bug away from his line of vision, and inched the chair snuggly against the table, covering the small device. She straightened pens, pencils, and miscellaneous items on the counter, trying to look busy while she watched him out of the corner of her eye. He paced around the room, stopped at the head of the table, and tapped his fingers on the back of the armchair. McIntyre had a sophisticated, polished demeanor and seldom showed any emotion, but today he seemed nervous. This further convinced Julie that it was not going to be a normal business meeting.

"Is there anything you would like me to prepare for the meeting?" she asked.

"No. I have everything."

A middle-aged woman wearing a white cafeteria uniform entered pushing a cart containing refreshments—breakfast rolls, juice, and coffee. McIntyre turned on his heels and headed out the door while the woman arranged the refreshments on the counter.

Julie lifted up the steno pad and dropped it on the floor, making sure it landed at the base of the chair concealing the bug. She stooped down to retrieve it, quickly attached the bug to the table's metal support, and stood up with her pad in her hand. Her muscles tightened and her heart beat rapidly as she brushed her hair away from her forehead. "Can I help you with anything?" she asked the woman, trying to appear calm.

"No, thank you. I'm almost finished."

Julie hurried to Pam's desk as her eyes swept over the area looking for McIntyre. Sinking down into the chair, she sighed when she didn't see him and noticed his door was closed. She plugged her earbuds into the receiver hidden in her purse. She also planned to record the meeting in case she needed to answer the phone or step away from the desk. Julie lightly swung her foot back and forth and squirmed in her seat as she checked her emails and waited for the meeting to begin.

Within a few minutes, Wilton's senior vice president Kent Fardown, a short, frail man in his early fifties, walked toward the conference room with three men. Julie assumed they were CT Oil executives and scrutinized their appearance. All three men looked to be in their forties. She knew from an article she had read that the CEO of CT Oil was in his sixties. He wasn't one of them. Two of the men were tall with slender builds; one had a dark complexion. She thought he could be of Middle Eastern descent. The third man was short and stocky. He appeared to be the oldest and, of the three, had the most pleasant expression on his face. Fardown smiled at her as he passed, talking to the men.

She turned toward the conference room. Her eyes remained fixed on the door until it closed. Of the seven in the room, only two were executives from Wilton: McIntyre and Fardown. McIntyre had entered with two men. One was Ethan Lemus, a tall, lean, former Wilton employee in his early sixties with recessed silver-gray hair. Julie wondered if he now worked for CT as she recalled seeing him having a heated discussion with Hadley, her boss, right before he left Wilton. The other man she didn't recognize. He was in his early forties and had a brawny, muscular build.

Julie began to listen. No introductions were made. She still managed to pick up four names — Abir, Ramza, Michael, and Luke. The phone rang, startling her. From the caller ID she knew it was her best friend, Gwynn, who worked in accounting. Julie didn't want to take out her earbuds, yet she had no choice.

"Hi, Gwynn. I'm pretty busy; can I talk to you later?"

"I'll make it quick. Did Taylor call or send you any emails over the weekend?"

"No. Why?"

"Cindy's been making the rounds. She wants to know if anyone heard from him. She just left my cubicle and asked me to call you."

"Why didn't she call me?"

"Her boss is giving her the evil eye because she's been chatting ever since she got to work. Anyway, Taylor never talked to her after he got fired. He didn't talk to any of us. She went to his apartment, and he's moved out. She thought he might have gone to his mom's, but he didn't. She's worried about him."

Julie felt anxious to listen to the meeting, but Taylor and Cindy were among her close friends. "That doesn't make sense. Cindy and Taylor were inseparable. He wouldn't just up and leave without saying anything to her. Did they have a fight?"

"She says they didn't. I'm starting to wonder," Gwynn said. "She received a package from him. It didn't have a personal note or anything like that in it."

"What was in it?"

"She didn't want to talk about it at work. She'll tell us tonight. You're still planning on going to Brody's after work, aren't you?"

"I'll be there."

"Good. I'm curious about the package and can't understand why no one has heard from Taylor."

Julie's eyes dropped to the desk. She stared at the earbuds, itching to slip them back on and find out about the meeting behind the closed door.

"Julie, you still there?"

"Yeah. I just have a lot of work to do." A red button flashed on the phone base unit as it rang. "I need to answer McIntyre's phone. See you after work." She disconnected, and then pushed the flashing button. "Mr. McIntyre's office. May I help you?"

After taking two phone messages, Julie stuck in her earbuds. Her eyes opened wider, her hands trembled as she listened. Frightened and confused at what she heard, she removed the earpieces and tucked them into her purse. She wished they had been discussing a merger; *that* she could handle.

"Are you okay?" Pam asked, standing next to the desk.

Julie jumped. She hadn't even noticed her approaching. "Oh … ah … I'm fine," she stuttered. "I was told you weren't coming in today."

"I had planned to stay longer in San Diego, but I thought John might need me. Is he still in the meeting?"

Julie nodded, "Yes."

"Since you're not taking minutes, John must be recording it."

Julie cleared her throat. "He told me he wasn't going to record it."

Pam pressed her lips together while she briefly glanced at the conference room door. "He's probably taking notes and planning to dictate them to me later. John wants minutes of all his meetings."

Not this one, Julie thought as she grabbed her purse, stood up, and tried to focus on the phone messages. She handed them to Pam. "Neither one left a number. They both said Mr. McIntyre already had them. I still wrote down the numbers on the caller ID."

Pam glanced at the messages. "John has their numbers. Thanks for helping out."

Holding tightly onto her purse, Julie headed to the elevator as she wondered how she could retrieve the bugs from the conference room with Pam sitting that close to the door. She couldn't watch for Pam to leave since her boss's office was on the floor below McIntyre's.

Settling into her chair, she inhaled deeply and clutched her hands together on her lap, hoping to stop them from trembling. When she felt her fingers relaxing, she pulled the receiver out of her purse, and slipped it in a drawer. Now she understood why McIntyre hadn't invited Hadley to the meeting. Every time there was a public outcry over something Wilton Oil had done, Hadley took care of the problem. McIntyre would profess he didn't know anything about it — he was always innocent. Hadley was known in the industry as the miracle man. It didn't matter how bad the problem; Wilton Oil always came through unscathed.

"I thought you were going to be at Pam's desk all day," Hadley said, stepping out of his office.

"She showed up," Julie replied.

"Did you find out what the meeting was about?"

"No. All I did was sit at Pam's desk. Mr. McIntyre didn't have me take minutes or do any work for him." Julie wanted to tell Hadley the truth about the meeting, but she wasn't ready to confess how she knew. Also, she wanted to hear the recording from the beginning in case she had misinterpreted something.

"So, you've had an easy morning," he smiled. "I'll have to make up for that." He dumped a huge stack of paperwork on her desk.

Later, when Hadley went to lunch, Julie connected the receiver to her computer and recorded the audio through line-in to a disk, and then she erased the meeting from the receiver. She planned to return the equipment to Barb, her friend, that evening. She put the disk in an envelope and mailed it to herself. That was the only way she was sure it would leave the building since Wilton had beefed up their security. The security guards did spot checks of employees' briefcases, purses, computer bags, and every container entering and leaving the building. Her purse had only been checked once, but she didn't want to take a chance. If the guards decided to look through it, they'd find the receiver and bugs. She'd tell them the truth — she was returning the stuff to a friend. If they turned on the receiver, they'd only hear the sound in the lobby being picked up by the bugs.

After she had listened to the disk and verified she hadn't misinterpreted anything, she planned to share it with Hadley and telling him how she managed to record the meeting. Even if that meant she'd be fired, she wanted to expose McIntyre, the "innocent."

She ate a stale, bland sandwich from the vending machine while she worked on Hadley's projects and felt grateful she'd be busy all afternoon as she waited to retrieve the bugs.

"Julie," Hadley said as he was ready to leave the office, "you don't need to finish everything today."

She glanced at her watch. It was past 5:30. "I just want to finish this letter."

"Okay, see you tomorrow," he said, strolling away.

When he was out of sight, she cleared off her desk, and hoped it was safe to go back up to the conference room. She figured that Gwynn was already at Brody's waiting for her. She called and said she'd be there soon.

After Julie stepped out of the elevator on the fortieth floor, she didn't see any employees as she walked toward the conference room. She noticed Pam's desk was cleared off and assumed she had gone for the day. McIntyre's office door was closed. It was like that most of time when he was at work, so she wasn't sure if he had left. The lights automatically went on when she entered the conference room. She recouped the bug hidden under the table. Then panic struck when she discovered the other two were missing.

"Is this what you're looking for?" she heard a man's deep, gruff voice behind her. She turned around and saw the dark, icy eyes of the brawny, muscular man McIntyre had escorted into the meeting. He glared at her as he held up the microphones. She clutched the third bug in her palm and stood frozen while he moved toward her, sending a shiver up her spine.

"Open your hand," he ordered. Julie kept her fist tightly closed. She'd give it to the security guards, but not to this man approaching her. Slowly, she took a few steps backwards. He inched closer. When she reached the corner of the room, her hands uncontrollably shook as she peered up at the stone-faced man hovering above her.

"Open your hand!" he demanded again as his eyes narrowed, boring into her. "Do you want me to take it from you?"

Julie knew that would be easy for him since he was built like a football player—his broad shoulders, his thick neck, and his muscles stretching out the fabric of his shirt. She swallowed hard. "Why don't you call the security guards?"

"That won't be necessary."

Reluctantly, she opened her fist and felt his rough, coarse, calloused hand as he grabbed the bug.

"I left one attached to the table so we could determine who put it there." He continued glaring at her. "Where's the receiver?"

"In my purse," she replied, suspecting he wouldn't let her leave until he had it.

The man snatched her purse from her shoulder, yanked out the receiver, and dumped out the remaining contents on the table. He ran his hands through all of it. Julie wanted to tell him he had everything, yet knew that wouldn't stop him. "So, you're a spy," he surmised.

"No. I'm not a spy," she said, her voice quivering. She sucked in a ragged breath and bit her lower lip.

"I could have located the receiver earlier, but it was turned off. Why?"

She didn't respond as she stood motionless, staring at his face.

"Who do you work for?"

"Wilton, no one else," she replied, sounding meek and scared.

"It will be easier on you if you tell the truth," he said in an even tone.

"That is the truth." She fidgeted with her fingers and felt her heart thumping against her ribs. "I only eavesdropped for personal reasons to find out if Wilton and CT were going to merge," she confessed. "That's all."

"I don't believe you. What do you want from us?"

"Nothing," she murmured, wondering who "us" was. Then she noticed McIntyre standing in the doorway and sighed with relief, until she saw the cold, hard expression on his face.

CHAPTER 2

Gwynn and Cindy sat at a table next to a wall of windows at Brody's, a bar around the corner from the Wilton Tower. It was a popular post-work meeting place with a white-and-black speckled, polished, marble bar lined with a row of stools that were seldom empty and tables scattered around in front of it. The buzz of customers chatting and laughing filled the air.

Gwynn lifted her napkin from her lap, placed it by her plate, and looked at her half-eaten steak. "What could be taking her so long?" she asked as her eyebrows creased with worry.

"Why don't you try calling her office phone again?" Cindy suggested.

Gwynn punched in the number and waited while it rang four times. Voicemail kicked in and she hung up. "Since I've already left her three phone messages, I'm calling her condo, just in case." She placed another phone call, pressed her lips together, and shook her head in confusion. "Well, she's not there." After glancing at her watch, she said, "If she's not here by eight, I'm going to look for her car in the parking garage."

"I'll go with you," Cindy said. "Hey, have you been able to figure out why Taylor sent me those contracts without a note or anything?"

"No," Gwynn said, picking up the documents from the chair reserved for Julie and thumbing through them. "I don't recognize the name of the purchaser, and I can't figure out why Taylor would've had these contracts. He did accounting for acquisitions and assets, not for sales. I haven't got the foggiest idea why he sent them to you."

"Do you think he wants me to take them to work and file them?"

"Doubt it. You better just hang on to them until he calls." Gwynn's eyes lowered to the contracts. "I wonder where he went."

"Something's wrong," Cindy said helplessly, as her eyes became moist. "Tomorrow, I'm going to the police station and reporting him missing. I want you and Julie to go with me. Will you?"

Gwynn stood and hugged her. "Of course. I'm sure Julie will go, too." They sat quietly as the waitress cleared the table, and then she continued, "Taylor cleaned out his apartment, so he must be okay. Maybe he's upset over whatever happened at work and he just wants some time by himself."

"I don't understand why he moved. He liked his apartment with the views of the city, and the rent was cheap. There'd be no reason for him to move unless he had a job in another city. He had money in the bank. Even without a job, he had plenty to get by on for a while. Why didn't he call me?"

Gwynn patted Cindy's hand as she wondered about the same thing. "Just give him a little time."

Holding back tears, Cindy inhaled deeply. "Do you think he met someone else?"

"No… No… Don't worry; he'll show up." Suddenly, Gwynn recalled seeing Taylor and Marilyn, his boss, whispering in the hallway and abruptly ending their conversation when they spotted her. Last week while Gwynn worked late, she saw them talking quietly in the corner of the cafeteria. Later, she noticed them heading into Marilyn's office and closing the door even though no one was within earshot. *Did Taylor and Marilyn have anything going?* Gwynn thought as she glimpsed at her watch. "I'm going to the garage." Rising from her seat, she held out the documents for Cindy.

"Those are copies I made for you. You're better at researching stuff than I am. Would you mind checking out the company?"

"I'll get right on it when I get home."

Cindy checked her cell phone as they walked out of Brody's. "Two of my sisters left text messages, nothing from Taylor."

****

They stepped into the garage elevator while car horns beeped, tires squealed, and engines roared on the busy street that ran in front of the Wilton Tower. As they began to ascend, the light flickered, the elevator jerked, a high pitched screeching sound reverberated, and then the overhead lights snapped off. The elevator came to a halt. Only the street noises that penetrated the walls could be heard inside. The buttons on the control panel shined, giving enough illumination so Cindy and Gwynn could see each other's form in the darkness.

Cindy reached for the phone. "I hate this. Last year, I was stuck in here for almost ten minutes; it seemed like an hour. I'm calling security."

The light blinked and hummed, then flashed on. A motor sputtered. The elevator vibrated, squeaked, and inched up. The door slid open on the third level, the one with a bridge to Wilton Tower. "I'm taking the stairs next time," Cindy said.

"Me, too." Gwynn's eyes darted around, looking at the deserted parking level with not one person in sight. She walked with Cindy toward Julie's reserved parking space as a helicopter blared in the distance almost drowning out the traffic below. She stopped and stared at an oil spot on the concrete floor where she had expected to see Julie's car. "She's gone."

"Maybe Borge's gig ended and he's back from Vegas."

Gwynn doubted that was a possibility since Borge, Julie's fiancé, wasn't due in Houston for a couple of weeks. The corners of her eyes wrinkled with worry. "I'll drive by Julie's condo on the way home to see if her car's there."

"I'd go with you, but I want to check my mailbox and email. Maybe I'll have something from Taylor."

As they headed toward the exit door leading to the stairwell, Gwynn glanced back at Julie's empty parking space and spotted a tall, dark silhouette emerging from behind a pillar at the far end of the structure. The image of the female Wilton employee who had been mugged in the parking garage a few years prior flashed into her mind. After that, security cameras were installed on each level. Gwynn thought it gave everyone a false sense of safety since she suspected the cameras were never monitored and the tapes were only viewed after a problem. She hated being in the dimly lit structure after everyone had gone home. Whenever she went to Brody's, she'd go with Julie to her car, and then Julie would drive her to wherever she was parked.

Moving up to the next parking level with Cindy, Gwynn heard a door below them squeak open and slam shut, followed by heavy footsteps pounding on the cement stairs. An uneasy sensation crept through her body. Cindy chatted about Taylor and wondered what type of forms she'd have to fill out at the police station, completely oblivious that they were not alone in the stairwell.

"What floor are you parked on?" Gwynn asked, feeling goose-bumps rising on her arms as the footfalls echoed below.

"Seven."

"I'm on six. Why don't I drive you to your car?"

Cindy's head swung back and forth, her eyes drifted over the area. "Yeah. It is pretty dark in here."

****

Gwynn stopped her car at the black wrought iron gate leading to Julie's condo complex. It consisted of four two-story white brick buildings with parking stalls underneath each structure for owners. Gwynn punched in the security code and waited while the gate slid open. As she drove around back to the guest parking area, she glanced at Julie's building and noticed lights on in her condo. She parked and then walked at a brisk pace into a brightly lit courtyard. Gwynn climbed the stairs, passed two condos, and knocked on Julie's door. No answer.

A loud thud rang out, like a chair tumbling over. Gwynn thought the sound came from inside Julie's condo. She gripped the doorknob and discovered it wasn't locked. She eased the door open and peered into a dark room. "Julie!" she yelled. No answer. Then she wondered why the alarm wasn't beeping and what happened to the lights.

Gwynn pushed the door open wider. "Julie!" She stuck her hand around the door jam, flipped on the light, and entered. "Julie, you here?" Gwynn peeked into each room. Everything looked in order, nothing out of place. She picked up a notepad next to the phone in the living room, tore out a blank page, and scribbled a message to Julie asking her to call when she got home. Gwynn laid the note on Julie's bathroom counter, knowing she wouldn't miss seeing it there.

Leaving the condo, she used the key Julie had given her and locked the front door. A feeling of dread washed over her as she trudged toward her car and worried about Julie. *Alarm turned off. Door unlocked. Not answering her cell phone. Something has happened.*

Gwynn slid into the driver's seat, took a few deep breaths, and pulled her cell phone out of her purse, ready to call Borge. Then she wondered if Cindy could be right—Borge came home early. *He surprised Julie. They're probably out having a romantic dinner.* She knew Julie would ignore her phone calls if she was with him; she had done that before.

****

Just as Gwynn leaned over to turn off her nightstand lamp, her cell phone rang. She grabbed it, thinking Julie was calling. "Hello." She heard someone breathing on the other end of the line as she waited for a response. "Hello." The phone went dead. Gwynn flipped through her cell phone menu for the caller's phone number. It showed: "Restricted." She sat on the edge of her bed, mulling over the call.

The doorbell buzzed, startling her. She slipped on her robe, hurried to the door, and peered out the peephole; there stood Cindy with sagging shoulders and a drooping chin.

Suspecting it was not good news and hoping nothing bad had happened to Taylor, Gwynn quickly unlocked and unchained the door. Opening it, she asked, "What's wrong?"

Fatigue and fear showed through Cindy's eyes as she entered. "When I got home I found my condo had been ransacked." Gwynn gently took her arm and led her to the sofa. Cindy's lips quivered and her hands shook. "The police came as soon as I called. Whoever it was didn't break in by damaging the door lock or climbing through a window. Besides me, the only one who has a key is Taylor."

"He wouldn't ransack your place," Gwynn assured her. "Was anything missing?"

"They didn't take my computer, television, sound system, jewelry, money — nothing like that. The only thing missing was the package Taylor sent me. There might be other things, but that's all I know for sure." She nervously rubbed her hands together. "I didn't tell the police about the package because I was afraid they'd think Taylor broke in. Even if it was him, I don't want to get him in trouble."

"Cindy, Taylor wouldn't do that!" Gwynn was emphatic. "He sent you the documents. If he wanted them, all he needed to do was ask."

"What do you think it means — someone breaking in just to steal those documents?"

"Don't know," Gwynn replied, shaking her head.

"Can I stay here tonight?" Cindy asked as gloom filled her face. "I could just sleep on your sofa."

Gwynn's apartment was small. It only had two rooms — a living room-kitchen combo and a bedroom.

"I want to do some research about that company mentioned in the documents," Gwynn said. "I should've done it earlier. Why don't you sleep in my bed?"

"You don't mind?"

"No." Gwynn stroked Cindy's arm. "I think you could use a good night's rest."

After she got Cindy settled and made up the sofa for herself, she turned on the computer. She searched the internet for Trulin Energy Company and found it was a new company incorporated in Texas, nothing else. Gwynn glanced through the contracts again. They were all standard agreements used by Wilton. However, the pricing provisions were unusual; all the contracts had a fixed unit price for gas and oil. None of them tied to a posting, bulletin, any market pricing where the prices fluctuate up and down almost daily. In the past, she had seen some fixed price contracts for gas. She couldn't recall ever seeing one for oil. Since Cindy's contracts had been stolen, Gwynn decided to make another set of copies, just in case.

She pulled out an old fax and copy machine from a bottom kitchen cabinet. The machine required several adjustments before it worked. She didn't have any plain paper, so she used pages from a notebook. The copies were yellow with blue lines running through them. By the time she finished, it was after 2 a.m.

****

The next morning Cindy still felt edgy. Nonetheless, she went home to get ready for work. Gwynn put the lined copies in a shoebox in her closet and hid the other set under the front seat in her car. She suspected the documents needed to be protected, even if she didn't know why.

Arriving at work, Gwynn saw her co-workers and her boss, Stan, huddled together chatting next to his office. A few of them looked at her and immediately turned away when she met their eyes. She wondered what was going on, but wanted to call Julie first. Her call went directly to voicemail; she assumed that meant Julie must be on the phone.

As Gwynn strolled toward the group, they dispersed and went to their cubicles. Stan held up his arm and motioned for Gwynn to come to his office. He was an overweight, middle-aged man who walked very slowly because of arthritis in his knees. When he wanted to talk to an employee, he either motioned them or called on the phone.

Normally, his office door stayed open, but when she entered, he asked her to shut it. The only thought that ran through Gwynn's mind was that Cindy must have told someone about the contracts.

"Gwynn, have you heard any news this morning?" he asked in a gentle tone while he held his hands together on top of his desk.

She cocked her head. "No."

"Last night." He paused, and he briefly lowered his eyes. "There was an accident."

She swallowed hard, fearing he was talking about Julie. "What happened?" she asked, biting her lower lip and gripping the arms of the chair.

"I'm sorry. There isn't an easy way to say this. I wanted you to know before you overheard someone talking." His brows slanted and his face creased with concern. "Julie Morgan died in a car accident. I'm so sorry."

"How?" she asked as her body went rigid and her face became stark white.

"All I know is that around ten last night, she was driving south of town toward Galveston and somehow lost control of her vehicle. It crashed into a semi."

Gwynn sat motionless, tears filling her eyes. *It happened right after I left her condo.*

"Is there anything I can do for you? Call someone?" he asked in a soft voice. He knew how close they had been.

Tears dribbled down her face. "No," she stuttered. "Could I be alone for minute?"

"Certainly." Stan stepped out of the room, closing the door behind him.

Gwynn didn't know how long she had been in Stan's office when she finally composed herself enough to leave. She shuffled out, retrieved her purse from her desk drawer, and left the building with tears streaming down her cheeks every step of the way.

She drove home on side streets so she could drive slowly. Her cell phone rang repeatedly; she didn't notice. It usually took her twenty minutes to get home. Today, it took her almost two hours.

The landline phone message light blinked as she sat on the sofa. Gwynn felt too numb to push the playback button. She put her head down on the armrest and sobbed.

****

Cindy heard about the accident during morning break. She immediately called Gwynn and got voicemail. She contacted Stan. He told her that Gwynn had gone home. Cindy rushed out of the office and headed to Gwynn's apartment. After buzzing the doorbell and knocking for fifteen minutes, she convinced the superintendent to unlock Gwynn's door and let her in. Cindy had just sat down when Gwynn opened her swollen, hazel eyes.

They held each other and cried. "Do you think Borge knows?" Gwynn stuttered between sobs.

"I don't know," Cindy sniffled, her face lined with sadness. "Do you want me to call him?"

"Please. I don't think I can talk to him yet."

Cindy straightened her spine and sucked in air. "Just give me his number."

Gwynn's hands trembled as she took her cell phone, pulled up contacts, and highlighted Borge. "Use my cell." She handed it to Cindy and watched her make the call. Gwynn knew from the conversation Borge had not heard about the accident.

"He's on his way home." Cindy laid the cell phone on the coffee table.

"I don't know what I should be doing. Julie and I were like sisters. She was raised by her grandmother. They haven't spoken since Julie got engaged. Maybe she's taking care of things." Gwynn fidgeted with her hands, and her mouth quivered. Tears kept flowing. "I just don't know."

Cindy rubbed Gwynn's back. "I know."

****

Julie's funeral service was on Saturday at a white church that sat on a hill overlooking a lush green valley. Her grandmother had made the arrangements and arrived in a limo, accompanied by two muscular men and one elderly gentleman. Gwynn wondered if the two men were bodyguards, like the security guards she had seen at the woman's estate when she went with Julie to visit. Julie's grandmother sat quietly at the front of the chapel.

Gwynn had known Julie for ten years, ever since they were roommates in college. She gave the eulogy. She spoke about a kind, loving person and the wonderful relationship they had. When Gwynn's boyfriend was deployed to the Middle East and didn't survive, Julie provided her with the strength she needed to get through the ordeal. Julie was her rock; she could always lean on her. Gwynn's voice cracked often as she spoke, yet she managed to stay composed for Julie. When she finished, there was not a dry eye among the mourners, including her own.

As the service ended, Gwynn, Borge, and Cindy wanted to give their condolences to Julie's grandmother, but she was escorted swiftly out of the building. Borge rushed after her.

Only family members were invited to the burial site in a private cemetery. Borge grabbed the side door of the hearse. "I'm going!" he yelled, pulling the door open. One of the muscular men who had accompanied Julie's grandmother yanked him away from the vehicle.

"You can't do this!" Borge screamed. "I love Julie. She was my life! We were going to be married!" The muscular man continued holding onto him as the hearse sped away from the church. Borge squirmed away from the man and charged after the vehicle, yelling,

"Julie! Julie! Julie!" He dropped to his knees, covered his face with his hands, and cried. Gwynn and Cindy hurried to his side and tried to comfort him. They held onto his arms as the devastated man stood up.

As soon as Borge's emotions were under control, the three of them went with a group of mourners to Florentine's, an upscale bar and restaurant. Gwynn felt drained and didn't plan on staying long, but she wanted to toast Julie. An hour later, she smiled to herself when she saw both Borge and Cindy were finally relaxing. She suspected the next day would be hard for Cindy; they were going to the police station to talk about Taylor's disappearance. His mother had filed a missing person's report. Gwynn said her goodbyes to the group and slipped away.

Driving home, she mulled over the car accident again. She knew something was missing. It had haunted her ever since she had been told the crash details. She didn't know why Julie was on that road, why she didn't answer her cell phone, or what happened after she called to say she'd be at Brody's soon. Gwynn suspected it wasn't an accident, but couldn't understand why. She wanted answers and decided she would talk to the police about it when she went with Cindy.

****

While she waited for the elevator in her apartment building, she noticed a tall, well-built, handsome, yet unfamiliar man walking toward her. Then she recalled seeing him at the funeral. Her body stiffened, fearing he had followed her. Relief came when another couple got on the elevator with her and the man. Trying to avoid him, she looked straight ahead and watched the couple push the fourth floor button. She planned to get off the elevator with them and take the stairs to her apartment on the fifth floor.

When she reached her apartment and opened her purse to get the key, the handsome stranger strode down the hallway toward her. Their eyes met, and she froze.

CHAPTER 3

Borge and Cindy left Florentine's together. She invited him to her place for coffee. When they got there, instead of drinking coffee, they drank wine. Borge talked about Julie, and Cindy talked about Taylor. They took turns crying on each other's shoulders. After they emptied the first bottle of wine, Cindy opened another one. That was the last thing either of them remembered.

****

"Don't be alarmed, Miss Reznick." The stranger calmly looked at Gwynn. "My name is Ruben Dordi. I'm working for Mrs. VanAusdell, investigating her granddaughter's death. I'd like to talk to you." He handed her a card with Mrs. VanAusdell's name and a phone number on it.

Gwynn's spine stiffened and her eyebrows arched as she examined the card. "Anyone could have a card like this printed. Do you have any other proof you're working for her?"

"Why don't you give her a call?" Ruben suggested.

She glanced at the card again; even if it had a phone number on it, she wanted to call the number Mrs. VanAusdell gave her when she asked her to give the eulogy. "I'll call her inside. You'll have to wait in the hallway."

"It would be better if you didn't use your landline and called her on your cell phone before you entered your apartment."

"Why?"

"Your apartment might be bugged."

Gwynn stared at him, wondering who would bug her apartment. "I'll call from here after I get her phone number."

"It's on the card."

"I want to make sure that's her number." Gwynn felt uneasy, but assumed if he was legitimate, he would understand.

"By all means," he said with a hint of a smile crossing his lips.

He stood next to the door while she unlocked it and stepped inside. Gwynn confirmed to herself that the numbers were identical. She took her cell phone out of her purse and walked out into the hallway. He watched silently as she placed the call.

After an elderly man answered the phone, Gwynn asked, "May I please speak to Mrs. VanAusdell?"

"Who may I tell her is calling?" the elderly man asked in a formal tone.

"Gwynn Reznick."

"She'll be with you shortly."

Gwynn and Ruben exchanged glances while she waited.

"Hello, Gwynn," Mrs. VanAusdell said. "How are you feeling, dear?"

"Better, thank you. Do you have a person working for you by the name of Ruben Dordi?"

"Yes, I do."

"Can you describe him?"

"Ruben is in his middle thirties, about six-foot-two, dark brown hair. A nice-looking man. He has a scar on his right forearm. I'm pleased you're cautious."

"Thank you."

"Do you need anything else?"

"No. That was all."

"Then I'll say good evening," she said and hung up, not giving Gwynn an opportunity to say anything else.

"Are you satisfied?" Ruben asked as Gwynn lowered her cell phone.

"Can you roll up your sleeve on your right arm?"

Ruben unbuttoned the cuff on his shirt then pushed up his suit coat and shirt sleeve to reveal a three-inch scar in the middle of his forearm.

"Where did you get that?" Gwynn asked, opening her door.

"It's a long story," he said, lowering his sleeve as they entered her apartment. He motioned for her to be quiet. He glanced around, closed the drapes, partially disassembled her phone, and took out a small object.

Gwynn began, "Wha ..."

He gestured again for her to be still. He pulled a cell phone-sized device out of his pocket, held it in his hand, and moved it around all the furniture and pictures. He stopped several times, removed, and crushed small, round, gray objects from a picture frame, under an end table, the side of her nightstand, and inside a vent. Gwynn's eyes grew wider with each item he found.

"That's all of them. I still want to run some interference." He slipped the device back into his pocket. Ruben reached into another pocket, took out a two-inch square gadget covered with open slits and two prongs sticking out one side of it, and plugged the prongs into an electric outlet.

"Why was my apartment bugged?" Gwynn asked, perplexed. "And why are you investigating Julie's death?"

"They're looking for something," Ruben replied. "There's a surveillance camera attached to the outside of this window." He gestured toward it.

Gwynn raised her hand to push the drape aside.

"Don't look," he said. "There isn't one on your bedroom window. It's easy to remove, but they can't see you if you keep the drapes closed. They could decide to install one inside your apartment. As a precaution, I would suggest that you dress and undress in your bathroom."

Gwynn nodded in agreement.

Ruben continued, "They could also use a directional mike. If they point it toward your windows, they can pick up anything said in your apartment. That's why I'm running interference." He pointed toward the plugged-in device. "I'm leaving that with you. Only plug it in when you're talking face-to-face about something confidential because it also interferes with wireless electronic signals. When you leave your apartment, take it with you. The back label says 'RD Room Refresher.'"

"It looks like one. Who are 'they'?"

"We don't know."

"What do they want?"

"We don't know that either. Mrs. VanAusdell wants you to be kept informed, so let me bring you up to speed."

"Please take a seat," Gwynn gestured toward the sofa, feeling good that Mrs. VanAusdell wanted her to know.

"Mrs. VanAusdell suspected something was wrong when she was notified about her granddaughter's car accident," Ruben said, sitting down. "According to her, Miss Morgan was always nervous driving around semi-trucks; she wouldn't have even pushed a button on her radio if she was near one."

As he spoke, Gwynn recalled seeing Julie staring out the windshield, not saying a word, whenever she drove near a semi.

He continued, "Mrs. VanAusdell had her secretary call me before she went to the funeral home. That's when I began my investigation. She didn't want me to approach you until after the funeral."

"Have you found out anything so far?" Gwynn asked. Although deep in sorrow over Julie's death, she was grateful that it was at least being investigated.

"Yes. The truck driver claimed Miss Morgan smashed into him. Forensic evidence suggests otherwise. Her car wasn't moving at the time of impact; the semi backed into her. Also, there were drugs in her system, and she wasn't wearing any jewelry, not even her engagement ring."

Gwynn trembled and gripped her hands tightly together. "Why didn't the police arrest the truck driver?"

"Mrs. VanAusdell wants this investigation handled independently. The police had the same information and came to an erroneous conclusion, which means that they're ineffective at best, or on somebody's payroll at the very worst. And Mrs. VanAusdell wants to know why her granddaughter was killed. Having the driver arrested won't answer that question."

"How do you know Julie's car wasn't moving?" she asked, feeling suspicious.

"The transmission was in park, the emergency brake was on, and we're relying on the forensic evidence. There was also an indentation in the back bumper, indicating something was behind her vehicle holding it stationary at the time of impact."

"Was Julie conscious when it happened?" she asked with moist eyes.

"No. With the drugs in her system, she might've already been dead."

"Didn't the police check any of that?" she asked in disbelief.

"An autopsy wasn't requested by the police for whatever reason. With Mrs. VanAusdell's permission, I had one performed."

A few tears trickled down Gwynn's face. She already knew the condition of Julie's body was bad; the coffin had remained closed. "Why did you think my apartment was bugged?" she asked, wiping her face.

"They're looking for something."

"How do you know that?"

"A person who works for me noticed a man, not Borge Haseman, opening Miss Morgan's locked mailbox and going through the mail. That same guy has gone through your mail every day since the alleged accident. I'm sure they searched your apartment when they planted the bugs."

"The night of the …" she began in a jittery voice, unable to state the traumatic event. "I drove to Julie's condo since she didn't meet us at Brody's, and she didn't answer her cell. I thought I saw lights on in her condo, went and knocked on her door. No one answered. I heard a loud noise, and it seemed like it came from inside her place. Then I found the door wasn't locked, and her alarm system wasn't on."

Ruben sat quietly for a minute and then reached inside his suit coat and pulled out a small notebook along with a pen. "What time was that?" he asked, scribbling down the information.

"Around 9:30," she said, her face strained and solemn, thinking Julie was still alive then.

"Did you enter her condo?" After Gwynn nodded, he asked, "Anything unusual?"

She shook her head. "No. Nothing appeared to be out of place."

"Did Miss Morgan give you anything to keep for her?"

"No. I have a friend, Taylor Denton, who's missing. Do you think his disappearance could be linked to what happened to Julie?"

"Possibly. I know about him along with his boss, Marilyn Anders, and two other Wilton employees."

Gwynn cringed. "Are they all missing?"

"Not all of them." Ruben laid the notebook down on the coffee table. "Two of Wilton's employees died ten days ago falling from an oil platform out in the gulf. Instead of the incident being investigated by the authorities, a safety inspector is checking into it. Marilyn Anders and Taylor Denton are missing."

"Marilyn isn't missing; she's on vacation," Gwynn informed him, as she wondered if Marilyn was with Taylor.

"Marilyn Anders' family just reported her missing."

Steering the conversation away from Taylor and Marilyn, Gwynn said, "Accidents sometimes do happen on platforms. Why are you looking into those?"

"One of the two men called an emergency number right before he landed in the water. His cell phone was found in a room twenty feet from where he went overboard, and the next day an employee quit. That employee adamantly refuses to talk about anything that happened on the platform. Now, he's working for another company."

"What connection could they have to Julie?"

"The last place anyone saw Miss Morgan alive was in the Wilton Tower. That's also the last place her cell phone functioned. I'm following up on other deaths that occurred among Wilton employees, along with anything that seems suspicious. I'm searching for a motive. There might not be a connection between Miss Morgan's death and the death of the two men who worked on the platform, but I'm not going to leave any stone unturned until I have answers. From everything I know Miss Morgan had no enemies, so her death is very suspicious."

"Everyone liked Julie," Gwynn confirmed. "Do you think something bad has happened to Taylor?"

"I don't want to speculate."

Gwynn felt a sharp spasm in her stomach. "Taylor sent his girlfriend, Cindy, some documents," she said, suddenly. "Her condo was ransacked. All that was taken were those documents."

His brows furrowed. "Do you know what those documents contained?"

"They were copies of contracts. Cindy made copies and gave them to me. She didn't know what it meant ... Taylor sending those to her."

"Can I see your copies?"

"They're in my car." Gwynn and Ruben left her apartment to retrieve them. When they reached her car, she discovered the documents were gone.

27

"I made another set of copies, but on lined notebook paper," she said, locking her car.

Back in her apartment, Gwynn went to get the copies. All of her shoeboxes were neatly stacked in her closet. Despite that, she knew they were out of order. She recalled leaving the contract copies in a pink-and-blue box buried at the bottom of a stack. Now that box sat on top. "They're gone," she said, disappointed, staring into the empty box.

"What can you remember about the contracts?" Ruben asked, picking up his notebook.

"So I won't forget, I want to write it down also." She took a notepad out of her desk, sat down, and wrote as she went on. "They were between Wilton Oil and Gas Company and Trulin Energy Company. Trulin was the purchaser. There were four contracts: two for oil and two for casinghead gas. I remember the term of the contracts was to begin within a month. I can't recall the exact date. The contracts couldn't be cancelled for five years. What struck me as being really unusual," she paused as she jotted it down, "the unit prices were fixed."

"How's that different?"

"Normally, the pricing provision is attached to bulletins, postings, market pricing of some sort that is publically available—prices that fluctuate up and down. The fixed prices seemed comparable to the current market, but I don't think Wilton Oil has any other contracts like that." She continued writing. "I tried to do some research on Trulin. All I could find was it's a new company incorporated in Texas."

"Why four contracts?"

"Two were for offshore production, one gas and one oil, and two for onshore production. That's common in the industry — separate contracts for each product. In fact, there are normally even more, with each being tied to production from specific wells, fields, units," she clarified. "These contracts didn't indicate any specific production; there were provisions for quality. The production could come from any of Wilton's wells. The delivery points were at various locations in Texas."

"Who signed them?"

"Kent Fardown, senior vice-president of marketing, signed for Wilton. He doesn't sign all of Wilton's contracts. I've only seen his signature before when there were significant quantities involved."

"What were the quantities?"

"I can't remember exactly. It struck me as being a lot — like maybe ten percent of Wilton's production. It surprised me that a new company would have resources large enough to commit to purchases of that magnitude."

"Who signed the contract for Trulin?" Ruben asked as he scrawled down the information.

"I couldn't read the signature and the name wasn't typed under it."

"Could Miss Morgan have seen those contracts?"

"Doubt it." Gwynn leaned back on the sofa and crossed her legs. "She worked for Steve Hadley, vice president of public relations. He doesn't get involved with contracts. The last day she was at work, she filled in for an hour or two for Pam, John McIntyre's secretary. McIntyre is the CEO of Wilton. Julie told me he was in a meeting, so she just sat and answered phone calls, but that kept her pretty busy.

"I was surprised that Taylor had access to those contracts. He did accounting for acquisitions and assets. He didn't work with any production sales."

"Do you know if Wilton Oil purchased anything from Trulin?" Ruben asked, tapping his fingers on the armrest.

"I don't know. I work in joint interest billing. That's on the same floor as accounting for acquisitions and assets. I'll see what I can find out at work on Monday."

"Be careful. I'd like to tell you not to check on it, but we need answers. Someone will be watching the lobby in case you are escorted out like Miss Morgan." Ruben slipped his notebook and pen back into his suit coat pocket.

"Who escorted her out?" Gwynn asked, bewildered, straightening her back.

"We've acquired the surveillance tapes for the last day Miss Morgan worked. She came in early and left at 7:25 p.m. A man walked by her side and talked as they left the building together. There was also a man walking right behind her. Additionally, we've acquired the tapes showing Taylor Denton leaving the building with his personal belongings and Marilyn Anders leaving before she allegedly went on vacation. The same man who walked behind Miss Morgan appears on the Denton and Anders tapes. He isn't a Wilton employee or, if he is, he doesn't work in that building. I'd like you to look at the tape to see if you recognize him. We're also using other resources to try to identify him."

"How were you able to get the tapes?" Gwynn inquired.

"A security guard. He liked Miss Morgan and was anxious to help. He regretted that the surveillance tapes by the elevators were no longer available. Those are recycled every forty-eight hours. We didn't get to him soon enough."

"You probably got them from Neil Trussen. He was always asking about Julie. I'm sure he hoped she'd break up with Borge. When Wilton implemented a new spot security check, he searched Julie's purse the first day. I stood and watched, thinking he just wanted to talk to her."

"It's better if I don't disclose the source. Are you willing to look at the tapes?"

"Of course. Do you want to bring them here, or would you like me to see them someplace else?"

"I'll bring the tapes here." He adjusted himself in the seat.

Gwynn flipped her pen around between her fingers. "Do you think I'm in danger?"

"Mrs. VanAusdell believes you are. Part of my job is to make sure you're safe while we're investigating the circumstances surrounding Miss Morgan's death."

"How are you planning to keep me safe?"

"You would've been safer had I not removed all the bugs. Now they know we're on to them. We need them to make a move. I'm no closer today in determining why Miss Morgan died than I was on Wednesday. You could help by letting me know if you see or hear anything out of the ordinary at work."

"How should I contact you?"

"Give me a call." He took a card out of another pocket and handed it to her. "Keep your cell phone with you at all times."

She glanced at the card. It only had a telephone number on it, nothing else. "This is too weird. I don't have anything, and I don't know anything. And I don't think Julie knew anything someone would kill to get or she would've shared it with me. Cindy received the contracts from Taylor. They were just contracts, not trade secrets.

If that's what they wanted, they've got 'em." She put down her pen and rested her hands on her lap.

Ruben took a small button-shaped gray device out of his pocket and gave it to Gwynn. "You can put this anywhere in here. It's a mike, more powerful than the bugs they installed. It'll pick up any noise in your apartment, providing you leave your bedroom door open and the interference is unplugged."

Gwynn looked around. "Where do you think I should put it?"

"The picture frame next to your kitchen cabinets would be a good place," he said, gazing in that direction.

She walked over to it and attached the mike to the side.

"It's late," he said, moving toward the door. "That brings you up to speed on the status of our investigation. What time would you be available to look at the tapes tomorrow?"

"In the morning I'm going with Cindy to the police station. The sergeant wants to talk to her about Taylor's disappearance. After that, I don't have any plans."

"I'll bring the tapes over then. One last question before I leave. When Miss Morgan was filling in for McIntyre's secretary, do you know what that meeting was about and who attended?"

"Julie said that McIntyre was meeting with CT Oil and Gas Company. She didn't know what it was about or who was attending from Wilton, except she knew Hadley, her boss, wasn't invited. That's all I know."

Ruben's forehead creased as he put his hand on the doorknob. "Just to be safe, you should keep your door bolted, and don't open it for anyone you don't know, regardless of what type of emergency they might claim."

"I won't," she assured him.

After he closed the door behind him, Gwynn locked, bolted, and chained it. She unplugged the interference device and put it in her purse. Then she checked all the windows, verifying everything was locked, and caught a glimpse of the small surveillance camera attached to the corner of the living room window.

As she fell into bed, her thoughts drifted to Julie. Someone had killed her. It wasn't an accident. She'd never see that glowing smile again. Gwynn's eyes welled with water, and she couldn't prevent the tears from flowing out.

CHAPTER 4

When Borge woke up in Cindy's bed, neither of them had any idea how he managed to get there. Both felt awkward and embarrassed as Borge quickly gathered up his clothes and darted to the bathroom.

She stayed covered in bed and sighed with relief when she discovered she had her underwear on. Cindy was attracted to him, his light blue eyes, ash brown hair, five-foot-eleven, perfectly proportioned body and boyish smile. Yet, she longed to be with Taylor and to feel his arms around her.

Borge came out of the bathroom, all dressed, and put on his shoes. "See you later," he said with a sheepish grin on his face, walking to the door.

Cindy heard the door close, then slipped out of bed and put on her robe. Her head throbbed as she made her way to the kitchen. After three cups of coffee and two aspirin, she finally felt somewhat human again. Her phone rang, and she noticed the ID. "Hello, Gwynn," she said, sounding groggy.

"Are you okay?"

"Yes, but I think I drank too much," Cindy replied, still wondering what happened.

"When I left, you and Borge were enjoying Margaritas," Gwynn commented. "I'm just calling to find out what time you want to go to the police station."

"Sergeant Fillmore told me he'd only be there until noon. Give me an hour and I'll pick you up."

"See you then."

****

As they drove to the police station, Gwynn noticed a black Ford Expedition behind them and a black Chevy Suburban behind it. Whenever Cindy turned a corner, she glanced at the side mirror — both cars followed. Worrying about the vehicles, Gwynn hoped one belonged to Ruben's team. She gazed at Cindy, thought she seemed awfully quiet, and assumed it was from last night's booze.

Parking the car, Cindy said, "I'm not going to mention anything about the contracts to Sergeant Fillmore."

"I won't say anything either." Gwynn looked out the side mirror, searching for either black vehicle.

They strolled into a bright, walnut paneled foyer with a high ceiling and a white-and-brown tiled floor. A long wood counter separated the police station's public area from the working area where only a few desks were occupied. Four people were leaning against the counter and talking in angry tones to the officer behind it. A man, dressed in a dark blue suit, came from around the counter, "Is one of you Cindy Wood?"

"I am," Cindy replied.

After brief introductions, Sergeant Fillmore escorted Cindy and Gwynn into a stark, gray room without any windows. A table and four chairs stood in the center. He motioned for them to take a seat. They sat on one side of the table, and he sat across from them.

Fillmore opened a folder and thumbed through the documents. "Miss Wood, can you tell me the last time you saw Taylor Denton and what you know about his disappearance?"

Cindy fidgeted with her bracelet and rotated it around her wrist. "Last time was at lunch on Thursday, July tenth," she recalled and turned toward Gwynn. "Gwynn was there."

"And where was that?" he asked.

"Wilton Tower's lunchroom on the second floor," Cindy said, and Gwynn nodded. "Later that day, I heard he had been fired. Taylor and I spent almost every evening together, but I didn't hear from him that night. I called his cell phone and his apartment. He didn't answer. When I got off work the next day, I still hadn't heard from him, so I went to his apartment. It was completely empty; he had moved out. I called everyone I could think of who knew Taylor.

No one had seen him." Her lips quivered. "I think something has happened to him."

The sergeant flipped through some documents, cleared his throat, and proceeded. "Miss Reznick, is there anything you can add to what Miss Wood has said?"

"No. Cindy's covered everything I know."

"Marilyn Anders, Mr. Denton's former supervisor, has also been reported missing. Do either of you know any details surrounding her situation?"

"Marilyn's missing?" Cindy asked softly, tilting her head and feeling bewildered.

"Yes," Fillmore said. "Her family reported her missing on Friday. Her parents couldn't reach her at home. They called her at work and were told she was on vacation. They thought that was strange since she hadn't mentioned it to anyone. She's going through a divorce, and they originally believed she just needed some time by herself. No one has heard from her for nine days, not even her children." He leaned further back in his chair. "Are either of you aware of any personal relationship Taylor Denton and Marilyn Anders might have had outside of work?"

Gwynn and Cindy looked at each other. Marilyn was in her early forties. Taylor had just turned thirty-one. Marilyn was an attractive, slender woman, but she had a very stern disposition. Taylor was the opposite — outgoing and fun.

Cindy squinted, bit her bottom lip, and folded her hands together. "Taylor felt sorry for Marilyn because of the problems she was having with her divorce, battling over the kids."

"Do you seriously think Taylor ran off with Marilyn?" Gwynn asked Fillmore, her face showing disbelief, although that idea had crept into her mind before Ruben's visit.

"We want to cover all possibilities. They worked at the same place and disappeared about the same time."

Cindy recalled all the times Taylor had mentioned hearing Marilyn arguing over the phone with her husband and how he had to wait until Marilyn calmed down before he could speak to her. "Have you talked to her husband?"

"Yes." The sergeant shuffled through another folder. "The investigation regarding Taylor Denton is moving along. We have a few leads." He pushed his chair away from the table and rose to his feet. "If you can think of anything else, please give me a call."

"I will," Cindy said.

Gwynn nodded in agreement and stood up with Cindy.

He shook their hands, "Thank you for coming in on a Sunday morning."

"Will you let me know if you find out anything?" Cindy asked.

"I'll keep you posted," Fillmore said, opening the door for them to exit.

****

Snapping on her seat belt, Cindy turned toward Gwynn and said, "That's so strange that Marilyn is missing, too. You don't think there's any possibility that Taylor is with her, do you?"

"Are you kidding? No! Taylor didn't even joke with her."

"Sometimes I wonder if he found someone else. Maybe somehow Taylor accidently took those contracts home. You know, maybe in his personal stuff when he left. Then he sent them to me, so he could run off with someone and leave everything to do with Wilton behind, including me." Tears welled in Cindy's eyes.

Gwynn leaned over, gave her a hug, and wanted to tell her about the investigation, yet knew it was better if Cindy didn't know. "You don't need to worry about Taylor being with another woman; he's crazy about you."

"He cleaned out his apartment. He left without saying a word." Cindy's lips trembled and a few tears trickled down her cheeks. "Taylor and Marilyn. I just can't believe that. But they're missing at the same time. I think I'd rather believe he ran off with Marilyn than had some kind of a bad accident." She sniffled.

Gwynn lightly stroked her arm. "I'm sure he's okay. I can't imagine he's with Marilyn." She pulled tissues out of her purse and handed them to Cindy. "Do you want me to drive?"

"If you don't mind."

They switched places. Cindy sat quietly shedding tears as Gwynn drove toward her place with the two black cars not far behind.

"Would you like to come in and talk?" Gwynn asked, pulling over to the curb in front of her apartment building.

"No," Cindy said, wiping her eyes. "I need to get some laundry done and see if I can do some cleaning."

"How about going to dinner later?" Gwynn said and gave Cindy a minute to think about it.

Cindy finally answered, "Sounds good. What time?"

"How about I pick you up around six? I think I'll ask Borge if he wants to go with us."

"Six works for me," Cindy replied without commenting about Borge. She wasn't sure if she wanted to see him so soon, but she knew Gwynn would think something was wrong if she didn't want Borge to go.

****

Gwynn walked into her apartment and closed the drapes. Five minutes later, Ruben rang the doorbell. He came with an average-sized man in his early fifties with grey-streaked light brown hair who looked tough and had a cold, unsettling smile. After Ruben introduced Gordon to Gwynn, she plugged in the interference device while Ruben set up and started the VCR player. The first tape showed Taylor in the foyer carrying a box.

Sadness crept through Gwynn's body as she watched and worried that she might never see him alive again, just like Julie.

Ruben paused the tape and pointed to a tall, muscular man with broad shoulders next to Taylor. "Do you recognize him?"

"No, but at least a thousand people work in the Wilton Tower."

"He's a hired thug," Ruben said. "His name is Luke Cromer, thirty-eight, born and raised in New Jersey, trained by the Marines."

"The Marines?" Gwynn questioned.

"He's not the first ex-Marine who's gone rogue."

"How do you know about him?" she asked, suspiciously.

"I just found out this morning," Ruben said without answering the question. "He's had run-ins with the police, but he's never been convicted of anything."

"Who does he work for?"

"We haven't been able to determine that yet since most thugs are paid in cash. But his presence strongly suggests something is going on at Wilton." Ruben bent down to eject the tape.

"Wait," she said, noticing the other people around Taylor. Gwynn moved to the screen and pointed to the man who stood next to the door. "That's Kent Fardown. He's the one who signed the sales contracts between Wilton and Trulin."

Ruben stared at the screen. "He doesn't resemble the picture I have."

"He didn't always look like that," Gwynn clarified. "He used to be stocky until two or three years ago when he developed some health problems. Do you have pictures of everyone who works in the building?"

"Almost everyone. Do you recognize anyone else?"

"The husky man talking to Kent. I've seen him before. I don't know his name, but I think he works for Wilton."

"See if you can find that out, and I'll do the same." Ruben removed the tape, put in another one, and started it.

Gwynn had a hard time holding her tears at bay when she saw Julie on the screen. Two men were walking close to her. "It looks like the men know where the cameras are, and they're blocking Julie. I can't see her face."

"That's probably deliberate," Ruben replied, pausing the tape. "Do you think there's any possibility that isn't Julie Morgan?"

"I think it's her. I can't say for absolutely sure. The outfit she's wearing is Julie's. She has long blonde hair like Julie." Gwynn's eyes remained fixed on the screen. "Do you think it isn't her?"

"I never met Miss Morgan." Ruben focused on the image. "This person's face is being hidden from the cameras, and she isn't being touched by either man. It appears she's leaving the Wilton Tower under her own free will."

"You never answered my question," Gwynn sounded annoyed. "Do you think it isn't her?"

"I don't know. Only one security guard was on duty in the foyer. If the tapes are any indication, there are normally two or three. Two were scheduled to be working there that evening. One of them had been called away from his post right before this woman left the building. The other refuses to talk about that evening. He seemed visibly irritated when Julie Morgan's name was mentioned to him. The parking garage security tapes didn't help—the cameras on her parking level weren't working. The tape from the one at the exit only showed the back of someone's head with long blonde hair leaving in Miss Morgan's car."

Gwynn continued studying the picture of the woman on the screen. "If that's not Julie, then who could it be?"

"I'm not sure yet," Ruben slowly replied.

Gwynn sat quietly in thought. She was the same size as Julie and remembered how people often asked if they were sisters, even though Julie had long blonde, wavy hair and hers was light brown and short. *Who else at work is Julie's size?* "McIntyre's secretary, Pam Simmons, is five-eight, slender, long blonde hair. In her five-inch heels, she looks taller." Gwynn paused. "Did you see Pam leaving the building on any of the tapes you watched?"

"Yes. After you mentioned that Miss Morgan filled in for Miss Simmons that morning, I checked the tapes again specifically for Miss Simmons. She left at 5:45. A woman came into the building around 6:40 wearing a coat and hat. Unusual for eighty degree weather."

"Do you have that tape with you?"

"Yes. Before I switch tapes, do you recognize any of the men on the screen?"

Gwynn pointed to one. "That husky guy was the one talking to Fardown on Taylor's tape."

"Anyone else?"

"No."

Ruben ejected the tape, started another one, and pushed pause. "Do you think that is Miss Simmons?" he asked, gesturing toward a woman wearing a coat with her face hidden under the brim of a hat.

Gwynn's eyes dropped down to the shoes partially concealed by the coat. Even if she couldn't see them well, she saw enough to know they were high heels. "It's hard to say with that coat on, but she's wearing stilettos just like Pam would wear. If that wasn't Julie on the other tape, how did she get out of the building?"

"Currently, we're working under the theory that Miss Morgan was drugged while she was in the Wilton Tower. Based on that assumption, we've developed one way they might have taken her out," he said, sounding hesitant. "That tape could be difficult for you to watch."

"I want to see it," Gwynn said, firmly, determined to know the possibility.

Ruben switched tapes. On the tape were two men; one was Luke Cromer, pushing a credenza on a flat handcart toward the freight docking doors. "We think she might be in there."

Gwynn's hands shook and her foot twitched. *How could they take her out like that? It's almost like a coffin.* Her breathing became labored and heavy as she continued glaring at the screen.

"Do you recognize the guy next to Cromer?" Ruben asked.

She stared at the short, slender man. "I don't know him, but he works in the building. I've seen him often in the elevator."

"His name is Carl Backman. He works on the fifteenth floor in the land department."

Gwynn had worked in the building for six years and didn't know his name. "Have you memorized the names of everyone that works for Wilton?"

"Not everyone," he replied casually. He ejected the tape and unhooked the tape player.

"Since you have the tapes, what time did McIntyre leave?" Gwynn asked, wondering if he was involved.

Ruben checked his notes. "He left at 7:10, thirty minutes before the credenza was removed from the building," he replied, heading toward the door.

Gordon, who hadn't said a word since he was introduced to Gwynn, followed. While the tapes played, Gordon, a surveillance expert, had scanned the apartment to verify proper security measures had been put in place and concluded that the bug Ruben had planted was sufficient for the area.

"Where are you going to dinner?" Ruben asked, opening the door.

"How did you know?" she asked, irritated, as she thought he had put a bug somewhere on her clothing or in her purse.

"We heard you talking to Miss Wood in the parking lot. Don't worry; you're not wearing a bug. If we feel that becomes necessary, we'll ask."

Gwynn sighed with relief. She didn't want them listening to her all the time. It would be bad enough letting them hear what she said in her apartment. "I don't know where we're going to dinner. I'll give you a call when we decide."

****

Borge showed up a little late. It was after seven when they reached the quaint, Italian restaurant with multi-colored ceramic tile round tables, wrought iron chairs, and pictures of Italy adorning the walls. Soft piano music came through corner speakers, giving the place a relaxing atmosphere. The smell of garlic, basil, savory dishes, and the aroma of fresh baked bread filled the air.

"Did you see your boss on *Meet the Press?*" Borge asked between bites.

Cindy and Gwynn exchanged glances. "What boss?" Gwynn asked.

"McIntyre," Borge replied.

"Why was he on?" Cindy asked.

"I only watched for a few minutes. It was something about the oil industry and the environment — clean water, something like that."

"McIntyre's big into the environment," Gwynn explained. "He's on the board of Preserve the Green, a pro-environment group. Normally, oilmen aren't actively involved in organizations like that. But his participation has endeared him to political leaders of both parties. He's convinced that with proper safety measures, maintenance, and monitoring, oil wells and pipelines won't harm the environment. He speaks often at conventions."

Cindy cut a piece of her eggplant parmesan. "He even sends copies of his speeches to all his employees. Some of them have joined environmental groups just to get on his good side. Not that I'm against the environment, but Nate, my boss, requires us to read all of his speeches. They're long and boring."

"It's nice that he supposedly cares about the environment, but if he was an environmentalist, he wouldn't work in the industry that he does," Borge remarked.

During dinner, Gwynn felt tension between Cindy and Borge; they kept avoiding looking at each other, even when one of them spoke. She wondered what had happened after she left the night before. A few times, she glanced quickly at Ruben, who was seated two tables away with Gordon. Once she briefly met his eyes and he smiled.

****

Borge drove Gwynn home first since Cindy lived closer to him. Gwynn didn't think that was the real reason, but hoped they'd clear the air between them.

"Oh, I almost forgot," Cindy said as Gwynn was getting out of the car. "I went to the chapel today — you know, Julie's, to get my sweater I left there. When a woman was getting it out of the office, I noticed a CD mailer with your name on it." She took it out of her purse. "She asked if I had your address. I told her I could give it to you."

"Thanks," Gwynn said, taking the mailer. "I'll see you tomorrow. Borge, give me a call at work if you need anything."

As Gwynn walked toward the apartment building entrance anxious to find out what was on the CD, she saw two black SUVs, a Suburban and an Explorer. She assumed they were the same two cars that had followed her and Cindy to the police station earlier and wondered which one belonged to Ruben.

Gwynn took the elevator to the fifth floor and hurried to her apartment. After she unlocked and opened the door, someone grabbed her from behind, pushed her in, and slammed the door shut behind them.

CHAPTER 5

Borge had thought often about Cindy during the day. He definitely was interested in her — her big brown eyes, long brown hair, her bronze Hispanic skin, her delicate, curvy, petite body, and her bubbly personality. Still, he ached for Julie and felt guilty about what he thought might have happened.

"We need to talk," he said, parking the car next to Cindy's condo complex.

"What do you want to talk about?" Cindy asked in a shaky voice.

"Last night."

She swallowed hard. "What about last night?"

"I don't know — that's the problem."

"I don't know either," she said, looking down and rubbing her hands together.

"The last thing I remember is drinking wine. Do you know anything that happened after that?"

"No," she said hesitantly, wishing she did.

On top of everything, Borge wanted to see her again. "We both had too much to drink. I probably just spent the night because I wasn't in any condition to drive home. Can we just leave it at that?"

"I'm sure that was all that happened," Cindy agreed as she was tempted to invite him in.

"It's dark out here. Let me walk you to your door."

****

A heavyset, square-jawed man with a broad, flat nose stood before Gwynn, his eyes fixed on her and his mouth smug. "What do you want?" she said, knowing Ruben could hear her.

"The CD."

She clutched her purse in her hands. "Why?"

Grabbing her handbag, he pushed her away. She stumbled and landed on the floor. He yanked out the cardboard case containing the CD, dropped the purse, and headed to the door. Gwynn scrambled to her feet, grabbed the vase from her coffee table, and smacked the back of his head with it. He turned and swung his hand across her face. She felt a throbbing pain as she fell to the floor screaming. The attacker pulled a knife out of his boot. She squirmed and rolled under the coffee table just in time to avoid the blade hurtling toward her. The knife stuck in the front wooden trim of the sofa's armrest, a foot away from her.

With an amused expression on his face, he looked at her peering out from under the coffee table as he held up the CD. The attacker opened the door and found Ruben and Gordon on the other side blocking him from leaving.

The man's eyes dropped to the CD case. He gripped it between his palms and snapped it before he could be stopped.

Gordon whipped out his pistol from the holster concealed under his suit coat and pointed the barrel at the man's head. "This way," he said to the attacker, motioning toward the hallway.

Ruben seized the disk case as Gordon escorted the man out of the room.

"He ruined it!" Disappointed, Gwynn held onto the coffee table and staggered to her feet.

Ruben gazed inside the case. "It's damaged but not completely shattered. Some of the contents might be recoverable."

"But how?"

"We know people," he replied, yanking the knife out of the armrest. He gently ran his fingers over Gwynn's nose and down the side of her face. "Does that hurt?"

Her eyes and mouth cringed. "A little," she said in a soft tone. She sank down on the sofa while he filled a plastic bag with ice cubes.

"Lay down," Ruben said. When Gwynn was stretched out on the sofa, he sat next to her and held the ice bag against her cheek. "This side of your face will be bruised, and it might be a little swollen tomorrow, but your nose isn't broken."

Someone knocked on the door. Ruben went and looked out the peephole. "Two policemen," he whispered.

"The neighbors probably heard me scream," Gwynn said quietly, sitting up.

After another rap on the door, Ruben gestured for her to answer it, and then he slipped into the bedroom.

"Can I help you?" she said, opening the door for the police officers. One appeared to be in his late forties and the other in his early twenties. Due to the age difference, she wondered if the younger guy was a new recruit.

"One of your neighbors reported hearing screaming coming from your apartment," the older officer said. "Are you okay, Miss?" Both policemen stared at her face.

From their gawking reaction, she suspected her face was red and swollen. "I just had a fight with my boyfriend, that's all." She couldn't think of anything else to say.

"Is your boyfriend still in your apartment?"

"No. He's gone."

The older officer pulled a notepad out of his pocket. "Can we come in and get the information?"

"I don't want to file any type of report. I'm not planning on seeing him again."

The officer handed her a card. "Give us a call if you change your mind or if you see him hanging around."

"Thank you, but I'm sure he won't be back."

The younger policeman raised his eyebrows. Gwynn surmised they had probably heard that often to the detriment of the victim. The two officers strolled away.

Gwynn closed the door and stretched out on the sofa again, and then Ruben placed the ice bag on the side of her face. "I can't use that same explanation tomorrow," she said since all of her co-workers knew she didn't have a steady boyfriend, and she would not tolerate being abused.

"You can tell everyone that you reached for a purse in the top of your closet, and you accidentally knocked down your bowling bag," he suggested.

She glared at him. "How do you know what's in my closet?"

"Remember? We looked for bugs yesterday."

She recalled and smiled, even though it hurt.

He smiled back and said, "Do you have a boyfriend we don't know about?"

"No. How about you, you married?"

"No."

"Good to know," she said, gazing into his radiant brown eyes.

"Your fifth floor apartment is a problem. It took too long for us to get up here. I had planned on coming up after you turned on your lights. We knew Cindy Wood had given you a CD, just like they did. We had observed one guy watching your apartment building all evening, and he was still in the same location when we heard you. Another guy must've been stationed in the lobby. That's never happened before. They must be anxious and concerned since their bugs are gone. At least now we know they were looking for a CD."

"But now I could go to the police and identify the man."

"We don't want the police involved," he reaffirmed.

"They don't know that. Do you think they had other plans for me?" Gwynn swallowed hard, thinking about the knife that she barely dodged.

"I don't know. This incident makes it clear that we'll have to keep an eye on you at all time. If you don't mind, I'll have Gordon sleep on your sofa tonight."

"No, that's fine," she replied, feeling safe but wishing it would be Ruben on the sofa. "What's Gordon going to do with the man?"

"He'll find an appropriate way to handle him," he said, avoiding directly answering her question.

Gwynn suspected the man was in serious trouble since they weren't going to involve the police. "Do you think Cindy and Borge are safe?"

"Probably. If their places were bugged, they still are. It appears they don't know anything, so we doubt there is anything incriminating they could say. Still, we're keeping track of them." He lightly touched her bruised cheek. "Anytime you are not going straight home from work, I want you to give me a call."

Gwynn nodded "I'll make sure to."

CHAPTER 6

Right after Gwynn sat down at her desk, a co-worker asked about the bruise that covered her cheek. As she was giving him the bowling ball story, several other co-workers joined him. It took her over forty minutes to get settled due to continued interruptions.

Alone at her desk, she logged into her computer and looked up asset acquisitions. Listed among the sellers was Trulin Energy Company, but she didn't have access to the application that showed the transaction details. All purchase documents were scanned into that program. Wilton only kept hard copies of major acquisitions. She had friends who worked in the asset acquisition accounting section and knew they could give her a computer printout, but she needed a business reason to request that information.

Gwynn determined she would first look for a hard copy. She planned on making a detour to the acquisition file room during morning break when most employees headed to the cafeteria. That would be her best opportunity to slip in and out of the room without being noticed. She mulled over the possible excuses she could give for being in there if someone spotted her.

Any hope of getting work done vanished when Gwynn found herself staring at the clock as she impatiently waited for breaktime. A thought occurred to her that Julie might have left something important behind at her desk. She got on the elevator and went up to check it out.

"Good morning, Gwynn," Hadley said, giving her a sympathetic smile as he walked out of his office.

"Good morning."

He pointed toward her cheek. "What happened?"

"My bowling ball attacked me," she replied. "I guess it's time to clean out my closet. I just came to pick up Julie's personal stuff."

"I'm sorry. I've already sent that to her condo, but I forgot to enclose her coffee mug. Would you like that?"

"Yes, please."

"Let me get it for you," he said and turned to go back into his office.

Gwynn scrutinized Julie's replacement, the woman sitting at her desk. She was in her early thirties, attractive, slender with shoulder-length brown hair. As the new secretary stood, Gwynn noticed her five-inch stilettos. Her movements and the sophisticated way she was dressed reminded Gwynn of Pam. She wondered if they were friends or maybe relatives. The woman smiled and introduced herself as Beverly Joran. Just as the introductions ended, Hadley walked out of his office.

"I'll give you a call if there's something else," Hadley said, handing Gwynn the mug.

"Thanks."

****

An elevator going up stopped, and its doors opened. Two people got off. Gwynn spotted Cromer, the hired thug, standing at the rear. Even though he only briefly glanced at her as the door closed, a chill still swept through her body. Within a minute, the same elevator stopped on its way down. She felt relieved it was empty as she stepped in.

Heading back to her desk, Gwynn ran into Cindy in the hallway. "What happened to your face?" Cindy asked.

"Bowling ball," Gwynn explained. "It attacked without warning when it tumbled off my closet shelf. Are you feeling okay? You look a little pale."

"I was just up late doing laundry," Cindy lied.

"See you at lunch," Gwynn said, anxious to get back to her desk since it was almost breaktime.

The message light on Gwynn's phone blinked rapidly when she reached her desk. She decided it could wait until after break. She twirled her chair around so no one could see the front of her blouse and pulled her cell phone out of her bra. Gwynn didn't want to take a chance it might ring while she was snooping. She turned it off, stuck it back in her bra, and wished she had a pocket.

Gwynn moved toward the asset accounting file room, checking cubicles along the way. The only employees still at their desks were talking on their phones. She quickly slipped into the room.

The light brown file room was brightly lit with fluorescent lights that covered the ceiling. Rows of six-feet tall, open metal gray cabinets lined the space with thirty-inch aisles between them. Wilton asset purchases were filed alphabetically by the name of the seller. Each seller had at least one folder, some had numerous, containing all the invoices and contracts applicable to that purchase.

It didn't take Gwynn long to find a folder labeled Trulin Energy Company. It contained only a checked-out card, indicating that Kent Fardown had the contents.

Disappointed, she turned to leave when she heard two male voices. She quietly eased around to the end of that row of cabinets. The talking grew louder along with heavy footsteps. She crouched down, held her breath, and inched to the next row. Out of sight from the open doorway, Gwynn went around the edge of the cabinets as the men stepped into the file room. Hunkering next to the floor, her shoulders knotted with tension as she craned her neck to listen.

The men's voices became softer. Straining her ears, she caught a few words, "Trulin...Lark Refinery...buy." She was tempted to creep closer, but knew it wouldn't be safe. Gazing from side to side, she found an opening between two file cabinets and wanted to peek through it to see who was talking. She began raising her head and moving toward it just as the cabinet vibrated and jerked. She held her breath as a wave of panic swirled through her.

A male voice rang out, "Watch it."

"That's all we'd need," another man said.

After that the men whispered. Gwynn couldn't make out anything they were saying as she sank back down to the floor, breathing deeply.

Five minutes later, she heard feet shuffling toward the door. Her knees ached when she stood straight up. She stealthily made her way toward the entrance. Gwynn hid by the open door and listened, just in case someone was nearby. Within a few minutes, she emerged, gradually relaxed when she didn't see anyone, and started walking toward her desk.

"Gwynn, do you need anything?" Jeff, an asset section employee, asked from behind her.

Trying to remain calm, she turned toward Jeff and spotted Carl Backman striding up the aisle. Her heartbeat spiked, and her palms became clammy, yet she was determined not to show any emotion. "Before Taylor moved," she said to Jeff, "he asked if I could get his coffee cup. It has his alma mater on it, but I didn't see it in your breakroom. Do you know what happened to it?"

"Isn't Taylor still missing?" Jeff asked, squinting and sounding confused.

She kept her eyes on Jeff as Carl Backman passed them. "He is. I just wanted to look for it before someone threw it out."

"If it's not in the breakroom, I can't think of anywhere else it would be. I'll let you know if I run across it."

"Thanks," she replied, and then headed back to her cubicle.

Sitting at her desk, she thought, *Carl Backman works on the fifteenth floor. What was he doing up here?*

The message light on her phone continued blinking while Gwynn researched Lark Refinery, the other company mentioned by one of the men in the file room. She had read that refinery had been closed because of some safety and environmental problems. Since she caught the name right after hearing Trulin, she wondered if they were somehow connected. The Lark Refinery's website stated it was still closed. There was nothing on the site about Trulin.

She picked up her office phone and listened to the message. It was from Barb, one of Julie's friends who lived in the same condo complex. Barb left her number and wanted Gwynn to give her a call. She dialed the number.

"Hello," Barb said.

"Hi, Barb. This is Gwynn returning your call."

"This is a little awkward," she began. "I loaned Julie something the weekend before her accident, and I hesitate to ask Borge for it. Could you get it for me?"

"What is it?"

"Well...ahhh," Barb stuttered. "It's...ahhh...receiver."

Gwynn couldn't understand Barb's reluctance. "Let me just call Borge and see if he's seen it."

"There's more to it than that. I don't know if Julie would want Borge to know she had borrowed something like that. Maybe you could just look for it in her condo."

"What more is there?" Gwynn asked, bewildered.

"Julie told me once that your phone calls at work are sometimes monitored. Are they?"

"Yes, sometimes. Why?"

"Can you call me on your cell?"

"Okay. I'll call you right back."

Wondering about the need for secrecy, Gwynn took her cell phone out of her bra, turned it on, and called Barb.

"Hey," Barb answered.

"Okay, what is it?"

"It's a receiver, a short wave radio, that you can listen to, and it records from three mini-microphones."

"You mean a tape recorder?"

"Something like that, but you can put the microphones in different rooms and hear what's being said someplace else."

"Why did Julie borrow it?" Gwynn asked as the bugs Ruben discovered in her apartment flashed through her mind.

"She never told me, but I thought she might be concerned about Borge. I bought it to find out if my boyfriend was cheating. To make a long story short, he was. I told Julie about what happened, and she asked to borrow it. So it might be better not to ask Borge about it. Anyway, now my sister wants to use it."

"I can't imagine Borge ever cheating on Julie. Anyway, I'll go there after work and look for it. How big is it?"

"Around five-by-eight and less than two inches thick. It easily fits in my purse."

"If I find it, I'll run it over to your place,"

"Thanks," Barb said and then clicked off.

Gwynn slipped her cell phone into her bra. She still found it difficult to get any work done as her mind was now preoccupied with the receiver that also records. *Why would Julie borrow something like that?* Gwynn couldn't imagine it was to spy on Borge. He called Julie every night when his band did gigs out of town. The way he looked at her—he adored her. No, Gwynn was convinced it wasn't for Borge. *Maybe Julie took it to work, but why?*

She wanted to call Ruben but decided it might not be safe to contact him from the office unless it was an emergency. Her cubicle could be bugged just like her apartment. If it was, whoever was spying on her had already heard too much.

****

Gwynn and Cindy stood, holding food trays, while they looked for an empty table in the crowded lunch room. Gwynn spotted Beverly, Julie's replacement, at Pam's table. Pam came across as stuck-up and arrogant to Gwynn because she never joined any of the secretaries at lunch. Instead, she ate at one of the vice-presidents' tables or went out to lunch with one or more of them. She also never joined in any conversations among the women, but today she was chatting and having lunch with Beverly. That further reinforced what Gwynn suspected—Beverly and Pam weren't just co-workers.

"There's one over there," Cindy said, nodding toward an empty table in the center of the room. She maneuvered around several occupied tables with Gwynn right behind her. Cindy put down her tray and settled into a chair. "Do you know who that is sitting next to Pam?"

"Beverly something. She works for Hadley."

"Did she take Julie's place?"

"Yeah. I met her when I went to get Julie's things."

"Borge told me that Hadley had sent a box of her stuff."

"Has Borge gone through it?"

Cindy shrugged. "Don't know." She took a bite of her sandwich.

"Hadley forgot to enclose her coffee mug. I'll give it to Borge next time I see him."

"Do you want me to take it to him?" Cindy asked, enthusiastically.

Gwynn normally would have noticed the excitement in Cindy's tone, but the recorder still monopolized her thoughts.

"Are you okay?" Cindy asked.

"Yes. I was just thinking about all the work piled on my desk. It's going to take me a month to get caught up."

"You don't need to worry about that. I'm sure they'll understand. I got so far behind, you know, because I'm always worrying about Taylor." She ran her fingers around the top of her Coke can. "Nate gave half of my work away. He's such a nice guy."

Pam and Beverly were heading toward the exit when they stopped at Gwynn and Cindy's table. "How are you doing, Gwynn?" Pam asked.

"Better," Gwynn replied, surprised Pam would want to know.

"I'm sorry I didn't have an opportunity at Julie's services to tell you what a wonderful eulogy you gave. It was a great tribute to Julie. Truly inspiring."

"Thank you," Gwynn said, doubting Pam's sincerity. She remembered the look of irritation, almost contempt on Pam's face, like she had been forced to attend the funeral.

"You're probably busy taking care of Julie's affairs."

"Borge's handling that," Cindy said.

"Yes, of course. Julie's boyfriend," Pam said. "Cindy, are the police making any progress locating Taylor?"

"They're working on some leads."

"I'm sure they'll find him," Pam said. "Mr. McIntyre is very concerned. Will you let me know if you hear anything?"

"Sure," Cindy nodded.

Pam and Beverly continued toward the door.

"Can you believe that?" Cindy asked.

"No. That's a first," Gwynn said.

"She didn't even introduce the new secretary," Cindy said. "And I'm sure McIntyre is being kept better informed about the investigation than I am. We only went to the police station yesterday. How does she even know I talked to them?"

Gwynn wondered the same thing. "Maybe she knows you're his girlfriend, so she just assumed the police would contact you."

"She never talks to any of us; how would she know who's dating who?"

Gwynn shrugged her shoulders. "Have you got any plans for tonight?" she asked, changing the subject.

"No. I'm just going to take it easy."

"Me, too."

****

Borge had called Cindy at work and asked her if she wanted to come over and have pizza and watch a video. Without hesitation, she said she'd be over right after work. They had talked for a long time the night before. She really enjoyed his company, even though the night ended with him crying on her shoulder. She also felt guilty about seeing him since she was Taylor's girl and hoped he'd show up or at least call her. In the back of her mind Cindy wondered if she was somehow using Borge. At the same time, she mulled over the possibility that Taylor might have run off with Marilyn.

****

Driving over to Borge's place, Gwynn noticed the two black SUVs behind her, the Expedition followed by the Suburban. She couldn't shake the feeling that whoever had bugged her apartment could hear her if she used her cell phone. Assuming one of the black vehicles belonged to Ruben's team, she figured he'd know her whereabouts even if she didn't contact him.

When Borge answered the door, he reluctantly opened it wider to let Gwynn in. She entered, meeting Cindy's eyes.

A puzzled expression crept across Cindy's face. Borge hadn't mentioned inviting anyone else. "Hi, Gwynn. I didn't know you were coming over."

"Would you like a glass of wine?" Borge asked Gwynn as he handed one to Cindy.

"No. I just came to get something. One of Julie's friends called today. She had loaned Julie a tape recorder and needed it back."

"A tape recorder?" Borge sounded perplexed. "What for?"

"Maybe she wanted to record a song or something."

"With all my equipment here, she could have recorded anything she wanted. The sound would have been great!"

"I don't know what she wanted it for," Gwynn said. She couldn't think of any reason she could give Borge that wouldn't hurt him. "Would you mind if I looked through her stuff?"

"No. Let me help you. What does it looks like?"

Even if she didn't want his help, Gwynn had no choice. "All I know is that it's about five-by-eight inches and around two inches thick. There are some small auxiliary sound pieces that go with it."

Cindy checked everywhere in the living room and helped Borge look through all the kitchen cabinets. Gwynn searched through the closet, even opening all the shoeboxes. All three of them went through the drawers in the bedroom. Before they gave up, Borge rummaged through the bathroom cabinets. There wasn't anything that matched, or even came close to the description Barb had given.

"I'll go and tell Barb it isn't here."

"Do you want to have pizza and watch a video with us?" Borge asked. He didn't want her to join them, but he felt awkward about her seeing Cindy there.

"No. I'm tired. It's been a long day." From what they had said while looking for the recorder, Gwynn knew Borge had invited Cindy over. Whatever they had going on, she didn't want to interfere. She thought maybe they needed each other since now they were both alone. Any hope she had that Taylor would be found alive had almost faded away. Her eyes felt moist as she walked over to Barb's condo thinking about him.

Barb answered the door. "Hi!"

"Hi," Gwynn said as she entered Barb's condo. "I looked for your receiver in Julie's condo. I'm sorry, but it wasn't there."

"Do you think it could be in Julie's desk at work?"

"No. Her boss sent all of her personal stuff to Borge. We went through it."

"I just bought it a few weeks ago," Barb said. "It was used. Still, it cost me three hundred bucks. The recorder doesn't work real well, but the receiver worked great. Could Julie have loaned it to someone?"

"I don't know. She never mentioned it to me."

"Well this is just great!" Barb hissed. "I'm out three hundred bucks. Julie said she'd return it the next day. Otherwise, I wouldn't have let her borrow it." Barb's jaw tightened as her eyes narrowed. "So what am I going to tell my sister?"

"The truth. It's lost."

"Maybe I should talk to Borge about it," Barb snapped.

Gwynn didn't want that. "Let me pay you for it," she said calmly.

"I don't know if I can find another receiver with three microphones at that same price."

"What do you think would be fair?"

"Four hundred. I think I can replace it for that."

Based on the hostile expression on Barb's face, Gwynn knew she wouldn't hesitate going to Borge about it. Reluctantly, she wrote Barb a check for $400 and left.

****

Driving home, Gwynn wondered how Julie and Barb ever became friends. Her cell phone rang. She glanced at the number. "Hello," she answered, knowing it was Ruben.

"Have you had anything to eat?" he asked.

"No. I was thinking of getting some Chinese."

"I want to talk to you about several things. How about if I get it and bring it to your place?"

"Okay," she replied.

When she reached her apartment building lobby, she noticed two men she didn't recognize sitting by the elevator. One was bald with a rugged, weather-beaten face and appeared to be tall. The other man was burly and had a round face with thick, bushy eyebrows. Gwynn decided not to go up to her apartment until Ruben arrived. She opened her mailbox and slowly went through the mail.

Ruben walked in as she finished reading all of her third class mail. He didn't say anything to her as they stepped into the elevator along with the two strangers. Only Gwynn and Ruben got off on the fifth floor.

"How did your day go?" Ruben asked while Gwynn unlocked her door.

"Fine. How about yours?" she asked, entering her apartment.

Ruben locked the door behind them and put a sack on the table. "The CD was exactly what I suspected it might be," he said, smiling and taking the food cartons out of the sack.

"What was on it?"

"A video recording of Julie Morgan's funeral service."

"So that's what the guy wanted? He must've missed the service." She put plates and utensils on the table. "What would you like to drink?"

"Have you got any beer?"

"Yes," she said, getting two out of the fridge. "Did you find out anything else?"

"Yes, but first why don't you tell me the reason you didn't call before you went to see Borge Haseman?" Ruben asked with an edge in his voice.

"I know I should've called, but I was afraid my desk and my car might be bugged. And I knew either you or Gordon would be following me."

"We are not the only ones following you. There's always the possibility that we could be cut off. Next time, call!"

Gwynn's eyes narrowed as she looked at him. She didn't like being ordered to do anything. At the same time, she didn't want to take a chance that he might stop giving her updates on the investigation if she didn't do as he requested. "Okay. I'll call."

"Now tell me about your day," he said, dishing up food.

"Wilton did purchase something from Trulin. There's a folder labeled Trulin Energy Company in the asset section file room, but the contents have been checked out by Kent Fardown. It's a Wilton procedure to sign a check-out card when you take a file. His name was the last one on it."

"So you don't know what Wilton purchased?"

"No. It had to be a significant purchase since there's a hard copy."

"What is considered a significant purchase?"

"A few years ago it was anything over $500,000. It might be higher now. I'll try to find out the current benchmark."

They ate for a few minutes in silence. Then he began again, "Let's get back to your day. Was there any special reason why you visited Haseman after work?"

Gwynn told Ruben about the receiver Julie had borrowed from Barb and how she, Borge, and Cindy had searched in vain for it. She also told him about her visit with Barb. He offered to reimburse her the $400, but she refused to take the money.

"That receiver may have some relevance to Miss Morgan's staged accident," Ruben said. "Was there anything at work she was concerned about?"

"She did wonder if Wilton was beginning merger talks with CT. That's all I can think of."

"Was there a reason she thought they were discussing a merger?" he asked, between bites.

She finished chewing and swallowed. "Last year's dividends were meager compared to the prior year and the stockholders weren't happy. Also, Julie had heard that some of the board members had talked about replacing McIntyre if the company's net profit didn't increase. CT's stockholders' dividends were five times greater than Wilton's."

"McIntyre could be ousted soon by the board. Interesting." He took a swig of his beer. "Potential mergers are in the works before they get leaked. Maybe she was trying to find out about that and accidentally overheard something else." Ruben's brow creased as he continued eating.

"Julie wouldn't eavesdrop on a meeting!" Gwynn said adamantly. "She might ask Hadley about it, but that would be all."

Ruben stared at her. "A taped recording could easily be put on a disk. They were looking for something, and so far the only thing that has baited them into explicitly acting was that disk. The missing receiver, the CD, Miss Morgan's staged accident, I suspect they're related.

"The fact that the CD was only a funeral service leads me to think it's not the one that the guy who attacked you was looking for. There must be another disk connected to Miss Morgan. Since it was not sent to her condo, and it wasn't sent to you, can you think of anyone else she would trust with something like that?"

"I know she had an attorney. Julie saw him right after she became engaged to Borge, probably to add him to the title on her condo. I doubt it was for a prenup. I don't know the attorney's name. And there's her grandmother. But you'd already know if she got it." Gwynn tapped her fingertips on the table. "Julie had a safe deposit box."

"Could she have gone to it during lunch that day?"

"I talked to her around noon. She said she was too busy to go to lunch and was eating at her desk. I guess it's possible she could've left the Wilton Tower."

"Do you know the location of her safe deposit box?"

"It's in the First National Bank, right around the corner from her condo. I went with her there a few times. I know where Julie kept the key. It's well hidden. I don't think Borge even knows."

"It must be. Her condo was searched and they continued looking for the disk. Unless they found the key, checked out the box, and it wasn't there."

"I doubt Julie left the building at lunch time on that Monday," Gwynn said, shaking her head. "She wouldn't have lied to me. Even with the key, how can you or how could they check out her safe deposit box?"

"That's not a problem if you have a key and know which bank."

Gwynn wanted to ask why but doubted she would get a straight answer. "I'll go to the condo tomorrow after work and get the key." She cleared off the table. "Something else kind of strange happened today."

"What?"

"Pam, McIntyre's secretary, came over and chatted to Cindy and me while we were eating lunch. She had the new secretary, the one that took Julie's place, with her. They must be buds."

"Why is that unusual?"

"She never talks to any of the women in the office unless she can't avoid it. I've never seen her eat lunch with a secretary."

"So she has a friend," Ruben said with a puzzled expression.

"That's not it. Pam asked Cindy how the police investigation was going. Cindy only went to the police station yesterday. Doesn't that strike you as strange?"

"Not necessarily. Someone probably told her Cindy was Denton's girlfriend."

"She asked Cindy to keep her informed because McIntyre wanted to know."

Ruben's eyebrows rose. "Let me know if she talks to you or Cindy again."

"I will."

"Anything else?"

"This might not be important," Gwynn said, and then proceeded to tell him what she heard in the file room and the research she did on Lark Refinery.

"It could very well be important. I'll have someone follow-up on that refinery."

"What did you find out today?" Gwynn rested her elbow on the table and cupped her chin in her hand.

"Trulin Energy Company deposited $200 million in their account a few weeks ago." He leaned back in the chair and stretched his legs out in front of him. "Two prior Wilton employees opened the account — Ray Sorenson and Ethan Lemus. Do you know either of them?"

"Ethan Lemus. He used to be Wilton's in-house attorney. I've heard the name Ray Sorenson before, but I don't know who he is."

"He was the guy you recognized on the video talking to Kent Fardown. The one you thought might be a Wilton employee since you had seen him in the building before."

"The husky guy?"

Ruben nodded. "He worked in marketing under Fardown."

"Did you find out anything else about Trulin?"

"Not yet. I have a person doing some research."

"Do you think there might be a connection between Trulin and what happened to Julie?" Gwynn asked, lowering her arms and adjusting her seat.

"Whoever searched your apartment wanted the contracts Taylor Denton had sent to Cindy Wood. That's all we know right now."

A loud rap on the door echoed through Gwynn's apartment.

"That must be Gordon," Ruben said, standing up. He looked out the peephole, and then opened the door.

Gordon strode in. "There are two of them in the apartment building, and one sitting in the car."

"Do you think they're the two guys that got on the elevator with us?" Gwynn asked Ruben.

"Probably."

"I've never seen them before," Gwynn said.

"It appears they've increased their workforce and hired more thugs," Ruben said. "Gordon will be staying here again tonight, if you don't mind."

"No," Gwynn replied, feeling good about it.

"I need to check on something," Ruben said. "So I'll say good-night."

CHAPTER 7

Cindy felt guilty about spending so much time with Borge and trying to hide it from Gwynn. She still thought about Taylor all the time; her hopes of him returning to her dimmed with each passing day. As soon as she got to work, she called Sergeant Fillmore to see if he had any news to report. The sergeant claimed they were still checking out some leads, but he didn't sound very hopeful. Cindy's stomach churned as she worried again that he had found someone else to take her place in his life.

She liked being with Borge and thought he needed her. He got visibly upset whenever he saw the back of a woman with long blonde hair, like Julie's, even while they watched a video. She felt good comforting him and loved his arms around her when she needed to be comforted. On top of that, he was handsome, interesting, and patient when she talked to relatives on the phone, which said a lot about him since she came from a large family. Julie had been crazy about Borge and now she understood why.

Cindy planned to fess up and walked into Gwynn's cubicle. "Have you ever heard Borge play his guitar?" she asked, her eyebrows bouncing.

"Yes," Gwynn replied. "If you can recall, we've all gone when his band played in Houston."

"Well ... yes ... I know. But I had never heard him play alone. He is absolutely wonderful. I could listen to him all night. I'm going with him to a movie tonight. Do you think it's okay?"

"Of course." Gwynn didn't want either of them to be alone and also thought, *Cindy going out with Borge might help her get her mind off Taylor.* "What movie?"

"I don't know. I'm sorry I lied to you yesterday about going home right after work."

"That's okay. Don't think anything about it."

Cindy's eyes sparkled, and she smiled. "See you at lunch."

****

Shortly after 5 p.m. Wilton employees started to clear out. Gwynn decided she'd stay a little longer and try to get into the computer system used by the asset section. She wanted to know the details of the transaction between Wilton and Trulin. Taylor had often joked about Jeff not following any of the computer security procedures. He left his user name and password in his top drawer that didn't lock. He was the guy Gwynn had talked to about Taylor's fictitious mug. She figured it was okay if she didn't call Ruben to tell him she'd be staying late since she wasn't leaving the building.

When her co-workers were finally all gone, Gwynn eased out of her chair and made her way over to Jeff's cubicle. She sat down at his desk, found his computer login information, turned on his computer, and entered his user name and password. Within a minute she located the right program. She drilled down through numerous screens, clicked on Trulin, and the contract appeared. Gwynn didn't want to read it sitting at his desk. She hit the print key knowing it would be noisy, but she didn't think anyone was within earshot. Shortly after the printer started, she heard talking.

"I'm sure he's gone," a raspy-voiced man said loudly.

Gwynn ducked down and anxiously waited for the document to finish printing. She grabbed it and slid out of the cubicle without turning off Jeff's computer. She crouched down and scooted along the floor toward the nearest hallway door.

"He left his computer on," another man said.

"What a waste of electricity. Turn it off," the raspy-voiced man said.

As soon as Gwynn reached the hallway, the elevator door opened and two janitors got off. She quickly stepped in and headed down to

Human Resources on the twentieth floor. There, she picked up a few brochures about retirement plans and went to the restroom. She folded the copied contract, stuck part of it under her bra, and the other part in her slacks. Then she looked in the mirror and adjusted her clothing to hide the bulges. She went back up in the elevator.

Cromer, dressed in a security guard uniform, stood in the aisle by her cubicle. "Why are you still at work?" he asked.

Gwynn held up the retirement brochures. "I'm leaving now. I just wanted to get some information from Human Resources, but everyone has gone for the day."

Cromer snatched the brochures out of Gwynn's hand and glanced through them.

"I've taken brochures before when no one was in Human Resources," she said, feeling goosebumps rising on her arms, yet maintaining her composure. "I didn't realize that was a problem."

He dropped the brochures on her desk. "It's not."

While Cromer remained close to her cubicle, Gwynn calmly took her purse out of her drawer, locked her cabinets, and walked to the elevator. Along the way, she saw several security guards opening and closing doors down the hallway. Cromer followed her into the elevator and stared blankly at her as it descended. Her body felt tense and her lips quivered slightly as she sensed his eyes on her. She moved farther away from him each time the elevator stopped and people got on.

When Gwynn stepped into the lobby, one of the security guards approached her and checked her purse. As she left the building, she wondered just how many of Wilton employees were involved in Julie's demise.

Ruben stood next to Gwynn's car talking on his cell phone until he saw her get off the parking garage elevator, and then he ended his conversation and put away his phone. "You're late. What were you up to?" he asked slowly, controlling his anger.

Gwynn noticed the hostile expression on his face, but didn't want to pull out the contract in the parking garage. "I'll tell you later."

"Give me your keys," he ordered.

From his harsh tone, Gwynn knew this wasn't the time or place to argue with him. She reluctantly handed them over.

"You're coming with me," he said, gripping her arm. "Dean will drive your car."

A tall, good-looking, well-built man with light brown hair and a close-clipped beard in his mid-thirties climbed out of a black Suburban. Ruben handed him the keys and led Gwynn to the front passenger door.

"Where's Gordon?" she asked, scooting into the Suburban.

"He's checking on something."

"Did you increase your workforce?"

"No." Ruben drove out of the parking garage. "Let's go over this one more time since you obviously weren't paying attention last night," he said, irritated. "You will — that is not a maybe, that is a must — call me if anything out of the ordinary occurs. You normally get off work at five, so when you leave the building at six, that is considered abnormal. Are you following me so far?"

"I'm not a child!" she hissed. "And I'm not one of your employees! Whether or not I call you is my choice, and I chose not to call you!"

Ruben pulled the car over to the curb and stopped. He glared at Gwynn. "Part of my job is to keep you safe. I can't do that if I don't know what you are doing. If you do not keep me informed, I will have no alternative but to have you stay in a well-guarded cabin until I finish my investigation. Do you understand?"

"You can't make me be your prisoner!"

"But I can, and I won't hesitate."

"You've told me that Mrs.VanAusdell doesn't want the police involved, but I think I might need their protection. I won't be your prisoner!" she said through gritted teeth.

"And what will you tell the police?"

Gwynn sat quietly thinking, flushing with anger. What could she tell the police? That a man wants her to be his prisoner; that something is going on at Wilton; that Julie's car accident wasn't an accident? If they asked for anything to substantiate her allegations, she had nothing to give. She had even lied about her bruised face when the police came to her apartment.

Ruben took her hand. "Relax. Breathe. I'm not going to harm you. I just want to make sure you are safe." He lightly stroked her face. "Breathe."

She hadn't realized she had been holding her breath as she exhaled and inhaled deeply and thought he might be right. *Inside the Wilton Tower could be a dangerous place after hours.*

"What would you prefer?" he asked calmly. "To go to a nice comfortable cabin and have a few leisurely days away from the city or call me if anything out of the ordinary occurs?"

Gwynn's shoulders slumped, and she lowered her head. "I'll call you."

"Just remember, if you find that too difficult, there is a nice place waiting for your visit."

"Don't you think I can help you?"

"I do. Otherwise, we'd be on our way to the cabin right now." He picked up her hand and kissed it. "Would you like to go out to dinner?"

She felt confused. A second ago, he was going to make her a prisoner since she didn't call him, now he was asking her to go out. "Yes, but I'd like to get some documents out of my underwear first."

"Can I help?" he asked as a faint smile creased his lips.

"No!"

He started the engine and drove to her apartment without asking about the documents. Given their discussion, he thought he needed to take it a little easy with her. Even if she said she'd call, he wasn't convinced she would. Usually, if clients feared they'd be harmed, they were anxious to stay in a secure protected place. Gwynn was the first person he had to protect who didn't follow his orders. He needed to change that. From the way she looked at him when he held the ice bag on her cheek, he suspected she was attracted to him. Maybe a little romance would help her trust him more. Ruben didn't like playing with her emotions, yet he had to keep her safe. It was part of his job. No one he protected ever died under his watch. He would use whatever means he had available to keep that record.

Dean handed Gwynn's keys to Ruben as they walked from the parking lot to her apartment building. Then he climbed into another Suburban and drove away.

As soon as Gwynn and Ruben entered her apartment, she went into the bathroom and removed the document from her clothing. "I printed off a copy of the contract between Trulin and Wilton," she said, heading into the living room. "Wilton purchased some leases from Trulin." She noticed Ruben's eyes light up. "I want to study the contract, but first I want to go to Julie's condo and get her safe deposit key. Borge and Cindy are at the movies, and I don't want to explain to him what I'm getting. I have a key to Julie's condo."

"We'll go there on the way to dinner."

"Oh, I almost forgot. Luke Cromer works for Wilton. He wore a security guard uniform today."

"That doesn't necessarily mean he works for Wilton. He could have acquired the uniform in a different way. We're still working on determining his employer."

Gwynn looked through her mail while Ruben went to freshen up. There was a letter from Babcock and Associates, Attorneys at Law. Opening it, she saw it was about Julie's will. The letter requested that she be at their offices on Friday at 3 p.m. If she couldn't make it, there was a number to call in the last paragraph. Gwynn felt surprised by the tone of the letter. She didn't think Julie had an estate other than her condo.

"I'm going to see Julie's attorney on Friday about her will," Gwynn told Ruben as he came out of the bathroom.

"I'll plan accordingly."

Gwynn put the Trulin contract in her purse. "I don't want to take a chance on leaving this here."

"I had already planned on taking it with us. We can stop and copy it."

****

Gwynn had Ruben stay in the front room of Julie's condo while she went into the bedroom. She didn't want him to see the hiding place in case Julie had put some personal items there.

She opened the third drawer of the bureau and emptied it, taking out scarves and sweaters. Next she turned the drawer handle and the bottom slid open, revealing a small compartment. Cash and three keys were in it. Gwynn picked up the keys — two went to the safe deposit box and one went to a post office box. Then she remembered Julie getting one when her checks were stolen from her apartment mailbox before she moved to the condo. Gwynn wondered, *Could it still be active?* She put one of the safe deposit keys back in the hiding place, closed the compartment, and laid the sweaters and scarves neatly back. Still irritated about the way Ruben had treated her earlier, she didn't want him knowing everything; she stuck the post office box key in her bra. Now she was curious if there was something in that box. If it contained a disk, she planned on copying it before she handed it over to Ruben. Even if Mrs. VanAusdell didn't want the police involved, she wasn't sure if she agreed. She'd keep her own file in case she decided to go to them.

"Here's Julie safe deposit key," Gwynn said, handing it to Ruben.

"We'll check it out tomorrow." He dropped the key in his sport coat pocket. "Do you like French cuisine?"

"Yes. It reminds me of the great time I had in Paris."

Ruben drove her to a small, secluded restaurant. The stone walls, the dark walnut furnishings, the white, linen tablecloths, the flickering candles in the center of the tables, the aroma of braised meats and baked breads: all added to the warm ambiance of the room.

The owner, dressed in a dark suit and white dress shirt, recognized Ruben and talked to him as he led them to a table in a private corner.

As they drank wine, they looked over the menu. There were some special items that Ruben wanted Gwynn to try so he ordered for both of them. During dinner, they talked about Paris and other places in Europe where they had both traveled. Neither one of them mentioned the case.

After they emptied the bottle of wine and finished eating, Gwynn felt completely relaxed as she looked at her handsome, charming escort.

Ruben held her hand as they walked to the car.

She glanced at his face, saw his glowing brown eyes in the dimly-lit parking lot, and hoped the evening wouldn't end when they reached her apartment. Then she noticed a Suburban just like Ruben's parked next to his and saw Gordon step out of it. Before that, she had thought about telling him about the other key. Now she decided against it since the romantic evening had been spoiled.

After she was seated in Ruben's car with the door closed, she watched as Gordon handed a small bag to Ruben, and they chatted for a few minutes.

Ruben opened the door. "Look in this bag," he said, giving it to her, "and see if Miss Morgan's engagement ring is among the items."

Without asking any questions, she dumped the contents of the bag in her lap and began rummaging through the rings. She picked up one with small rubies on each side of the diamond, just like Julie's.

"This looks like hers, but I can't say for sure. Where did Gordon get it?"

"Hang onto it." Ruben gathered up the other rings and slipped them back in the bag. "Gordon needs to get these back. We'll talk about the ring when we get to your place." He shut the door, gave the bag back to Gordon, and resumed talking to him.

Five minutes later, Ruben drove out of the parking lot. He stopped on the way to Gwynn's apartment and made two copies of the contract. "You never told me how you were able to obtain a copy of the contract," he said, easing back into traffic.

"It wasn't a problem," she said with a smirk on her face. She was just as capable as he was in giving vague answers.

He glanced at her, frowning. She smiled to herself.

****

Back in her apartment, Gwynn took the ring out of her purse and thoroughly examined it under her desk lamp. "Where did Gordon get this?" she asked again.

"Out of Pam Simmons's jewelry box," Ruben replied, sitting down on the sofa.

"Did Gordon search her house?"

"Yes. She was meeting someone at Brody's after work. Also, McIntyre is out of town with Fardown."

"Did you also have their places searched?"

"We tried. McIntyre had a security guard at his place and Fardown's wife was home. We'll try again on Friday night."

"Why was Pam's place searched?" Gwynn asked. "And how did you know she was going to be meeting someone?"

"Since you thought that the blonde woman on the security footage might be her, I had Gordon search her house. I have an employee on the inside. That's how I knew Miss Simmons wouldn't be home. We don't know if she's somehow involved in this case. Until we have more answers, everyone Miss Morgan came in contact with at Wilton is a suspect. Tomorrow evening, Hadley's house will be searched."

"Hadley?" Gwynn asked, her eyes opening wider. "He really liked Julie. I can't imagine he could be mixed up in this."

"He might not be. For now we're not ruling out any possibilities."

"Who works for you at Wilton?"

"Someone who can help find answers."

Knowing that was all the information she was going to get, Gwynn held up the ring. "Do you want me to ask Borge about it? I could tell him that the ring was found in the remains of the car. He'll be upset, but if you need to know."

"Why don't you try to ask Borge about the ring, but not in the condo. If it becomes a problem, let it go." He paused. "Do you know the name of the jewelry store?"

"Celeste. I saw the box."

"Let me check that out before you talk to Borge." He rubbed his chin with his knuckles. "There's more—Miss Simmons isn't just a secretary at Wilton. She handles the books for some small corporations. They're only shells; all they have is a checking account. Money is funneled through them from Wilton and paid to various senators and representatives. Money is also funneled through her personal checking account and paid to the same legislators. I'm sure the politicians would rather not say the total actual amount of their donations they receive from Big Oil."

"I wonder how Wilton indicates that in their books?" she said, thinking out loud. "It's probably still shown as political donations with supporting documentation showing the trail. The Wilton officers are always schmoozing with Dalton & Meyers, the company's auditors. Given the size of the gifts I've been told the auditors receive, I can't imagine they'd ever say Wilton was doing anything unethical."

"Gordon found out some additional information and said it was of a personal nature. I didn't want to keep you waiting any longer in the car, so he'll fill me in later."

"Personal nature — what does that mean?"

"Probably her love life."

For years Gwynn had heard the rumor that Pam was having an affair with McIntyre, even when he was married. She assumed it was about that. Yet, whether it was true or not, that didn't have any bearing on finding who was responsible for Julie's death. "Anything else?"

"Since you mentioned that Wilton had a meeting with CT Oil and Gas Company that morning, we've been doing some research on that company. We discovered they recently lost a few employees to casualties. Those employees worked for various CT pipelines."

"That reminds me of another reason why Julie wondered about that meeting." Gwynn adjusted herself on the sofa and crossed her legs. "Last year, one of the major gas pipelines used by Wilton had to undergo a significant repair. Wilton wanted to move some gas on one of CT's pipelines. CT claimed they didn't have any capacity left to move the gas, but that wasn't true. McIntyre got the Federal Energy Regulatory Commission, FERC, involved and CT was forced to move Wilton's gas."

"And now they're teaming up on something — but what?" Ruben tapped his fingers on the sofa's armrest.

"What were the casualties?"

"There have been a total of five in the past month that we questioned. None of them occurred while the employee was at work. Two died in climbing accidents. They worked for CT's gas pipeline division and monitored a large compression station along with some pipelines running through Wyoming." Ruben had spent the morning in Wyoming checking on one of the casualties and knew from the reaction of the victim's wife that it wasn't an accident, although he wasn't able to obtain any information from her. "Three worked for CT's offshore oil pipeline division. One died when a crane supposedly malfunctioned and some steel beams hit him. Two drowned in separate boating accidents.

"Wilton and CT both employ a significant number of people. There were more deaths than these casualties, but the others didn't appear to be out of the ordinary — illnesses, natural causes, car crashes. I briefly looked at those involved with car crashes; in all the cases injuries were sustained in both vehicles. We're still researching these five casualties. Some might turn out to be just accidents— nothing more."

"Those poor families," Gwynn said sadly, thinking about Julie.

Ruben stood up. "I need to make a quick call," he said, walking into the bedroom.

She leaned down, picked up a contract from the coffee table and started reading it.

When he returned, she said, "Wilton purchased oil property and leases located in North Dakota and Wyoming from Trulin. The Wyoming property is currently producing. The North Dakota property has proven reserves but needs to be developed. There's a petroleum engineer's report attached verifying the reserves and a memo from the Land Department supporting the purchase. Carl Backman signed the memo. Ethan Lemus signed the contract for Trulin, and Kent Fardown signed it for Wilton. Next to his signature, he wrote 'for John McIntyre'."

"Was the purchase price $200 million?" Ruben asked. After Gwynn nodded, he went on, "That seems high."

"Not if this reserve report is accurate."

"I'll check that out tomorrow." He casually glanced at his watch to see how much time he had before Gordon arrived — less than a half an hour. He knew there wouldn't be enough time for anything to get out of hand when he put his arm around Gwynn's shoulders. "It will be nice when this is all behind us." He slid her closer to him.

She liked his arm around her. At the same time, she wondered if he was just using his good looks and charm to get closer to her so she'd completely obey him. She didn't want another confrontation like they had in the car, but she wasn't his employee. She was curious how far he would go; she put her head on his shoulder and her hand on his thigh.

He raised her chin and kissed her. She kissed him back, remembering how much she enjoyed being with him at the restaurant. He kissed her again and her lips parted slightly. She felt his tongue and a rush of excitement ran through her body. It had been a long time since she was this close to a man and she wanted him.

His breathing became heavier as he moved his hand down her body and slowly unbuttoned her blouse. He kissed her neck, unhooking her bra.

She unbuttoned his shirt and her pulse spiked when he ran his hand up her leg. Hearing a knock on the door, they withdrew from each other and sat straight up.

His brilliant eyes closed briefly as he kissed her hand. Neither one of them said anything while they buttoned their clothing. He occasionally looked at her delicate hands, her pretty face with high cheek bones, and her well-proportioned slender body. He didn't want to stop, but she was business. He stood up and opened the door to let Gordon in.

Ruben turned toward Gwynn. "If you don't mind, Gordon will be staying here again tonight."

She wished Ruben would give Gordon some excuse and stay in Gordon's place. Even if he was using his charms to get what he wanted, she liked the closeness.

Ruben picked up all the copies of the contract.

"Can you leave a copy here so I can read it over again?" she asked.

He handed her one.

"Tomorrow after work, I'm stopping at the post office to mail a present to my aunt," she said, wanting to check out Julie's post office box.

"I'd rather you come straight here after work. You can give the present to me, and I'll have someone mail it."

"No, I'll take care of it," she insisted.

Ruben felt annoyed as he said goodnight. He believed he had made some progress with Gwynn, but obviously not enough.

CHAPTER 8

A post office stood right around the corner from Julie's former apartment; Gwynn guessed that was the location of Julie's box. She decided she'd go there during lunch so she could go "straight home" after work like Ruben had requested. She called Cindy and told her she had to run some errands during lunchtime.

A black Suburban and a black Expedition followed her as she drove out of the parking garage. Now she knew the black Suburban belonged to someone on Ruben's team—maybe Ruben.

She parked and walked at a brisk pace to the post office entrance carrying a wrapped empty box. It didn't take her long to find the post office box that matched the number on the key: 268. She looked over her shoulder. When she didn't spot anyone watching her, she inserted the key and turned it. The box opened and she pulled out two items, a disk mailer and a letter from Babcock & Associates. She stuck them in her purse and locked the box. On the way to the restroom, Gwynn dropped her wrapped box in the garbage can. She went into a stall, pulled the disk mailer from her purse, and tucked it under her camisole.

Moving toward the post office door, she noticed a bald man wearing a suit standing near the entrance. When she stepped closer, she saw his face. He was the man with the rugged, weather-beaten face she had seen in her apartment building. She avoided eye contact as she passed him and hurried to the sidewalk. Sensing he was right behind her, Gwynn picked up her pace as she rushed toward the parking lot. She heard his feet pounding against the concrete, and then he grabbed her arm.

"Give me what you just took out of the box," he hissed.

"Let go of my arm!" she shouted. "I didn't take anything out of a box."

"I saw you!"

Gordon approached. "Is there a problem here?"

"Yes," Gwynn said. "This man won't let go of my arm."

"Let go of her arm!" Gordon ordered.

"She has something that belongs to me," the bald man said.

Gordon grabbed the man's other arm, folded it behind his back, pulled the man's elbow toward his spine and his wrist to his neck. "If you don't let go of her arm right now, you won't make it out of this parking lot alive," he whispered.

"And who do you think you are?" the man said sarcastically.

"Someone who doesn't like to see women hassled," Gordon replied.

A crowd began to gather as Gordon twisted the man's arm. A few seconds later, the bald man let go of Gwynn. Gordon yanked out and flashed a badge toward the spectators. "This is police business," he shouted. "This man is wanted for questioning."

The crowd dispersed as Gordon led the man toward his car. He secured him in the back seat with handcuffs attached to a steel pole that ran across the roof of the Suburban. Gordon snatched a cell phone out the man's shirt pocket and dropped it into a nearby garbage container.

Gwynn spotted another man she had also seen before standing next to a black Expedition and wondered if he would make a move. With people constantly coming and going from the parking lot, she hoped that would deter him from trying anything.

"I'll take you back to work," Gordon said to Gwynn.

"What about my car?"

"We'll get it later."

Without hesitation, Gwynn scooted into the front passenger seat of Gordon's car since she didn't want to take a chance of anyone getting the disk from her. As she secured the seat belt, she speculated about what could be on it.

Gordon made a quick call to Ruben, and then drove out of the parking lot. He turned onto a side street lined with two story industrial buildings and glanced at Gwynn. "Did you get anything in the post office?"

"Yes," she confessed.

Looking at the rear view mirror, Gordon saw the barrel of a gun protruding from the window of the Expedition right behind them. "This car is bulletproof."

"Do you think they're going to shoot at us?" she asked with concern evident in her voice.

A loud ping rang out from a bullet striking the back of the Suburban. Gwynn covered her head with her hands and bent her neck.

"I sure hope not," he said with a tinge of sarcasm as a burst of gunfire hit the vehicle. Gordon slammed the accelerator to the floor. He skidded around a bend onto a major highway with the Expedition only twenty feet behind. Tires squealed and cars swerved as Gordon darted in and out of traffic. He gunned the engine and glided through an intersection as the light turned red.

Gwynn focused on the side mirror and saw the black Expedition stopped at the light with heavy traffic moving in front of it.

Cars honked while Gordon continued barreling around them. He executed several sharp turns. Gravel and dust spun up as he peeled down an alleyway. He eased up on the gas pedal and pulled into a parking lot behind a motel. He stopped, dug his cell phone out of his pocket, punched a number, and gave his location.

"Stay in the car," Gordon said, climbing out of the vehicle. He strolled around it, checking for damage. "Only a couple of small dents," he said, standing by the door.

A black Suburban pulled into the parking stall next to them. Ruben stepped out of it. His eyebrows rose with irritation as he opened Gwynn's door. "Is it really that difficult for you to call before you do something out of the ordinary?" he snapped.

"Well...well," she stuttered. "You wanted me to go straight home right after work so I thought it would be better if I went to the post office during lunch."

"Come with me. I don't want our prisoner listening to this conversation."

Gwynn had completely forgotten about the guy in the back seat. "What are you going to do with him?"

Ruben glimpsed at the bald man. "Gordon will handle it."

After they were seated in Ruben's car, he handed her a small object. "I want you to wear this. Do you think that will be too difficult?" he asked with his eyes fixed on her. "Or are you ready for a few days in the cabin?"

She studied the object. "This doesn't look like the bug in my apartment."

"It's more powerful since you'll be wearing it in the Wilton Tower. I want a clear signal. Sometimes electronics interfere."

"I'll wear it." She looked down and ran her eyes over her clothing. "Where would be the best place?"

"Probably in your bra."

"I'm already carrying my cell in my bra. And yesterday I had to tuck a few pages of the contract under it. At this rate, I'm going to need to buy a bigger size."

Ruben's face relaxed, and his mouth curled up into a smile. "There might be a better place. Would you like me to find one?"

"Of course," she replied in a flirtatious tone. "Would you like me to lie down, or should I stand up?"

Ruben leaned over, took the bug out of her hand, and slipped it into her bra. "What did you pick up at the post office?"

"Julie had a post office box. I found a disk in it."

"And you didn't think it was important to tell me about her box?" he asked in a cool tone.

Gwynn's eyes dropped to her lap, and she caught a glimpse of her watch. "I had forgotten about it until I saw the key next to her safe deposit box keys. I need to get back to work. Can we talk about this later?"

"Do you have the disk on you?"

"Yes. It's hidden."

"I don't want you to go into the Wilton Tower with it."

"Will you promise you won't listen to it without me?"

"Like *your* promises?"

"Then I'm not going to give it to you."

"Okay. I promise I won't listen to it without you being present. And I keep my promises."

"Turn around so I can get it."

"Do you think that's necessary?"

"Yes," Gwynn replied adamantly.

Ruben turned away from her. Gwynn unbuttoned her slacks and pulled the disk container out from underneath her camisole.

"You can turn around now," she said, buttoning up her slacks. "Here." She handed Ruben the mailer. "Remember your promise."

"I won't forget." He drove to the Wilton Tower. "If you give me your car keys, I'll have someone drive it to your apartment building. I'll pick you up at five."

Gwynn fished her keys out of her purse and gave them to him. "See you later," she said, getting out of the car.

****

It was around three o'clock when she sat down at her desk and noticed her message light blinking rapidly. After telling her supervisor she was late coming back from lunch because of car problems, she checked her messages. Two were business, and one was from Cindy. She returned Cindy's call first.

Gwynn told Cindy the same car problem excuse she had given her boss for getting back to work late.

"Sergeant Fillmore called," Cindy said.

"Did he find out anything?"

"Nothing about Taylor, but they found Marilyn Anders' car in Arizona. It was abandoned, and everything was stripped out of it. The sergeant said all that was left was the frame. Then he asked me again about Taylor and Marilyn's relationship. I told him that if Taylor was with Marilyn, he'd still call his mom since he talked to her at least twice a week. Taylor wouldn't want to worry her."

Gwynn suspected Taylor was dead. Still, until his body was found, there was a flicker of hope. "I know Taylor's mom didn't know where his dad was; have the police been able to locate him?"

"Yes. I asked the sergeant about him. He said Taylor's dad was living in South Carolina. They've talked to him. He hasn't seen Taylor for seven years. We all knew that."

"Does the sergeant have any leads?"

"He says he does. I think he's hung up on Marilyn and Taylor being together," she said in a voice heavy with despair. "I guess there isn't anything I can do but wait."

Gwynn tried to think of something to say about Taylor that might comfort Cindy, but nothing popped into her head, so she changed the subject. "How was the movie?"

"Great. We saw a 3-D Disney show. We didn't want to see anything too serious. It was a fun movie. Oh, yeah, I received a letter from Julie's attorney. He wants me to go to his office on Friday. It said it was about Julie's will. Borge got a letter, too. I can't imagine Julie had anything but her condo."

"Neither can I," Gwynn agreed. "I also got a letter. I need to get back to work." She clicked off, unzipped her purse, and pulled out the letter she took from Julie's post office box. She stared at it as she contemplated opening it since it was addressed to Julie. Feeling uneasy about it, she slid a pencil under the flap, and eased it open. She unfolded the letter and found it was a bill for amending Julie's will. Gwynn's mouth fell open as she gazed at the amount due and thought, *now I know why I don't have a will.*

****

At 5 p.m., Gwynn picked up her purse and headed to the elevator. She stepped into it along with Cromer and four other employees. As the elevator moved downward, she felt him staring at her. Each time the doors slid open, she tensed slightly, fearing she'd be forced to get off. She sighed with relief when it reached the lobby. Just like yesterday, her purse was targeted and searched before she left the building.

Ruben's car was parked next to the curb, and he opened the door for her. "How did the rest of your day go?" he asked, driving away.

She told him about her conversation with Cindy. "Do you think there is any possibility that Taylor is being held somewhere for some reason?"

"I've already told you that I don't like to speculate."

She lightly stroked his thigh. "Please, just this once."

"No."

"No, you won't speculate; or no, you don't think he's being held prisoner somewhere?"

"I won't speculate."

Her eyes drifted to the side window and she gazed at the traffic as she mulled over the possibility that Taylor could be a prisoner. She sat quietly, deep in thought until Ruben reached her apartment. "Will Gordon be staying at my place tonight?" she asked, breaking the silence.

"That's the plan." He got out of the car and opened her door. "There's a pizza place about a block from here. Would you like pizza for dinner?"

"Sounds good."

"I have an appointment at eight. I'll get a pizza and we can listen to the disk while we eat. Gordon should be here around seven-thirty." Ruben scanned the parking lot. "I don't see any of their cars." He looked at her suspiciously. "You are still wearing the bug, aren't you?"

"Yes. It's right where you left it."

"Would you like to go with me to get the pizza?"

"No. I'd like to change clothes," she said, climbing out of the car. All Gwynn wanted to do was curl up with a good book. She had experienced enough excitement for one day.

"Do you want me to go up with you?"

"No, I'll be okay. If I see any of them or someone I don't recognize in the lobby, I'll stay there until you get back."

Ruben stuck his hand in his glove compartment and pushed a button.

"What's that for?" she asked.

"Shhh," he whispered. A minute later, he said, "I was just checking your apartment. I wanted to make sure you didn't have any uninvited guests." He watched her enter the apartment building, and then he drove off.

When the door slammed behind her, she paused in a deserted lobby and slowly walked over to her mailbox. Several people got off the elevator and she recognized all of them. Even if she didn't know their names, she knew they lived in the building.

The elevator stopped on her floor and her eyes flitted back and forth as she scanned the empty hall. After Ruben had told her about his investigation, she had often gone to her apartment unescorted, but today, every step sent a chill through her body. The closer she got, the more nervous she became. Finally, Gwynn reached her apartment. She quickly unlocked the door, slipped in, and locked it as she took a deep breath.

As she eased out of her shoes, someone grabbed her from behind and covered her mouth. A scar-faced man stepped in front of her.

CHAPTER 9

Gwynn had never seen the short, thin man whose face was streaked by several long scars before. He moved his hands down her body as his accomplice restrained her. She trembled while his hands lingered on her breasts. He stuck his hand in her bra and pulled out the bug. He put it in a padded, steel box that sat on the table. He continued feeling every inch of her body as she squirmed. When he finished, her eyes were moist and she felt violated.

He took a small oval-shaped object from his sport coat pocket and glanced at it. "Clear," he said with a straight, emotionless face.

The man behind Gwynn released his grip over her mouth as he continued holding firmly onto her arms. She recognized the round-faced, burly-looking stranger who had been in the apartment elevator with Ruben and her.

The scar-faced man glared at her, his eyes narrowing. "Where's the disk?"

"What disk?"

He slapped her face. She winced in pain, but held her composure.

A hard knock shook the apartment door. The burly man clutched Gwynn's mouth with his hand again.

The scar-faced man drew a pistol from under his coat and aimed the barrel at her. "Tell whoever it is that you aren't feeling well," he whispered. "Nothing else."

The burly man led her to the door and lowered his hand from her mouth.

The next knock caused the door to rattle on the hinges.

"Gwynn?" Ruben said loudly.

"I'm not feeling well," she yelled, leaning against the door frame.

"Why don't you take this pizza? You can have it later when you're feeling better."

The scar-faced man whispered, "You're going to bed. You couldn't eat anything."

Gwynn relayed the message.

"See you tomorrow," Ruben called through the door.

Her captors remained silent while Ruben's footsteps drifted away from the door.

"Where's the disk?" the scar-faced man asked. "The one you got at the post office."

"I didn't get any disk."

The man switched his gun to his left hand and flung his right hand across her face again. The pain brought tears to her eyes. She swallowed hard, holding her lips tightly together. Blood trickled from her nose, running over her mouth and down her blouse.

"I don't know what you're talking about," Gwynn said as tears drizzled down her cheeks.

"You'll talk." The scar-faced man strutted to the coffee table, pulled a narrow, rectangular-shaped, plastic container out from the inside of his sport coat, and snapped it open. He lifted up a syringe and began filling it.

Suddenly, the apartment door burst open. Ruben lunged at the scar-faced man, knocking the syringe out of his hand as he punched the man's face and kicked his side. The burly man let go of Gwynn and joined in the fight.

As Ruben swung his hand into the back of the scar-faced man's neck, he smashed his elbow into the burly man's stomach, sending the assailant reeling backwards. The scar-faced man fell to the floor, unconscious. The burly man staggered, but caught his balance and yanked a gun from under his coat. Ruben hurled his foot into the assailant's chest. The pistol flew across the room. Gasping for air, the burly man's knees buckled. As he struggled to gain his footing, Ruben kicked the side of his face. The man swayed. He struck his head on the coffee table. As he attempted to rise, he collapsed in a heap, motionless.

Gwynn's face was wet with tears. Ruben put his arms around her. "I should have taken you with me." He led her to the sofa. Then he got a wet towel, wiped the blood from her face, and felt her nose. "It isn't broken."

The scar-faced man regained consciousness and crawled toward his weapon.

Ruben noticed the man's movement. He yanked a knife out of his boot.

Gripping his gun in his fist, the scar-faced man pointed the barrel at Gwynn. "Where's the disk!" he demanded to know.

In a split second, Ruben leaned in front of Gwynn, blocking her from the weapon. He flung his knife. It hit the man in his chest, and the gun went off. The bullet ricocheted off the metal edge of the coffee table and lodged in Ruben's arm above the elbow. Blood squirted from the wound.

Gwynn gasped, grabbed the towel, and held it against Ruben's arm. She saw the pain on his face as he raised the towel and examined the wound. "It's not serious," he said. "But the bullet needs to be removed."

"I don't know how to do that," Gwynn said sadly, forgetting the throbbing pain she felt earlier.

"I don't expect you to do it," he said with hazy and drawn eyes. He caught a glimpse of the burly man stirring.

"What can I do?"

"Take that syringe," he said, nodding toward the coffee table. "And stick it into that man's arm."

Gwynn gingerly picked it up. "I've never given a shot before."

"He isn't conscious yet. He won't notice if you do it right now."

She rose to her feet, went to the burly man, and pulled up his sleeve. She held the needle against his arm and hesitated.

"Just stick it in," Ruben said.

The burly man unconsciously flung up his arm, plunging it into the syringe. Gwynn sucked in a sharp breath and pushed the serum into the man's body. She sighed as she pulled out the needle. She stood, dropping the syringe on the floor. "Now what?"

"Stick your head out the door; see if any of your neighbors are wondering about the gunfire."

She cracked open the door and saw people milling around. "What was that noise?" she yelled into the hallway.

"I don't know," a woman said. "It sounded like a couple of gunshots."

"Probably someone has their television too loud," Gwynn blurted out.

"Everyone on this side of the hallway has been accounted for now," a man said.

The neighbors continued talking about the noise as Gwynn eased the door shut. "Anything else?"

Ruben briefly closed his eyes, attempting to control the pain surging through his arm. "Can you drive me somewhere?"

She nodded. "Can I get you something for your wound first?"

"Ace bandages?"

"Sorry, I don't have any."

"Do you have a scarf?"

"Yes." She hurried into the bedroom and opened a drawer. "What color?"

Ruben rolled his eyes. "Any color."

How could I have asked that? Gwynn grabbed one and rushed back into the living room.

She helped Ruben get his arm out of his sports coat sleeve. Following his directions, Gwynn got a dishtowel. He held it against his injured arm while she wrapped the scarf twice around the covered wound and tied it in place. She took a clean towel and secured it around his arm over the scarf. "I'm going to put on another blouse."

"Hurry, we need to get out of here."

She quickly changed her blouse, camisole, and bra since they were all saturated with blood. Stepping out of the bedroom, she looked at the scar-faced man's body lying on the floor in a pool of blood. Her lips trembled, and her hands shook. For a minute she froze as she stared at the dead man.

"Gwynn, we have to go," Ruben said.

She forced herself to turn away from the scar-faced man and walk toward Ruben.

"Put this where you had it earlier," Ruben said, holding the disk in his hand.

Without a second thought, she undid her slacks in front of him and slipped the disk up under her camisole. After she buttoned her slacks, she helped Ruben take off his sports coat. She noticed the handle of a pistol protruding from a holster attached to the back of his belt.

Ruben pushed the bloody sleeve to the inside of the sports coat, put the other sleeve back on his good arm, and draped the coat over his other shoulder.

Gwynn wiped away the splattered blood on Ruben's face with a wet dishtowel. She stuck her head out the door again and scanned the hallway. Empty. Ruben laid his arm around her shoulder for support as they left the apartment.

In the parking lot, he handed over the keys to his car and a scanning device.

"How do I use it?" she asked, helping him into the passenger seat.

"Flip the switch. Hold it in the palm of your hand and move it over the vehicle. If it starts blinking red, there's a tracking device."

She proceeded to check the Suburban. "All clear," she said, handing the scanner back to Ruben.

"Thanks." He put the device in his pocket.

While he secured his seat belt, she noticed blood had seeped through the towel. "Do we have far to go?" she asked, feeling her muscles tighten and a lump forming in her throat.

"It's about a forty-five minute drive." He gave her the first of the directions.

As she drove out of the parking lot, he dug his cell phone out of his pocket and punched in a number. "There's clean-up work... Gwynn Reznick's apartment...No...Two men... One...Yes, a coffee table." He hung up, laid his cell phone on his lap, and held the palm of his hand against the wrappings covering his wound, applying pressure. "Your living room will be spotless when you get back."

She looked at his pale, drawn face. "What did you do with the pizza?"

"Gave it to one of your neighbors. He was grateful."

Ruben made two more calls. One to Gordon, telling him he needed to cover for him at the eight o'clock meeting. The other call was to Dr. Dimitri Kozlov. Ruben described his wound and told him he'd be there shortly.

Worried, Gwynn glanced at him a few times and saw his eyes flickering. "How are you doing?" she asked, tenderly.

"I'll be okay."

"We're almost at Exit 32. Where do I go from there?"

Ruben didn't answer.

She glanced at him and saw he was slumped in the seat. "Ruben?"

Still no answer.

Panic-stricken, Gwynn exited and pulled off the road. She leaned over and touched his arm. "Ruben?" After no response, she shook him.

"Aah ... aah," he moaned.

"Ruben, where do I go?"

His eyes popped wide open. He swung his head back and forth. "Can you get a small metal box out of the glove compartment?"

She pushed open the compartment, rummaged through it, and pulled out a box. "This one?"

He nodded as he continued applying pressure to his wound. "Take out two orange pills."

Raising the lid, she saw a collection of various colored pills. She scooped up two orange ones. "Can you take them without water?"

"Yes."

She plopped them in his mouth.

He swallowed. "Thanks." He nodded toward the windshield. "Turn left at the stop sign. Follow the road."

Gwynn pulled away from the curb, inched toward the intersection, and took the turn.

Ruben adjusted himself in the seat. "I'll tell you when to turn again."

Dense trees lined both sides of the road. Clouds snuffed out the moon and stars. All that lit her way were the headlights. There were no other cars. If houses stood beyond the trees, their lights didn't shine through. She never would have ventured on a road like this at night by herself. Driving farther into the woods, Gwynn felt more uncomfortable with each curve of the pavement as she worried about Ruben's condition.

"Are we almost there?" she asked in a jittery voice.

"Turn right at the next mailbox."

She followed his instruction and stopped next to a closed gate.

A uniformed guard walked out of a small building carrying a square metal basket. Ruben rolled down his window. "Hello, Scott."

"Hello, Ruben," Scott said. "Dr. Kozlov is expecting you. Do you have any weapons?"

"Yes." Ruben, wincing in pain, leaned down and pulled three knifes out of his boots and dropped them into the basket held by Scott. Then he clamped his teeth together as he reached behind him, retrieved his pistol, and placed it into the basket.

"Any more?" Scott asked.

"No."

"Cell phones?"

Ruben turned off his cell and put it in the basket. "Gwynn, give me your cell."

She plucked it out of her purse, stretched over Ruben, and dropped it in the basket.

"Thanks," Scott said and walked back into the guardhouse with the basket.

The gate swung open and Gwynn drove to the end of the long driveway, stopping by a large Victorian house. "This doesn't look like a doctor's office," she commented, climbing out of the car.

"It's not supposed to look like a medical facility."

A man dressed in a white uniform came out of the front door, pushing a wheelchair. He opened Ruben's door. "Dr. Kozlov is ready for you," he said, holding Ruben's arm and helping him sit down in the wheelchair.

"Thanks, Matt," Ruben said.

Gwynn walked behind them as they entered the house.

Dark rosewood paneling covered the walls of the huge foyer. All the doors inside the house were closed.

Matt moved the hand of a female bronze statue that stood in the corner. The paneling against the one wall separated, revealing an elevator.

Gwynn scanned the elevator and felt edgy entering with Ruben and Matt. She was surprised when the elevator descended. She expected it would take them to the second floor.

Ruben took her hand. "Don't worry," he said softly.

The elevator opened into a bright, wide hallway. The walls and doors were all painted white. Medical equipment stood against one wall. She thought it looked like a wing in a hospital, certainly not a basement. Gwynn continued holding Ruben's hand as Matt pushed him down the hallway past a door that stood ajar. She caught a glimpse of a bed inside covered with white linens and the edge of a table. From what she saw, it appeared to be just like a hospital room.

Matt stopped next to a double door with a small round window on each side. A heavyset woman with graying hair peered out the window and opened the doors.

"Hello, Ruben," she said, giving him a warm smile. "It's been a long time."

"Not long enough, Stella."

Stella smiled again, knowing Dr. Kozlov's guests came out of necessity, not choice. She went around the wheelchair, and Matt released his hold.

Ruben let go of Gwynn's hand as a short, middle-aged man with thinning white hair and wearing a lab coat, walked toward them. "Let's get that arm taken care of," Dr. Dimitri Kozlov said with a heavy Russian accent.

"Dimitri, Gwynn could also use some medical attention," Ruben said.

"I can see that," Dr. Kozlov said, moving toward Gwynn. He gently ran his hand over her cheek. "How long ago did this happen?"

"A little over an hour," Ruben answered.

"Matt, take care of this young lady," Dr. Kozlov said.

Matt took Gwynn's arm and began leading her down the hall.

"Dimitri, I want her in my room," Ruben said.

"Matt, put her in room four."

Gwynn glanced behind her and saw Stella wheeling Ruben through the double doors.

Room four contained two single hospital beds, two nightstands, two chairs, and a television hung high in the corner. Medical equipment was attached to the back wall.

"If you need to contact anyone, let me know and I'll place the call," Matt said.

Gwynn nodded. "Okay."

Matt had her take off her shoes and lie down on the bed farthest from the door. "I'll be back; I need to get some supplies."

After Ruben had been shot, Gwynn hadn't even thought about her injury. Now her cheek, jaw, and teeth throbbed as she ran her fingers over her face and knew it was badly swollen. Her bruise from Sunday's "bowling ball" incident had just started to clear up prior to the blows inflicted by the scar-faced man.

Matt returned pushing a cart. "Are you in pain?"

"A little."

"Take these." He handed Gwynn two pills and a glass of water.

"What are they?"

"They'll help with the pain and swelling."

"Will they put me to sleep?" she asked, not wanting to fall asleep in this strange place.

"No. You won't even be groggy."

Reluctantly, she swallowed them and put her head down on the pillow.

He gently wiped her face with a sweet smelling, moist cloth. Then he unscrewed the cap on a jar of pink ointment and applied a thick layer on her face.

It felt soothing and Gwynn closed her eyes. She didn't want to sleep, but now she could finally relax knowing Ruben was being taken care of.

****

Stella touched Gwynn's arm. "Miss?"

Slowly Gwynn opened her eyes.

"Ruben would like to leave now," Stella said.

Gwynn, sitting up, wondered how long she had slept.

Ruben sat on the edge of the other bed. He looked pale, his eyelids drooped, and his left arm was bandaged from his mid-forearm to his shoulder. He wore an oversized blue smock, slacks, and boots.

"How long have I slept?" Gwynn asked, standing up.

"I don't know," he replied. "It's almost four. I want to be back where I'm staying before daylight."

"How are you feeling?"

"Better."

Gwynn swept her hands over her clothing to make sure the disk was still securely in place. She touched her face. Her cheek didn't hurt or feel swollen. She scanned the room looking for a mirror. She couldn't see one. "Is my face bruised?" she asked, slipping on her shoes.

"A little, probably from Sunday," Ruben replied.

"What was that stuff Matt put on me?"

"One of Dr. Kozlov's secret mixtures," Stella said. "It doesn't have a name." She carefully put a sling around Ruben's arm and tied it behind his neck.

"He should patent it," Gwynn said. "He could make a fortune."

"I think he already does," Ruben commented.

Matt strolled into the room with a wheelchair.

"Thanks for everything," Ruben said to Stella as he moved into the wheelchair.

"You're welcome." She handed him two pill containers. "The instructions are on the side. Keep taking the pills until they're gone." Stella looked at Gwynn. "Maybe you better keep these," she said to Gwynn, taking the containers from Ruben. "Make sure he follows the instructions."

Gwynn nodded, even though she didn't think Ruben would do anything she said.

"Try to keep him in bed for at least a day," Stella said. "I know that won't be easy."

"I'll try," Gwynn said, doubting she could manage that.

"Have a safe drive back," Stella said as Matt pushed the wheelchair into the hallway.

****

After the gate closed behind them, Scott brought the basket to the car. Ruben retrieved his weapons and their cell phones. "Thanks, Scott," he said, giving Gwynn her phone. Then he put his knives back in his boots and slid the pistol into its holster.

"You'll have to give me directions again," Gwynn said. "I wasn't paying attention driving here."

"I'm not surprised."

When they reached the freeway, he called Gordon and filled him in on his visit with Dr. Kozlov.

The directions Ruben gave Gwynn led them to a Residence Inn close to Houston's Galleria. He had her park by the building farthest away from the street. It had two floors, and all the rooms opened to the outside. She noticed several black Chevy Suburbans in the parking lot.

"You don't live in Houston?" she asked, feeling bewildered.

"I do. But when I'm involved with an investigation that appears to have numerous players, some of my employees and I stay at a Residence Inn. It gives us an opportunity to discuss the case face-to-face daily, and it helps keep our personal lives private."

"Why don't all your employees stay here?"

"Some of them aren't involved with this case. Others stay where they are needed."

Gordon walked around the car and opened Ruben's door. "How are you feeling?" he asked, taking Ruben's arm.

"Tired," he replied, stepping onto the ground.

"How can I get your car back to you?" Gwynn asked, leaning over the passenger seat.

"Your apartment isn't safe for you to be there alone," Ruben said. "You're staying here."

Gwynn got out of the Suburban, thinking Gordon had rented her a room. She followed Ruben and Gordon up the stairs. They went inside a one-bedroom suite, almost as large as her entire apartment. On the table were cheeses, vegetables, crackers, and a box of cookies.

"I thought you'd be hungry," Gordon said.

"I am. Thanks," Ruben replied, sitting down at the table.

"Let me know if you need anything," Gordon said, then left.

"What would you like to drink?" Ruben asked, starting to rise.

"No, let me get it," Gwynn said, jumping to her feet. She opened the fridge. "What would you like?"

"A beer," he replied.

"Should you be drinking that?" she asked, thinking he shouldn't have alcohol with drugs in his system.

A brief smile flickered across his lips. "Okay, Mother Gwynn, how about a Coke?"

She opened a bottle of Coke, a bottle of water, and put them on the table. They ate in silence. "Is there anything I can do for you before I go to my room?" she asked, clearing off the table.

"Your room?" he asked, furrowing his brow.

"You didn't rent me a room?"

"No. You're staying here."

She glanced around the suite. "I want you to sleep in the bed, so I'll sleep on the sofa." Wondering if it made into a bed, she lifted up a cushion and saw the folded box springs. The image of the scar-faced man touching her flashed through her mind. "Is it okay if I take a shower?" she asked, wanting to feel clean again.

"Yes. I could use one too, but I'm not up to it right now." He pushed himself away from the table, rose to his feet, and held onto Gwynn's arm as he walked slowly to the bed. He sat down, pulled the knives out of his boots, and placed them in the nightstand drawer.

Gwynn took off his boots and noticed a leather band running around the inside of each one with loops for knives.

"Thanks," he said. "I can manage the rest. You can sleep in one of my T-shirts. They're in the top drawer."

She eased the disk out from under her camisole, laid it on the bureau, got a T-shirt, and went into the bathroom. Gwynn scrubbed her body and her hair, trying to wash every trace of the scar-faced man away.

After she blow dried her hair and slipped into Ruben's T-shirt, Gwynn quietly opened the door, trying not to wake him up.

He stirred in the bed and their eyes met.

"What took you so long?" he asked, sounding groggy.

"I had to blow dry my hair. I didn't mean to wake you up."

He raised the covers next to him and patted the bed. "I'm sure we can both sleep in the bed."

She smiled to herself, climbed in bed, and turned off the nightstand lamp.

CHAPTER 10

Gwynn awoke slowly to a telephone ringing with an unfamiliar sound. Feeling dazed and disoriented, she tried to focus.

The phone continued ringing.

She brushed against Ruben's bandaged arm and remembered. She didn't want the phone to wake him so she moved her leg over Ruben, straddling him, and reached for the phone on his nightstand.

Picking up the receiver, she whispered, "Hello."

"Gwynn?" a male voice asked.

"Yes."

"I need to talk to Ruben."

She looked down at him, his eyes still closed and sleeping peacefully. "He's asleep," she whispered.

"This can't wait."

"Okay. I'll wake him," she said reluctantly. She laid down the phone and nudged Ruben's shoulder.

He raised his eyelids abruptly and saw her sitting on him. His eyes lit up. "What have you been up to?" he asked with a mischievous smile.

She quickly moved her leg so she was sitting next to him. "Well, not that."

"Are you sure?" he asked, still smiling.

"Yes," she replied, embarrassed. "You're wanted on the phone."

Lifting the receiver to his ear, he felt his arm throbbing. "Hello?"

"Sorry to wake you, but you said you didn't want to sleep late. Do you want me to bring you breakfast?" Gordon asked.

The clock on the nightstand indicated it was almost nine. He had slept less than three hours. "Yes. I need to get going." Ruben clicked off.

"I'm late," Gwynn said, jumping out of bed. "I need to get to work."

"You didn't sleep very long. Can't you call in sick?"

"I will if you'll stay in bed," she answered, knowing he needed rest more than she did.

"Are you planning to take advantage of me again?" he asked, giving her a crooked smile as the pain increased.

"I didn't do anything! I just answered the phone."

His brows drew together, and he gritted his teeth.

She saw the contorted expression of agony on his face and suspected the pain he must be suffering. "You need some medicine," she remembered, rushing to her purse. She fished both containers out of it, took out the prescribed amount of pills, and filled a glass with water. "Take these." She handed the pills to Ruben.

He swallowed two of the three pills and drank some water. The remaining pill he laid on the nightstand.

"You need to take that one, too," Gwynn insisted.

"No. Not now. That pill will put me to sleep. I need to get some work done first."

"Can I take your car today?"

"You're not going to call in sick?"

"Not unless you stay in bed."

He gazed at her for minute. "Will you call in sick if I promise to stay here?"

"Will you sleep at least part of the day?"

"You've got a deal."

They heard a knock on the door. "That must be Gordon," Ruben said, getting out of bed. He stumbled into the bathroom, freshened up, and threw on a pair of pajama bottoms and a T-shirt. He went into the other room, closing the bedroom door behind him.

Since the phones in the Wilton Tower had caller ID, Gwynn didn't want to use the hotel phone to call her boss. She got her cell, turned it on, and discovered she had five new messages — three from Cindy and two from Borge. She wondered what was going on and decided to listen to them before calling the office. All the messages were about her not being at work. From Cindy's trembling voice on the last message, Gwynn thought she was crying. She immediately punched in Cindy's number.

"Where are you?" Cindy asked in jerky breaths.

"I'm home," she replied, attempting to sound sick and pathetic. "I've been throwing up all night. I finally got to sleep around five or six this morning. I didn't mean to worry you."

"Borge went to your apartment this morning. You never answered the door."

"I must have really been out of it. I haven't even called in to work yet."

"You don't sound well. You're not going to try and come to work today, are you?"

"No. I'm calling in sick and then going back to bed. I've already unplugged my landline. Do you want me to leave my cell on?"

"No. Turn it off. Will you call me tonight?"

"Yeah. I'll call when I wake up."

"Good. I'll let Borge know."

"Thanks. Talk to you later." After Gwynn hung up, she called the office and told Stan she wasn't feeling well, so she wouldn't be in.

"Kent Fardown wants to see you," Stan said. "Do you know what that's about?"

During all the years with Wilton, she had never dealt with Fardown directly. In fact, she couldn't think of a business reason for him to talk to her. "No."

"I'll tell Fardown you won't be in today. Get well soon."

"Thanks." She turned off her phone and dropped it in her purse. She put on her slacks and opened the door to the other room.

Ruben looked at her. "Come and have something to eat."

She poured a cup of coffee, sat at the table, and drank.

"Did you call your office?" Ruben asked between bites of his bagel.

"Yes. My boss, Stan, said that Fardown wants to see me. He'll tell him I won't be in today."

"That's not possible," Gordon said, sounding bewildered, putting down his cup. "Fardown is out of town with McIntyre. They won't be back until tomorrow."

"Let me call one of my agents just in case he came back earlier," Ruben said. "Gordon, can you get me an N-cell?"

Gordon stood and took a cell phone out of a kitchen drawer.

"What's an N-cell?" Gwynn asked.

"It's a non-traceable phone." Ruben punched in a number. "Can I speak to Mr. Fardown?"

"I'm afraid you have the wrong extension, but Mr. Fardown won't be in until tomorrow. Would you like me to transfer you to his secretary?"

"No. That won't be necessary," Ruben replied. "I'll try to reach him tomorrow." Ruben disconnected. "He's not in the office."

"So what do you think that was all about?" Gwynn asked, buttering a bagel.

Ruben and Gordon glanced at each other. "Not sure. Have you got any ideas, Gordon?"

Gordon tapped his fingers together. "It might be business; someone under Fardown using his office. Nothing more. On the other hand, assuming whoever wanted the disk was connected to Wilton, it could be a dangerous situation."

Gwynn's hands slightly shook as she pondered the second possibility. On two occasions she had been slapped in the face, and once had a knife thrown at her. *What will happen the next time?*

Ruben put his hand on hers. "Don't look so worried. You're safe."

"I'm planning on going to work tomorrow."

"You'll be wearing a bug," Ruben said. "We'll know where you are all the time."

Gwynn exhaled a long breath, wishing she didn't have to go back to the Wilton Tower. Yet she couldn't stay away, and she needed to work.

Ruben lightly squeezed her hand. "It'll be okay."

"Have you found out anything new?" she asked.

"I'm having the casualties looked at — both Wilton's and CT's, even those I've already checked out," Ruben said. "One of my men has made contact with a guy who worked on the platform when the two deaths occurred."

"You told me about those," she said. "Is he the same guy who wouldn't talk to you earlier?"

"No. This guy stayed on the job for a couple of weeks after the incident. He wants to get paid for what he knows. We always pay for information if it's valuable, but he wants to be paid up front. He didn't accept our initial amount. He won't give us a hint about what he has to offer. Gordon and I were talking about how high we should go."

"Have you found out if that was Julie's ring?"

"It was," Gordon replied. "The jeweler verified it."

"So was the woman who appeared to be Julie on the security footage Pam?"

"Not necessarily," Ruben explained. "One of her admirers could have given her the ring, either McIntyre, Fardown, or an unidentified person. She's been personally involved with McIntyre for years and now we know Fardown is also interested in her."

"But he's married," Gwynn said, squinting.

"I didn't tell you everything Gordon found in Simmons's house when he searched it." Ruben turned toward Gordon as Gwynn recalled *the personal nature stuff* and he continued, "Tell Gwynn what you found in Simmons's closet."

Gordon leaned back in his chair and stretched out his legs. "Several suits hanging up belonging to McIntyre and, tucked in the corner behind a stack of shoeboxes, a duffle bag. It contained male workout clothing smaller than the size worn by McIntyre along with a woman's sheer undergarment. At the bottom of the bag was a grocery list on a piece of stationery with Fardown's name at the top."

"Undergarment?" Gwynn questioned.

"Like women wear under blouses or maybe to sleep in," Gordon said.

"Why would he have that?"

"Simmons probably gave it to him as a remembrance," Ruben said. "Or he took it."

"Maybe it belongs to his wife," Gwynn said.

"No," Gordon said. "Fardown's wife is a plump woman. She'd never be able to squeeze herself into that garment."

"How do you know the suits were McIntyre's?" Gwynn asked.

"Size and initials. One of the drawers in her bathroom was devoted to male toiletries — shaver, shaving lotion, male cologne. In that drawer was a set of cufflinks with initials 'JM' on them. Also, there were numerous messages on her answering machine from various people: two from Fardown, one from McIntyre, and two from another admirer anxious to see her. I didn't recognize his voice."

Gordon took a sip of his coffee. "Regarding McIntyre and Fardown. If Fardown can come up with some excuse why he has to go to Simmons's dinner party without his wife, she'll have two men who plan on staying after everyone else has gone."

"Pam will know someone listened to her messages since the light wasn't blinking when she got home," Gwynn said.

"I fixed that," Gordon replied.

"Do you think they know about each other?" she asked.

"From information an inside person has gathered," Ruben said, "it appears Simmons is interested in McIntyre. We suspect she might just be using Fardown."

"Maybe it has something to do with Trulin," Gwynn suggested. "It was Kent Fardown who signed the contracts. Did you find out anything else?"

"Yes. If you're through eating, let's listen to the disk first. Gordon has an appointment later this morning."

"I'm finished," Gwynn replied, picking up the dirty dishes and stacking them on the counter.

Gordon opened a kitchen drawer, took out a computer, set it up on the table, and turned it on. Gwynn got the disk from the bedroom and inserted it. They stared at the computer, waiting for it to begin. The recording started out with five minutes of static, and it continued intermittently as the disk played on.

"… we all set … financial end …" a male voice said. Gwynn thought it was McIntyre, but she wasn't certain.

"Trulin contract … engineer wanted more money … no longer … twelve … all cleaned up," another male voice said.

"Yes … refinery ... July …" another voice.

"Pipeline ... pig … computer software … metal fatigue … safety waiver … PHMSA."

Several male voices were heard laughing.

"Centar … compression station … offshore pipeline … they've been taken care of."

"Luke ... not yet ... no water pollution … Centar … Sander is a computer genius … no injuries … still need him … Ramza … surface transportation … no environmental impact … senator ... chairman … Brent in line … meeting with Jenkins about refinery … clean air," a male voice said.

"That was McIntyre," Gwynn informed.

"Can the failure … traced … not him … won't look … Trulin," another male voice said.

Gordon stood up and paced around the room while the disk played on.

"Yes … Arlene … EPA … OSHA … Maxine dating … married …won't be a problem … the board …"

They heard laughter again and gave each other darting glances.

Ruben shifted in his chair, staring glumly.

Gwynn rested her elbows on the table, glared at the computer, hoping the static would end. This was what she had feared after Barb told her the recorder didn't work properly and felt irritated she had paid $400 for a broken receiver.

"She doesn't … anything … everyone else … gone."

"Loose ends … disaster … CT … severely damaged … three weeks … four …"

"Months to repair … wells shut-in … no, Abir …"

The track ended.

"That was disappointing," Ruben said, rubbing his chin. He looked at Gordon. "Any thoughts?"

"All I got out of the CD was something was going to happen — maybe in three weeks and an engineer wanted more money. We already suspect there's a connection with Trulin. We know Trulin is trying to buy a refinery."

"Trulin's buying a refinery?" Gwynn asked.

"Yes. A refinery outside of Houston," Ruben replied. "The owners, two oil and gas companies, have done a significant amount of updating trying to meet all the EPA standards, but there are still some safety and site clean-up issues. Trulin will take it off their hands and do whatever is required to get it operating again and assume all the environmental liabilities. Getting back to the disk, Gwynn, any thoughts?"

"Julie went missing at Wilton the same day she talked about a meeting between Wilton and some CT guys. Then we find out she borrowed a receiver. She made a disk. Some men want it. Now, we know it was a recording of that meeting. Whatever it was about either someone else really wants to know, or they want to keep it a secret.

"From what I could pick up on the disk, it might have something to do with a computer system since they mentioned software and a computer expert. It might also have something to do with a pipeline or a refinery. There just wasn't enough recorded."

"Whatever they said in the meeting must have been damaging, probably criminal." Ruben pushed back his chair, stood up, grabbed a notepad lying on the counter, and dropped it on the table. "Otherwise, they wouldn't be concerned about getting the disk. They don't know the quality of the recording." He paused. "We'll have to guard it as if it's valuable and see what develops. I want to listen to it again so I can write down the names and anything else that might help."

"I want you to sleep," Gwynn insisted. "I'll listen to it again and make notes."

"Gordon, before you leave, let's copy the disk and you can take it to Abby. Maybe she can do something about the static."

Gordon nodded. He took a blank disk out of the cabinet and copied the original.

"So how much should we pay the platform guy?" Gordon asked, putting the copied disk in a large envelope.

"Elliott has always been a good negotiator on these matters." Ruben eased back down in a chair. "Tell him he can go up to fifty. If that's not enough, the guy has to give us something before we go higher."

"Sounds good," Gordon said. "Do you need anything before I go?"

"No. Gwynn will be staying here. Check with our man and find out if he was able to get on the security team for tomorrow night's party."

"I'll let you know how the meeting goes," Gordon said, picking up a briefcase next to the door and putting the envelope in it.

"What party?" Gwynn asked after Gordon left.

"Pam Simmons is having a dinner party."

"One of your men might be going?" she asked skeptically.

"Hopefully," Ruben replied. "We're still not sure who's on the guest list besides McIntyre and Fardown. Simmons has arranged for some of Wilton's security guards to be there."

"Is she expecting something might happen?"

"Maybe. It could be one of the attendees wanted the security guards present."

"Before the CD started, you said you had found out something else. What was it?"

"Trulin purchased the North Dakota oil and gas properties from Marshall Roberts."

"McIntyre's ex-wife's father?" Gwynn asked in disbelief.

"Yes, while they were still married," Ruben replied as a hint of a smile flashed on his face. "For twenty million."

Gwynn smiled. "If she only knew the resale."

"The engineer who prepared the report estimating the reserves has disappeared," Ruben drummed his fingers on the table.

"Maybe he's the engineer they talked about on the disk."

"That's exactly what I was thinking."

"The two men Gordon took away — the one from my apartment and the one from the post office — did he find out anything from either guy?"

"We couldn't get anything out of the one, the guy who met you at the post office. The other guy thought he was retrieving a disk that contained corporate secrets."

"Like I was involved with espionage?" she asked, raising her eyebrows.

"Yes," he answered. "He also believes he was working for Fardown. I'm not convinced Fardown is the one in charge."

"Did you go to Julie's safe deposit box?"

"Yes. There wasn't anything in it that would have a bearing on this case. I'll give you back the key. That brings you up to where we are."

"It seems like everything is getting more complicated. Do you think you're closer to finding out who is responsible for Julie's death?"

"Yes, but I also need to know 'why.'" Ruben's bloodshot eyes blinked often and his skin was pale white.

"You look tired." She gently touched his face. "Why don't you try to get some sleep?"

"Will you join me after you listen to the disk?" he asked, gazing at her.

"Yes," she said, stroking his arm. Wanting to make sure Ruben took his pill, Gwynn followed him into the bedroom and watched him swallow it, take off his T-shirt, and stretch out on the bed. She closed the door behind her as she stepped into the other room.

Carefully she inched open a cabinet door, took out a blank disk, and laid it on the table. She sat down and hooked up earphones to the computer. Then she proceeded to listen to the disk again and made two sets of notes. When it ended, she copied the disk, and put the copy in her purse along with one set of notes.

CHAPTER 11

Pounding on the door awakened Ruben and Gwynn. Dazed, they sat up and stared at each other.

"What the ..." Ruben said.

"I'll get it!" Gwynn leapt out of bed.

"Look out the peephole first!" Ruben yelled.

Gwynn peered through the peephole, saw Gordon, and unlocked the door.

"I've been trying to reach Ruben for over an hour," he said angrily. "Why didn't you answer the phone?"

Ruben strolled into the living room in his T-shirt and pajama bottoms. "The phone didn't ring."

"That's my fault." Gwynn looked at Ruben. "I wanted you to sleep so I unplugged the phone and turned off your cell."

Gordon glared at her. "I was ready to break down the door," he huffed.

Staring at Gwynn, Ruben's eyes narrowed. "I know you meant well, but my people need to be able to reach me."

"I'm sorry. Remember I told Stella I'd keep you in bed," she said in her defense.

Ruben's gaze relaxed, and he turned toward Gordon. "What's happened?"

Gordon pulled a necklace, a gold chain with a pendant, out of his pocket. "Here." He handed it to Ruben.

Ruben fell into an upholstered chair and held up the necklace.

"That's Julie's," Gwynn said, taking the necklace. "Where did you find it?"

"Simmons's desk," Gordon replied, sitting down on the sofa. "Our inside person wasn't able to slip it to Dean until this morning."

"Let me see it," Ruben said.

Gwynn gave it back to Ruben. The pendant had the initials *JM* delicately formed out of gold. On the back of the necklace was inscribed, *Love B*.

"Simmons probably wanted to keep it since JM is also John McIntyre's initials," Gordon said.

"I didn't even think about that." Gwynn sat on the arm of Ruben's chair.

"Simmons is going to know this is missing," Ruben said, examining the necklace. "She'll know someone at work is on to her."

"Yes," Gordon said with a smug expression on his face. "Let's see what she does. Last night, our inside people searched McIntyre's and Fardown's offices along with Simmons's desk and file cabinet. They discovered a receiver and three mini-microphones in a bottom drawer."

"How big was it?" Gwynn asked, thinking it might be Barb's.

"It matched the description Ruben had mentioned," Gordon said. "Fingerprints were lifted from it."

"Whose drawer?" Gwynn asked.

"Simmons's."

"Have the fingerprints been matched?" Ruben asked.

"Julie Morgan's and Luke Cromer's were on it. There are two sets we haven't been able to identify yet."

"Whose prints are we missing?" Ruben asked.

"We suspect a set might belong to Barbara Lange."

"Julie's friend?" Gwynn asked.

Gordon nodded. "The set we had of McIntyre's was smudged. Our inside person will get another one today and I'll get Lange's."

"Do we have prints of all the other Wilton suspects?" Ruben asked.

"Yes, along with all of Miss Morgan's close friends."

Gwynn looked at her hands. "Mine?"

"Yes," Ruben said. "Pam Simmons's weren't on it?"

"No."

"That's strange … What else did we get?" Ruben asked Gordon.

"Photos of various documents. Dean's downloading and printing them now."

"Why didn't they send them through a cell phone to Carlos?" Ruben asked.

"Wilton's increased security. They're able to track cell phone calls made and received in the building on floors twenty-seven and higher. All the security guards were told that an employee is stealing corporate secrets so they're hoping to catch the individual. They even have the police helping them."

"Don't they need to tell their employees about the new security?" Gwynn asked.

"Not if they're trying to catch someone," Ruben replied. "It could be considered an invasion of privacy, but with the police involved, who knows."

"They obviously want to make sure no incriminating information leaves the Wilton Tower through cell phones," Gordon said. "Calling after hours in the building would definitely send up a red flag."

"If something happens at work tomorrow, I better not call you," Gwynn said.

"Gordon, can you pick up a couple of buttons?" Ruben asked. "I'll have Gwynn wear one."

Gordon nodded.

"I take it these buttons are not used to hold up pants," Gwynn said.

"You're right," Ruben said. "They're beepers that can't be traced. You'll also be wearing a bug so we can hear everything said, but we're not always listening. All you need to do is push the button if you are in danger. That will get our attention. Then talk normally; we'll hear you."

"Holly called," Gordon said, glancing at Gwynn with a cocked eyebrow. His eyes moved to Ruben.

Ruben nodded, go on.

Gordon continued, "She tried to reach you on your cell."

"Has she found out something?" Ruben asked.

"The wife of one of the CT workers who perished might talk, but not to her."

"Which guy?"

"Ian Daniels, a climbing accident victim."

"Her name's Carrie or something like that?" Ruben remarked.

"Karlee," Gordon clarified.

"She trembled all the time I talked to her. I knew something wasn't right. I'm surprised she's even considering saying anything. Why doesn't she want to talk to Holly?"

"Holly didn't know. Karlee told her she'd only talk to Ross. The stickler is Karlee wants to talk to Ross and his wife." A lopsided smile creased Gordon's lips. "I didn't know Ross had a wife."

"He doesn't," Ruben said. "I'll call Janet and see how their investigation is going. Maybe she can go with me."

Up to this point, Gwynn had easily followed the conversation. "Are you Ross?" she asked Ruben.

"Yes. We use an alias when we're asking questions unless we already know that person."

"Why did you tell Karlee you had a wife?" Gwynn wanted to know.

"She was nervous. Sometimes women feel more comfortable if they're talking to a family man. Also, I told her I was investigating the death of one of my wife's relatives."

Gwynn felt anxious to find out what was going on. "How about I go with you and pretend to be your wife?" she asked, hoping to obtain more information if she decided to go to the police. She wanted Julie's killer punished.

"You don't have the needed skills," Ruben replied.

"I don't know how to shoot a gun, if that's what you mean. Since you're not planning on shooting her, I do know how to comfort someone. And I won't seem like a professional because I'm not."

"You've got a point. Let me think about it."

"Did you get the names from the disk?" Gordon asked.

"I made notes," Gwynn said. "All the names I heard are included."

"Give them to me. I'll check the names," Gordon said.

She went to the table, picked up the notes, and handed them to him.

"Dean should be by soon with the document pictures," Gordon said, walking toward the door.

"I'll make sure my cell remains on," Ruben said as Gordon left.

"Who are your inside people?" Gwynn asked.

"It's better if you don't know."

She checked the clock on the microwave. "It's almost three. Do you want me to go and get us some lunch?"

"A few things are in the fridge. Let's eat something here."

Gwynn thought Ruben still looked pale. "You need to take some medicine," she said, going into the bedroom. She returned with three pills and handed them to him.

Just like earlier, he only took two of them.

Gwynn pulled cheese and lunchmeat out of the fridge and made toasted bagel sandwiches. When they were almost finished eating, someone knocked on the door.

"I'll get it," she said, jumping to her feet.

"Don't forget ..." Ruben said.

"I won't," she interrupted, looking through the peephole. She recognized the man on the other side of the door and opened it.

Dean entered with a large envelope and handed it to Ruben. "Here are the document photos. I need to get back to the Wilton Tower," he said, leaving.

Ruben moved to the sofa and sifted through the pictures. Among the documents from McIntyre's office were handwritten notes with Trulin scribbled along the top. One note only stated that McIntyre had talked to Senator Stenson about the refinery. Another one indicated he had talked to OSHA's Maxine Alexander about Trulin — nothing more.

Gwynn sat down beside him and he gave her the documents after reading them.

Another note stated McIntyre had talked to Senator Jenkins and Jenkins was on board. That page had stars drawn in the top two corners. The last note said the engineer problem was resolved.

"They didn't get very much from McIntyre's office," Ruben said. "He's careful. Let's see what they got from Fardown's." Ruben continued looking through the documents. He smiled when he ran across the purchase contracts Gwynn had told him about — Wilton selling crude oil and gas to Trulin. The Fardown stack also included handwritten notes. The first one mentioned the meeting with CT. It said, "Luke's taken care of that. Pipeline set. Won't be long. Pam. Stevenson. Trulin. EPA. Refinery opening. Purchase deal, John handled. All lined up." On the edge Fardown had jotted down, "CT disgruntled employees." Ruben flipped through Fardown's other note pages. He had written Trulin often along with two or three words.

"Fardown doesn't make good notes," Ruben said, sounding frustrated. "McIntyre's were short, but at least they were complete sentences. Fardown's are as bad as listening to the disk. Maybe when we have more pieces of the puzzle this will all make sense."

"I need to go home and put on clean clothes," Gwynn said. "Can I take your car?"

"I'll go with you."

"Don't you think you should stay here and rest?"

"No. I'm feeling better. Just give me a few minutes to take a shower."

"Can you manage by yourself?" Gwynn asked.

"Yeah. I'll be fine."

"Just holler if you need help," Gwynn snickered.

While Ruben showered, Gwynn gathered up all of the documents, put them back in the envelope along with the disk, and stuck it in her purse. Even though half of the envelope protruded, she didn't want to take a chance of leaving it behind.

"Can you help me button up my shirt?" Ruben called out from the bedroom.

"Yes," Gwynn replied, opening the bedroom door. She helped him with his shirt, pulled on his boots, and put his arm in the sling. She watched him take his gun and knives out of the nightstand and slip his gun in one of his boots and the knives into the other.

"Is it okay if I wear your T-shirt? My blouse has blood on the front."

"Sure."

****

As Ruben and Gwynn walked toward her apartment elevator, the doors slid open. Borge and Cindy stepped out of it. Borge carried a large sack.

"Where have you been?" Cindy asked, gazing at Gwynn. "We were going to ask the superintendent to open your door." Before Gwynn could answer, Cindy noticed the T-shirt and continued, "You weren't sick today, were you?"

"No," Gwynn replied sheepishly.

"You probably sounded groggy this morning because you just got out of bed." Cindy eyed Ruben.

Gwynn's cheeks became rosy as she smiled and introduced Ruben to Borge and Cindy.

"What did you do to his arm?" Cindy asked Gwynn teasingly.

"It's just a basketball accident," Ruben said, looking at his arm. "Basketball can be a dangerous sport."

"I know what you mean," Borge agreed. "I've sprained my ankle twice and my arm once. But I love it!"

"We were bringing you some soup." Cindy gestured toward the sack Borge held.

"Thanks. I should have told you I wasn't sick," Gwynn said in an apologetic tone. "Is there enough soup for all of us?"

"No," Borge answered. "Since you're not sick, why don't we all go out to dinner?"

Gwynn glanced at Ruben.

"Sounds good," Ruben replied.

"I need to change first," Gwynn said.

Cindy smiled. "But I think you look so cute in Ruben's T-shirt."

"So do I," Ruben said as his eyes focused on Gwynn's face.

She beamed and her hazel eyes sparkled. "I can't go to dinner like this."

They went up to her apartment. Gwynn heard them talking and laughing while she cleaned up and felt good how well Ruben was fitting in.

He took her arm when she walked out of the bedroom. "I need to talk to you for a minute." Then he looked at Cindy and Borge. "Excuse us."

They went back into the bedroom. "What is it?" she asked.

He raised his index finger to his mouth. "Shh!" he whispered and moved his hand around the room. "Bugs."

She nodded.

"I wish we could just stay in here all night," he said in his normal voice. "But we do have to eat sometime."

"I heard that," Cindy chuckled as they walked back into the living room. Her eyes flashed to Gwynn. "We have a lot to talk about tomorrow, so don't call in sick."

****

Borge drove them to a Mexican restaurant. They drank Margaritas. Gwynn occasionally squeezed Ruben's hand and motioned, trying to tell him he shouldn't be drinking alcohol. He ignored her. Ruben and Borge talked about sports. Gwynn and Cindy tried to join in on the conversation whenever they mentioned a player they had heard something about, but most of the time, they laughed and joked during dinner.

By the time they were through eating they had consumed two pitchers of Margaritas. Cindy and Gwynn giggled walking to the car. Ruben put his arm around Gwynn. "And you were worried about *me* drinking," he whispered.

Ruben and Gwynn were dropped off at her apartment building. When they reached the lobby, he said, "I want you to stay at the Residence Inn tonight. I don't think you're safe here, and Gordon won't be able to stay tonight."

She raised her arms and put them around his neck. "Can't you stay with me?"

He smiled, thinking about it. "With my arm, I wouldn't be able to protect you if any thugs show up at your apartment."

"I need some clothes for work," she said, lowering her arms. "Can I get a few things?"

"Yes. I'll go with you. Don't say anything inside your place." He pulled his cell out of his pocket and turned it off.

Ruben drew his gun as soon as they entered her apartment. He paced while she put a change of clothes and toiletries in a tote bag.

When she was ready to leave, she raised the bag strap over her shoulder, took his arm, and led him to the door. He slipped his pistol into his sling as they took the elevator down. They walked at a fast pace to the Suburban. Ruben settled into the passenger seat, and Gwynn checked for tracking devices on the vehicle. After they were both buckled in, Ruben took the small metal box out of the glove compartment and handed it to Gwynn. "Take out a blue square one, and chew it like gum."

"Is it a breath mint?" Gwynn asked, lifting up a square-looking pill.

"No," Ruben said. "It's one of Dimitri's inventions. It offsets the effect of alcohol in your system."

"So if we should be stopped, I could pass a sobriety test?"

"Yes, because you'll be completely sober."

Gwynn put the blue pill in her mouth and chewed it. "It tastes sweet. I could use a box of these," she said, driving out of the parking lot.

"I'll see what I can do." He put his pistol in his boot, reached in his pocket, and took out his cell. As soon as he turned it on, it started vibrating. He checked his messages and returned a few calls on their way to the Residence Inn.

****

All the parking spaces behind the main building were taken, so Gwynn parked in front. Heading toward Ruben's suite, suddenly she felt the same sense of impending danger that had plagued her the previous night in her apartment building hallway. She swallowed hard, grabbed his arm, and stopped walking.

"What's wrong?" Ruben asked.

"I don't know. Something isn't right."

"What makes you think that?"

"Maybe it's my imagination. Can you have someone check out your room?" she asked, trembling. "Please."

"Let's go to the lobby. I'll have it checked. Will that make you happy?"

She nodded.

When they entered the lobby, some people, including a couple of kids, were playing board games. Ruben and Gwynn sat down as far away from them as possible. He called one of his men. No answer. He punched in another number. No answer. He called Gordon. "Where's Travis and Carlos?"

"They should both be in their rooms. Why?" Gordon asked.

"Neither one of them answered their cells. I had planned on having Travis check my room."

"Is there a problem?"

"We just got back from dinner and Gwynn felt uncomfortable when we walked toward it. I told her I'd have the room checked.

111

We're in the lobby. Now I'm starting to think something is wrong. Both of their cars are in the parking lot. If they did leave with someone else, one of them would've answered his cell."

"It'll take me over an hour to get there."

"I'll call Dean."

"I'm on my way if Dean can't leave."

"Good," Ruben said. "Check the lobby when you get here."

Ruben hung up and called Dean. "There might be a problem here. I'm in the lobby with Gwynn. Travis and Carlos don't answer their cells. I need you to check it out."

"I'll be there in about fifteen minutes."

Ruben ended the call. After verifying Travis or Carlos hadn't returned his call, he put his cell back in his pocket, stood up, and held out his hand. "Car keys. I want to check something."

Gwynn pulled them out of her purse and gave them to Ruben. "What do you want to check?" Her shoulders felt knotted with tension. She didn't want him to leave her.

"My door. I want to see if it has been compromised. I'm not going to enter."

"How can you check that with your car keys?"

He held up one of the keys. "With this," he said, pushing a button on it. A light appeared. "I've marked the doorknob. You can only see the marking under ultraviolet light. If the marking is gone, someone has entered, or at least attempted to enter."

"I didn't see you mark the doorknob."

"It only takes a second."

"Let me check it," she said. "You can't move that fast with your injured arm."

He stared at her for a minute. "We'll both go. I'll stay at the bottom of the stairs." He held the key up in front of her face. "Push this," he said, referring to the 'unlock' button. "And shine it on the doorknob. You should see one or more red streaks."

"What did you mark the doorknob with?"

"With this same key." He pushed the 'lock' button and out came a small marker tip. "You just run this over what you want to mark."

"Got it." Gwynn took the keys from him.

As they moved through the parking lot, Ruben scanned all the cars, searching for anyone who might be watching them. They passed a few people on their way, but he wasn't concerned about them.

Reaching the stairs, he leaned down, drew his pistol out of his boot, and placed it in his sling again. He stayed close to the building, almost hidden in the shadows.

A couple walked by them and went up the stairs, talking. Gwynn immediately followed. Her hand twitched as she pointed the key at the doorknob to Ruben's suite and pushed the 'unlock' button. She slowly moved the ultraviolet light around the doorknob. No red streaks appeared. She crept back down the stairs. "There isn't a mark," she whispered.

Ruben held onto his gun as they walked at a brisk pace toward the lobby. He stopped when he saw a black Suburban pulling into the parking lot and waited with Gwynn while Dean parked the car and got out.

"Have you heard from Travis or Carlos?" Dean asked, heading toward them.

"No," Ruben replied. "Someone has entered my room. They might still be there."

"I'll start with Carlos' room first," Dean replied.

"Gwynn, stay in the lobby," Ruben said. "Make sure you're not alone. I'm going with Dean."

"But you can't with your arm," she said as an uneasy feeling vibrated through her body.

"I'll stay at the bottom of the stairs."

Gwynn doubted he would. Reluctantly, she went back into the lobby. She sat by the window and watched Ruben and Dean go up the stairs and out of sight. She bit her lower lip, tapped her hands on the armrest, crossed her legs and swung her foot as she waited, hoping they'd be back soon.

CHAPTER 12

Gwynn could no longer stay seated. She paced around the lobby, picked up a magazine, and thumbed through it. She dropped it on a table and stared out the window. She buried her head in her hands, worried that something terrible must have happened. Finally, the door to the lobby flew open and Ruben walked in, carrying a duffle bag over his shoulder.

"We can't stay here," he said. "We need to get going."

"Why?"

"I'll explain later."

They were driving out of the parking lot as another black Suburban pulled in. Ruben had Gwynn stop the car. Gordon stepped out of the other vehicle and came over to Ruben's car.

"We're going to the Hilton down the street," Ruben said.

"I'll stay here until everything is cleaned up. Should I go to your room when I get there?"

"No. We'll talk in the morning after I drop Gwynn off at the Wilton Tower."

"Let me get the buttons," Gordon said. He went to his car, returned with a bag, and handed it to Ruben.

"Thanks," Ruben replied.

As they drove toward the Hilton, Gwynn knew something was really wrong, and suspected that either someone was badly wounded or dead. Ruben sat quietly with narrowed eyes and a clenched jaw so she decided not to ask any questions until they reached the hotel.

****

"What happened?" she asked as Ruben closed the drapes and locked the door.

"Carlos is my computer expert on this case," he explained. "He's capable of hacking into almost anyone's system. Part of his job was to monitor all of the rooms we occupied at the Residence Inn with surveillance cameras and mikes."

"In the bedroom?" Gwynn asked with raised eyebrows and wondered if he saw her put the copied disk in her purse.

"No. The bedroom and bathroom are private. Had the bedroom been monitored, Gordon would have known there wasn't a problem when I didn't answer the phone."

Then she recalled she had put the disk in her purse in the living room. Since Ruben hadn't mentioned it, she assumed Carlos wasn't watching at that moment. "Did something happen to Carlos?"

With his features lined with worry, Ruben sat on the sofa scratching his forehead. "Carlos and Travis were in my room. I suspect, Carlos saw someone in there and went with Travis to check it out. Travis was a skilled fighter, expert in all weapons. He was capable of protecting anyone. Both Carlos and Travis were shot."

Gwynn's eyes popped wide open. "Are they both dead?"

"There had to be more than one assailant. Travis was shot in the back. He died from his injury. Dean's taken Carlos to Dimitri's."

"Will he be okay?" Gwynn asked, easing down in the chair across from Ruben.

"When we got to him, he was unconscious, his hands were bound, and he'd lost a significant amount of blood. The bullet hit him in the side. His arms and face are badly bruised. Dean stopped the bleeding and got Carlos in the car. Based on the color of the blood surrounding the wound, it appeared the gunshot was inflicted within the past hour."

"Do you think the shooters were hurt, too?"

"Carlos knows how to use weapons," Ruben said sadly, drumming his fingers on his leg. "But he isn't a fighter. I suspect the bruises are a result of trying to acquire information from him."

"Wouldn't someone have heard noise?"

"The assailants might've had the television volume turned up and used suppressors. People who know what they're doing can do it without stirring up any attention."

"How did the attackers know where you were staying?" Gwynn asked. "Did they follow us yesterday?"

"No one followed us to Dimitri's," Ruben answered firmly. "Travis relieved Dean for a few hours today. Maybe they followed him."

"Where did he relieve Dean?"

"Dean waits in Wilton's parking garage to make sure there isn't a problem since we have inside people. Today, Travis took his place. Before Dean leaves the garage he makes sure a tracking device hasn't been attached to the vehicle. He also knows how to lose tails."

"Didn't Travis do that?"

"He should have. If he did, I have no idea how they tracked us. On top of that, I can't figure out how they knew which room was mine. Everyone had a suite." Ruben's lips were pressed tightly together as he rubbed his wounded arm. "All of our rooms were next to each other. Mine was closest to the stairs. Maybe they planned to search all of them."

"Have Carlos and Travis worked for you long?" Gwynn asked, gazing at his pale face creased with sadness.

"Carlos has been with me for a long time." Ruben's eyes briefly closed and his jaw tightened. "Travis, less than a year."

"So he was new at your line of work."

"No. He worked for someone else before I hired him." He paused. "I'm sure you're as tired as I am. Let's go to bed."

Gwynn got Ruben's pills out of her purse and made sure he took them. This time he even swallowed the third pill. She insisted that he get ready for bed first, and he didn't disagree.

Ruben was stretched out on the bed sound asleep when Gwynn climbed under the covers next to him.

****

"Remember I have an appointment today with Julie's attorney," Gwynn said to Ruben, driving to work. "Maybe I can get a ride with Cindy."

"I'd rather Gordon or I drove you, but Cindy might want you to go with her since she mentioned it during dinner. Then one of us will follow."

"My desk is stacked with work I need to finish. I hope Stan doesn't insist I go and see Fardown. Since I have to leave early, I'll try to stall him."

"If you can't, push the beeper and get out of the building. We'll be listening. Someone will be by the entrance to pick you up."

Gwynn wore a rose pin secured to her blouse. The beeper button was disguised as rose petals. She touched her bra to make sure the bug was securely in place.

When the car stopped in front of the Wilton Tower, they both got out. Ruben moved to the driver's side.

"Are you sure you can drive?" Gwynn asked.

"I could've driven yesterday, but I enjoyed being chauffeured around," he said smiling.

****

Gwynn had just sat down at her desk when Cindy walked into her cubicle. She knew the early visit was about Ruben, and she was prepared.

"Where did you meet him?" Cindy asked with glowing eyes as she sank down into a seat. "You've been holding out on me. I didn't even know you were dating anyone. And here I was feeling guilty for not telling you about Borge. So tell me everything."

Gwynn began her planned lies, laced with a bit of truth, "I met him in my apartment building. He was visiting a friend on my floor when the fire alarm went off. Someone ran past me on the stairs and knocked my purse out of my hand and he picked it up. We talked in the parking lot while we waited for the all-clear sign. Then he asked me out."

"So how long have you known him?"

"A week."

Cindy squinted and a puzzled expression darted across her face. "When was the fire alarm?"

Gwynn hesitated trying to remember the prior week's evenings. "It was after Borge dropped me off on Sunday."

"The night your bowling ball hit you in the face?"

"Yes," Gwynn replied, nodding, and then quickly changed the subject. "Ruben dropped me off at work. Can I get a ride with you to the attorney's office?"

"Sure. Borge will meet us there." Cindy stood up. "I need to get to work. You'll have to tell me more about Ruben at lunch."

Gwynn felt a little awkward that Ruben had heard her lie; at the same time, she wouldn't need to worry he might say they had met in another way. She opened her file cabinet and mingled the copied disk among other papers in a used file folder. Her file cabinet already contained CDs, so if anyone saw it, it wouldn't arouse any suspicion. She also figured that would be the last place anyone would look for it. She put the rest of the documents she had obtained in another folder. If she decided to get the police involved, she'd find a way to take the documents and disk out of the building.

Brad, one of Gwynn's co-workers, strolled into her cubicle carrying a newspaper. "Did you see the article in the paper about McIntyre this morning?"

"No."

Brad spread the newspaper out on her desk and pointed to a headline. *Houston's Lark Refinery purchased by Trulin Energy Company.*

Gwynn cocked her eyebrows. "That's not an article about McIntyre."

"But it is," Brad replied. "That refinery had been closed down by the EPA and also had OSHA violations. The article goes on to say that two of Trulin's officers had worked for Wilton under McIntyre."

"Just because McIntyre is mentioned in the article doesn't mean it's about him."

"He's mentioned more than anyone else. The EPA Administrator is quoted saying the Trulin officers had adopted McIntyre's philosophy on the environment, and because of that the administrator knew they could tackle the water pollution and air quality violations. Senator Stenson also chimed in by saying how the American people needed the Lark Refinery production and said the refinery would operate under an environmentally-friendly manner since Trulin's officers were going to follow McIntyre's example. He didn't even mention the names of the officers."

"Trulin's officers probably weren't happy about that. Did the article say when the refinery will reopen?"

"EPA implies that the refinery will be able to open again in a week or so. The prior owners couldn't get it reopened after all the improvements they made. What could Trulin possibly do about the refinery's pollution problems in a week?" He tapped his fingers on the article. "Read it."

"I will."

"Let me know what you think." He left her cubicle.

She knew Brad hated the emails employees received about McIntyre's speeches on the environment. He'd say, "McIntyre always likes to toot his own horn." Last year, Brad, as well as all the stockholders, was irritated with the size of Wilton's dividends. His retirement fund was all in Wilton stock. Since then he complained whenever a newspaper article showed McIntyre hobnobbing with some politician in Washington, D.C. and traveling around the country preaching about the environment. He regularly opined that McIntyre should be working on improving Wilton's financial picture and not spending his time gallivanting around.

Gwynn used to think McIntyre's political contacts helped Wilton and she felt good working for a company whose CEO cared about the environment. Now she wondered if McIntyre played a role in Julie's death and if everything he did was self-serving.

She read the article and agreed with Brad. The Trulin officers were insignificant compared to the praise McIntyre received. It almost sounded like the refinery would be run by McIntyre. She mulled over a possible connection between Wilton and Trulin: *Did McIntyre or Fardown have a stake in the private company? That would certainly explain why the contracts were so closely guarded.*

During lunch, Cindy tried drilling Gwynn about Ruben. Since he might be listening, Gwynn kept all of her answers vague. When she saw the frustrated expression on Cindy's face, she made up a couple of lies, "Ruben's a sales rep for a pharmaceutical company, and he constantly travels."

At 1:45 p.m., Cromer stepped into Gwynn's cubicle. "Mr. Fardown would like to see you," he said, politely.

Gwynn maintained a neutral expression despite the fact she felt a cold chill creeping up her spine. "I have to leave early today. We all work closely together in this section; maybe someone else could talk to him. Can you tell me what it's about?"

"He didn't tell me."

"Maybe my boss, Stan, could go. He knows everything I do at work," Gwynn said, fidgeting with her hands.

"No. He specifically asked to see you. No one else.

"Let me just finish summarizing this report and I'll be right up."

"How long will that take?"

"Only a few minutes."

"I'll wait and escort you to his office." Cromer moved to the other side of her cubicle wall, his shoulders and head towering above her.

Gwynn's breathing became tense as she wondered how to escape with him lurking. She pushed the rose petals. *How long will it take Ruben or one of his men to get here?* Fear consumed her every thought, yet she needed to look busy while she waited for help. She keyed in meaningless numbers on her computer.

Another security guard walked past her cubicle and stopped to talk to Cromer about security measures at a party. Gwynn assumed it was about Pam's dinner party.

While they spoke, she noticed Cromer turned away slightly from the cubicle entrance. She quietly slipped her purse out of her drawer and eased around the corner of her cubicle and stayed low until she passed the next cubicle. As she inched into another aisle she looked back and saw the two men were still talking.

Gwynn opened the exit door in the hallway, the noxious smell of fresh paint hitting her as she sprinted down the stairs. "I'm in the stairwell," she said, hoping someone was listening. She heard noise in the stairwell above her and took the first exit door. "I'm on the eighteenth floor." She encountered two people getting on the elevator and joined them. "Don't you think the elevators in this building are slow?" she asked, wanting Ruben to know her location.

"I don't think they're any slower than other buildings," a woman replied.

When the elevator stopped on the twelfth floor, Gwynn inhaled deeply, eased to the back corner, and anxiously waited as a few people got on. One was Pam's friend, Beverly, Hadley's new secretary. She gazed at her wondering if she could be somehow involved.

Beverly squeezed around people toward her.

Gwynn's heart pounded in her chest when Beverly touched her arm. The elevator stopped on the eighth floor. Gwynn contemplated making a beeline for the door and then running down the stairs. She took a step forward.

"Stay here," Beverly whispered, gripping her arm. "Give this to Ruben." She slid an envelope into Gwynn's hand.

Gwynn's eyes shot wide open and her forehead creased as she turned and stared at Beverly. Beverly didn't meet her eyes; she was looking straight ahead. Beverly moved in front of Gwynn, shielding her from the other elevator passengers.

Gwynn briefly gazed at the envelope, unbuttoned the bottom button on her blouse, and slipped it in. While she tucked in her blouse, making sure the envelope was well hidden, the elevator stopped on the fourth floor. Beverly got out.

Walking out of the elevator on the main floor, Gwynn exhaled a long deep breath when she saw Ruben standing by the entrance.

A security guard approached her. "Mr. Fardown needs to see you before you leave the building," he said, blocking her.

Another security guard came and stood on the other side of her.

She heard the elevator bell, then turned and saw the elevator door opening. Out stepped Cromer. A wave of terror swept through her body and her spine stiffened as Cromer came closer.

"Thanks, Harold," Cromer said, gazing at Gwynn with a stern expression.

Ruben moved between them. "Miss Reznick is wanted at the police station to go over some mug shots regarding the disappearance of Taylor Denton."

"And who are you?" Cromer asked in a tone full of disdain.

"He's Lieutenant Baxter and I'm Sergeant Tillman," Gordon said, walking toward them. He flashed a badge in front of Cromer's face. Cromer yanked it from him. Gordon held his hand under his jacket while Cromer carefully examined the badge.

Cromer's eyes scanned their faces. "I'll inform Mr. Fardown of the situation."

Ruben led Gwynn out of the building. Her body shivered. He wrapped his uninjured arm around her shoulders as they walked swiftly toward a parking lot across the street. Opening his car door, he said, "You're okay."

"Do you want me to drive?" she asked, clutching her hands together to prevent them from twitching.

"No. I better do that."

Sliding into the passenger seat, she said, "Beverly gave me something for you. Do you want it now?"

"Do you have to disrobe to get it?"

"No." She unbuttoned part of her blouse, pulled out the envelope, and handed it to him. After Ruben closed her door, she felt the tension in her body dissipating. Looking out the window, she saw Ruben passing the envelope to Gordon while they spoke. Gordon laid it on the front seat of the Suburban parked next to Ruben's, and then he pulled a scanner out of his pocket and moved it over both vehicles.

As Ruben buckled his seat belt, Gwynn said, "I never would have suspected Beverly worked for you."

"She's good."

"How's your arm?"

"I took the pain pills a couple of hours ago. Right now it feels fine. Did you make arrangements with Cindy to drive you to the attorney's office?"

"Yes."

"Tell her the pharmaceutical rep is taking you," he grinned, handing her a cell.

"I thought you might've heard that," she said, returning his smile.

CHAPTER 13

Gwynn and Ruben were the first to arrive at Babcock & Associates. A short, elderly man with thinning white hair strolled down the hall and met them by the receptionist's desk. He introduced himself as Julie's attorney, Frank Young. Ruben sat in the outer office as Gwynn was escorted to the conference room.

Three o'clock came and went with no sign of Cindy or Borge. Young and Gwynn chatted about the weather and the oil industry while they waited for them. Twenty minutes later, Gwynn started feeling anxious as she feared those involved with Julie's death might have gone after Cindy or Borge. *Had Cindy been detained at the Wilton Tower?* She restlessly swung her foot under the table as she worried and kept glancing at the clock hanging on the wall.

At 3:38 p.m., the receptionist led Cindy and Borge into the conference room. Gwynn jumped up and gave them both a big hug. "Sorry we're late," Cindy said. "The security guards at Wilton were busy checking everyone's stuff before they could leave. It took me forever to get out of there."

After Cindy and Borge had been introduced to the attorney and everyone was seated at the conference table, Young began, "You all have my condolences on your loss. Miss Morgan was a wonderful person. I've known her since she was ten." He shuffled through the documents in front of him. "She recently amended her will. Taylor Denton is also listed as a beneficiary. I haven't been able to locate him. Do one of you know his address?"

Cindy swallowed hard and tears filled her eyes.

Borge held her hand and said, "Taylor Denton has been missing for over two weeks. The police are investigating his disappearance."

"I'm sorry to hear that," Young said, and then he straightened the pile of papers in front of him. "Julie Morgan's Last Will and Testament." His eyes remained fixed on the document as he read it.

Borge's eyes became moist when Young read his name. Cindy tenderly caressed his arm. Julie had bequeathed him the condo along with her stocks and bonds. The next name read was Gwynn's. Julie had left her all her certificates of deposit held by First National Bank along with her jewelry in her safe deposit box except for the emerald necklace and earrings. She had bequeathed those to Cindy along with $200,000. Taylor was also left $200,000.

When Young finished reading the will, he handed Borge a schedule of the stocks and bonds along with their current value. He gave Gwynn a list of the certificates of deposit and their value. He presented Cindy with an envelope.

Gwynn sat silently with Borge staring at the documents. She was numb when Young requested their signatures and social security numbers on some of the forms. They signed and filled in the information on the lines he indicated without asking any questions.

"Do you know where Julie Morgan kept her safe deposit key?" Young asked Gwynn.

"Yes," Gwynn replied softly, feeling confused and bewildered.

"Take this letter along with the key to the bank," Young said, handing an envelope to Gwynn. "Then they'll allow you access to the box. After you remove all the contents, the box will be closed." He paused. "Will you make sure that Miss Wood receives the emerald jewelry?"

"Yes," Gwynn nodded, glancing at Cindy.

"Let me know if you encounter any problems," Young said. "I have another appointment, so I'll excuse myself, but feel free to stay in here as long as you like."

Borge, Gwynn, and Cindy thanked him and shook his hand. Then he left.

"I didn't know Julie was rich," Borge said with an uneven voice. "We were going to be married. Why didn't she tell me?" He raised his elbows to the table and held his face in his cupped hands. "Julie," he murmured.

"She didn't tell any of us," Gwynn said quietly, clasping her hands together. "I knew her grandmother was rich. From what she told me about her father, he wasn't. She once mentioned she had inherited from her mother. But the way she said it, I thought it was a small amount."

"Julie," Borge said again as tears welled in his eyes. "I wanted to give her everything. There wasn't anything I could give her she couldn't have."

Cindy pushed her chair back as she rose to her feet. She put her arms around Borge's neck, pulled his face to her chest, and gently stroked his head. He wrapped his arms around her waist and cried.

Gwynn leaned over the table and touched Borge's arm. "Julie loved you. All she wanted was you," she said with moist eyes.

Borge's sobs became louder, and Cindy held him tighter as she softly ran her fingers through his hair. "Why do you think she worked?" she asked Gwynn, scrunching her face in confusion as her eyes drifted over the documents lying on the table.

"Maybe she wanted to make her own way," Gwynn said, tears trickling down her cheeks. "She lived within her salary. She was never flamboyant." She wiped her face with her fingertips. "Even when we went shopping, she looked at the price tags."

Clinging to Cindy, Borge cleared his throat and stuttered, "I'm still going to play with the band. That's my life."

"This is going to take me some time to absorb," Gwynn confessed, pulling a tissue out of her purse. "This is overwhelming. Ruben is waiting. I better get going."

"I want to talk to you about something privately," Cindy said to Gwynn as she continued comforting Borge. "Is it okay if I come to your apartment tonight, or will Ruben be there?"

"Why don't I go to your place?" Gwynn replied, thinking it wasn't safe to talk in her apartment.

"Okay. When?"

"How about now? I'll have Ruben drop me off."

"I don't know," she said hesitantly, glancing at Borge. "I'll be there as soon as I can."

"I'll wait," Gwynn said, leaving the conference room.

"That took awhile," Ruben said as she walked toward him. Then he noticed her red eyes and pale lips. Grief covered her face. "It must've been rough." He reached out and took her hand.

"Yes," she said sullenly. "Poor Borge is really having a hard time."

"I'm sorry to hear that," he said in a gentle tone as he led her out of the building.

"How's Carlos doing?"

"It was touch and go for a while, but he'll be fine. He'll be staying at Dimitri's for a week or ten days."

"Cindy wants to talk to me about something. Can you drop me off at her place?"

"Can I go with you?"

"No. It's something private."

"Then I'll wait in the car."

****

On the way to Cindy's condo, Ruben stopped at a drug store and picked up some medical supplies. When they reached her place, Cindy's parking spot was empty.

"Cindy wasn't sure how long it would take her to get here. I told her I'd wait," Gwynn said. "What time does Pam's dinner party begin?"

"Seven."

"I wonder if they're celebrating Trulin purchasing Lark Refinery."

"You saw the article," he said as his eyebrows slightly flickered.

Gwynn nodded.

"The way Simmons acted, Bev thought it was to celebrate something. That's probably exactly what it is."

"Is Bev going to Pam's party?"

"Yes." He turned toward Gwynn with an amused expression. "Remember, they're buds."

Gwynn smiled as she recalled that was how she referred to them. "Who do you think has interest in Trulin — McIntyre or Fardown?"

"Both. Carlos researched that angle. He found out that McIntyre and Fardown were both slowly and discreetly dumping their Wilton stock. He traced the transactions. Their proceeds went directly into Trulin's account. Carlos was surprised by the measly size of Fardown's holdings." He pushed a button and his window slid down. "McIntyre's been talking to Hadley almost every day. From the pieces of information Bev's gathered, it appears McIntyre is recruiting him to work for Trulin."

"Is Hadley going to?"

"She doesn't know."

Cindy's car pulled into the parking lot. She parked, got out, and walked over to Ruben's car. "I'm sorry I'm so late," she said without giving an explanation.

"I understand," Gwynn said, suspecting it was probably difficult for Cindy to leave Borge.

"I'll drive Gwynn home," Cindy said to Ruben. "You don't need to wait."

"No, I'll wait. It'll give me a chance to read the newspaper," he said, holding it up.

"Call if you change your mind," Cindy said.

****

As soon as they stepped into Cindy's condo, she opened a bottle of wine and poured two glasses. "I need this," she said, handing a glass to Gwynn.

"So do I," Gwynn replied, lifting the glass to her lips.

"I don't want to keep you long since Ruben's waiting and I need to get back to Borge. So I'll get right to it." She took a sip of her wine.

"Before you start, how is Borge doing?"

"I drove him home. We'll get his car later. I gave him a couple of aspirins, had him lie down, and sang him a song."

"You did what?" Gwynn asked. She had heard Cindy sing before and knew she couldn't carry a tune.

"I didn't know what else to do to get him to sleep. He must've liked my singing because he fell asleep."

Curious, Gwynn asked, "What did you sing to him?"

Cindy's lips quirked up into a crooked smile, and she slightly shook her head. "Don't laugh. The only song I could even think of was *Row, Row, Row Your Boat.*"

Gwynn's face broke out in a wide grin, yet she managed to stifle her impulse to laugh. "And it worked?"

Cindy nodded and began, "Borge's leaving for Vegas tomorrow. The guy who filled in for him has another gig. He talked to me about it last night and again before we went into the attorney's office." She took another sip and fidgeted with her glass.

"Is something wrong?"

"No. I just don't know what to do. He wants me to go with him." She gulped down the rest of the wine in her glass. "I think he needs me. I want to go with him, but what about Taylor?" Her eyes shined with unshed tears as she ran her finger around the rim of her empty glass.

Gwynn reached out and touched her hand. "You can't worry about Taylor forever. I can see Borge needs you, but you should do what makes you happy."

"It's been hard to go to work since Taylor isn't there," Cindy said as her lips trembled. "And then when I found out Marilyn was also missing, I began to think something is going on at Wilton. Especially since Taylor sent me those contracts and someone broke in just to steal them. Am I being paranoid, or do you think something's going on, too?"

"You might be right. I don't know if Taylor's or Marilyn's disappearance has anything to do with Wilton," she said, guessing Cindy's condo might be bugged. "I don't like working there anymore, either. Maybe I'll feel different if Taylor is found. I'm going to start to look for another job."

"You don't need to work anymore," Cindy said, realizing the fortune Gwynn inherited.

"But I want to."

"Borge doesn't need to work either. I'm not sure if he's ready to go back yet, but I know he'd never give it up. Maybe performing will help him. Do you think it's okay if I go with him?"

"Yes," Gwynn replied without hesitation. Until Ruben's investigation was finished, she'd feel better if they were both away from Houston.

Cindy gave her a warm smile. "Thanks. That's what I wanted to hear."

"When will you be leaving?"

"Borge has to play tomorrow night, so we'll have to fly. Earlier, he said he'd try to get tickets for the first morning flight heading to Vegas. I don't want to wake him, so I'll have to see what's available."

"How long will you be gone?"

"I don't know. He wasn't sure when the gig ended."

"What about work?"

"I'll call in sick on Monday. Then try to figure out what I'm going to do."

"Will you let me know when you're leaving and when you get there?"

"Yes, Mom," Cindy said with a smile.

Gwynn stood. "I better get going." She set her glass down on the kitchen counter. "Thanks for the wine."

"You're welcome." Cindy and Gwynn hugged each other.

"Have a safe trip," Gwynn said. "Say 'bye to Borge from me."

"I will."

CHAPTER 14

After Gwynn filled Ruben in about Cindy's plans, he said, "Good. They might have decided to go after her to get to you." He turned into a strip mall parking lot. "I'm going to pick up a pizza, so I'll be available to take calls this evening."

"Sounds good. I want to relax if that's possible."

"We got to bed late last night. Maybe things will go smoothly at the party and no one will call me, but I wouldn't count on that."

As they drove back into traffic, Gwynn noticed Ruben heading in the opposite direction from the Galleria. "Is there somewhere else you need to go?"

"No. We're staying at a different Residence Inn across town where Holly has all the video and audio equipment set up."

"Is she also a computer expert?"

"Yes."

****

Gwynn and Ruben were eating pizza and watching a movie when he received the first call.

"What's the problem?" he asked, answering the phone. Gwynn pushed the mute button on the television remote.

"Don't let Gwynn use her cell phone," Dean said.

"Just a minute." Ruben moved the phone away from his ear. "Turn off your cell phone," he said to Gwynn. He kept his eyes on her as she took it out of her purse and pushed a button.

"Her phone doesn't have GPS," he said into the phone. "Go on."

"She's being monitored. There are two guys waiting in her apartment."

"Anything else?" Ruben scratched his chin as he slid farther back on the sofa.

"Besides McIntyre hitting on Bev whenever he gets a chance," Dean said, sounding irritated, "and Simmons making her rounds with Jurovski, Lemus, and Cromer, everything's going smoothly."

"Flirting with them?"

"Yeah. I'll give you the guest list later."

"Let me know if any problems develop," Ruben said and hung up.

"What's happened?" Gwynn asked.

"Two guys are in your apartment waiting for you to return, and your cell is being monitored. Even without GPS, if you're on it long enough, they'll be able to trace your location. You said Cindy was going to call you later?"

"Yeah," Gwynn confirmed.

He stood up, got an N-cell out of a drawer, and handed it to Gwynn. "Call Cindy. Tell her you broke your cell phone and give her the number on the side of this one."

"Okay." She went into the bedroom and called Cindy. Gwynn relayed the broken phone story and gave her the temporary number.

"Borge and I are leaving at six tomorrow morning," Cindy said. "I'll give you a call when we reach the hotel."

After Gwynn clicked off, she put the N-cell on the kitchen counter and sat down beside Ruben. "Who was it that called?"

"Dean."

"Has anything happened at the party?"

"McIntyre's hitting on Bev. Dean doesn't like it. Simmons is probably too busy to notice."

"Are Dean and Bev dating?"

"They're married."

Her mouth dropped open. "Married?" she asked, surprised Ruben had team members who were that close.

He nodded.

"Having his wife hit on must be hard for Dean."

"It's part of the job, and it's a matter of trust. Sometimes Dean's the center of someone's desires. We have a job to do and use whatever means necessary."

Gwynn looked down and stared blankly at the floor. She thought she had become more than a job to Ruben; now she wasn't sure.

"Are you okay?" he asked, leaning toward her and stroking her hand.

"I'm fine," she replied, raising her head and gazing at Ruben. "What did you mean when you said Pam was too busy to notice?"

"She's been giving her attention to Jurovski, Lemus, and Cromer. That was probably her assignment for the evening."

Gwynn knew Pam was crazy about McIntyre and felt sorry for her, thinking she was just being used by him. "Jurovski? Who's that?"

"He's a CT guy who attended the meeting. We heard his first name, Abir, on Miss Morgan's disk."

"Yeah, I remember writing it down."

"With an unusual name like that, it wasn't difficult to find his last name."

"Was your tech person able to do anything about the static on the CD?"

"She couldn't get behind it for the missing dialogue; she removed the static so it'll be easier to listen to."

Gwynn's mouth curled with disappointment. Though she already suspected if the missing information had been recovered, Ruben would have told her about it sooner. "Has Elliott talked to the guy who worked on the platform yet?"

"He's talking to him sometime tonight."

"Have you decided if I can go with you to see Karlee Daniels?"

"Yes, if I'm going. Gordon's searching McIntyre's and Fardown's houses. He might come up with something so the trip won't be necessary." He gripped Gwynn's hand. "If we go, you have to promise me you'll let me do all the talking."

"What should I do when we're there?"

"Just sit by your husband's side, like the dutiful wife," he said as a faint smile touched his lips.

She grinned, thinking no way.

"I know that will be hard for you. Do you think you can manage?"

"Yes. I can do role playing."

His cell rang again.

"I knew it wasn't going to be a relaxing evening," he said, putting the phone next to his ear. "What's the problem now?"

"Fardown's wife just left in a huff," Dean said. "I can't reach Gordon on his cell. Cromer's having another pow-wow with the guys, so I hate to leave."

"Fardown's house isn't far from here. I'll have Holly go."

Ruben ended the call and punched in Holly's number. "Fardown's wife is on her way home. Gordon isn't answering his cell. He might be in Fardown's house. Go and check it out."

"I'm on my way." Holly disconnected.

Ruben called Gordon. No answer. He stood up, paced around the suite, drank a glass of water, and flopped back down on the sofa. His body was rigid as he stared at the wall with hazy and drawn eyes.

"Maybe Gordon turned off his cell because someone else was in the house," she said, trying to ease his tension.

"Gordon would have put it on vibrate."

"Even if it was vibrating, he still wouldn't be able to answer it if anyone was close by."

"Yes, but he would've found a way to call by now."

She caressed his arm. "I'm sure he's okay. Aren't most of their guys at the party?"

"I don't know how many men are working for them. Whenever we think we have a count, more appear." He tilted his head and tapped his fingers on the armrest. "I wonder how many of them know what's really going on. Most of them might believe the story we heard about stolen corporate secrets."

"Everyone we saw on the tapes has to know the truth."

Ruben's cell rang again. He immediately answered it. "Did you find him?" he asked in an anxious tone.

"It's me," Gordon said. "I'm using Holly's cell. Fardown has a security system and a small dog. I emptied my pockets to find the tool I needed to disconnect the system. The dog ran off with my cell. I spent half an hour chasing the little bitch around the house. She dropped it in the toilet." He chuckled. "She sat next to the toilet and watched me fish it out. I think she was mocking me."

Ruben laughed.

Gwynn smiled, feeling good hearing him laugh.

"Holly and I were both at the top of the stairs when Mrs. Fardown came home. Boy, was she mad! She slammed the front door, threw her purse against a wall, and punched in her security code. She didn't notice it wasn't on. She went in the kitchen and we heard pots and pans flying around the room. Oh, was she noisy! I didn't even have to creep around to hook up the security system. After I finished, Holly and I just walked out the front door. We could still hear her slamming and banging things around when we were in the front yard. I feel sorry for the dog."

"Were you able to find out anything?"

"Yes. I'm going back to McIntyre's. I want to check out his garage. Do you want Holly to stay with me or should I send her back?"

"Keep her with you. It appears Fardown will be staying with Simmons so McIntyre won't be. If he goes straight home from the party, you might not have very much time there. Be careful." Ruben laid his phone down on the end table.

"What was so funny?" Gwynn asked.

Ruben told her what had happened.

Gwynn laughed, happy Gordon was okay. She cleared off the coffee table and put the rest of the pizza in the fridge. "Can I get you anything?"

"A Coke," Ruben replied, playing with the remote. He started another movie.

Settling down on the sofa, Gwynn gave him a Coke and attempted to watch the show. Her eyelids kept getting heavier, and she dozed off.

"Why don't you go to bed?" Ruben said, nudging her.

"I think I will." She staggered to her feet.

Ruben's cell phone came to life with a loud ring, and Gwynn sank back down beside him.

"I'll put on the speaker," he said, answering it. "What is it?"

"The party is breaking up," Dean said. "McIntyre wanted Bev to go to his place. She turned it around and invited him to her condo so she could change into something more comfortable. We all know what that means," Dean lightly laughed. "McIntyre's going to his place first to pick up something. Poor bastard probably thinks he's going to get lucky."

"I'll let Gordon know McIntyre's on his way home and get Holly in action," Ruben said. "You'll have to let Holly know when she should make her appearance."

"Will do," Dean said, hanging up.

Ruben called Holly.

"Yes," she answered.

"Tell Gordon that McIntyre's dropping by soon to get something. You'll be playing cousin tonight."

"Okay."

"Give Dean a call when you're parked by Bev's building. He'll let you know when you should go in. Hurry, we don't want any problems," Ruben said and disconnected.

"How does the cousin thing work?" Gwynn asked.

"She just drove in from Galveston because she had a fight with her boyfriend."

"And she'll make her appearance when things start getting cozy between McIntyre and Beverly?"

"You got it. Until then we want to know if McIntyre discloses anything."

"What would you have done if Holly wasn't here?"

"Carlos was going to be Bev's brother-in-law. He would've had a fight with her sister — similar scenario, different players."

"How many roles have you played?"

"Too many."

Gwynn no longer felt tired as she looked at Ruben's colorless complexion and knew he wasn't well enough to stay up this late. "Why don't you go to bed? I'll wake you if someone calls."

"No. You go to bed. You were having a hard time staying awake during the movie."

"Do you think anything else will happen tonight?"

"There's always a possibility, especially since everyone is still out."

She picked up the remote. "Then I'll stay up with you. We haven't seen an entire movie yet."

Around 2 a.m., Gordon called on the hotel phone and said he was back in his room. Ruben finally agreed to go to bed. Gwynn made sure he took his pills.

****

When Gwynn awoke, she found herself lying in bed alone. She heard voices coming from the other room and smelled freshly brewed coffee. She threw on her sweatpants as she glanced at the clock on the nightstand. It read: 7:23 a.m.

Dean, Gordon, and Ruben sat around the table. They stopped talking when the bedroom door opened, and Gwynn entered the room.

"Why are you guys up so early?" she asked, making her way to the coffee pot. "None of you could have slept more than five hours."

"Something is going to happen next week," Ruben said, lifting a coffee mug. "We don't know what it is, so we need answers."

"How do you know something's going to happen?" Gwynn asked, pulling a chair up to the table and grabbing a donut.

"There was whispering going on last night," Ruben said. "One of our inside people heard someone say, 'By next weekend it will all be over.' Later, when the male guests went into the den, he tried to listen, but couldn't hear enough to put it all together. All we know is it has something to do with a pipeline or pipelines. Based on what we could pick up on the disk, that's probably what they were discussing when Miss Morgan overheard them. Gordon was just starting to tell us how he handled the security guards at McIntyre's house." He looked at Gordon. "Go on."

"There wasn't anything to handle," he said with a crooked smile. "McIntyre has a huge home theater. The screen's at least six by eight feet. Last night, there was a game on between the Spurs and the Bulls. I heard the television blasting outside before I entered. The security guards were cheering when I went upstairs. They hovered by the screen all night. Occasionally, one of them walked around the main floor, checking to make sure the doors were locked and glancing in each room. They never went upstairs.

"Searching McIntyre's den was my only challenge, but the guards talked to each other about the game even when one was walking around. That gave me plenty of warning when someone was on the move."

"Did you find anything?" Ruben asked.

"Not in the house, but in the garage. The first time I was there, I noticed the garage seemed deeper than it appeared from the inside. When Fardown arrived at the party with his wife, I left to check out his house. You already know how that went." He took a sip of his coffee. "After that, Holly and I went to McIntyre's garage. It took us a while, but we finally found the entrance to the hidden room. That's when Holly left. McIntyre keeps all of his important papers in that room. I don't think the guy ever does anything without a profit plan. He even has a file cabinet drawer labeled 'marriages'." Gordon chuckled.

"There's a pre-nup for each one. I thumbed through the files until I came across Nina, Marshall Roberts's daughter. Remember, he's the guy who sold Trulin oil properties and leases in North Dakota. McIntyre planned to marry her as soon as he discovered she was Roberts's daughter. He didn't even know her before that. He had a game plan written — where they'd meet, places he'd take her, proposal, and marriage date. The guy is thorough.

"I wasn't able to get into one of his file cabinets. It's built and locked like a safe. I couldn't break in. You might have to call Rosie. She can crack it."

"She's in New York. I hate to call her off that case." Ruben paused and softly tapped his fingertips on the edge of the table. "Let's see what we can find out over the weekend first. Did you run across anything else at McIntyre's?"

"He's leaving Wilton sometime soon," Gordon said. "He's working on his farewell speech. In the margin he wrote the names of a couple of senators and a few other dignitaries. I'm not sure what that meant — if they're going to be there when he gives his departure speech, if they'll also be talking, or if he listed them for another reason. After Holly gets through with her slumber party," he said jokingly, referring to her staying at Bev's, "I'll have her check to see if any of those senators or dignitaries are going to be in Texas soon or if they're already here."

"Did you find out anything at Fardown's besides you're an animal lover?" Ruben asked, chuckling.

Everyone laughed with him.

"He's leaving Wilton with McIntyre. In his locked, top desk drawer were documents showing he was in debt over poor investments. He also had three mortgages on his house. Those documents were clipped together with a sticky note on top. On it he had written, 'John is a lifesaver. All paid off.' That might be the reason Fardown became involved."

"That's exactly what I'm thinking," Ruben said. "When Fardown recently sold his stock, I wondered why his holdings weren't larger and so did Carlos. He's probably been selling it off to cover his debt."

"A notebook was also in that drawer..." Gordon stopped abruptly and gazed at Gwynn. "This might be hard for you to hear."

"Gwynn, why don't you go in the bedroom for a few minutes," Ruben suggested.

Assuming it was about Julie, "No. I want to hear," she said as her hands trembled. She intertwined her fingers and held them under the table.

Ruben stared at her, and she stared back. He turned to Gordon. "Go on."

"I would've taken pictures of some of the pages if my cell had been functioning. To summarize, Fardown had written several notes about Julie Morgan. He felt guilty about what happened to her." He thumbed through his notepad. "On one of the pages next to Miss Morgan's name he wrote, 'Luke should have waited. Luke said it was McIntyre's order. John would never do that. Luke acted too hastily. Why? Why? Poor Julie. It's Luke's fault the recording is missing. If only he had waited. Julie would have given it to us. Poor sweet Julie.'"

A few tears trickled down Gwynn's face.

Ruben slid his chair closer to her and laid his arm around her shoulders. "You should have gone in the other room."

"No. I wanted to know."

Dean handed her a box of tissues.

"Thanks," she said.

"Why do you think he wrote that down?" Ruben asked Gordon.

"The whole notebook contained confessions. Maybe he needed the outlet. He also felt guilty about Simmons, but he didn't want to stop. He wrote numerous pages about their relationship — some graphic. We already knew they were having an affair. He had a brief note about Carl Backman, 'Carl's a nice guy, but he can't control his temper. John's right, he shouldn't work for Trulin.'" He shuffled around in his chair. "Carl Backman might be their next victim."

"They can't leave him at Wilton," Ruben said, turning toward Dean. "Was Carl Backman among the guests?"

"No," Dean replied.

"He won't be around long," Ruben said. "Gordon, try and get some information from him. He might not believe his days are numbered, but it's worth a shot."

"I'll see if I can persuade him," Gordon said, pouring coffee.

Gwynn sat quietly listening with dry eyes.

"I'd like a copy of the page in Fardown's notebook that mentions Miss Morgan," Ruben said.

"That was already on my to-do list for today," Gordon replied.

"We already suspected McIntyre was behind her death," Ruben said. "Cromer wouldn't have acted without orders. Anything else?"

"No. That covers it," Gordon said.

"Dean, your turn," Ruben said, taking another donut.

"The party guests," Dean began, "McIntyre, Fardown and his wife, Cromer, Lemus and his wife, Ray Sorenson, Abir Jurovski, Ramza Delucia, Michael Baskar, and Bev."

"Now I understand why Bev didn't have any problem getting invited with that many guys," Ruben said, pushing back his chair and standing up. "I know Carlos was checking out Jurovski and Delucia since they were mentioned on the disk." His eyes darted between Gordon and Dean. "Do either of you know how far he got?"

"With those first names, Carlos didn't have any problem finding them among CT's employees," Dean said. "They work under the vice president over midstream operations. Jurovski lives in an apartment in Houston. Delucia lives in Louisiana. He's married, but his wife lives in a house and he lives in an apartment. Jurovski has never been married. He has gambling debts. That's as far as Carlos got with the CT guys."

"I'll have Holly pick it up from there," Ruben said. "Were you able to get pictures of them?"

"Yes." Dean pulled an envelope out of his pocket and handed it to Ruben.

"I'll look at them later," Ruben said, placing it on the table.

"There were six security guards at the party," Dean said. "That includes our guys. One found out that the guards were operating under the pretense that corporate secrets had been stolen by a vicious group." He chuckled. "A guard had been killed and that vicious group might be responsible for Marilyn Anders' and Taylor Denton's disappearances."

Ruben shook his head.

Dean continued, "Wilton and the police are working on trying to recoup the stolen documents. The guards were there to protect everyone in case the perpetrators showed up."

Dean, Gordon, and Ruben laughed while Gwynn smiled.

"With Lemus' wife there, how did Simmons manage private time with him?" Ruben asked.

"Lemus' wife spent most of the evening talking to Fardown's wife before she stormed out. And Simmons didn't spend a lot of time with Lemus, just enough for a passionate kiss and an embrace," Dean smirked. "She spent more time with Jurovski, but away from prying eyes."

"It was probably either Lemus or Jurovski who left a couple of messages on Simmons's answering machine," Gordon commented. "The voices I couldn't identify."

Ruben nodded in agreement. "Did Bev-," he began, and he was cut off by a knock on the door. "That's probably Holly." He went to the door.

Gordon and Dean rose quickly to their feet. Gordon pulled a gun out of his holster. Ruben peered out the peephole and then opened the door.

Holly, an average-sized woman in her early thirties with brown eyes and shoulder length auburn hair, strolled in. She wore a pair of jeans, a black T-shirt with "BUZZ OFF" scrawled in sparkling, yellow letters on the front, and a floppy, purple fedora.

"How did it go?" Ruben asked.

"Smooth," she said as she moved toward the table. Looking at Gwynn, she handed Ruben a note. Dean pulled up a chair for her.

Ruben read the note. It contained the contact information for Karlee Daniels, the wife of recently deceased CT employee, Ian Daniels. "Holly, this is Gwynn Reznick. Gwynn, this is Holly."

As the women said hello to each other, Gwynn realized Ruben didn't give the last names of any of his employees when he introduced them.

Gordon offered Holly a donut.

"No, thanks. I've already eaten, but I'll have a cup of coffee if you have any left."

"Just made another pot." Gordon filled a mug and handed it to Holly.

"Thanks," she said, setting it down on the table. "McIntyre wasn't happy to see me last night." She scoffed. "Can you believe that?"

The guys nodded.

"After I told them why I was there," Holly said, "McIntyre said he had to leave and then talked to Bev privately for a few minutes at the door."

"I know," Dean said, irritation evident in his tone. "He invited her to his place and kissed her goodnight. She's going there on Sunday evening."

"Did Bev find out anything?" Ruben asked.

"Why don't you tell him since you heard everything?" Holly said to Dean between sips of her coffee.

"McIntyre told her he was leaving Wilton because of disagreements he had with some of the board members. That isn't exactly what Simmons told Bev on Tuesday evening. Simmons was upset with the board because they were talking about replacing McIntyre if the profits didn't improve." Suddenly, a smile lit up his face. "McIntyre wants Bev to work for him at Trulin."

"Interesting," Ruben remarked. "Did he say in what capacity?"

"No. So she didn't know if that meant he was replacing Simmons or if she'd be someone else's secretary. She'll find out more on Sunday evening. Outside of that, he just wanted to get cozy."

"Okay, let's move on to Elliott. Gordon, did you talk to him?" Ruben asked.

"Yes. For fifty grand and a promise his identity would remain anonymous, the guy talked."

Gwynn's eyes popped wide open. *Fifty thousand dollars.*

Gordon went on, "The guy saw Kirk Randolph beaten and thrown off the platform by two men. One of the attackers was short with a scarred face."

Gwynn and Ruben exchanged glances. They both remembered him from Gwynn's apartment. He was the one who shot Ruben.

"The other attacker was average size," Gordon said. "No remarkable features. The guy heard the attackers talking before they finished off Kirk. They knew someone had seen them — probably throwing the first man in the water. Then they said a guy by the name of Luke was on the platform and he'd make sure the witness didn't talk." He paused. "That's all Elliott got. I think the guy was overpaid."

"So do I," Ruben remarked. "He confirmed what we suspected — two men didn't accidentally fall off the platform. But we didn't know Cromer was there when the *accident* happened. I had hoped the guy could've enlightened us about what Kirk Randolph saw or did before he landed in the water." Ruben stood and paced while Gordon poured Dean and Gwynn another cup of coffee.

"Elliott's staying in Louisiana to check on one of the guys who worked for the offshore pipeline again," Gordon said. "The drowning victim. Last Wednesday, his wife suffered a fatal injury in a two-car crash. She was alone in the car."

"And the other vehicle?" Ruben asked.

"A pickup truck driven by a thirty-six-year-old man. He ended up with a couple of scratches; didn't need to go to the hospital."

Gwynn stared at Gordon. She felt numb, too stunned to move, and thought, *another innocent person died — for what?*

Ruben lightly squeezed her shoulder. "Are you okay?"

"Yes," she said softly, her voice barely audible.

"Is there anything else we need to discuss?" Ruben asked.

Gordon, Dean, and Holly looked at each other. "No," Gordon replied. "I'll tell Holly what she needs to check on after we leave."

"Dean, are you still planning to see Carlos today?" Ruben asked.

"Yes. I'll know later this morning if he's allowed visitors."

"I need to know what his attackers wanted as soon as possible," Ruben said. "Gordon, I'll let you know when we're leaving for Wyoming."

Gordon nodded as he left the room with Holly and Dean.

Ruben caressed Gwynn's arm. "Do you still want to go with me to Wyoming? Or would you rather go to a nice cabin out in the wilderness? It's only an hour away. You'll be safe there."

"I want to go with you."

"Why don't you lie down while I make arrangements with Karlee Daniels?"

She nodded in agreement, feeling exhausted. She headed into the bedroom and closed the door behind her.

Ruben called the number on the note.

"Hello," a female voice answered.

"Is this Karlee Daniels?" Ruben asked.

"Yes, and who are you?" Karlee responded.

"This is Ross Olson. I talked to you about Ian."

"Oh, yes, I remember you. You have such a kind smile."

"A few days ago you talked to Joann Shelton," Ruben said, knowing Holly used that name in Wyoming.

"Yes, I did. She said she worked for you and wanted to know about Ian's accident, just like you. I thought I should talk to someone, but I lost your card. Do you have other cards?"

"Yes."

"Good. I have Joann's card, but she didn't have anyone in her family who worked for CT and died; your wife did. So I want to talk to your wife. What's your wife's name?"

"Ellen. I'll bring her."

"That's good. Your wife shouldn't travel alone. Ian stayed next to me whenever we traveled. That's how it should be."

"Is it possible to talk to you today?"

"Today's Saturday," Karlee said. "That's a good day. I'm going to Ian's cabin to clean it. Mom's at my house, and I don't want her to know about this. Max will be there at seven. You can talk to me there at five, if you want to."

"Where's the cabin?"

"It's north of town. Just stay on the main road until you see an old gas station. You can't get gas there; it's closed down. Turn on the dirt road next to the gas station and follow it to the end. That's where the cabin is. It's easy to find. I find it all the time."

"We'll see you there at five," Ruben confirmed.

"Now, don't be early and don't be late. Be on time."

"Okay," Ruben said hesitantly.

As he hung up, Ruben wondered if it would be a waste of time going to Wyoming to talk to her, and then recalled, *sometimes the people you think know the least are the ones who know the most.*

CHAPTER 15

Ruben had arranged for a private plane to take them to Pinedale, Wyoming. Right before they boarded, Cindy called. She gave Gwynn the hotel information. Gwynn heard Borge in the background telling Cindy to hurry.

"I've got to go," Cindy said. "Borge has a list of things for us to do before the performance tonight. I'll call you tomorrow."

When the plane was airborne, Gwynn said, "I forgot to ask. Were the other fingerprints on the receiver identified?"

"Yes. McIntyre's and Lange's."

Gwynn laid her hands on her lap and gazed at the floor. She had suspected that, but she couldn't understand how anyone who had known Julie could have hurt her.

Ruben put his hand on top of hers. "Just because his fingerprints are on the receiver doesn't mean he was responsible for Miss Morgan's death. Let me bring you up to speed about Karlee Daniels. The last time I talked to her in Wyoming it was in a store parking lot. Since she seemed apprehensive, I told her I was investigating the death of my wife's brother. He had worked for CT at their offshore pipeline subsidiary and my wife wasn't convinced his death was an accident. She became extremely agitated and her body trembled.

"Then a truck pulled into the parking lot. A man got out and hurried to Karlee. He embraced her, apologized for being late, and told her everything was going to be okay. He asked me why I was talking to her. I said I was asking her how she was doing since I knew she had recently lost her husband. He glared at me, and then he carried her to his truck. As he was leaving, he yelled out the window, 'Don't talk to her again.'

"When I made today's appointment, she seemed anxious to talk. She didn't want her mother to know about the meeting, so we'll be seeing her in a cabin."

"Does she live with her mother?"

"No. Her mother's staying at her house, probably helping out with the kids." He paused. "Karlee seems a little slow."

"Did Holly have any problem talking to her?"

"No, but Holly talked to her on the front porch and only for a few minutes. Karlee's mother came out and questioned Holly. Holly told her she was from CT and checking to make sure Karlee was doing okay. Her mother led Karlee back into the house and told Holly not to come back again."

Gwynn sat silently, thinking about Karlee and wondering if they should see her. It might be too hard on her and the poor woman just lost a husband. "Maybe we should leave her alone."

"If she seems at all agitated, we'll leave," Ruben assured her. "In case she mentions the name Joann Shelton, that's the name Holly used."

****

Ruben drove up the dirt road next to the old gas station; when he saw the cabin he made a U-turn. "We're early," he said. "Karlee Daniels was very specific that we had to arrive exactly on time."

Checking her watch, Gwynn felt puzzled. "But we're only ten minutes early."

"She was adamant," he said, stopping at the abandoned gas station. "We'll wait."

At three minutes to five, Ruben drove up the dirt road again. At five, he knocked on the cabin door.

The door opened. In front of them stood a five-foot-six, blue-eyed, twenty-eight-year-old beautiful woman with long wavy strawberry-blonde hair and rosy cheeks.

Gwynn couldn't help but stare at her. She had envisioned Karlee to be a woman of average appearance, not the beauty before her. Ruben hadn't even mentioned the way she looked.

"You must be Ellen Olson," Karlee said, reaching out and hugging Gwynn. "I'm sorry your brother, Ted, died."

"I was sorry to hear about Ian," Gwynn said.

"So am I," Karlee said, her face lined with sadness. "Hello, Ross. Please come in."

It was a large one-room cabin with a sofa and a cushioned chair in front of a stone fireplace. In one corner a television stood on top of a chest. Against the far wall was a double bed with two nightstands. A kitchen with a table for four and a small bathroom were on the other side of the cabin. Everything was spotless, including the windows. The smell of fresh baked bread filled the room.

As soon as they entered, Karlee lightly touched Ruben's bandaged arm. "What happened?"

"It's a basketball injury."

"Does it hurt?" Karlee asked, gently stroking the bandage.

"No," Ruben replied.

Karlee smiled. "That's good."

Ruben and Gwynn sat down on the sofa. Gwynn assumed Karlee would sit in the chair, but instead she squeezed in between them.

"Karlee, what would you like to talk to us about?" Ruben asked.

"I think it's better if I start at the beginning."

"Okay," Ruben said.

It surprised Gwynn when Karlee reached out and took her hand. Karlee's hand felt baby soft and velvety smooth.

"Ian was my boyfriend since the sixth grade," Karlee began, holding firmly onto Gwynn's hand. "Everyone loved Ian. We were king and queen of our junior prom." Her face lit up with a proud smile. "Max and I were king and queen of senior prom. Max is a real nice guy, but I wanted Ian to be king again. Max was the football captain and that year we won state. That's probably why he got voted for and not Ian. I was a cheerleader so I got to go to all the games. Ian played on the basketball team. He was real smart. He went to Stanford."

Ruben lifted an impatient eyebrow. He didn't want to hear her life story. "Can we jump to Ian's accident?" he asked.

Gwynn noticed Karlee's hand trembled slightly. "Karlee, take your time. Tell us about your life with Ian."

Karlee smiled at Gwynn. "I knew you'd understand. It's important to start at the beginning. Ian asked me to marry him the night of senior prom. I'll always remember that night. We were engaged all the time he was in college. He'd come home to see me whenever he could." She gazed into Gwynn's eyes. "You're real pretty. I wanted to get my hair cut short like yours, but Ian always liked my hair like this. Do you think I should get it cut?"

"No. It's the perfect length."

Karlee blushed. "You're so sweet. Then I won't get it cut. Ian graduated in computer science. He got a job in Pennsylvania. We were going to move there after we got married, but I was in a car accident. It was real bad." A few tears trickled down Karlee's cheek.

Gwynn hugged her. "You don't have to tell us about the accident."

"But I do, so you'll understand about Ian and me," she sniffled.

Gwynn took a tissue out of her purse and handed it to Karlee.

"Thank you," Karlee said, wiping her eyes. "I used to be smart, not as smart as Ian. I have awards I won in high school. One in math. Now I can't figure out how much money I spend on groceries or anything. Dad's taking care of the money since Ian's gone. Where was I?"

"You were telling us about marrying Ian," Gwynn said, patting Karlee's hand. She glanced at Ruben who was rolling his eyes. She wanted to tell him to wait in the car, but that wasn't an option.

"I was in the hospital for over a month," Karlee said. "Our wedding invitations had already been sent out. Mom and Ian had to call everyone. After that, I wondered if Ian still wanted to marry me. I forget things. Not big things, but little things — like how to get to the doctor's office, phone numbers, and things I need to pack for a trip. Ian always made me lists. Then I just needed to check things off. I still can't go to the doctor's office by myself. I'd never find my way home. If I get nervous, I can't do anything. Now where was I?"

"You were telling us about marrying Ian."

"Oh, I remember. He still wanted to marry me. He said he'd always love me and take care of me." Her face was wet with tears.

Gwynn gently dabbed a tissue over Karlee's eyes. "Maybe this is too hard for you to talk about."

"But I need to," Karlee said in an uneven tone. "Someone killed Ian, and I want whoever it was put in jail."

Ruben perked up. "Why do you think Ian was killed?"

Gwynn stroked Karlee's trembling hands as she flashed Ruben a silencing glare. Her squinting hazel eyes sent a clear message: *Be quiet. Don't rush her.* "I'm sure you and Ian had a wonderful wedding," she said, giving Karlee a sweet smile.

"We did," Karlee said, returning the smile. "Everyone came and said they had never seen such a beautiful bride." Her cheeks glowed. "We never moved to Pennsylvania. Ian thought it would be better if we stayed in Pinedale where I knew people. That's when he went to work for CT. I used to work there when Ian was in college. I was their receptionist." She beamed with pride.

"Dad's company moved to Cheyenne so Mom and Dad went there. They want me to come and live with them, but I don't want to leave my friends and my house. Ian wanted my name on the title, so we had to go to the title company three times. Every time that guy told me what I was signing, I got nervous, so we had to keep going back. Then Ian told everyone there not to talk to me, and he showed me where I should sign my name. Signing papers to get my name on that title was real hard. I don't ever want to do that again. That's why this cabin only belongs to Ian. Dad says it's mine, but I'm not going to sign any papers." She looked at Ruben and Gwynn. "Can I get you something to drink?"

"No, we're fine," Ruben replied.

"Ian and I have two children — Tyler and Sami. Sami is short for Samantha. You know, *Bewitched.* I love that show. After Tyler was born, Ian started calling me his 'Baby Girl.'" She smiled again. "Tyler was his baby boy and I was his baby girl. Sami came and then he joked about having two baby girls. He was such a wonderful husband. He brought me flowers every Friday night. He'd have his mom watch the kids and we'd come here." She stood up and pulled Gwynn's hand. "Let me show you." She led Gwynn out the back door and Ruben followed.

"We'd lie here and look at the stars," Karlee said, standing beside a trampoline. "When we started kissing, he joked about not wanting the bears to watch us. Then he'd carry me inside." She looked around. "Don't worry; there aren't any bears around here. So you don't need to be afraid." She continued holding Gwynn's hand as they walked back into the cabin.

Ruben sank down in the chair while Gwynn and Karlee sat on the sofa.

"Now do you understand why I want Ian's killer in jail?" Karlee asked.

"Yes," Gwynn replied.

The phone rang.

Karlee stood up, motioned for them to be quiet, hurried to a nightstand, and picked up the phone. "Mom, I'm okay. ... Yes, I'll use my beeper ... Bye."

"Mom calls all the time," Karlee said, sitting down. "I have two beepers." She held out her necklace. "See. Aren't they cute?"

"Yes," Gwynn replied, smiling at her.

"The blue bull is to call Max and the pink lamb is to call Mom. I used to only have one beeper. But Mom and Max both wanted me to beep them, so now I have two. Max had them made into a bull and a lamb. I only push a beeper if I start shaking." She held Gwynn's hand again.

"I tried to tell Mom and Dad that it wasn't an accident," Karlee said. "But they acted like I didn't know what I was talking about. That's why I don't want them to know I've talked to you. You won't tell them, will you?"

"No, we won't tell them," Gwynn reassured her.

"Good," she sighed. "A few days before Ian died, he forgot something at work. We were going out to get ice cream. Do you like ice cream?"

"Yes."

"Max is bringing some ice cream. We're going to eat it when we watch a movie. Now where was I?"

"Ian had forgotten something at work."

"I remember. On our way to get ice cream, Ian drove me and the kids to his office so he could get it. The kids and I stayed in the car. When he came out, he noticed a man standing by the corner of the building. Ian stared at him as he got in the car. I asked him who the guy was. He just said it was a guy who worked for CT. Then I wanted to know what the guy did since I'd never seen him before. Ian told me it was better if we didn't talk about him.

"The day of the accident, Ian came home early without calling and telling me. That made me nervous. So he had to calm me down before he told me that we were going on a little trip to Houston. The kids were going, too. I was excited. I've never been there. Ian was going to talk to one of CT's vice-presidents. He had an appointment and everything. Ian wanted to pick up a few things at the store for our trip. He made me a list so I could start packing. We were going to leave as soon as we were ready. I don't know if we were going to drive to Houston or fly. I can't remember if he ever told me.

"He wasn't home when I was through packing. The store isn't that far away. I got nervous and kept pushing my beeper, but he didn't come or call. I couldn't stop shaking so I pushed the fire alarm." She paused. "That's what I'm supposed to do if I need help. My neighbor, Diana, came over and she watched the kids while I took a pill and lay down." She looked at Ruben. "When I shake all over, I need to go to sleep. That's what I need to do.

"When I woke up, the police were at my house. Diana told me what had happened. But it's all wrong. Ian's never been rope climbing before and we were going on a trip. I couldn't talk to anyone for a few days. Max, Ian's best friend, came and saw me every day. He even drove me to the police station when I told him something was wrong. I think he believes me, but he's not an investigator or anything. When we were at the police station, I saw that same guy that Ian stared at when he went to get something at work. That guy was talking to Captain Milt, and he kept looking at me. He made me nervous, so Max took me home. I don't know why Captain Milt was talking to that guy. They were smiling and everything. So I don't want to go back there, and Max doesn't think I should."

"Do you think if you saw a picture of the guy, you could recognize him?" Ruben asked.

"Yes, I'd remember him," Karlee replied.

Ruben rose to his feet, pulled an envelope from his inside sport coat pocket, and took pictures out of it. "Is it one of these guys?" he asked, handing the photos to Karlee.

Karlee flipped over the first picture and stopped at the second one. "This is the guy. How did you get his picture?"

"I took pictures of some of the people who work for CT," Ruben replied.

"Then you're lucky you got a picture of him," Karlee said, giving them back to Ruben.

Ruben glanced at the man she had identified. It was Abir Jurovski.

Karlee went to the kitchen area and took a folder out of the cabinet.

"Here," she said, handing it to Gwynn. "Ian put this in the bottom of the suitcase before he went to the store. He wanted me to pack our clothes on top of it. I've looked through the folder, but I don't know what it means. This is what he picked up the night we went to his office. He had it hidden under his jacket. At our house, he put it under the mattress. So whatever it is, it's important." She touched Gwynn's cheek. "You're so pretty. Will you make sure whoever killed Ian is punished?" Karlee's eyes were moist.

"Yes, I'll make sure," Gwynn promised, hugging Karlee.

"Do you know Dan Massey, the other guy who died the same day as Ian?" Ruben asked.

"No," Karlee replied, noticing the clock on the wall. "I'm sorry; you have to leave right now."

"Okay," Gwynn replied, bewildered.

"I'll explain in the car," Ruben said, taking Gwynn's arm.

Karlee waved to them as they drove away.

"Max will be there at seven," Ruben said. "Karlee had to get us out of there."

"Stop when you reach the gas station," Gwynn said.

"Why?" Ruben asked, pulling into the gas station parking lot.

"Do you think Karlee could be in danger?"

"She isn't capable of going to the authorities and testifying even if she knew something. They'll leave her alone."

"Why didn't you tell me she was beautiful?"

"It wasn't important."

"The guy who picked up Karlee in the store parking lot probably thought you were hitting on her."

Ruben half grinned. "You might be right."

They heard a loud diesel truck approaching. "That's probably Max. The guy from the parking lot drove a diesel truck, and it's almost seven."

The truck turned onto the dirt road, and they watched until it was out of sight.

Ruben drove out onto the main road. "When I was here before, I ate at a great steak restaurant in town. Would you like to give it a try before we leave for Houston?"

"Sounds good," she replied, wondering if it would be a romantic place.

****

The restaurant stood on top of a hill overlooking a golf course. Rustic, unpainted wood covered all the walls. In the center, a fireplace warmed the room. Lit candles enclosed in glass holders hung on the walls. Each table also had a lit candle in the center.

The cozy restaurant surpassed Gwynn's expectations. She smelled the aroma of steak cooking over an open flame. "Doesn't that smell good?"

"Yes," Ruben replied. They were seated at a small table in a quiet corner next to a window with a spectacular view of the dark, deserted golf course. He ordered a bottle of wine and a platter of stuffed mushrooms. He wanted to wait to order the main course. Their knees touched each time either one of them moved slightly in their chairs.

"This place is wonderful. How did you find it?" Gwynn asked.

"The rental car agent recommended it."

The waitress brought the wine and appetizer.

"You were great," he said, pouring wine. "I don't have that kind of patience."

"I know," Gwynn smiled. "How's your arm? You haven't taken any pills since we got on the plane."

"Right now, it's a little sore, but it's getting better. How would you like to spend the night in a motel and fly out tomorrow morning?"

"I'd like that," Gwynn said, sipping her wine, wondering if Ruben had anything else in mind.

"Can I use your cell to call the pilot?" Ruben asked.

"The N-cell?"

Ruben nodded.

She handed him the phone and listened while he talked to the pilot. Her hopes of sleeping in vanished when she heard him say, "We'll be leaving at six."

"We're all set." Ruben handed back the cell phone.

"Don't you need to tell Gordon you won't be back tonight?" Gwynn asked.

"No. He already knew we could be staying here."

After the waitress took their order, they admired the great view of the golf course and discovered they both played. Gwynn had once played in a golf league. Ruben wished he had more opportunities to work on his game.

The waitress brought their orders; the steaks sizzled and smelled wonderful. While they talked about places they had traveled and the ones they enjoyed the most, Gwynn savored every bite.

They both wanted to visit Paris again. They laughed when Ruben told about his first experience scuba diving. He started to descend when a man dived off the boat and landed on him. The guy became flustered and pulled off Ruben's mask. After that, Ruben wasn't too anxious to get back in the water, but he managed. They had both gone scuba diving in the Caribbean.

Gwynn felt surprised by how much they enjoyed the same things. The evening was turning out just like she had hoped, not talking about the investigation.

Ruben ordered another bottle of wine. After he poured, he held and kissed her hand. They sat quietly and gazed into each other's eyes.

"If we don't finish the wine here," he said, breaking the silence, "we'll take it with us. After going through the documents, we might want another glass."

That was not how Gwynn had anticipated the evening would end. As her expectations faded, she took another sip of wine.

****

In the motel room, Ruben spread the documents out on the coffee table.

Gwynn decided she still wanted romance. After all, they had enjoyed polishing off one-and-a-half bottles of wine at the restaurant.

She went in the bathroom to freshen up, hoping to look alluring when she emerged. Her Victoria's Secret bra and panties appeared suggestive and sensual. *Would that be enough to entice him?*

When she came out, she only wore her bra and panties. She snuggled up to Ruben on the sofa and kissed his neck.

"Did you have too much wine to drink?" he asked, trying to concentrate on the documents.

"No," she replied, moving her hand under his shirt.

"Gwynn," Ruben said, sounding irritated. "This isn't the time or place."

"When will be the time or place?" she asked with a smirk on her face, still determined to get what she wanted.

He pulled her hand out from under his shirt. "You are my client," he said in a firm tone. "I don't mess around with my clients."

"I'm not your client!" she snapped. "And you didn't have any problem undoing my blouse or bra on the sofa at my place after we went to that secluded restaurant. You only stopped because Gordon came." She suspected that night he was just trying to get closer to her so she'd obey his orders. Now she wondered how he would justify that, and she wanted him.

Ruben had never planned on that evening going any further than it did. "I had a moment of weakness. You aren't directly my client, but you are part of the agreement."

"Well, I guess I'll just have to call Mrs. VanAusdell and ask her if it's okay if we mess around," Gwynn said sarcastically.

Ruben rolled his eyes. "Do you have her number memorized?" he asked, playing along.

"No, but it's in my cell."

"If you'll recall, you left your cell in Houston."

"I'm sure I can call information and get her number," Gwynn said, hoping he'd give in.

"Go for it," he smiled.

She knew it wasn't going to be that easy, if not impossible, to get Mrs. VanAusdell's number. "I'm sure her number is in your cell phone, and I know you have it with you. Can I see it?"

He shook his head. "No."

"Don't you think I deserve a reward for helping with Karlee?" she asked, scanning his face for any sign he'd relent.

"I do," he replied immediately. "How much would you like me to pay you?"

"Money," she said, irritated, jumping off the sofa. "You want to pay me money!" She clenched her teeth. "Money!" She glared at him. "Forget it." She walked over to the counter, poured herself a glass of wine, climbed in bed, leaned against the headboard, and stared at Ruben while she drank.

Looking through the documents, Ruben occasionally glanced at her, regretfully. Yet, no matter how much he felt tempted, he had a code not to get physically involved with a client. Some investigators he knew had been destroyed over that type of involvement. He certainly found her desirable and wanted more than only to share a bed with her.

The first documents he examined contained information about the other CT victims — the three employed by CT's offshore oil pipeline division. He remembered those three had only died a week or so before Ian and wondered, *What did Ian hear or see that caused him to look for CT's casualties?*

The last document he reviewed had numerous pages stapled together. The heading read: "Software Enhancement." The document consisted of printed pages written in computer programmer jargon, a flow chart, and several pages of diagrammed equipment, labeled in plain English with a Fig. number ranging from 1 to 6 next to each piece of equipment. Those numbers coincided with handwritten numbers at various locations in the margin on the computer jargon pages. Outside of that, he had no idea about the substance. But he pretended to be engrossed in the document, waiting for Gwynn to fall asleep. Tonight, he'd sleep on the sofa since he felt vulnerable and didn't want to take a chance on being tempted by her again.

CHAPTER 16

At 5:30, they ate breakfast at the airport without saying a word to each other. Ruben had made several attempts to talk to her after they woke up. Each time, Gwynn brushed him off with brief replies. She picked up a newspaper before they boarded in order to avoid conversation. He sat down in the seat beside her on the plane. She moved to the row behind him.

After the plane took off, Ruben leaned over the back of his seat. "Gwynn, I'm sorry that I disappointed you last night. It won't always be like that."

"I am not your client," she reiterated in a cold, harsh tone, her eyes narrowing. "But that's obviously the only way you view me. At least now I know exactly where I stand."

"Gwynn," he said, reaching for her hand. "When this investigation is over, things will change."

She pushed back as far as she could in the seat with her hands tucked next to her body so he couldn't touch her. "I know they'll change. You'll be working on another investigation."

"If that's the way you want it to be," he said, sounding annoyed.

"No," she said calmly. "I'm a realist. That's the way it will be."

His eyes drooped as he turned around. He couldn't reassure her that she meant more to him than a client without letting down his guard. Ruben took his notepad out of his briefcase, summarized the meeting with Karlee, and sifted through his notes. Since he had other investigations waiting for his attention, he wanted to be able to finalize this one within the next week. He thought McIntyre's safe-

156

like file cabinet might hold valuable information. Ruben determined he'd send for Rosie soon. With her skills, he knew she could easily crack it.

Gwynn read the newspaper and took a nap on the plane. Once they landed, she planned on making notes on what she had learned so far from the investigation. She wanted to be prepared with as much information as possible if she decided to go to the police. Sleeping next to Ruben no longer held any appeal for her since she now knew it wouldn't go anywhere. Yet, she suspected it would still be dangerous to return to her apartment. She also knew she had to stay close to Ruben in order to be kept informed about the investigation.

****

Driving toward the Residence Inn, Ruben stopped and made copies of the documents they received from Karlee. When they reached the hotel, he called Gordon. Within five minutes, Gordon and Holly walked into Ruben's suite and sat down at the table by Ruben and Gwynn.

Gordon handed Ruben a large envelope. "These are copies of Fardown's notebook pages."

"Thanks," Ruben said. "Were you able to find out anything from Carl Backman?"

"I went to his house several times yesterday. I couldn't catch him at home. Can I talk to you privately for a minute?"

"Sure," Ruben replied, and went with Gordon into the bedroom.

Ten minutes later, they returned to the living room. "That was about another case," Ruben said. "Gordon has to check on something after this meeting so I'll be paying a visit to Backman. Holly, what have you found out?"

"Do you want me to start with the CT guys, the dignitaries, or the other names from the disk list?" she asked, thumbing through her notes.

Ruben snapped off the cap on a Coke bottle and took a swig. "The dignitaries."

"It appears McIntyre will be giving his farewell speech on Tuesday. Everyone on Gordon's list will be in town then. The two senators are flying in Monday evening and leaving Tuesday evening. After that, they don't have any airline tickets reserved to fly to Houston."

"That's good. Now we know McIntyre's departure date. But that isn't the reason for the trail of victims." Ruben rubbed his chin with his knuckles as he briefly stared at the wall. "What did you find out about the CT guys?"

"Last year, at the recommendation of CT's CEO, their Board voted not to give bonuses below the executive level. No one below a vice president got anything. Before that, everyone at the supervisor level or above received a bonus. They were significant. I suspect CT has a lot of unhappy employees."

"CT made skyrocketing profits," Ruben remarked. "Obviously, they didn't want to share that with their employees. On Fardown's notes about the meeting between Wilton and CT, he wrote 'disgruntled employees' next to CT."

"So that wasn't a meeting between Wilton and CT?" Gordon questioned.

"I suspected the CT employees weren't representing CT's interest," Ruben said. "Since the meeting was with the CEO of Wilton, CT would've been represented by an executive, not Jurovski, Baskar, and Delucia. The CT guys must be planning to work for Trulin. McIntyre might have been recruiting them, but why?" He gulped down the rest of his Coke and then proceeded to brief them on the meeting with Karlee Daniels. When he finished, he looked at Holly. "Did you find out specifically what the CT guys did for CT?"

"Delucia and Baskar work for the offshore oil pipeline division in Louisiana," Holly said, gazing at her notes. "Jurovski works for the onshore gas pipeline division. Jurovski is a gas transportation expert and a supervisor. He follows new developments in gas pipeline technology and maintenance. If he determines a new product or technology will enhance performance, he can authorize a purchase up to a certain amount and have it implemented. He also visits the various gas pipeline control stations if they're implementing something new. That's all I was able to find out about his position at CT.

"Baskar is an engineer and also has a degree in computer science. His title is Oil Transportation Specialist. He's a supervisor. Outside that, I wasn't able to find out specifically what he does. Delucia is an engineer. I'm still working on trying to locate additional information about him. I did find something interesting about all three," Holly said with a smirk on her face.

Ruben raised his eyebrows. "What?"

"A few months ago corporate papers were filed for a company named Starling Pipeline. Those guys are listed as the principals along with Ethan Lemus."

Ruben stood up and paced around the room. "Interesting. Did Starling list any assets?"

"No."

"Since Ethan Lemus is involved with both Trulin and Starling, maybe Starling Pipeline will become a subsidiary of Trulin. Holly, see if Starling has acquired any pipelines or if they're trying to buy any." Ruben sank into his chair, rested his elbows on the table, and tented his fingers. "What did you find out about the other names from the disk?"

Holly shuffled through her folder and pulled out a page. "Centar is the name of a company that develops software for the oil and gas industry. At least, that's what their incorporation papers say, but the company doesn't have any employees. I researched all the officers listed and all but one is in a nursing home. Bogus company. The one that isn't in a nursing home is Fred Sander — another name from the disk. He worked for Wilton until six weeks ago. Centar does have a checking account and there have been checks deposited from CT and Wilton. I managed to get into both CT's and Wilton's computer systems and looked up the invoices. CT's invoice said it was for pipeline enhancements. On Wilton's invoice it just showed computer services and an hourly rate."

"Where is Centar located?" Ruben asked.

"The address on the incorporation papers is an empty lot. The checks went to a post office box. That box was closed last week along with the checking account. I haven't been able to locate an address for Fred Sander."

"Good work," Ruben said. "That ties into this." He handed Holly a copy of the document in computer jargon received from Karlee. "See if you can decipher it before you check on Starling."

Holly breezed through the pages. "Is this what you got from Ian Daniels' wife?"

Ruben nodded. "Yes."

"I wonder why she didn't give it to me when I was there," Holly said.

"Because she wanted to talk to my wife, Ellen," Ruben said, smiling at Gwynn.

Gwynn forced an awkward smile, not wanting Gordon and Holly to suspect anything was wrong. Ever since the exchange of information began, she had sat quietly listening, absorbing everything said.

Ruben continued, "Karlee Daniels told us her life story, every detail, before she handed over the document. If it wasn't for Gwynn's patience, I don't think we could have gotten it. Look it over and let me know if I need to solicit the help of an engineer to decipher it." After Holly nodded, Ruben turned toward Gordon. "Was Dean able to visit Carlos yesterday?"

"No, Dr. Kozlov didn't want him to have any visitors until today. Dean's planning to go there after he gets back from Galveston."

"So that's where he's visiting Bev."

"Yep," Gordon said. "Bev's there trying to patch up things between her cousin and the cousin's boyfriend."

"But I'm here," Holly piped in.

"And they don't want you there," Gordon remarked.

"Tell Dean I'm going to go and see Carlos," Ruben said. "If Carlos is up to it, I want him to look over that document, also. How long do you think it'll take you to handle the other matter we discussed?"

"I should be back this evening."

Ruben checked his watch: 12:15 p.m. "I want to see Carlos and try to talk to Backman today. Let's finish this briefing after Gordon gets back."

"Sounds good," Gordon said, heading toward the door.

"Since your arm is in a sling, do you want me to go with you to Backman?" Holly asked.

"No," Ruben replied. "I want you to work on the computer jargon document." His eyes moved to Gwynn. "Are you ready to go?"

She nodded.

"We'll get lunch on the way to Dimitri's."

****

When they had driven a couple of miles, Ruben noticed a plain white paneled truck behind them and recalled seeing a truck like it leaving the Residence Inn parking lot. He thought it could be a coincidence since they were still on the major road that ran by the Residence Inn, but he didn't want to take any chances. He stopped at the next restaurant. If the truck was following them, he'd know when they got back in the car.

After they were seated, Ruben asked, "How long are you planning to give me the silent treatment?"

"I don't think it's a requirement for your clients to talk to you all the time," Gwynn replied, looking down at the menu. "Have you talked to Mrs. VanAusdell since you started your investigation?"

"Only briefly a couple of times."

"That sets the bar. We only need to talk briefly."

Ruben glared at her as the waitress took their orders.

They ate in silence.

"Do you mind driving?" Ruben asked, leaving the restaurant.

"No," she replied, taking the car keys from him. "Does your arm hurt?"

"No. I took a couple of pills before we left."

She had the urge to say "good," but kept her mouth shut.

While Gwynn turned the key in the ignition, Ruben saw the white paneled truck parked across the street. "Zigzag up and down a few streets on the way to the freeway."

"Do you think we're being followed?"

"It's just precautionary."

Gwynn assumed it was more than that since Ruben didn't zigzag when they drove anywhere. Each time she looked at the rear view and side mirrors, she spotted a white paneled truck a few car lengths behind them. She decided to move into action in case that truck was tailing them. Gwynn gunned the engine and made three sharp right turns, a left turn, drove down an alley, backtracked away from the freeway, and maneuvered through heavy traffic. She hadn't seen the white truck for a while, but continued weaving in and out of traffic, executed several turns, and entered the freeway.

Ruben had not said a word during the driving experience. "Where did you learn to drive like that?" he asked as they glided along the freeway.

"Growing up, I lived in Los Angeles. My first job was a forty-five minute drive from my house. I never allowed that much time, so I needed to improvise."

"By speeding and driving recklessly?"

"I never drove recklessly," Gwynn clarified.

"How long did it take you to get to work?"

"Eighteen minutes," she answered, grinning from ear to ear.

"I'm impressed. Sometimes I need drivers. Let me know if you want to make a career change."

"I will," she said, feeling pleased with herself. "Why didn't you tell me that a white paneled truck was following us?"

"I thought it might upset you; obviously, I was wrong. Next time, I'll let you know. We're going to change hotels again. The first time I saw the truck, it was driving out of the Residence Inn parking lot."

"How did they know where we were?"

"That's the same question I've been asking myself. I need to call Holly." He took his cell phone out of his pocket. "I'll put the speaker on." He pushed a few buttons.

"They know we're staying there," Ruben said after Holly answered.

"How?" Holly replied.

"I don't know. Get all our stuff out of there. Check in someplace where we can exit easily without relying on an elevator. Use a different hotel chain. There aren't that many Residence Inns in Houston, maybe they just drove around looking for our cars. Or maybe they tapped into the Residence Inn computer system and looked for someone reserving several rooms. Book each room separately."

"Will do. Any particular name you'd like to use?"

"Any name that's on one of the driver's licenses."

"If this keeps up, Gordon's going to have to get some more made."

"I hope that won't be necessary. I'll call on our way back." Ruben put away his cell phone.

Gwynn wanted to ask Ruben about his phony IDs, but decided against it. She still felt annoyed about the way he treated her the night before and figured she had already talked too much to him.

She took exit 32, turned left, and followed the road. "I know I make another left turn somewhere."

"At the second light," Ruben said.

After she made that turn, the curvy road looked familiar with the trees lining the pavement on each side. It was dark and uninviting the last time she drove on this road. Now she enjoyed the scenery and saw glimpses of houses tucked behind the trees. She heard a helicopter and glanced through all the windows as the sound kept getting louder. "That helicopter sounds close, but I can't see it through the trees."

"Several of the homes around here have a place for a helicopter to land," Ruben said. "Go right at the next mailbox."

She turned and followed the asphalt to the gate.

A security guard walked out of the small building. He wasn't the guy who was on duty the night Gwynn drove Ruben here. "May I help you?" he asked.

Ruben leaned toward the driver's window, touching Gwynn's arm. "Anton," he said.

"Hello, Ruben," the guard said.

Gwynn wondered how many times Ruben had been there.

"I'm here to see Carlos," Ruben said.

"Let me check to make sure he can receive guests." The guard went into the security building.

Ruben leaned back into his seat and pulled out his cell phone. "Remember, he'll want your cell," he said, turning off his.

The guard returned, carrying a metal basket. He collected their weapons and cell phones and carried them into the guard house. The gate opened.

Gwynn drove down the long driveway, seeing the magnificent Victorian in front of them. As she got closer, she saw part of a helicopter behind the house.

"Why didn't you tell me the helicopter was going here?" she asked, parking the car.

"Some of the other houses do have helicopters landing occasionally," Ruben clarified. "Dimitri doesn't want attention brought to his facility. Having a helicopter land here isn't a novelty for this area."

Matt, dressed in blue scrubs, stood on the porch waiting for them. He smiled as they headed up the stairs toward the entrance. "Ruben, how are you feeling?" Matt asked, escorting them into the house.

"Better, Matt."

"Gwynn, how are you today?" Matt asked in a formal tone.

"Fine. I'm still impressed by how well the cream worked that you put on my face."

"I'm glad you were pleased," he said as the elevator door opened. "I'll leave you here. We're expecting another guest. Carlos is in room two."

"Thank you, Matt," Ruben said, taking Gwynn's arm and leading her into the elevator.

When they stepped into room two, Carlos, a thirty-six-year-old, small-framed man with a dark complexion and dressed in a hospital gown, was leaning against a pillow watching television. A large bandage covered his forehead, but his black wavy hair draped over most of it. Only a few bruises were visible on his face. A blanket covered his body up to his arms. One of his hands and an arm were bandaged. He had a splint on the index finger of his other hand.

"Hello, Ruben," he said with a big smile.

"How are you doing?" Ruben asked.

"A lot better today. All I've done since I got here is sleep. Finally, I'm getting a chance to catch up on my favorite television shows," he said, jokingly.

Ruben introduced Carlos to Gwynn, and then he asked, "Do you feel like talking about what happened?"

"Yeah."

"I'm not sure how long Dimitri will allow us to stay," Ruben said, holding up a copy of the computer jargon document. "After we leave, if you're up to it, can you look this over?" Ruben gave it to Carlos.

Carlos glanced at the first page. "Is this part of the investigation?"

"Yes, we got it from a victim's wife. The way her husband protected it, she believed it was valuable. Her husband worked at a gas pipeline control station."

"The way they keep me doped up," Carlos said, "I'll probably fall asleep right after you leave. Do you need to know about it right away?"

"I'd like to know soon. If that's not possible, don't worry about it. Holly's also looking at it. Since a few pages contain diagrams of equipment, maybe it will take an engineer to decipher it."

"I'll see what I can do. I'll have Matt let you know if I'm making progress, but I won't say anything explicit."

"Since you've been here, Gordon gets a message from Matt every day. Now tell me what happened on Thursday evening."

"On the monitor, I saw a man entering your suite. He was around six-foot-four with a slender build. He didn't look all that tough, but I knew he was more than I could handle. I got Travis, and we went to your room."

"You did what?" Ruben snapped, clenching his jaw.

"I know … I know … but I wasn't planning on fighting the guy," Carlos explained. "I was just going with Travis."

"Let's go over this one more time," Ruben said each word slowly, controlling his anger. "What are you supposed to do if you see an intruder on the monitor?"

Gwynn couldn't understand Ruben's hostile tone since he already knew Carlos had gone with Travis to his room. She felt sorry for Carlos.

Carlos' dark eyes dimmed and his eyelids drooped. "I'm supposed to call someone to check it out and stay next to the monitor."

Gwynn thought, *I'm not the only one who doesn't follow orders.* She felt uncomfortable watching Ruben chastise Carlos in front of her. Yet, she suspected she wouldn't be allowed to freely roam the halls while Ruben talked to him.

"Then why did you go?"

"I promise I won't do it again," Carlos said, fidgeting with his bandaged hand.

"You've made that promise often," Ruben said in a solemn tone. "Each time you say it won't happen again. Up to this point, you've come away with only a few bumps and scrapes. This time you weren't that lucky. When you get out of here, we're going to have to discuss your future with the organization."

"Oh, come on, Ruben," Carlos pleaded. "I've learned my lesson. I won't do it again."

"We'll talk about this later," Ruben said sharply. "Go on; what happened next?"

"When Travis opened the door, the guy held a gun, pointing it toward us," Carlos said with a shaky voice as he looked down at the covers. "Travis kicked it out of his hand and had the guy on the floor in a split second. Travis aimed his pistol on him as the guy got up. I went in the bedroom to see if anything looked disturbed. When I came out, I saw the door opening. Travis also took care of that guy. The door was still open and that's when the third guy appeared. I yelled, but it was too late. The guy came in shooting. He used a silencer."

"There were three?" Ruben asked, wrinkling his brow.

Carlos nodded. "Yeah. I thought the guy was going to shoot me, too. Instead, he told one of the guys to tie me up so he could get some information. That's when I heard the third guy's name—Luke."

"They must be tired of sending out two guys and not getting results. Cromer probably waited in the car and when they didn't return, he went to check it out." Ruben paused. "Did any of the hotel guests see you?"

"I don't think so," Carlos said, fiddling with the splint on his finger.

The door opened. In walked a woman wearing a nurse's uniform.

"Hello, Becky," Ruben said.

"Hello, Ruben. How's your arm?" Becky asked.

"It's getting better."

"Good," Becky said. "Carlos needs his rest, so you can't stay much longer."

"Can I have five minutes more?" Ruben asked.

"Yes, but that's all," Becky said, leaving and closing the door behind her.

"When he interrogated you, what did he want to know?" Ruben asked.

"It was mainly about the disk — who had it, had I heard it, had it been copied ... stuff like that. He also wanted to know who was leading the investigation, who was financing it, and where Gwynn was."

"What did you tell him?"

"Nothing, Ruben. Honest! I kept my mouth shut."

"Glad to hear that," Ruben said. "We better go before Becky comes back. I normally don't get a five-minute warning, so I don't want to abuse it."

"Ruben, I promise I won't do it again," Carlos pleaded, squirming under Ruben's steady gaze.

Ruben lightly patted Carlos' shoulder. "Get some rest. I'm sure we can work out a solution to the problem."

Carlos raised his chin and his eyes glowed. "Thanks," he sighed.

"Get well soon," Gwynn said.

Carlos gave her a warm smile, and then she left with Ruben.

Standing next to the Suburban, Gwynn handed Ruben the car keys. "Don't you think you were too rough on him?" she hissed, staring at him.

"So now you're going to tell me how to run my business," he said, his jaw tightening.

"Forget it." Gwynn tossed her hands in the air.

Watching the trees blow freely in the wind as they drove toward the freeway, Gwynn remembered Ruben's sad eyes and drawn face the night Carlos was shot. "Stop the car," she demanded.

"Why?" Ruben asked.

"Please, stop the car," she said in a calm tone.

He pulled over to the side of the road. "What is it now?" he asked with an edge to his voice.

Gwynn unhooked her seat belt, leaned toward his seat, and hugged him. "I'm sorry," she said softly. "I should have realized you were worried about him, and you didn't want it happening again."

"I expect my employees to follow orders," he said abruptly, feeling awkward about Gwynn's empathy.

Settling back in her seat, she smiled at him and buckled up her seat belt. "I understand."

Driving back on the road, Ruben flashed her a curious expression. "Does this mean you're talking to me again?"

"No," she said, her tone cool again. "Nothing between us has changed." She turned and looked out the side window.

CHAPTER 17

As Ruben exited the freeway, he said, "You're going with me to Backman's house."

"He'll recognize me from work," Gwynn said.

"Assuming he's home, you'll stay in the car and keep watch if any black Expeditions or white panel trucks park close to his house."

Gwynn didn't want to talk to him, but at the same time, she felt excited about being included. "How can I let you know?"

"I'll be wearing a hidden receiver earpiece. My cell phone is equipped with special software. All you'll need to do is talk into it." He cut to the curb and turned off the engine.

Gwynn looked out the passenger window and saw a white, two-story framed house. "Is that where Backman lives?"

"No." Ruben pointed to a red single-story brick house next to the one directly across the street. "That's Backman's. There's a dark green Honda in the driveway." He yanked his cell phone out of his breast pocket. "I'm checking with Holly to see if Backman owns a car like that. He placed the call.

"Hi, Ruben." Gwynn heard Holly say and knew Ruben had put on the speaker. "We're moved to another hotel. Ready for the info?"

"Not yet. We're out in front of Backman's house. Does he own a late model, green Honda Accord?"

"Give me just a sec."

They listened to pounding on a keyboard as they waited.

"Yes, he does," Holly said.

"I'll call later for the hotel information." He disconnected, punched various buttons on his cell phone, and handed it to Gwynn. "It's all set." Ruben pulled a small plastic container out of his glove compartment, took out a gadget, and stuck it in his ear. "I'm going to stand outside. Talk into the cell. I want to make sure it's working."

After he shut the car door, Gwynn said, "Ruben, can you hear me?"

He opened the door. "Loud and clear!" Ruben stuck his hand under the front seat and dragged out a pair of gloves and a small pistol.

"You didn't turn that in at Dr. Kozlov's."

"I did. It was among my knives." He inserted a magazine into the weapon. "If you should be in danger while I'm inside, flip off the safety." He showed her where it was.

"I don't know how to use a gun."

"Just point and shoot. Even if you miss, it might scare them off."

Gwynn's hands shook as she took the pistol from him.

"Don't worry. I won't be gone long."

She noticed a blue paneled truck parked three houses away from them. "That paneled truck," she said, pointing at it. "Do you think we need to worry about it?"

Ruben saw something written on the side and moved across the street to get a better look. A large advertisement for "Murphy's Carpet Cleaners" was plastered on it. He went back to the Suburban. "Carpet cleaners. Keep an eye on it."

Gwynn nodded. "What are you going to say to Backman to get him to talk?"

"I'll start with the truth—I'm here about an investigation. If he asks what investigation, I'll mention Marilyn Anders. If you do see any of the vehicles I mentioned, duck down so they can't see you when you warn me."

"Got it."

Gwynn watched Ruben go to Backman's front door and saw the door swing open. From her location, she couldn't see the person inside. A few seconds later, Ruben entered and the door closed. Her eyes darted around as she searched for anything out of the ordinary in the peaceful residential neighborhood.

Hearing the clanging of metal, she swung her head toward the windshield and saw the back door of the blue van opening. Two men leapt out, wearing jackets and jeans. Gwynn's eyes remained fixed on them as one took a narrow, three-foot long black plastic bag out of the vehicle. He held it firmly under his arm and ran across the street with the other man toward Backman's house.

She slid off the seat and sank down to the floor. "Ruben, two men are coming," she said in a quivering voice. "Get out of there!" In Ruben's condition, she knew he couldn't fight two guys. She raised her head and peeked out the side window. She couldn't see the guys and feared Ruben was in trouble.

Gwynn pushed the pistol under the waistband of her slacks and stepped out of the car. She sprinted across the street as she kept track of the paneled truck, thinking someone else could be inside. Reaching the corner of Backman's house, she stood flat against the brick wall, wondering which way to go.

A gunshot rang out! "Aaaah," she screamed, and then covered her mouth. Another shot echoed from inside the house. She heard footsteps pounding against the ground, heading her direction. She ducked between two bushes. Chills swept through her body as the two men ran past, only a few feet away.

Terrified that Ruben had been wounded again, she gathered her nerves and moved stealthily to Backman's back door. Holding the gun in her trembling hand, she gripped the doorknob and turned. Her heart beat frantically and she bit her lower lip as she slowly pushed the door open.

She peered into the kitchen. Quietly, she entered. She heard drawers being slammed closed. It sounded like the noise was coming from the front of the house. She cautiously moved into the hallway. Suddenly, silence descended through the house. Gwynn held her breath as she inched forward.

Someone grabbed her arm from behind. She screamed as the pistol tumbled to the floor.

"Didn't I tell you to stay in the car?" Ruben said.

Gasping for air, Gwynn said, "I thought … I thought … you were in trouble."

"Well since you're here, you can dig a slug out of a wall in Backman's bedroom. I suspect we'll have company soon. Probably the police. First, grab the dishtowel hanging in the kitchen and wipe your fingerprints off the back door and everywhere you might have touched something. Keep the towel with you so you can wipe what you touch in the bedroom."

"Where's Backman?"

"In the bedroom. Dead. I'll fill you in later." Ruben picked up the pistol. "You didn't release the safety," he said, sticking it in his belt, and then he headed down the hall. Gwynn grabbed the dishtowel and went to work wiping every place she recalled touching along with a few other places.

When Gwynn entered the bedroom, Ruben gave her a knife and pointed to the wood frame around the window. "You don't need to do it neatly." He went into the closet.

She caught a glimpse of a body lying face down on the other side of the room. She willed herself not to look at Backman as she dug the knife into the frame next to the bullet and forced it out. "What should I do with it?"

"Keep it."

The sound of a siren blared in the distance and kept getting louder.

"We need to get out of here now," Ruben said.

Gwynn spotted a book lying on the nightstand that she had read. However, there was something unusual about this one. It appeared much thicker. "I'm taking this book," she said, grasping it in her hand.

"If anyone is outside, don't look at them. Keep her eyes focused on the car."

They rushed out the front door. A few neighbors stood on their lawns, looking toward Backman's house as Ruben and Gwynn bolted to the Suburban.

Ruben started the engine and sped out of the neighborhood. "Why did you want the book?" he asked.

She spread it open on her lap. "I have this novel. This particular book is bigger."

"I've already flipped through it," Ruben said as he drove behind an apartment building.

"Why are we going here?"

Ruben climbed out of the vehicle. "To change the license plates."

Gwynn laid the book on the floor. "Let me help," she said, getting out of the car. "With your arm like that, I can probably do it faster."

He agreed and showed her where the license plates were along with a screwdriver. While she replaced them, Ruben scanned the vehicle for tracking devices. Then he called Holly for the location of the hotel and gave her the new license plate numbers. Within fifteen minutes, they were back on the road.

Gwynn spread the book out on her lap again. The book cover seemed too thick. She noticed a wide seam on the inside of the back cover. She tried to lift the edge of it from the top. It didn't budge. Then she attempted at the bottom of the seam. It rose easily.

"Find anything?" Ruben asked.

"Maybe." She slid her fingers into the cover and pulled out two pages and three photos.

Ruben glanced at what she had discovered. "Don't look at them."

He had said it too late. Gwynn's eyes were already focused on the top picture. Tears were drizzling down her face. "Julie."

Ruben eased the car out of the traffic and stopped. He wrapped his arm around her. Neither one of them spoke as she cried on his shoulder. He gently opened her hand and removed the pictures. He stared at the image of a credenza with Julie being tucked inside by Cromer. Next to it stood Fardown. He looked at the second picture while Gwynn's head remained buried in his shoulder. It also showed the credenza. One of the hinges on the cabinet doors was being screwed on or off. Julie's face was clearly visible. Three men were in the third picture—Lemus, Cromer, and the third one lying on a cement floor, his chest covered with blood. Part of that man's face could be seen. Ruben suspected the man could be Denton. He slipped the pictures under his shirt, out of Gwynn's sight.

Ruben brushed her hair away from her face, kissed her forehead, and picked up the dishtowel dangling between the seats. He dabbed her face. "You okay?" he said, tenderly.

She inhaled deeply. "I will be when those monsters are punished," she sniffled, and then swallowed hard. "I had hoped that wasn't how they took her out." She sat up straight. "Your shirt is soaking wet."

"It'll dry."

"What do you think it means—Backman having those pictures?"

"Probably blackmail. After he led me into his den, I jumped right into asking questions about Trulin. Backman didn't hesitate telling me he planned on leaving Wilton and working for Trulin. I mentioned that didn't agree with information I had acquired. He blew up and demanded proof. I showed him Fardown's note. He started ranting about how everyone had lied to him, and how he was going to get even. Then he headed into the hallway to get some documents. That was when you warned me."

"Were you ready for them?"

"Yes. Did they come from the carpet cleaners' truck?"

Gwynn nodded. She picked up the two pages that had come from the book.

"Let me see them first," Ruben said, taking the sheets from her.

He unfolded them and saw they were reports. "What do you make of these?" he asked, showing them to Gwynn.

She studied them. "The one is an engineer's report about reserves. I have no idea what the second one is."

"It looks something like one of the pages in the documents Holly and Carlos are looking at."

CHAPTER 18

After they arrived at the new hotel, Candlewood Suites, Ruben went into the bedroom to call some of his people working on other cases.

Gwynn sat on the sofa with her feet propped up on the coffee table. She closed her eyes and mulled over everything she had learned so far about the investigation. A theory popped into her head about the gas pipeline. Even though she didn't want to go to work, that was the only way to check it out.

She didn't have anything clean she could wear to the Wilton Tower. Gwynn stood up, took off her blouse and camisole, and went to the kitchen sink. She washed her clothing and hung it in the bathroom over the shower rod.

Leaving the bathroom, she ran into Ruben.

He gazed at her bra. "Why aren't you wearing your blouse?" he asked with a puzzled expression.

"I'm not dressed like this for you, if that's what you're thinking," she said in a firm tone. "I had to wash my blouse so I'd have something to wear to work."

"Right now, you're not safe at Wilton."

"I have a theory. Before I get started, can I wear one of your T-shirts?"

"I'll get you one," he said and headed into the bedroom.

Gwynn opened the fridge. "Do you want a Coke?"

He handed her a T-shirt as he looked into the fridge. "How about a glass of wine?"

"I could probably use a glass," Gwynn said, slipping the T-shirt over her head.

Ruben took out a bottle of sauvignon blanc, opened it, and poured two glasses. "What's your theory?" he asked, sitting beside her on the sofa.

"I told you that McIntyre had to get FERC involved so some of Wilton's gas could be transported on one of CT's gas pipelines. I want to check if it was a pipeline Ian monitored."

Ruben's eyebrows rose and he locked his eyes on hers. "Do you think McIntyre is after revenge?"

"It's a suspicion I have about the gas pipeline."

"According to the reports I've read, Wilton makes most of its money on oil," Ruben recalled. "How much money did Wilton lose over the gas pipeline problem?"

"Most of Wilton's revenue does come from oil. Wilton's oil wells in Wyoming also produce casinghead gas. McIntyre's an environmentalist, so he wouldn't allow anyone to get special permission from BLM to vent the gas when the gas pipeline that Wilton uses was shut down for a major repair. Since the gas quantities were significant, BLM might not have approved the venting, but he wouldn't even let anyone try. Wilton transports the casinghead gas to two plants in Wyoming."

Gwynn noticed a perplexed expression on Ruben's face. "Casinghead gas is wet gas. Liquids are removed at gas plants — propane, butanes, and other hydrocarbons. Since CT wouldn't transport the dry gas, the gas after the liquids have been removed, it caused a whole chain reaction. Wilton had to shut-in the oil wells, idle the gas plants, and find product to satisfy some of their contracts. Everyone at work talked about CT. Some employees believe that was the reason for Wilton's bleak profits. I don't know exactly how much money Wilton lost because of CT, but it was significant."

"Whatever is contained in the documents from Karlee, I doubt it's to enhance the pipeline system," Ruben said. "Maybe it is revenge. The Wilton board wouldn't be talking about replacing McIntyre if the profit picture had been better. How can you determine if it was that pipeline?"

"I have access at work to the system that contains the information."

"Let's see if Holly can access Wilton's system from here," Ruben said, putting his wine glass down on the coffee table. "You might be able to help guide her to the right location once she gets in."

****

Holly's suite was laid out like Ruben's — a living room/kitchen combo with an adjacent bedroom, except the living room area had been converted into a makeshift office. Two folding tables had been hauled in along with three computers. A desktop computer stood on each table, and a laptop sat on the kitchen table. The monitor on one computer was divided into four sections. Three suites were displayed and the fourth section showed the hallway.

Next to that computer were two headphones and a receiver with numerous buttons and switches. Holly was working on the other desktop computer.

"I want you to get into Wilton's computer system," Ruben said.

"What am I looking for?" Holly asked.

"Pipelines," Ruben said. Then he turned to Gwynn. "What would it be called?"

"Transportation contracts or transportation invoices," Gwynn said. "I'll try to help you sift through the results after you get in."

Ruben and Gwynn watched as Holly clicked and moved around on several screens. When she needed to enter a password, she used another software program to bypass it. Gwynn's hand twitched and her skin tingled with anticipation when Holly accessed the Wilton database.

A warning sign flashed in the corner of the screen and a soft beeping sound came from the speakers. "What do you want me to do?" Holly asked.

"Shut it down," Ruben replied.

Holly quickly unplugged the computer.

"What was that?" Gwynn asked, bewildered.

"Someone knew we were in Wilton's system and attempted to trace our location," Ruben replied. "But it takes time with our system. I don't want to change hotels again today."

"We probably won't be able to get back in tonight," Holly said. "Do you want me to set up more secure proxies and try again tomorrow?"

"Let me think about it," Ruben said.

"So they weren't able to trace us?" Gwynn wanted verification.

"Nope. We weren't in there long enough," Holly said. "Last time I was in Wilton's system, I didn't have any trouble."

Ruben explained to Gwynn, "Normally, we don't need to worry about being traced when we tap into a company's computer system, but Wilton has stepped up their security. Someone must be concerned about something getting out." He glanced at the computer screen. "Holly, how are you progressing on deciphering the document?"

"It's a software program that will override a monitoring system," she replied. "It will give answers of clear, good, okay without checking the component. No one will be alerted about a potential problem. Some of the valves on the equipment diagrammed will be closing when they should be opening. A cooling unit will register it is working even if it isn't. Stuff like that. I know these changes will have negative consequences, but right now I don't know the function of each piece of equipment diagrammed. I'm in the process of researching that to determine what will happen if these changes are implemented — stop functioning, blowing up, or just causing a kink in the system."

"The cooling unit is part of a compressor system," Gwynn said.

"How's it used?" Holly asked.

"If gas is coming from a low pressure pipeline and it's going to a pipeline with a higher pressure, the gas needs to be compressed before it can enter that pipeline. Depending on the pressure variance, it might require several stages of compression. After each stage, the gas is cooled. Also along the pipelines are compressors that are used to maintain the pipeline pressure. I don't know what would happen if hot gas entered the pipeline."

"Thanks," Holly said. "That information will help."

Ruben asked Holly, "Have you had any calls about Bev?"

"No. I guess everything must be going smoothly."

"Since Gordon isn't back yet, we'll finish today's briefing tomorrow morning at six."

****

Ruben's cell phone chirped as he opened the door to his suite.

Based on what she could hear, Gwynn knew he was talking to Gordon. She motioned for him to turn on the speaker, but he ignored her. Seeing the solemn expression on his face, she wondered if there was a problem. She poured herself another glass of wine and sat down on the sofa.

Ruben continued talking on his phone while he moved into the bedroom.

Even though she could still see him, she no longer could hear any of the conversation. The clock on the wall said it was 9:50 p.m. when she picked up a *TV Guide* and thumbed through it.

At 10:20, Ruben walked out of the bedroom, putting away his cell phone.

"Anything new?" she asked, turning off the television.

"No. How long do you think it'll take you to find the pipeline information at work?"

Gwynn leaned back on the sofa. "A half hour."

"Don't stay longer than an hour," Ruben said, getting his computer out of the cabinet.

"I'm feeling tired. Will it bother you if I sleep on the sofa while you work at the table?"

"Sleep on the sofa? You don't want to sleep in the bed?"

"When we got back to the motel after dinner last night, you made it quite clear that you only viewed me as your client. I don't want to sleep with you again."

"You don't need to sleep with me again," Ruben said, his voice dragging. "I can sleep on the sofa."

"No. You take the bed. I'll sleep on the sofa."

"It'll be safer if you're in the bedroom."

That wasn't what Gwynn wanted. She thought he should sleep on the bed because of his arm, but she didn't want to argue with him. "I'll get it set up for you," she said, removing the cushions.

Ruben turned around, shifting his attention to his computer.

She pulled out the sofa bed, straightened the linens and blanket on it, and then went into the bedroom.

Sleeping restlessly, Gwynn stretched out her arm, wanting to touch Ruben. She opened her eyes and realized she was sleeping alone. Then she remembered Ruben was in the other room on the sofa. She rolled over on her side, trying to find a comfortable position so she could fall back to sleep. Instead, she jerked and squirmed around in bed as she continued thinking about him.

At 1:30 a.m., she sat up and longed to be next to him, even though she didn't believe he felt the same way. She crawled quietly out of bed, opened the bedroom door slowly, and saw Ruben sound asleep on the sofa bed. She crept over to him, slid under the covers, put her arm on his bare chest and closed her eyes.

She didn't know how long she had slept when she felt him wrapping his arms around her.

CHAPTER 19

Knocking on the door suddenly woke them up.

"I forgot to set my alarm," Ruben said, getting off the sofa bed. He looked through the peephole and cracked open the door. "Just give us a minute." He hurried into the bedroom while Gwynn collapsed the sofa bed and put back the cushions.

Ruben came back in the room wearing a T-shirt and a baggy pair of cotton pants. Gwynn went into the bedroom to put on a pair of slacks as Ruben let Gordon, Holly, and Dean into the suite. A minute later, she joined them. A box of sweet rolls and styrofoam cups filled with coffee sat in the center of the table. Ruben handed her a cup of coffee, and she took a roll.

"How did it go at McIntyre's last night?" Ruben asked Dean.

"Bev has him eating out of her hand," Dean said with a smirk. "She wants to take it slow since she really enjoys his company." He paused. "I understand how McIntyre must have felt; just listening to her made me wonder if we should slow down." Dean laughed along with everyone else. "He wants her to be his secretary at Trulin. He's planning on making Simmons an assistant administrator — whatever that means. When he talked about Simmons, it was strictly business — not the slightest hint it was more. Bev's seriously thinking about working for him at Trulin, but she's concerned about dating her boss."

They laughed again.

Dean continued, "He did tell her he'd be leaving Wilton on Tuesday, and he wasn't planning on sticking around until they found his replacement. They ate lobster and drank wine on the patio with three security guards roaming around. A real romantic evening."

"Holly, besides the names we discussed earlier, there were others on the disk," Ruben said. "Did you find out anything about them?

Holly handed Ruben a sheet with names on it. "These are the committees the two senators, Brent Stenson and Albert Jenkins, serve on. Stenson is the chair of the Energy and Natural Resources committee. Jenkins is on Environment and Public Works. He's chair of the Clean Air and Nuclear Safety subcommittee."

"It makes sense that McIntyre would be their buddy," Ruben commented.

"Maxine was mentioned after OSHA," Holly said, "that's probably Maxine Alexander, the assistant secretary. Arlene Gregson is the administrator of EPA. That's everyone mentioned."

"Anything new about Starling?" Ruben asked.

Holly took a sip of her coffee. "They're in the process of acquiring two Wyoming gas pipelines. I'm still searching for the purchase details."

"Gordon," Ruben said.

"I've told you what one of our inside guys found out last night," Gordon said. "Did you get to see Backman yesterday?"

Ruben started to brief them about the visit, when Gwynn noticed the clock on the stove. "I need to get ready for work," she said, jumping to her feet. She ran into the bedroom and closed the door behind her.

****

Ruben parked in front of the Wilton Tower and checked her beeper and bug to verify they were both working properly. He took a small bandage out of his pocket and placed it over a small scratch on her forearm. "This is also a beeper," he said. "To activate it, you can either remove it or just pull up one side."

"Why do I need this?" she asked.

"Because it can't be detected." He leaned over and kissed her. "I want you to be safe. Leave your purse in the car. It'll be easier for you to leave if you're not taking anything with you. When you locate the document attach it to an email." He gave her a simple email address.

She nodded.

"The document will automatically be relayed before it's opened and it will be removed from your business mailbox." Ruben looped around the hood of the car and opened the passenger door as Gwynn took her employee ID card out of her purse. "One hour, no more," he said emphatically. "Leave whether or not you've emailed the document."

"I will," she assured him, and he hugged her.

Walking at a brisk pace toward the elevator, she noticed two security guards staring at her. The taller one, in his early forties with dark, deep set eyes and a broad face, she had seen before. The other one with brown eyes, a slender face, and a dark complexion, she wondered if he worked for Cromer.

On the twenty-seventh floor, Gwynn got off the elevator, hurried to her cubicle, and flipped on her computer. Within a few minutes, she found the information, including several maps. It was CT's main pipeline in Wyoming that McIntyre got FERC involved with so Wilton's gas could be transported on it, the one with the compression station monitored by Ian. After she emailed the documents, she opened a file on her computer and spread out work papers on her desk.

She had just reached the hallway when Cromer stepped out of the elevator. Gwynn turned and rushed down the hall to the women's restroom. She felt relieved when she saw a muscular-looking female security guard inside.

As the guard came closer, Gwynn saw a smug, hostile expression on her face. Thinking Cromer had recruited a woman, a wave of terror swept through Gwynn's body. She raised her hand to push the beeper, but the woman grabbed her wrist. Before she could press the button with her other hand, the woman lunged for her, knocking her to the floor. With the woman on top of her, Gwynn struggled and kicked. Yet, she was no match for the skilled thug with strength that surpassed most men. It didn't take long before the woman had Gwynn's arms pinned down.

"What's going on?" Betty, a co-worker, asked, walking into the restroom.

"Call 911," the uniformed woman said. "She's having a seizure!"

"Betty ... Betty," Gwynn yelled, but it was too late, Betty had gone. "Get off me!" She wiggled and squirmed, trying to free her arms. She managed to strike the woman's leg with her foot. In return, she received a painful blow to her right arm.

Still pressing Gwynn against the tile floor, the woman glared at her. "I wish we could have a more interesting fight, but you can't look injured leaving here." She swung her legs up to Gwynn's arms. "How does that feel?" she asked, digging in her knees.

Gwynn screamed and winced in pain as she continued struggling and kicking her legs.

Cromer entered and slapped a piece of duck tape over Gwynn's mouth. He took a small metal case out from the inside of his sport coat, lowered his knees to the floor beside Gwynn, and opened it, revealing a syringe. He filled it with clear liquid from a small bottle. "Get off her arm," he demanded.

The woman followed his order while she held tightly onto Gwynn's wrists.

Gwynn felt the searing pain as Cromer plunged the needle in her arm. She stared at him and saw his stern face, completely immobile. As he put away the syringe, the woman released her hold and yanked the tape off of Gwynn's mouth.

Gwynn attempted to raise her hand, but she couldn't summon the strength. "Mhhh," she mumbled and tried to open her mouth to speak; the words wouldn't come. Her breathing became labored and her body felt numb. *Was this how Julie felt?*

The restroom door opened. She heard talking. The voices folded into each other as her eyes closed.

CHAPTER 20

Gwynn awoke slowly with tape covering her mouth again, her wrists firmly tied together, and her body aching. She saw the back of a man dressed in a Wilton security guard uniform sitting a few feet from her. Glancing down, she saw she was lying on a cot and her blouse had been torn, the rose pin gone. She managed to move her forearms over her bra and found the bug was also missing. The bandage was still securely attached to her arm. With her hands and mouth bound, she couldn't pull it up.

She smelled a musty odor and wondered where they had taken her. Looking around, she saw a high ceiling with rusty metal trusses, several broken insect-infested skylights, and walls covered with masonry and metal siding. Pigeons fluttered around in the large open space; their droppings marked the walls. Old abandoned equipment stood in the center of the room, puddles of water on the cement floor. Off in the distance, she saw large double doors standing ajar with daylight shining through the opening.

The security guard turned around. He was the guard with the deep set eyes who had stared at her when she entered the Wilton Tower.

"You're finally awake," he said, rising to his feet. "Now don't go away while I get Luke." He gave her a malicious smile as he turned and strode toward the door.

She held onto the side of the cot with her bound hands, raised herself up to a sitting position, and saw the rope tightly wrapped around her ankles. Her feet were bare. She swung her legs over the edge as Cromer walked toward her.

His eyes were locked on her as he yanked the tape off of her mouth. "You're moving around too freely. Looks like I have to sit down with Todd and criticize his hostage binding technique."

She sat silently, immobile, staring at him.

"Don't tell me you're going to be difficult like your friend, Julie," he said with a stone, cold, emotionless face.

She took a few deep breaths but remained silent.

"When I questioned Taylor, he was very concerned about his girlfriend, Cindy. She's also your friend. Will you be as concerned about her as Taylor was?"

Gwynn felt her stomach churning as she continued staring at him.

Cromer picked up a chair, lowered it down next to her, and sat, looking at her intensely. He loosened his necktie, and then pulled a knife from under his sport coat. He ran the side of the blade against his fingers. He leaned forward and caressed her neck with the tip.

Gwynn forced herself not to move as he wielded the knife around her.

"You're in for a treat; a technique that was used on me in Iraq." He popped off her buttons with the tip of the blade. "I screamed, bled tears, and begged for death. Like you'll be doing if you don't answer my questions."

She flinched and pressed her lips together.

"I suppose I should be thankful for that experience. Otherwise, I wouldn't be the well-adjusted person I am today." He pushed the tip into her side.

Gwynn couldn't prevent a scream from escaping as the blood ran down her blouse.

"That's just to give you a little taste." He stood and took off his sport coat, revealing a gun in a holster strapped across his shoulder, ready for the final assault. He hung it over the back of the chair and sat down. "Now that we've had some fun, let's get down to business." he said, rolling up the sleeves on his blue shirt.

"What was on the disk you took from Julie Morgan's post office box?"

Gritting her teeth, Gwynn held her bound hands over her wound as she tried to decide how to answer.

He wrapped his fingers around her arm. "Do you want your little friend, Cindy, to join Taylor out back?"

She shook her head.

"In case you think Cindy Wood is safe because she's in Vegas, you're wrong. Are you ready to give me answers?"

She nodded, feeling the throbbing pain in her side. "The disk was blank," she said, thinking it no longer mattered. Julie's killers were in a photo.

He tightened his grip, digging his fingers deeper into her flesh. "You expect me to believe that?"

The pain surged through her arm down to her fingertips. "It's true," she said, squinting with moist eyes. "The recorder was broken on the receiver Julie used." She swallowed hard, struggling to hold back tears. "Julie died because of that meeting. If there was anything on that disk, I would have already taken it to the police."

He slowly released her arm.

She sighed, wiggled her fingers, and closed her eyes briefly as she felt the unrelenting pain in her side and arm.

He ran the tip of the blade down her chest and asked, "Who's financing the investigation?"

"What investigation?"

He inched the tip under her hands that protected her wound; forcing her to move them. He stuck the blade in again. She gasped and moaned as pain shot through her body. She bit her bottom lip in a determined effort not to scream.

"Don't play naïve. I want answers."

"I'm financing the investigation."

He stroked her bare feet with the bloody blade, leaving a few small scrapes along the way. "And how did you get that kind of money?"

"I borrowed it," she said, clenching her jaw.

"You couldn't borrow that much." He moved the tip over her slacks up to her waist.

"But I did." Her voice quivered, believing any minute he'd plunge the knife into her body again. "It didn't matter if it took the rest of my life to pay off the loan, I wanted to find Julie's murderer."

Readjusting himself in the chair, he pulled the knife away from her and wiped it on the side of the cot. "Why did you think she had been killed?"

"She was supposed to be meeting me at Brody's, and she was afraid to drive close to semis. There was no way Julie would have accidentally driven into one." She squeezed her eyes shut and grimaced from the reeling pain.

"Interesting." He brushed the tip of the blade against her arm. "We knew Julie's grandmother was a wealthy woman. If she disappeared, someone would come looking for her. That's why she didn't join Taylor and Marilyn."

"Will I be joining Taylor and Marilyn, or are you planning on staging another accident?"

"We'll have to see," he said. "When Julie knew she couldn't escape, she asked me to tell her grandmother she was sorry. Did she actually expect me to be her errand boy?"

Gwynn knew he was trying to get a rise out of her. She tightened her mouth and remained immobile, hiding the pain she felt.

He leaned back, stretched out his long legs before him, and drummed his fingers on the arms of the chair. "Who's leading the investigation?"

"I don't know his name." She bent over, holding onto her side, trying to stop the bleeding. She noticed a knife handle protruding from his boot, his pant leg draped above it.

"You don't know the name of the man you were kissing this morning?"

"He's not the one leading the investigation," she said, gazing at his face.

Cromer sat up straight and moved the blade to her side again. 'Then who is?"

"I hired the Anderson Investigation Firm," she lied calmly, giving him a made-up name. "Someone there is running the investigation. I've never seen him. He calls and talks to one of the guys every night. I've talked to him a few times, but he doesn't identify himself."

"I've heard of them," Cromer said, surprising Gwynn. "It's either Lynn Anderson or Carter Stone. What's the status of their investigation?"

"They don't tell me much. All I know is they are focusing on someone at Wilton. I hear the name Fardown a lot. So they must think Kent Fardown is behind Julie's murder." She paused. "Is Kent Fardown responsible? Did he hire you to kill Julie?"

"Yes," he replied without hesitation.

Gwynn held her breath as he circled her face with the tip of blade. She sucked in air when he lowered it to her shoulder and glided it down her arm. "Do you know what the meeting was about Julie recorded?"

"Supply and demand," he said as he caressed the seams of her blouse with the blade. "The pipelines ..."

"Luke," the security guard shouted from the door.

"What?" Cromer yelled.

"You're wanted on your cell. It's important."

"I'll be right there." He turned toward Gwynn and slipped the blade into her side again.

She screamed as the pain raked through her body.

"We'll have to finish our discussion later."

Determined to get the knife from his boot, Gwynn leaned forward and fell on top of his feet. "You never finished your answer," she said, gripping the handle. She yanked it out, slid it under her blouse, and held her arm firmly over it, securing the knife in place.

He grabbed her shoulders, raised her up, and pushed her down on the cot. "I said we'd talk later." He strode toward the door.

When he was out of sight, she eased the knife out from under her blouse. If she was going to survive, she knew she couldn't dwell on the pain. She rolled over on her side and held the knife handle between her teeth while she moved the rope binding her hands up and down against the sharp edge.

After her hands were free, she pulled the bandage off, and pressed a hand against her wound. Gwynn's eyes were fixed on the entrance while she cut the rope around her ankles, leaving it in place. Lying on her uninjured side, she held the knife handle between her hands and the blade under her arm. With her teeth, she draped the cut rope over her wrists. She stared at the door and wondered how long she'd have to wait for Ruben.

The security guard entered the building and sauntered toward her. With a malicious smirk on his face, he sat down on the chair.

"Isn't Luke coming back?" she asked.

"No. We're all alone." His eyes riveted over her body. "You're bleeding. How did that happen?" he asked, perplexed.

"Luke stabbed me," she moaned, water filling her eyes, hoping he'd show some compassion.

"He should have finished the job," he said, bluntly. "Now he's left it up to me." He scanned her face. "All the time I worked for Wilton, I wanted to get to know you better. Right before I whacked Taylor, I asked him about you. Do you know what that bastard said?" he growled.

Gwynn shook her head, thinking of ways to escape as the pain in her side escalated. Her blouse was completely saturated with blood.

"He said you'd never date a scumbag like me. I had the barrel pointed at him and the stupid bastard said that to me!" His brows drew together in an angry frown. "But it was the last thing that asshole said."

Gwynn felt a lump in her throat and moistened her dry lips with her tongue. "I didn't know you were interested in me. You never said anything," she said, attempting to keep him talking.

"I searched your purse twice, and you didn't even look at me! You just kept talking to your friends!"

"I'm sorry," she said in a soft tone. "You could've called."

"As if that would have made a difference." He tightened his jaw. "You don't even know my name."

"But I do," she assured him. "Todd."

"How do you know that?" he asked, leaning forward in the chair.

"I did notice you." She forced a smile.

"It's too late." He drew a pistol from under his blazer.

"Did you also shoot Marilyn?"

"Certainly did," he replied, sounding pleased. "This would be so much easier if you looked more like her."

She needed to stall him. "Do you have anything you can wrap around my side? My blouse is covered with blood."

He rose to his feet in one quick motion. "You won't need to worry about your blouse much longer," he said, raising his gun.

"I feel so alone," she said, wanting him closer. "Can you hold my hand when you pull the trigger?"

His eyes opened wider. "Yeah." He leaned down and reached for her hand.

She plunged the knife into his chest.

Blood poured through his shirt. "You little cunt!" he yelled, wobbling, trying to point the pistol at her.

With all her strength, she leapt up, knocking the gun out of his hand. He struck her in the face as he bent down to retrieve it. She raised her leg, flung her foot into his back, and landed on the cot. He swayed and fell, pushing the blade further into his chest. His body convulsed and then became motionless.

She staggered to her feet and saw the pool of blood surrounding his body, trickling down the cracks in the floor. Holding onto her side, she stood still and listened. No sound, no movement. Then she slowly made her way to the door, leaving a trail of blood in her path. Chills swept through her body as she stumbled through the doorway. Off in the distance, she saw another building, but knew she couldn't go that far. Wincing in pain, she imagined something had happened to Ruben. She fumbled around the corner and leaned against the wall as she moved to the back of the building, wanting to see where Taylor had been buried.

When she reached her destination, her arm still ached and throbbed, but her side felt numb. Scanning the area, she couldn't see any disturbed dirt. A large pile of freshly cut wood stood only a few feet ahead of her. Her jaw tensed and tears poured down her cheeks as she suspected Taylor and Marilyn must be buried under it. Her trembling legs could no longer support her weight. She collapsed to the ground, crawled over to the wood pile, and stretched out her hand. "Taylor, I'm here."

CHAPTER 21

Gwynn opened her eyes and found herself cradled in Ruben's arms. She felt too weak to utter a sound. His brown eyes met hers and she managed a weak smile.

"You'll be okay," he said in a gentle tone, carefully easing her down in the passenger seat. "I'm taking you to Dimitri's." He secured the seat belt around her.

"Where were...," she said, her voice barely audible.

"Shhh," he interrupted, leaning down and kissing her forehead. "We can talk later."

"Do you want me to call clean-up?" Gordon yelled.

"Yes," Ruben replied, getting into the driver's seat. "I don't want any of Gwynn's fingerprints found."

"Taylor's buried in the back," she mumbled, trying to stay awake.

"We know," Ruben said, stroking her face. "That was the first thing you said when we found you."

"Cindy ... they're watching Cindy," she anxiously murmured.

"I know. I have someone watching her, too," he said, driving away from the building.

Gwynn tried to touch her side and discovered her body had been completely wrapped.

"Am I still bleeding?" she asked.

"No," Ruben replied. "Close your eyes and try to sleep. It will take us a couple of hours to get to Dimitri's."

"Why?"

"We're not in Houston."

She wanted to know where they were, but couldn't muster the strength to ask. Slowly, she closed her eyes and heard Ruben talking. She no longer could understand what he said; the words became intertwined.

******

Ruben lightly squeezed Gwynn's hand as she opened her eyes. "Good morning," he said, kissing her cheek.

She smiled, glanced around the room and knew she was at Dr. Kozlov's when she saw medical equipment secured to the white walls and a white nightstand next to the bed. A television hung on the wall in front of her, tuned to a news program. She ran her fingers over the wrapping around her tortured upper arm and the bandage on her stabbed side. Raising her hand, she touched her face and felt no pain.

"Your face isn't bruised," Ruben said. "Dimitri took care of that. Your arm is swollen; it will be back to normal in a couple of days. The stitches in your side will dissolve and there shouldn't be any scarring, but if there is, Dimitri will take care of it. The cuts on your feet should heal quickly. The blood you lost has been replaced. I'm glad we found you in time." His eyes glowed as his lips eased into a smile.

"Did you have trouble finding me?" she asked, remembering it took her a long time to drag herself to the wood pile and Ruben still hadn't arrived.

"We were already headed in your direction when we received the signal," he replied. "It took us awhile to get there. The last time I heard your voice I could tell you had been sedated. We knew you were in the restroom from what was being said around you. It was being heavily guarded. I couldn't get anyone in there before the paramedics came out with a patient on a gurney, wearing your bug and beeper. In the ambulance, they talked as if they were transporting you. Gordon and I listened through the microphone as we followed it.

"Dean went after a semi that left from the receiving dock at the same time. It was going in the opposite direction. He secured a tracking device to it and returned to the Wilton Tower in case you were still there. In the interim we kept track of departures from the receiving dock. Holly tracked the semi on her computer.

"Forty minutes later, the ambulance stopped in front of a farmhouse. That was when we discovered you weren't the patient. The woman, wearing a security guard uniform, was the decoy."

"What happened then?"

"It wasn't pleasant," he said with a solemn voice. "But I needed to know where you were. All she told us was that you had been taken elsewhere. That might've been all she knew. The two men disguised as paramedics didn't even know that much."

Gwynn felt uneasy. "Are they okay?" she asked timidly.

"We let the two guys go. They had just been hired to pick up and drive a patient. They had no idea what they were getting themselves into. The male voice we heard from your bug came from a cell phone."

"She was alone without anyone there to help her?"

"She had served her purpose and was judged dispensable," Ruben said.

Gwynn lay quietly and thought how cruel to send out a decoy without anyone to protect her.

"The woman isn't dead, but she won't be returning to that type of work until this investigation is over."

She broke into a wide, open smile and wanted to hug him. "Good," Gwynn said, relieved.

Ruben lifted up her hand and kissed it.

"What day is it?" she asked, wondering how long she had been there.

"Tuesday. Do you feel like talking about what happened?"

Gwynn recalled those were the exact words Ruben used when they went to see Carlos. "Yes," she replied and proceeded to tell him everything that she could remember from her abduction to stabbing the security guard, Todd.

"I'm impressed that you did so well, given your lack of training."

"Was it okay that I told Cromer there wasn't anything on the disk?" she asked hesitantly.

"Yes," he replied, "because it wasn't blank. It's been helpful."

"Yesterday in the car you said that you had someone watching Cindy."

Ruben nodded.

"How long has that person been watching her?"

"Since the day after I was shot. I thought they might try to get to you through her. Paul, my employee, knows someone else is also keeping track of her. Their guy isn't very clever. Paul is a master of disguises. He sat next to Cindy several times during Borge's performances. Once when he was disguised as an old man, she even flagged down a server for him."

Gwynn smiled. "Why didn't you tell me?"

"I didn't want you to worry about her."

"So if Cromer hadn't said anything about Cindy, you wouldn't have told me?"

"You believed she was safe in Vegas, and I didn't want you to believe anything different."

She mulled it over and decided he was right. "How long will I be here?"

"Dimitri said you can leave if you're feeling up to it, or you can stay another night. What would you like to do?"

"I'm feeling pretty good," she said. "When I emailed the information about the gas pipeline, I remembered something about an offshore oil pipeline."

Ruben's brow wrinkled as he leaned forward, stroking Gwynn's arm, and asked, "What?"

With a mischievous smile, she squeezed his hand. "We're going to have to negotiate."

"You're in no condition to get what you wanted in Wyoming," he said and winked.

She scanned his face. "Are you sure?" she asked with bouncing eyebrows.

"I'm sure," he reaffirmed. "What do you want?"

"I don't want to go to the cabin, and I'm afraid that's where you'll take me when we leave here. I want to help solve the case."

He hesitated, assessing her for a moment. "Will you follow my orders?" She nodded, and he said, "You can stay with me as long as you do as I say. If you disobey one order, you have to agree to go to the cabin without any fuss. Understood?"

"Agreed."

"Okay. What did you remember?"

"McIntyre started the problem with CT," she began. "It was his fault that CT didn't want to transport Wilton's gas." She rested her elbow on her pillow, cupped her chin in her hand, and adjusted herself in the bed. "A year or so ago, McIntyre gave a speech somewhere — I can't remember exactly where — about keeping pipelines maintained to make sure they were safe and wouldn't cause any environmental disasters." She paused. "McIntyre and the board have been at odds for years over spending money to add expensive refinements that would ensure Wilton would never be responsible for any ecological problems. I liked all of McIntyre's positions about that. Now I'm having a hard time separating his goals from what happened to Julie."

"What did the speech have to do with CT?"

She took a deep breath and proceeded. "In it he mentioned that most pipelines weren't being properly maintained. Then he gave an example of one of CT's offshore pipelines. CT was the only company he named. He implied other companies, but didn't name them.

"Some board members were angry because Wilton had a small interest in that pipeline. I guess McIntyre's always had a love-hate relationship with the board. He's never had any trouble getting anything Wilton wanted from regulators, but at the same time the board wants to maximize profits. I can't remember the name of CT's offshore pipeline McIntyre mentioned. If he's trying to destroy an offshore pipeline, it makes sense it would be that one. Do you know the name of the offshore pipeline connected with the Louisiana victims?"

"I've got it in my notes," Ruben said, standing up and pacing the room. "How can you find the name of the pipeline in McIntyre's speech?"

"All of his speeches are on Wilton's website."

"We need to look that up today," Ruben said. "Since McIntyre's leaving Wilton, they could be removed from the website soon."

"I noticed a library next to Exit 32. We can go there on the way back."

A thoughtful smile curved his mouth. "I didn't say we needed to look it up immediately. We can wait until we get back to the hotel." He slowly stroked her cheek. "Are you ready to go?"

"Yeah," she said, nodding.

****

Leaving Dr. Kozlov's facility, Gwynn wore hospital scrubs and carried a bag filled with bandages and pills. Now she knew everyone's name who worked there, including the security guards stationed at the gate.

"How's Carlos doing?" she asked as Ruben drove toward the freeway.

"He's getting better. He was able to analyze the document from Karlee. He says it's changing two systems — one is the operating system and the other is the monitoring system. He went into all the technical specifics, but in summary, the operating system won't operate appropriately and the monitoring system won't recognize anything malfunctioning."

"That's what Holly told you. So what did he think would happen?"

"He's not sure. He thinks the compressors might blow up, or at least be destroyed beyond repair along with possibly a section of the pipeline."

"Are you going to get an engineer to look at it?"

"No. Even if Carlos and Holly weren't positive what would happen, they've given me enough information."

"We need to warn CT," Gwynn said in an anxious tone.

"Just because we have a computer software document doesn't mean it was installed. That's all we have, and it was given to us by the wife of a deceased CT employee." He paused. "How do you think Karlee will handle being questioned?"

"We can't give anyone Karlee's name," Gwynn said emphatically. "She'd go to pieces."

"Exactly."

"You think there's a chance the software wasn't installed?"

"I suspect it was, but we don't have any proof."

With painful realization, Gwynn knew Ruben was right. They couldn't warn CT. Then she thought if a compression station was destroyed it might not result in the loss of any more lives. Gwynn gazed out the window at the landscape as it flashed by and recalled that Cromer mentioned pipelines when he told her about the meeting.

Ruben reached over and touched her hand. "Gwynn, my assignment is to determine who is responsible for Julie Morgan's death and why she was killed. Nothing more."

"I know. Do you know when McIntyre will give his departure speech?"

"Sometime this afternoon."

Gwynn pulled her cell phone out of her purse and saw eight messages from Cindy. "Have you called the police and told them where Taylor's buried?"

"The police will be given that information anonymously after my investigation is closed."

"I'm calling Cindy, but I'm not going to say anything about Taylor." She pushed in the number.

Cindy told her she had tried to reach her at work and talked to Stan, Gwynn's boss. He told her that Gwynn had some kind of a seizure and was taken to the hospital. Gwynn explained that the security guard overreacted when she tripped in the restroom and how embarrassing it was to have paramedics take her out of the building on a gurney. Nothing was wrong with her, but she didn't feel like going back to work, so she called Ruben. They went to Galveston for a night.

Ruben smiled at her.

After Gwynn hung up, she called her boss and told him she didn't feel well so she wouldn't be in the rest of the week. He was sympathetic, believing the seizure story.

****

Ruben put a protective arm around Gwynn as they walked into the Candlewood Suites. Gordon and Holly were seated on the sofa in Ruben's suite when he opened the door.

"What's going on?" Ruben asked, gently helping Gwynn sit down.

Gwynn smiled to herself when she noticed Holly's forest green floppy fedora and her T-shirt that read: "Warning: I'm a Bitch so don't mess with me."

"McIntyre just finished his speech," Gordon said. "It was televised to all Wilton employees. Holly streamed it through your television."

"I also recorded it," Holly said. "Do you want to see it?"

"Yes," Ruben said, walking to the fridge. "Let me get a piece of pizza first."

"It's in the oven," Gordon said. "We kept it warm for you."

"Can I get you some?" Holly asked Gwynn.

"No, thanks. I ate at Dr. Kozlov's."

Holly got everyone a drink while Ruben dished up some pizza. As soon as he sat down on the arm of Gwynn's chair, she started the recording.

McIntyre stood at a podium in a large room with rows of seats in front of him.

"That room is in the Wilton Tower," Gwynn said. "I recognize some of the people sitting next to the podium: Senator Brent Stenson, Senator Albert Jenkins, OSHA Assistant Secretary Maxine Alexander, Arlene Gregson from EPA, and Jack Wilson, a railroad commissioner."

McIntyre spoke: "As an oil man who gradually climbed the corporate ladder, I learned just how vital fossil fuels are to our nation. Not just as an energy source have they augmented our lives by forming a practical and robust cornerstone of our infrastructure; they have also played an inseparable role in the economic and social foundation of modern-day America. The world we live in today has been formed the way it is, for the better, through the brilliant advances possible only through harnessing the power of petroleum.

"As a proud environmentalist, I understand that nature is utterly essential for American society and humanity as a whole not just to function, but to even exist. This is something other individuals in leadership oppositions of the oil and gas industry take for granted.

"I have been called a hypocrite from the environmental left— those unwilling to make actual progress through compromise—and an obstructive nuisance from within the industry. I have seen unfettered greed in the pursuit of wealth, and headstrong, steadfast attachment to compelling but misguided naïve idealism. I have made enemies all across the political and industrial spectrum, but withstood their attacks and found great success without resorting to irredeemable sacrifice.

"Without oil, society cannot function, and would collapse into stagnant depression. Without concern for the environment, society would wither and die in the rancid wasteland of pollution and death we would make for ourselves through overzealous impetuousness. This is a sacred, fundamentally symbiotic relationship I have spent my career protecting and making others aware of the importance of preserving both.

"Now, I have been given an unprecedented opportunity to put my philosophical agenda into action by becoming the Chief Executive Officer of Trulin Oil. This great corporation will be molded into an industry paragon of sensible, progressive, practical, and efficient practices. This will be advancement for myself, Trulin, and the oil and gas industry as a whole. We will be breaking entirely new ground on America's corporate landscape.

"At Wilton I was met with obstruction and argumentation at every step as the board fought tooth and nail to block environmental mandates of mine that they found too radical. These difficulties ranged from cautious appeal to tradition to full-blown idiocy, but never once did they serve as anything but harmful obstacles to progress. With the support of Trulin's officers, I am free to push progress forward with determination.

"As I take this step forward, I will be joined by others with great wisdom and integrity. Kent Fardown and Steve Hadley, two great men who have taken my philosophy to heart, enhanced it with constructive criticism, and helped me with their decades of combined experience to form a business plan that will make Trulin into a sensible and progressive juggernaut of the American industrial world. Steve Hadley will serve at the helm of Trulin's public relations. He will keep the American people informed of Trulin's growth and innovations as we move forward in molding a company that will bridge the gap between the oil industry and the environment we cherish.

"Trulin will explore and harness more needed energy for the American people to ensure a bright future for generations to come. We will create jobs, promote research, and invest in communities throughout this great land. The Earth's delegate eco-systems matter and Trulin will always put them first in all decisions.

"I wish to thank all of you at Wilton who share my philosophy and worked diligently to implement it against the obstacles that we strived to overcome. I am proud to have worked with so many dedicated men and women." The audience clapped as McIntyre took a seat.

Each of the dignitaries said a few words. All of them praised McIntyre and knew Trulin would be the company that set the standard. Each one mentioned something specific McIntyre had accomplished.

When it was all over, Ruben stood up. "I think I'll apply for a job at Trulin," he said.

"Did you hear any news this morning?" Gordon asked Ruben.

"I watched part of the news," he replied. "Did something happen?"

"A refinery in Texas City was shut down for OSHA and EPA violations."

"Interesting," Ruben said. "The same day McIntyre becomes CEO of Trulin and in charge of the Lark Refinery. So much for eliminating some of the competition."

"Don't tell me you think the nice honorable John McIntyre played a role in that?" Holly said, cocking her brow.

Gordon leaned back on the sofa and said, "I'm picking up Rosie at the airport at seven."

"Take her out to dinner before you bring her here or you will never hear the end of it," Ruben said with an amused expression.

"That was already part of the plan," Gordon said.

"Don't worry," Holly said. "I'm going grocery shopping to make sure her fridge is stuffed with everything she likes."

Gwynn wondered why they were all catering to Rosie and looked forward to meeting her.

Ruben took his computer out of the cabinet and put it on the table. "Gwynn, I want you to lie down after you look up McIntyre's speech." He held onto her arm while she shuffled over to the table.

"But you just saw his speech," Holly said.

"This is another speech," Ruben clarified and proceeded to tell Gordon and Holly about Gwynn's oil pipeline theory.

It didn't take Gwynn long to locate the speech. Skimming through the document, she found the name of CT's pipeline McIntyre mentioned. "I want to print off his speech; do you have a printer I can use?"

"Let me get one," Holly said, leaving.

Ruben was looking through his notes, "What's the name of the pipeline?"

"It's the First Outland," Gwynn replied.

"That's the one," Ruben said. "The oil pipeline victims worked at its monitoring station. Do you know if any of Wilton's offshore platforms transport oil on that pipeline?"

"Wilton transports oil on it," Gwynn confirmed. "Are you thinking about the platform associated with the two victims?"

"Exactly."

Holly returned, plugged in the printer, and put in several sheets of paper. "It's wireless, so just send your print job."

The computer screen went black. Gwynn assumed the screen saver had come on and shook the mouse to get the speech to reappear. "Something's wrong," she said, staring at the blank screen.

Holly sat down beside her, took over by refreshing the internet browser, and then went to Wilton's site. The webpage read: "404 the page was not found."

"That was quick," Holly said. "I guess Wilton didn't like McIntyre's speech and immediately shut down their site. It'll probably be up and running later today without any of McIntyre's speeches."

"You don't think they shut it down to add his current speech?" Gordon suggested with a solemn expression.

Knowing he was joking, Holly smiled at Gordon and said, "No, I don't think that's the reason."

A recollection flashed into Gwynn's mind. "Wait — I just remembered," she said, rubbing her forehead. "The pipeline speech will be out on the 'Preserve the Green' website."

Within three minutes, Holly found the speech and printed it.

"Nap time," Ruben said, escorting Gwynn into the bedroom.

"I'm sure you didn't sleep very much last night," Gwynn said. "Why don't you join me?"

He handed her some pills along with a bottle of water. "I will in a few minutes."

CHAPTER 22

As they were getting out of bed from their afternoon slumber, Ruben said, "When Rosie gets here you can't talk about the investigation. She is only coming to open McIntyre's file cabinet, nothing more. I don't allow my people to share information between teams about ongoing investigations." He reached out and took her hand. "Can I count on you?"

"Yes, I won't tell her anything."

A rap on the door echoed through the suite. Ruben dressed quickly and went to see who was knocking.

Stepping out of the bedroom, Gwynn smelled the aroma of Chinese food: pot stickers, egg rolls, sweet and sour pork, and various beef dishes.

Ruben sat at the table with Holly and Dean. Open take-out containers stood in front of them. He pulled out a chair for her. "Dean had just started telling us what Bev found," Ruben said. "She sat at Simmons's desk after McIntyre's speech while Simmons went over to Trulin's office." Ruben nodded toward Dean as he lifted up an egg roll. "Go on."

"Simmons maintains a transcript file of McIntyre's meetings. In it was a transcript for the July fourteenth meeting between McIntyre and some CT employees. The names of the attendees were listed — McIntyre, Fardown, and the three CT employees, but not Cromer. To sum it up, the transcript stated that the three CT employees were starting a pipeline company, and they wanted McIntyre's input regarding potential environmental issues since they had heard a speech he had given regarding maintaining pipelines."

"We know the speech," Ruben said, dishing up sweet and sour pork. Then he told Dean Gwynn's theory and what they had discovered about the oil pipeline. "It appears McIntyre is covering all his bases."

"Bev thinks Simmons is pretty savvy," Dean said, "but can't understand how she can believe everything McIntyre tells her. He told her he only flirted with Bev at the party so Fardown wouldn't be suspicious about their relationship. Simmons said she hoped Bev understood, and now McIntyre has Simmons trying to convince Bev to work for Trulin."

"He must be smooth," Holly said, getting several beers out of the fridge and putting them on the table. She opened one as she sat down. "Trulin bought an oil tanker. I haven't been able to locate how much they paid or if it was financed."

"That purchase makes sense," Ruben said, "if what they've planned for the oil pipeline prevents it from being able to transport oil for a while. Holly, check on the three CT guys and verify they're still working for CT."

She nodded and ate the fried rice on her plate.

"Did Elliott find out anything else about the oil pipeline victims?" Gwynn asked between bites.

Ruben gave her a puzzled look. "That's right. You left to get ready for work before Gordon filled us in." He took a swig of beer. "Marie Kessler, the wife of a drowning victim who worked for CT's pipeline, recently died in a car crash."

"Who did he work for at CT?" Gwynn asked.

"Michael Baskar," Holly said.

Ruben continued, "Elliot talked to Sana Garcia, Marie Kessler's best friend. She doesn't believe Marie's car crash was an accident. Garcia told Elliott that Josh, the CT victim, was concerned about a computer program upgrade and a chemical coating applied to a section of the pipeline. He had been told the coating would help preserve the pipeline, but that explanation didn't sit right with him since it was applied at night. Josh only knew about it because he was on the graveyard shift. When he mentioned it to his co-workers, his boss said all they did was inspect part of the pipeline. They'd never have any work done on it at night. Josh tried to talk to his boss,

Baskar, about the computer software upgrade. He wouldn't listen. Josh copied some documents and planned to fly to Houston so he could talk to his boss's boss. He died before he got a chance. Marie told Sana she thought that was why Josh had been killed."

"People do have drowning accidents," Gwynn said. "What made her think it wasn't an accident?"

"Josh Kessler swam on a swimming team in college and he didn't like fishing," Ruben said. "He was alone on a fishing boat when he fell overboard and drowned. Marie had the copies Josh had made in her purse when the car accident happened. After that, Marie's purse went missing."

"That was probably software CT had purchased from Centar," Gwynn said.

Ruben nodded. "But we hadn't heard about a chemical coating before."

"Do you think Sana will be okay?" Gwynn asked.

"They won't harm her," Ruben said. "She suspects something is wrong, but she doesn't have any proof."

They heard a loud knock on the door. "That must be Gordon and Rosie," Holly said, jumping to her feet. She looked through the peephole and opened the door.

"Hello, Rosie," Holly said, giving the five-foot-three, heavyset woman with short red spiked hair a hug.

Gordon closed the door and flopped down on the sofa without saying a word.

Rosie went over to the table and gave both Ruben and Dean a big bear hug. Then she turned toward Gwynn. "Aren't you a pretty little thing," she said with a smile.

Gwynn blushed as a faint smile creased her lips.

After Ruben introduced Rosie and Gwynn, he asked Rosie about another case, "How did it go?"

"That was the hardest goddamn safe I've ever opened," Rosie said, falling into the cushioned chair.

"Ralph told me it only took you six minutes to crack it," Ruben said.

Rosie stared at him. "That doesn't mean it wasn't goddamn hard! Then there wasn't a fuckin' thing in it! That asshole had emptied it."

"Did you find what you were looking for?" Dean asked.

"Yeah," Rosie replied. "In the bastard's house. It only took us five minutes to find that safe. It was behind the fuckin' asshole's picture. But Ralph made me climb a fuckin' fence to get to the bastard's house."

"Rosie," Ruben said, calmly. "Ralph said the fence was only two feet tall."

"It was still fuckin' hard," she said.

Ruben looked at Gwynn and rolled his eyes.

Gwynn noticed the amused expression on everyone's faces, but no one laughed. She couldn't help but smile to herself.

Rosie glanced at Gordon. "If there's a fence between me and your safe, then you're going to have to carry me on your fuckin' back and make goddamn sure you don't drop me."

"Relax," Gordon said. "There isn't a fence." His eyes lit up. "But you will have to climb through a second story window."

Everyone laughed, except Rosie.

"Gordon," Rosie said, glaring at him. "That wasn't fuckin' funny!"

Ruben sat down on the sofa and asked Gordon and Rosie, "What did you two decide — are you going to break into the safe-like file cabinet tonight or tomorrow?"

"Tonight," Gordon said.

"Yeah," Rosie said. "My goddamn new fridge isn't working. I need to be there when the bastard replaces it and he fuckin' fills it. He said he would, but I need to make sure he isn't a goddamn liar."

"Dean's going with you," Ruben told Gordon. "He'll bring Rosie back here while you look through the cabinet contents."

"Good," Rosie said with a wide smile stretched across her face. "Then he can help Gordon lift me to that fuckin' second story." She chuckled, and then she held onto both arms of the chair and raised herself up to a standing position. "I want to freshen up a little so I can look as pretty as Gwynn when I go with these two handsome studs. Is there any fuckin' food in my room?"

Holly leapt to her feet. "Rosie, I got everything you like."

Rosie slipped her arm around Holly's shoulders. "Come to my room, and we can gossip about these guys. You can tell me if Ruben and Gordon are still available and if you're gettin' any. Girl talk. Gordon, what time are we leavin'?"

He checked his watch. "Twenty minutes."

Walking out of the suite with Holly, Rosie turned her head toward Gordon. "Don't be fuckin' late!" As she pulled the door shut, "Men," she said, cocking her eyebrows.

"Where did you go for dinner?" Ruben asked Gordon.

"Longhorn Steakhouse. It was good, but Rosie complained about the dessert. Too much cake, not enough frosting."

"She can be a challenge," Ruben said. "But I've never had a better safecracker."

Gordon took a deep breath. "She's interested in her neighbor and from what she said, he's interested in her. That's why she wants to go home. Her fridge is broken, but her niece is taking care of it."

"Oh, that's too bad," Dean said, shaking his head.

Assuming they were being mean to Rosie, Gwynn said, "I think it's nice she has a boyfriend."

"She's had a lot of boyfriends," Ruben said. "She tires of them and doesn't know how to end it."

"We've all had to play like we were her new boyfriend at some point," Gordon said. "That's how she ends it."

Gwynn wondered how Rosie found the time for numerous relationships with her line of work. Her mind wandered to Ruben and she mulled over if he would ever adjust his work schedule for a relationship.

"Gwynn?" Ruben said, gazing at her.

Snapping out of her pondering, she stammered, "Oh…aah… aah… Is McIntyre going out with Bev tonight?"

"No," Dean said. "He's celebrating his departure from Wilton with Simmons at her place. That's how we know he won't be home. He'll celebrate with Bev tomorrow night."

Gordon stood up. "We better get going or we'll never hear the end of it." He looked at Ruben. "If I run across anything interesting in McIntyre's file, do you want to see the copies of the documents tonight or first thing in the morning?"

"Tomorrow. Let's meet at six."

CHAPTER 23

Ruben tapped the alarm clock at 5:30 a.m., ending the loud buzzing sound.

"Do we have to get up?" Gwynn asked, looking at his handsome face, wishing he would relent. The pain in her side and arm was just a memory when she was this close to him. She snuggled up to him and kissed his neck.

His eyes glowed as he looked down and met her eyes. He wrapped his arms around her and passionately kissed her lips, sending shivers of desire racing through her.

Her pulse leapt with excitement as she felt the movement of his hands against her body.

Without warning, he pulled away from her. "I can't do this," he said, exhaling, sitting up. "You're still my client."

"Don't say that again! I'm not your client!"

"I promise I'll make this up to you after this case is closed," he said between deep breaths. "Your side will be better by then. We can enjoy being together at my house. Not in a hotel room."

"How long do you think it will take to close the case?" Gwynn wanted to know.

"My report to Mrs. VanAusdell is almost complete, but something is missing and I'm hoping documents from McIntyre's file will help clear it up."

"What's missing?"

"McIntyre's been an environmentalist all his life. Whatever is planned for the pipelines could have an environmental impact.

Would McIntyre turn his back on something he's been preaching about all these years?"

"Maybe he took the environment into consideration. Compression stations are located in large fenced-in clearings. Even if Carlos is right and several compressors blow up, there's a possibility the damage from the explosion could be contained within the compression station. If the pipeline next to it is destroyed, pipeline sections can be shut off. It might only have a minor effect on the surrounding area. Whatever is planned for the offshore oil pipeline could include environmental safeguards."

"I'd like some documentation stating that. Then I can finish my report and close the case." He lightly kissed her lips.

"But … but …" Gwynn stuttered. "Whatever is going to happen might not have happened by then."

"It doesn't matter. My assignment was to find who was responsible for Julie Morgan's death and why," he reiterated. "We've known who was responsible for a while and the 'why' — she had overhead a meeting, but that wouldn't be enough to satisfy Mrs. VanAusdell. I needed to know the specific substance of that meeting."

"So Julie's killer won't be punished?" Gwynn asked, squinting, unable to believe the murderer wouldn't be brought to justice.

"That wasn't my job," he said, getting out of bed. "Even if we felt compelled to go to the authorities, the type of information we've gathered wouldn't be enough to convict McIntyre. He's been very clever. Most of the evidence we have points to Fardown, and it was acquired illegally." He grabbed some clothing out of a drawer.

"McIntyre's not in the pictures we found at Backman's house," Gwynn said with a forlorn expression and feeling helpless. "His name isn't on any of the contracts. He didn't sign anything. If I went to the police with the pictures and told them about Cromer kidnapping me, I can't tie anything to McIntyre."

"We lack hard proof that Cromer even works for McIntyre," Ruben said, flipping through his clothing hanging in the closet. "We heard his name on Miss Morgan's recording, but he isn't listed on the meeting transcript created by Simmons."

"Do all your cases end like this?" Gwynn inquired.

"If you want, we can talk about this later. Right now I need to shower before Gordon gets here." Ruben headed into the bathroom.

Gwynn pondered over the evidence she had put in her file cabinet at work. She wanted justice for Julie and hoped something from McIntyre's cabinet would point to his guilt. Then she planned to turn that along with everything she had over to the authorities. Even though the documents hadn't been obtained through legal methods, she couldn't imagine the police wouldn't still try to put the perpetrators behind bars.

Ruben, wearing a yellow T-shirt and a baggy pair of dark grey chinos, came out of the bathroom. "Your turn. Let me take the bandage off your arm first." He undid the hooks and eased it off carefully. "It's still swollen. I'll wrap it when you get out of the shower. Try not to get your side wet, but I'll also put another dressing on it. Holly bought you a pair of sweatpants and a T-shirt. They're in the second drawer," he said, gesturing toward the bureau. Then he headed to the kitchen to brew a pot of coffee.

Ten minutes later Gwynn stepped out the bedroom and saw Ruben and Gordon hunkered over a newspaper. She poured herself a cup of coffee without either one of them looking up.

"Has something happened?" she asked as she settled into a chair by the table.

"CT's One Outland pipeline has been shut down," Ruben said, moving toward the counter. He picked up an elastic bandage roll and wrapped Gwynn's arm. "Let me check your side." He motioned for her to stand, and then he ran his hand over her bandaged side. "I'll change it later."

Gordon gave Gwynn the newspaper. The article began in the bottom corner of the first page and continued at the top of the fourth page. While Gordon and Ruben ate bagels, Gwynn focused on the article. It stated that around 2 a.m. part of CT's One Outland offshore oil pipeline collapsed as a result of metal fatigue, corrosion, and pressure. The internal inspection tool should have identified and located potential problems before the pipeline failed, but the integrity management computer system had malfunctioned. CT was able to shut-off that section of the pipeline and the well operators transporting oil on it shut down their wells, preventing oil from seeping out into the gulf. Those actions appear to have prevented an environmental disaster. Currently, CT was working on determining why the computer system failed. Several experts discussed the age of the pipeline. One said the pipeline's design life had ended years ago, that it had been operating on borrowed time.

CT couldn't estimate how long it would take to repair the pipeline since the damage was still being evaluated. Another expert said the pipeline couldn't be repaired and that it needed to be replaced, which would take months. The article included a picture of the damaged pipeline.

Gwynn put down the paper and took a bagel. "It's not even a headliner."

"With this pipeline failure," Ruben said, "no lives were lost, and in comparison to catastrophic oil disasters that have occurred in the Gulf of Mexico, this is minor." He filled his coffee cup, drank half of it, and sat back down at the table. "It doesn't appear it'll have a significant environmental impact, if one at all. I'm sure that's how it was planned; McIntyre will be pleased."

"I wonder when the gas pipeline will fail," Gwynn said.

"Sometime before the week ends," Gordon said as he opened the door for Holly.

Gwynn read the slogan on Holly's light brown T-shirt, "Man-Eating Alien Inside." Glancing at her floppy burnt-orange fedora, she became curious about how Holly met Ruben and decided she'd ask him about it later.

After everyone greeted Holly, Gordon continued. "One of McIntyre's notes indicated something was going to happen on Wednesday, and everything would be taken care of by Saturday." He handed the newspaper to Holly and pointed to the pipeline article.

"How did it go last night?" Ruben asked Gordon.

"Rosie didn't have any problem opening the file cabinet. It took her less than two minutes."

"She'll probably tell us how hard it was," Ruben said with a tinge of amusement in his voice.

"McIntyre's been busy shredding documents," Gordon said. "His wastebasket was full along with a large plastic bag, and several empty file folders labeled 'CT's Wyoming Gas Pipeline' and 'CT's One Outland' were on his desk."

"That's too bad." Ruben rubbed his chin. "Were you able to find out anything about those two?"

"No," he said, and then a brief smile flickered across his lips. "But he hadn't shredded the Centar file. That was in the cabinet

Rosie cracked." He went and got a folder off the coffee table. "It's all in here." He handed it to Ruben. "Notice everything is printed, except for a few handwritten stars and lines drawn on some of the documents."

"We both know what that means," Ruben said as his eyebrows rose.

"Nothing traceable to McIntyre," Gordon said. "Anyone could have written those notes."

Feeling disappointed that Gordon hadn't uncovered anything that she could take to the police to establish McIntyre's guilt, Gwynn thought about how devious he was. McIntyre made sure if anyone found any of his notes he could claim they were planted. He was always innocent, just like Julie told her whenever Hadley questioned him about something. *Mister Innocent.*

"In the folder are notes he made about meetings with Sander," Gordon said, "and how he'd make sure Wilton and CT paid him for his services along with a bonus."

"It is pretty funny how McIntyre had the companies pay for his plan and their problems," Holly commented.

Raising his eyes from the folder to Holly, Ruben asked, "Have you been able to locate Fred Sander?"

"No. He's a computer expert. Maybe he erased all traces of himself, or he's joined Denton and Anders."

"McIntyre wouldn't want anything happening to him until he saw the software's results, just in case it needed to be tweaked. Maybe Sander took the money and ran for his life, knowing about the other victims." Ruben flipped to another document and glanced at Gwynn. "Here's a note from Sander assuring that the software enhancements would only have an insignificant effect on the environment. Next to it McIntyre has placed several handwritten stars."

"That answers your concern," Gwynn said, smiling at him.

Ruben resumed going through the folder. "I had speculated about a connection between Wilton's offshore platform and the CT guys. This confirms there wasn't one," he said, tapping his index finger on a document.

"What did McIntyre's men do at the platform?" Gwynn asked.

"It wasn't just one platform," Ruben clarified. "Sander created a software program that would override the operating system for Wilton's wells that transport oil on CT's One Outland. If the wells are shut-in, even temporarily, the valves won't open again. The system will indicate there is a problem with the valves, but the problem will be with the software. The men were probably installing it when the victims spotted them."

"McIntyre sure wants to sock it to Wilton," Holly said and turned toward Gwynn. "How long do you think it will take them to figure that out?"

"No idea," Gwynn replied, shaking her head. "Wilton transports a significant amount of oil from those wells. This will cut deep into their profits." The Trulin contracts flashed into her mind. "As a result of CT's pipeline problem, the price of crude will probably rise on bulletins and NYMEX, but Wilton won't be able to take advantage of that increase on all their other production because of the fixed price in the contracts with Trulin. McIntyre certainly knew how to screw Wilton."

"It appeared he sold Wilton stock to raise money for Trulin," Ruben said. "It might have also been because he knew Wilton stock would plunge."

"The Lark Refinery's capacity isn't large enough to handle all the crude Trulin's purchasing from Wilton," Gwynn said. "McIntyre must be planning on reselling it at a profit. And Trulin will come to the rescue of the other operators affected by the closure of the One Outland pipeline by offering, at a profit, to transport their crude on the tanker Trulin just purchased."

"That's most likely the plan," Ruben said as his eyes became fixed on a document in the folder. "Gordon, what do you think it means that McIntyre crossed off all the names of the CT guys on the summary?"

Gordon shrugged. "Who knows?"

"After this week, they won't be CT guys anymore," Holly said. "They all gave their notice a couple of weeks ago. That information showed up in CT's computer system last night. So that's probably what it's about." She took a sip of coffee.

"Were you able to find out anything more about the pipelines Starling is purchasing?" Ruben asked.

"The sales are final," Holly said. "Neither pipeline runs completely across Wyoming like CT's. From the map, it looks like the two pipelines aren't far from each other. Maybe they're planning to extend one of the pipelines to the other one."

Ruben continued studying the documents and held up the last one. He looked at Gordon and chuckled.

Gordon laughed. "I thought you'd enjoy that one. It was on his desk, not in the file cabinet."

"We'll have to tell Dean," Ruben said. "He's losing Bev."

"What?" Gwynn asked, puzzled.

"McIntyre's planning on taking Bev with him to Paris, and it isn't on business," Ruben replied.

"It isn't just Dean who would have a problem," Gwynn said. "How about Pam?"

"McIntyre would give her some excuse," Ruben said.

"How could he possibly justify that to her?" Gwynn asked.

Ruben's cell phone beeped, and he fished it out of his pocket.

"Who knows," Holly said. "But he's smooth."

"It's Dean," Ruben said after he answered his phone.

Gordon, Holly, and Gwynn sat staring at Ruben while he talked.

"When?" he asked Dean. "No ... How long? ... Keep me informed." Ruben laid his phone down on the table. "Fardown's going to the hospital later this morning. He has a lump on his liver. He'll have some tests done today, and he'll be operated on tomorrow."

"If it's related to his last bout with cancer, it's probably malignant," Gwynn said.

"Was it just discovered?" Holly asked.

"No," Ruben answered. "He's known about it for weeks. He's gone through radiation and chemo."

"Do you think he knew about it all the time he was involved with Pam?" Gwynn asked.

"We don't know when his relationship started with Simmons. She told Bev about Fardown's operation when Bev arrived at work."

"Do you think that's why he got involved with this whole thing?" Gwynn asked, recalling Fardown had written a note indicating he felt bad about Julie.

"Maybe," Ruben said. "He might have wanted his debt cleared up before this operation in case it didn't go well."

"Is Simmons still working for Wilton?" Holly asked.

"She's cleaning out McIntyre's files there," Gordon said. "Her last day will be Friday."

"How about Bev?" Gwynn asked.

"Sometime today," Gordon said, "she'll tell McIntyre she's decided to work for Trulin, but she'll stay at Wilton until Hadley leaves. He's not leaving for a few weeks."

"But she'll never work for Trulin," Ruben smiled, "even after McIntyre's inspiring speech."

"I want to visit Fardown in the hospital," Gwynn said.

"Why?" Ruben asked, furrowing his brow.

"I want to confront him."

"Confront him about what?" Ruben inquired.

"Cromer told me that Fardown was responsible for Julie's death."

"But he's not well," Holly remarked.

Gwynn clenched her teeth. "I don't care. Even if he isn't the one in charge, he knew what was happening. He was in the picture and on the surveillance tape. McIntyre paid off a huge debt Fardown had amassed, but that doesn't justify standing on the sidelines while people were being killed. Julie, Taylor, Marilyn, Ian, Josh Kessler, his wife and the others, maybe more we don't know about. All for money. I want him to realize people know. Let him go into that operating room knowing that!" she said, her eyes red with rage.

Ruben sat motionless for a minute staring at her. "I don't know how many people know Fardown will be operated on tomorrow. We can't blow Bev's cover."

"That kind of information travels fast at Wilton," Gwynn said. "I'll call one of my co-workers to verify it."

"If other people know," Ruben said, "I'll take you to the hospital late this afternoon. McIntyre, Cromer, and others might visit Fardown after work. I don't want to take a chance on running into any of them."

"I'll check on it." Gwynn went into the bedroom and called a co-worker. Just as she suspected, everyone heard about it when they got to work.

CHAPTER 24

At three o'clock, Ruben drove Gwynn to the hospital. "I want you to wear this," he said, handing her a bug. "Since I won't be going with you into Fardown's room, I'll be listening in the hall. Don't tell him anything we know about the pipelines."

She tucked the bug into her bra. "What if he mentions something about the meeting Julie overheard?"

"If he brings it up, tell him what you told Cromer — the disk was blank."

Ruben held Gwynn's hand while they rode the elevator up to the fourth floor. Stepping out of it, they came face-to-face with Pam. As Pam moved past them to get on the elevator, her eyes narrowed, and she gave Gwynn an awkward smile without saying a word. Returning a fake smile, Gwynn remained silent.

Ruben glanced at Pam with a stoic expression on his face as he watched the elevator doors slid shut. "I didn't expect her to be here this early. Make your visit with Fardown short. I don't want us to be here if and when reinforcements arrive."

"I won't take long."

Ruben stopped next to the open door leading to Fardown's room, but out of sight from anyone in the room.

Before Gwynn entered, she peeked in to make sure Fardown was alone. He was sitting up in bed with a pillow behind his back and tubes attached to his arms, reading a book. Walking toward him, she noticed his pale, wrinkled skin, and his thin, white hair that no longer covered his scalp. "How are you feeling?"

Fardown looked up, his eyes darting back and forth. Fidgeting with his book, he answered, "Fine."

"That's too bad!" She stared at him.

His jaw clenched. "Why are you here, Gwynn?" he asked in a jittery voice.

"Julie always spoke highly of you. She really believed you were a nice person. You even went to her funeral and gave your condolences. I want to know why you killed her!" she snapped.

"I didn't," he protested, grimacing.

"Luke told me you were responsible for her death when you had him kidnap me." She continued glaring at him, and her hands trembled as the hatred for the man before her consumed all her thoughts. "How can you look at yourself in the mirror?"

"I'm not responsible ... for Julie's death ... I swear."

Her upper lip twisted in a sneer. Her hazel eyes darkened with rage as they bore into him. "Then who is?"

"Luke."

"But you gave the order."

"No ... No. It wasn't me. Please believe me."

"If you're not responsible, you know who is," she said in a harsh tone. "Tell me!"

"I don't know," he said, gasping for air.

A buzzing sound erupted from the equipment beside his bed.

"You pathetic little man. I hope you don't survive the operation."

Two nurses ran into the room. Gwynn slipped out.

Ruben grabbed her arm. "This way." He led her in the opposite direction from the elevator and opened the exit door. "Are you okay?" he asked, pulling her into the stairwell.

Gwynn felt numb. She had never treated anyone that cruelly before. "Yes," she replied with moist eyes.

Ruben hugged her. "We need to get out of here. Gordon is waiting for us. Try to walk down the stairs. Let me know if your side starts hurting." He held onto her arm and they crept down the stairs.

"Why can't we take the elevator?" she asked.

"At least one of their goons is already in the hospital. He kept checking the hallway from the waiting room near the elevator." After going down two flights of stairs, Ruben stopped, moved his gun from his holster to his outside sport coat pocket and picked up Gwynn. "Hold on tight."

She clamped her arms around his neck. Ruben went at a quick pace down the stairs and out the exit to Gordon's car. He eased her into the back seat and slid in beside her. Gordon tore out of the parking lot as they buckled up.

"What about your car?" Gwynn asked.

"I'll get it later."

"We have a tail," Gordon said, pressing down on the accelerator. "Sit tight." He swerved in and out of traffic, nearly clipping another car, and meandered through various streets.

An hour later, Gordon pulled into the hotel parking lot. Feeling the pain from being swung back and forth in her seat belt, Gwynn held onto her side as she climbed out of the vehicle.

"Are you okay?" Ruben asked, putting his arm around her shoulders.

"My side hurts."

"I've got some ointment to put on it when we get to our room."

As soon as they reached the suite, she lay down on the bed and Ruben helped her take off her blouse. He carefully removed the bandage, rubbed ointment over the wound with his fingertips, and handed her three pills along with a glass of water.

"Do you think I was too hard on Fardown?" she asked.

"What do you think?"

She stared at the ceiling as she gathered her thoughts. "No. I wonder if he'll confront McIntyre about what Cromer said to me."

"He might say something, but he'll be careful not to put McIntyre on the defensive. He's planning to have a future with Trulin."

Her eyelids became heavy. "Can I work for you when this is over?" she asked, her voice just above a whisper.

He caressed her arm. "We'll talk about it later."

"When?" she mumbled, dozing off.

"Later."

****

Darkness filled the bedroom with only a beam from the moon lighting Gwynn's way as she moved toward the door and opened it. Ruben sat on the sofa reading a document. When his eyes met hers, they both smiled.

217

"I thought you might sleep all night," he said.

Gripping the arm of sofa, Gwynn sank down beside him.

He laid the document on the coffee table. "You made quite a stir with your visit to Fardown. Simmons complained to Bev about how you had upset him in the hospital. She told her you were deranged and hallucinating, and you've had a hard time working since Julie Morgan died. She went on about how worried McIntyre had been about you since you had a seizure and were taken to the hospital on Monday. He wanted to make sure you were getting the help you needed, but no one knows where you're staying."

"What did Bev say?"

"She sympathized and asked her how Fardown was doing. Simmons had just talked to him on the phone. He hasn't been able to sleep or concentrate on anything since your visit. She's going to see him this evening." He checked his watch. It said 8:15 p.m. "Simmons is probably there now."

"How about Fardown's wife?"

"It's not a problem if they're visiting at the same time. She doesn't know anything about Fardown's personal relationship with Simmons. I thought that might have been the reason his wife left in a huff from Simmons's party, but apparently they argued about something else."

"He deserves to be upset," Gwynn scoffed. "Is Bev still seeing McIntyre tonight?"

"Yes. He picked her up at seven and took her out to dinner." Ruben leaned back and placed his arm on the top edge of the sofa behind Gwynn. "After dinner, they're going to his place to discuss Trulin. He's probably hoping he'll get lucky."

She smiled and gazed into his eyes. "I know the feeling."

He grinned. "After the case is closed."

Her eyes dropped to the unfamiliar-looking document on the coffee table. "What were you reading?"

"I'll tell you while we're eating. Holly made enchiladas." Ruben stood up and put away his computer and printer.

As soon as the table was set and the food dished up, Ruben opened a bottle of wine and poured. "To the end of this investigation," he said, toasting, clicking her glass.

She took a sip and tilted her head toward the coffee table. "Is that document your report?"

"A draft. Just a few loose ends to tie up."

"But it doesn't seem like it's over," she said, her voice heavy with despair, knowing that meant he'd be leaving soon for another investigation.

"It's not over until I deliver the report. Most of my cases don't have this many players, but they all end when the client has been provided with the information requested—when the contract has been satisfied."

"What do your clients do then?" Gwynn asked, hoping McIntyre wouldn't walk away unscathed.

"I don't know. It's up to the client. All of them know we won't testify in any court of law or to any authorities. We're finished."

"Do you kill people if that's what your client wants?"

"I don't take that type of assignment. Sometimes people die along the way, but that isn't by design," he said as he continued eating. "I'm planning on delivering the report tomorrow afternoon. I thought we'd sleep in." Looking at her, his radiant brown eyes crinkled in the corners. "If you can behave yourself."

She gave him a mischievous smile.

"Tomorrow night, you won't be my client and we can celebrate."

"Do you think Cindy and I are safe now?"

"In my report I've recommended that you be assigned a bodyguard for a few weeks. As far as Cromer knows, the only focus of the investigation was to find Julie's killer. His men won't see any of my guys or cars around. We're hoping they'll think the investigation was closed for lack of evidence. Since you don't have any hard evidence against them, they'll leave you alone."

"But Cromer kidnapped me. Won't he be worried about that?"

"That's why I've recommended a bodyguard. At the same time, you need to leave them alone. If they think you're still snooping around, you could be in trouble." He filled their wine glasses. "Holly will be watching you while I give my report to Mrs. VanAusdell. I'll know when I leave her if she's going to follow my recommendation."

"How about Cindy?"

"Paul, my employee, hasn't seen any trouble to be concerned about since Monday afternoon. Cromer might have called off that surveillance after he left you in the abandoned warehouse. Cindy doesn't know anything. She was only a bargaining chip. I think she's safe now, but Paul will continue keeping track of her until I notify him otherwise."

"What about your other people? Will they leave tomorrow?"

"A couple of them are already on another assignment. Bev's next assignment doesn't start until a week from Monday; Dean's starts on Thursday."

"They won't be together?"

"No. Bev wanted to stay another week to help out Hadley, but decided to leave with Dean on Tuesday. Gordon will go with me tomorrow to drop off the report. Then he'll leave. Holly will leave as soon as I return from seeing Mrs. VanAusdell."

Gwynn felt depressed that the morning briefings were over. "Can I work for you?" she asked again. "I have a degree in accounting. I was an auditor before I went to work for Wilton. I know the oil and gas industry."

"Why do you want to work for me?" he asked, scanning her face. "You don't need to worry that you won't see me again." He caressed her hand. "Holly is taking you to my place tomorrow. We'll see each other as soon as I've delivered the report."

"I still want to work for you. I know your work is dangerous, but on top of everything, I've enjoyed feeling like I was part of your team. You don't need to pay me anything."

Ruben gave her a puzzled look, yet didn't ask why, as he wondered if she had inherited money. "All my employees are paid — no exceptions. I already know your background. You lack fighting skills and knowledge about weapons."

"I can learn!"

He gazed at her while he finished eating. "If you worked for me, I wouldn't give you any special consideration. All my employees are treated equally."

"I wouldn't expect anything different. Don't think I want to work for you just so I can be with you." She lightly ran her fingers around the rim of her wine glass. "I want to be with you, but that's not the reason. Since I've been part of your investigation, I've never felt so much alive. Even when I was scared, the excitement bubbled inside me. That's why I want to work for you."

"Let me think about it."

"How much time do you need?" she asked, lifting an impatient brow.

"I'll tell you tomorrow night," he replied in a firm tone.

While Gwynn cleared off the table, she bit her lower lip and asked, "Do you have any rules about not getting personally involved with your employees?"

"No." He pulled her down to his lap. "But I try to separate business from pleasure. Sometimes it's not a straight line. Tomorrow night won't be business."

She flushed with pleasure as he held her close and his lips pressed against hers.

CHAPTER 25

Pounding on the door abruptly woke them up. "What the …" Ruben said, stumbling out of bed in his pajama bottoms. "I told everyone not to disturb us. This better be an emergency!" he huffed, putting on his T-shirt and hurrying toward the door. He peered out the peephole, unchained the door, and opened it.

"Turn on the television," Gordon said, entering, carrying a pot of coffee.

Ruben grabbed the remote, pushed the on button, and then closed the bedroom door.

Gwynn threw on her sweatpants and joined them in the other room. Gordon and Ruben sat on the sofa with their eyes locked on the television screen. She eased into the chair, looked at the screen, and saw flames covering a hillside. Then she heard the announcer say, "A swath of flames can be seen across Wyoming running the path of CT's Oxbow gas pipeline. Over five thousand homes have been evacuated. Sixty people are confirmed to have perished and hundreds more are unaccounted for as the raging fire burns on. Two small towns, numerous trailer parks, campsites, and backcountry hikers have been completely cut off from any escape routes and have limited communication. The smoke, flames, and gusting winds have slowed down helicopters trying to get them out as firefighters across the country are converging on Wyoming."

Gordon stood up, handed her a cup of coffee, and refilled his as they continued following the news story.

The reporter said there was a small forest fire when the first section of the pipeline exploded. CT and the forest service were trying to determine if the forest fire was responsible for the pipeline explosion.

Ruben opened the door for Holly and raised an index finger to his mouth. "Shh," he whispered. She put a box of donuts on the coffee table and sat down on the sofa between Gordon and Ruben as they heard an estimated half a million acres were burning.

A room full of reporters interviewed a CT spokesman. He couldn't understand why that section of the pipeline had not been shut down after the first explosion occurred. He kept saying that CT had safety measures in place to prevent this type of accident. There are multiple places along a pipeline to shut it down. He went on to mention it could've been shut down manually, but when the workers got close, the heat was too intense.

The reporters continued badgering him about CT's safety measures, and one reporter brought up the failure of CT's offshore oil pipeline. The spokesman seemed flustered as the questions kept coming, and he couldn't answer any of them. Finally, he said that CT was investigating what went wrong and apologized for not being able to provide them with more information. The television station broke for a commercial.

"CT needed Hadley," Gwynn commented. "Even if he couldn't answer all the questions, he would have been more polished than this guy."

"I'm sure you're right," Ruben said, rising to his feet. "CT's spokesman didn't come across very well." He paced the room.

"When did it start?" Gwynn inquired.

"The first explosion was around four this morning," Gordon said. "It started a chain reaction of explosions that ended shortly before five. One reporter said that if it had occurred later there would've been more casualties since sections of the pipeline run close to industrial areas and roads traveled by school buses. Looking at the area burning, I think his statement was premature. If it happened later people would have been awake and they might have been able to respond earlier."

"I thought only one compression station along with a section of the pipeline would've been damaged. So much for McIntyre being an environmentalist," Gwynn said, wondering if she could have helped prevent the disaster if she had warned CT. She had no idea it could possibly be this devastating.

"I don't buy it," Ruben said. "Sander assured him the enhanced software would have an insignificant effect on the environment. I'm missing something." He continued pacing.

The commercial ended and everyone's eyes became glued on the television screen again as scenes from the disaster appeared — charred remains of houses completely burned down to their foundations, flames and smoke shooting above tall buildings, firefighters digging trenches as dust whirled around them, and victims being loaded into ambulances. The reporter said that in some areas the firefighters were hampered in fighting the blaze by the high winds, in other areas due to the destruction of the water mains, and in other places the fire was too intense. Approximately one-hundred-fifty-three structures had been destroyed so far. Over ten thousand homes had now been evacuated, thirty thousand homes were without electricity and their gas service had been cut off. A call had gone out for blood donations.

Ruben and Gwynn exchanged glances when McIntyre appeared onscreen being interviewed by a reporter. The reporter had heard his speech the prior year about pipeline safety and the environment. He wanted McIntyre's opinion on the disaster. McIntyre's shoulders slumped, his eyes drooped, and his lips quivered slightly as he attempted to rationalize the devastation. It would take decades before the forests and landscape returned. His hands trembled as he lowered them down to his side. In an uneven tone, he offered his sympathy to all the families who had lost loved ones and said he prayed for the safe return of those still missing.

"He certainly doesn't act like a man responsible for the disaster," Gordon said, shaking his head.

McIntyre's voice broke a few times as he talked about how it could have been avoided if more emphasis and money had been put into maintenance and less into profits. He lambasted PHMSA, the Pipeline and Hazardous Materials Safety Administration, for not properly regulating pipelines to ensure their safety.

The interview was momentarily interrupted to give the latest death toll numbers after another burnt campsite had been discovered without any survivors.

When the interview resumed, McIntyre's face had turned ashen and lined with sadness. He took several deep breaths and cast his eyes down. Within a few seconds, he raised his head, straightened his shoulders, gazed at the news reporter, and continued by taking a jab at Wilton's Board of Directors, reiterating what he had said in his departure speech — how he was often at odds with the board over spending money for upgrading and maintenance so Wilton wouldn't be responsible for this type of catastrophe and how Trulin would never let the American people down. He gave a few more plugs about Trulin and how the Lark Refinery would increase capacity to help fill the void from the lost energy as a result of this disaster.

Gwynn adjusted herself in the chair. "Production from all the wells transporting on that gas pipeline will be stopped until they can find other transportation for their gas, even oil wells if they produce casinghead gas. I wonder how much of that gas volume can be handled by Starling."

"The timing of Starling purchasing those pipelines couldn't have been more perfect," Holly said in a sarcastic tone.

McIntyre went on to say that the oil and gas industry rely on the American people to buy their products, and they owe it to their customers to produce and deliver those products safely and in an environmentally friendly manner. He talked about Senators Stenson and Jenkins working on legislation that would require pipelines to use steel that can handle high stress levels in both urban and rural areas and not allow PHMSA to issue safety waivers. Currently, companies had the ability to request and possibly receive permits to use steel below the minimum stress level requirements. The legislation would also make it mandatory for pipelines to improve their monitoring systems with the latest technology to ensure safety so that the environment is always preserved. He hoped their legislation would sail through on Capitol Hill.

"That's good as long as Centar isn't involved," Gordon said.

Ruben paced while more pictures of the disaster were displayed, and several reporters interviewed people who had been evacuated, including a sobbing pregnant woman whose husband and son had gone camping and were among those missing. The camera panned in on an elderly woman staring sullenly through grief-stricken eyes at the burning mountain in the distance. The reporter said her husband, along with their three children and extended families, had gone on a three-day family reunion camping trip. She had only stayed behind because she recently had a hip replacement. She had not heard from any of her relatives since the previous night.

They continued watching the news report while Ruben went into the bedroom and made several calls on his cell phone.

Thirty minutes later, he walked out and declared, "The investigation isn't over." He picked up his report on the counter and tore it in half and then put the television on mute. "McIntyre was supposedly dealing with pipeline experts from CT. Even on the disk recorded by Miss Morgan, we heard enough to know he was concerned about the environment. I'm convinced McIntyre started the ball rolling, but was he misled by someone or did another player take control along the way? If someone else called the shots, did that happen before or after Miss Morgan's accident? Then who's responsible?"

"Do you think it could be Fardown after all?" Gordon asked. "Even if his notes indicated otherwise, maybe he's smarter than we think and he planted them in case someone suspected anything."

"No," Ruben said. "It's not him. He wouldn't have signed the contracts between Trulin and Wilton. He would've had an employee sign so he could pretend he didn't know about them until after they were executed."

"I also don't think it's Fardown," Gwynn said in agreement. "If Cromer worked for him, he wouldn't have easily confirmed Fardown gave him the order. And the way Fardown acted when I visited him in the hospital ... I just know it's not him." She gazed at Ruben for a minute. "Who do you think it is? One of the CT guys?"

"I have my suspicions, but we need proof," Ruben replied, getting a folder out of the cabinet and sitting down at the table.

Holly moved the donuts to the table and made another pot of coffee.

After everyone was situated, Ruben began, "Gordon, I want you to plant bugs in McIntyre's house again, his office at Trulin, and monitor his cell calls. He appears to be upset, so he might say or do something out of character. Use equipment that can be monitored from a distance." Gordon nodded. "After you've set up that equipment, search Cromer's place." He opened the folder and took out a printed page. "When you finish that, give me a call. Depending on where we are, I might want you to search Ethan Lemus's house.

Here's the address." Ruben handed Gordon the page. "Since his name wasn't picked up on Miss Morgan's recording, he wasn't seen on any of the surveillance tapes that evening, it appeared he wasn't in the loop, but he's on one of Backman's pictures and he's the only one who has access to Trulin's and Starling's bank accounts."

"Good point," Gordon said. "What about the CT guys?"

"None of them have enough money to finance that type of an operation," Holly said. "Even if they pooled their resources, I doubt if they'd have enough to pay Cromer's salary. The funds used to buy the two pipelines in Wyoming came from Trulin."

Ruben drank his coffee and thumbed through the folder. "Dean will be tracking Simmons. She's still going back and forth between Trulin's offices and the Wilton Tower. After work, Bev's going with her to the hospital to visit Fardown. Gordon, if you need help give Dean a call. He can monitor the bugs or McIntyre's cell calls even if he's tracking Simmons."

"Got it," Gordon said.

Ruben turned to Holly. "I want you to gain access to Simmons's computer files, both at her house and at Wilton. Gwynn and I will be going with you to her house."

Gwynn crossed her legs and started slowly swinging her foot under the table, excited that she was included.

"Her home computer is password protected," Gordon said. "I tried to access it when I searched her house, but the screen flashed after my first attempt. I didn't try again since it appeared she wasn't a prime suspect."

"Thanks for the heads up," Holly said.

"We need to wrap up this investigation as soon as possible." Ruben pushed back his chair and stood up. "Holly, dress in business clothes. We'll be leaving in twenty minutes."

After Holly and Gordon left to get ready, Ruben said to Gwynn, "This investigation needs to be finished before Tuesday, even if that means working through the night."

Gwynn didn't ask why, but the way he had said it gave her the impression there wasn't a contingency plan.

****

As Holly drove toward Pam's house, she asked, "What will be my cover at Wilton?"

"Tomorrow is Simmons's last day," Ruben said. "She's expecting someone from the temp agency to fill in for her."

"I'll be a secretary?"

"Yes. Drive past Simmons's house and park where the car can't be seen from her place."

Holly turned around a corner, eased over to the curb, and stopped less than a block away. Gwynn and Holly waited in the Suburban while Ruben checked out the inside of the house. Fifteen minutes later, he called and said the alarm system was off. He wanted them to enter through the back door.

On Pam's back porch, Holly and Gwynn put on latex gloves and went into the house. Ruben, also wearing latex gloves, had already turned on the computer and was looking through the desk drawers. He found a small post-it note stuck to the side of one of the drawers with "01!" scribbled on it and thought that might be part of the password.

Holly attached a device to one of the USB ports. "This shouldn't take long," she said. While she worked on the computer, Gwynn and Ruben searched the den.

"I'm in," Holly said. "Is there anything you want me to do before I leave?"

"Can you recover or tell Gwynn how to recover data Simmons has erased in the past month?"

"I'll handle it," Holly said, pushing a memory stick into a USB port. She opened a program and started clicking through the numerous windows it produced.

Ruben put his arm around Gwynn's shoulders and led her away from the computer. "I want you to look at all the emails, correspondence, and any files that might have a bearing on this case." He handed her a memory stick. "Copy it on this." He took a marble-sized object out of his pocket. "This is a tracking device. Put it somewhere on you."

Gwynn eyed her pocketless clothing and couldn't see anywhere else to hide the object except inside her bra. She stuck it in and flinched as she felt the cold surface against her breast.

Ruben reached in another pocket and pulled out a cell phone. "If something happens — a car pulling in her driveway, someone entering, an alarm goes off — call me on this cell, but leave it turned off unless you need it."

Gwynn bobbed her head up and down, feeling good Ruben trusted her enough to give an assignment. "Okay."

A few minutes later, Holly said, "I'm finished." She removed the device and the memory stick from the USB ports. "If for some reason you have to turn off the computer, here is a password you can use to get in. Also, when you're finished you need to remove a program. Follow the link I've written and delete it." Holly handed her a note, and then headed toward the door with Ruben.

Gwynn slid into the chair Holly had just vacated, laid her hand on the computer mouse, and double-clicked on the email icon. A login screen appeared. "Holly," Gwynn yelled, but no one answered. She knew it was too late; they were gone. She decided to wait and guess a password after she'd looked through Pam's documents. She started with spreadsheets and discovered several that showed bank account numbers along with all the transactions. Gwynn was surprised by the size of the cumulative totals and copied all of them onto the memory stick.

Then she noticed a folder named "recipes." Doubting Pam did much cooking, she clicked on it. Her face lit up when she glanced at the first recipe called SD Brownies and saw an ingredient named liame, email backwards, with alpha and numerical characters next to it. There were also other ingredients she didn't recognize with random digits by them. After copying the recipe onto the memory stick, she printed it and sighed with relief when the print job ended. Staring at the printed page, she was tempted to try out what she suspected could be the email password. However, she decided to finish looking through the other documents in case it wasn't and there were further security counter measures.

She glanced through the text documents, finding only one that appeared relevant. It contained information about Cromer. Gwynn copied it, then went through some PDF files and breezed over two that had general information about pipelines. She saved them to the memory stick. Gwynn ran across a few documents addressed to McIntyre and several other ones that included a Centar header. She copied all of those without reading them.

Gwynn went into Pam's picture files. There was a folder for each of McIntyre's weddings, but the first folder she opened was labeled Bad Boy.

Tears blurred her vision as she looked at a picture of McIntyre standing beside Julie with his hands gripped around her shoulders. Determined to keep her emotions under control, Gwynn sucked in air and wiped her eyes with her fingertips. Yet, she couldn't prevent her shoulders from sagging or her lips from trembling as she scanned through the photos. Several showed Julie crying while McIntyre held onto her. One showed Julie unconscious and McIntyre taking off her shoes. Another showed McIntyre carrying Julie. Gwynn stopped and glared at that picture since McIntyre had a relaxed, almost happy, expression on his face. *Strange.* As much as she didn't want to, she flipped back through the other pictures. In all of the photos McIntyre's expression seemed pleasant, not grim or angry.

After Gwynn copied that file, she spotted a folder labeled July 14, the day Julie died. With shaking hands she opened it. The first picture showed Cromer holding onto Julie in the same manner as McIntyre had in the prior folder. She studied the picture for a minute, and then clicked back to the first picture in the Bad Boy folder. Julie's body and expression were identical in both pictures. Gwynn looked through all the pictures in the July 14 folder. Every picture appeared to be the same as those in the Bad Boy folder except Cromer was in the place of McIntyre, and his face held a cold, hostile expression. *Why would Pam have photoshopped that? Could she be blackmailing McIntyre?*

With all her attention focused on the pictures, she never heard the front door open.

CHAPTER 26

Suddenly, a man's voice drifting down the hall caught Gwynn's attention. "Pam must've just forgotten to turn on the alarm."

She listened with bated breath as heavy footsteps pounded on the hallway floor and the sound of voices grew louder. Gwynn unplugged the computer, grabbed Holly's note, and slid under the deep desk into the knee space. She eased the chair snug against the desk, curled into a ball, and held tightly onto her legs. Her side ached, but she forced herself to remain motionless. Recalling the memory stick attached to Pam's computer, she pressed her lips together and hoped it wouldn't be problem.

"Everything looks okay in here," a man with raspy voice said.

"Hold on, I see something," another man said in a tenor voice. "Come over here."

Their footsteps stopped and the house became quiet. Gwynn perked up her ears as she tried to figure out where they were. A few seconds later, the silence was broken by the humming of the computer, and she knew one of the men had plugged it in. She saw a pair of legs in dark gray slacks by the chair and felt a rush of adrenaline, fearing she might be discovered soon. She jerked as the edge of the chair leg bumped against her foot.

"What the hell?" the tenor-voiced man said, pulling out the chair. "What's this memory stick doing here?" He sat down and Gwynn turned to the side and tried to make herself flat as possible so his feet wouldn't brush against her.

"What are you doing?" the raspy-voiced man asked.

"I'm going to hit my girl up on facebook real quick. Her cell's broken. Also, this memory stick was in the USB hub. Never seen one there before. You think we should take it to Pam?"

"If she wanted it she would have brought it with her."

"Damn, I need a password."

"Put back the memory stick and get out of there."

"What are you doing with your gun out?" the man sitting centimeters away from Gwynn asked.

"To shoot your ass if you don't turn off that damn computer. Let's go."

The tenor-voiced man pushed back the chair, stood up, and walked away.

"Go put the chair back where it was when we got here," the raspy-voiced man said.

The other man jammed the chair under the desk, striking Gwynn's injured side with one of the legs. She cringed in pain, closed her eyes, and clenched her teeth to prevent a sound from escaping her mouth.

"I'm going to set the alarm and then we're out of here," the raspy-voiced man said.

A door slammed shut, but Gwynn wanted to make sure they had gone so she stayed under the desk, listening.

Five minutes later, the tenor-voiced man said, "Alwyn, I told you there wasn't anyone here. You're just being paranoid. Can we leave now?"

"Yeah," Alwyn replied. "Let's get back to the Wilton Tower."

After Gwynn heard a door close, she remained under the desk for a few more minutes as she continued suffering from the pain in her side. When she felt certain they had gone, she let out a sob before gathering her composure. She emerged, gently rubbed her sore side, and glanced around the room, looking for motion detectors since the alarm had been reset, but didn't see one.

Though the pain had not dissipated, she refused to let it slow her down. She logged into the computer using the password Holly had given her, went back to the pictures files, and copied the folder labeled July 14. Assuming the Bad Boy pictures had been photo shopped, she opened the folder named John's Birthday, thinking McIntyre's face might have come from one of those photos. He had a nice expression on the first picture, and then she proceeded to copy the folder. Anxious to get started looking through Pam's emails and worried that the two men could return, she copied the folders labeled Ethan, Sander, and Luke without viewing any of them.

She clicked on the email icon, entered the digits from the recipe page she had printed, and smiled ear-to-ear when Pam's inbox opened. Gwynn began with emails dated the first part of April and copied each one after reading only a couple of sentences.

A shrill alarm cut off her concentration. She jumped, almost knocking the computer mouse on the floor.

"Gwynn, it's me," Ruben yelled.

She stepped out into the hallway and saw him adjusting the alarm system. "I had company — two guys. They set it when they left."

"I saw them." He glanced at her a few times while he continued working on the alarm system. "Did you hide under the desk?"

"Yes. How did you know?"

"Just a guess," Ruben replied without mentioning he had seen her through the window.

"With the alarm turned off, they'll be back."

"I'm turning it back on," he said. "But the motion detectors will be off."

"Where are the motion detectors?"

Ruben pointed to one above his head. "There's another one by the back door." He moved closer to her. "Are you almost finished?"

"I'm still going through Pam's emails. I found some pictures with…"

He interrupted, "We need to leave here as soon as possible, so finish the emails. You can fill me in later."

Ruben pulled up another chair and sat beside Gwynn while she continued scanning and copying the messages until his cell rang. He glimpsed at it and went out into the hallway.

Feeling drawn to the email Pam had sent to Lemus on July fourteenth, Gwynn quickly skimmed over the rest before copying them. Staring at the remaining email, her hand lingered above the computer mouse as a tinge of uneasiness swept through her. She licked her dry lips and clicked on it.

The heading read, "More trouble with John." The message said, "I went back to work after John called me. He hesitated doing anything about the spy since he was concerned about her grandmother. What does he think her grandmother will do – hit him over the head with her walking cane? What a wimp! He laid into Luke when Luke had taken appropriate action. What did he expect? He told me he wanted the spy kept safe while she slept it off. He actually believes if he talks to her, he can work it out. John was furious when he left, but I took care of it and told Luke what to do. I just wanted you to know about it so you're prepared when John complains to you. I wish I could see you tonight, but I understand. Love, Pam"

Gwynn held back tears while she copied the email, ejected the memory stick, deleted Holly's program, and turned off the computer. As a few tears trickled down her face, she sat with her eyes fixed on the blank screen.

"Are you okay?" Ruben asked, standing in the doorway.

"Yes," she murmured, wiping her cheeks with her fingers. "How could I have been so wrong?"

Ruben strode around the desk and stood behind her. "You're not the only one," he said, putting his hands on her shoulders. "We need to leave."

He reset the alarm and they departed out the back door. As they made their way toward the front of the house, Ruben came to an abrupt halt and grabbed Gwynn's hand. "Shh!" he whispered, turning around and pulling her back.

She wondered what was wrong, but didn't ask as he quietly led her between a row of bushes to a six-foot-high wooden fence.

"They must've entered the house just as we were leaving," Ruben said softly. "I saw one of them through the window."

"I don't think I can climb that fence with my side," she whispered, anxiously.

"This is the only way we can leave undetected. I'll give you a boost." He lifted her up.

Gwynn gripped the top edge of the fence and managed to get her legs over it. Her side burned as she dropped down, but she forced herself to hide the pain she felt rippling through her side. Ruben scrambled over the fence as a burst of gunfire hit it. He grasped her hand, and they ran toward the Suburban parked around the corner.

"They're coming," Gwynn said with her head twisted around and looking out the rear window as she buckled up.

Ruben gunned the engine and sped away as a bullet struck the back bumper.

Gwynn saw the men charging after them on foot, and then they gradually vanished. "I think they got the license plate number."

"That's not a problem. We have others."

Still attempting not to show the pain she was enduring, Gwynn leaned back in the seat, pressed her lips together, and gently stroked her injury.

Ruben laid his hand on her leg. "Close your eyes and try to relax," he said with concern evident in his voice. "The medicine at the hotel will help."

****

While Ruben applied antiseptic and wrapped her side, Gwynn talked about what she had discovered from the documents on Pam's computer. "How do they dare use email to correspond with each other?"

"They have a high security email server. The only way we could access Simmons's email account was through her computer." Ruben handed Gwynn three pills, including a sleeping pill, and insisted she take them.

Reluctantly, she stuck the pills in her mouth and swallowed them along with a big gulp of water. Within five minutes, she was sound asleep.

Three hours later, Gwynn strolled out of the bedroom and heard Ruben on his cell giving someone names and numbers that sounded like passwords. While she continued listening, she sank down on the sofa.

"Yes, I'm sure the first one is Lemus's. Unless he recently changed it," Ruben said into the phone as he looked and smiled at Gwynn. "Give it a try ... Come straight to my room." He clicked off. "It appears Simmons's recipe has passwords for Ethan Lemus's computer, Fardown's, and Jurovski's. Recipe makes sense. It's her recipe to get into their systems. The ingredients are their names with the letters backwards."

"Have you gone through all of Pam's documents?"

"Almost, but I haven't finished going through her emails," he replied. "Holly's going to love Simmons's attempt at photoshop." He chuckled.

"Why?"

"Let me show you," he said, turning toward the computer. After Gwynn was by his side, he tapped on a Bad Boy picture and pointed at one of McIntyre's arms. That arm was large and muscular, like Cromer's, and it didn't match the other one.

Gwynn couldn't help but smile even though she had a hard time looking at the photo with Julie in it. "Maybe this was a work in progress."

"I wonder what Simmons planned to do with the pictures."

"Despite professing her love to Ethan and Abir in emails, I still think the one she wants is McIntyre," Gwynn said. "When McIntyre married his fourth wife, Hadley had the wedding pictures so he could pick out one for the news release. I looked through them with Julie. From Pam's expression in the pictures, we both thought she was on the verge of tears. I've seen the adoring look on her face when he's giving a pep talk to the employees. She's crazy about him. But I can't understand why she overrode his decision about Julie. That can't endear her to him."

"You didn't read enough emails," Ruben said. "McIntyre believes Cromer acted on his own. Holly called while you were sleeping. Simmons had access to his emails. McIntyre wanted to fire Cromer after the Miss Morgan problem. I don't know what changed his mind. He questioned the two deaths on the oil platform since Cromer was there and also suspected Cromer's involvement in the disappearance of Denton and Anders. McIntyre wanted Denton and Anders fired and planned to discredit them, but the emails didn't say why."

"Did he really not know what was going on or was he just playing dumb?"

"It doesn't appear he knew," Ruben said, rising from his chair. "You missed lunch." He took a sandwich out of the fridge, led her to the sofa, and handed it to her.

"Have you been able to figure out what Pam was going to get out of this?"

"Several of the documents indicate that Lemus planned on making her a vice president at Trulin, and he was adding her name to all the Trulin accounts," Ruben said, sitting down by her. "And Jurovski's going to put her on the Starling board. McIntyre had planned to give her a bonus and a raise for helping him through this, but obviously she wanted more. It appears what she really wants is more money and power."

"Do you think Lemus could make her a vice president with McIntyre around?"

"Not likely," he said, rubbing his forehead, "but there are a couple of emails that make me suspect she might have something on him and Fardown."

"What?"

"In one to Lemus she mentions she has McIntyre's fingerprints, so she can handle him. In another one she talks about Fardown's duffle bag. She says that should keep him in line."

"Duffle bag?"

"There was an exchange of emails between her and Fardown. He asked about his duffle bag and she told him she hasn't been able to find it."

"Maybe she'll use it to threaten him that she'll tell his wife about them if she doesn't get what she wants. Blackmail."

"Possibly. Although, I doubt that would be a strong enough reason for him to go against McIntyre. The guy thinks he's a saint."

"Then what?"

"When Gordon gets here, I'll ask him about it again." He picked up the remote. "Let's see what's happening on the fire."

A burnt hillside appeared on the television and a reporter talked about the devastation Wyoming had already suffered with only twenty percent of the fire contained. They stared at the screen as the catastrophe continued to unfold with news of more deaths and rescues, and footage of the Wyoming landscape covered in smoke and flames.

Ruben's cell rang, and he headed into the bedroom to talk. Gwynn ate her sandwich while she watched, wishing they had known more, and then maybe they could've prevented the disaster.

****

Shortly after 6:30 p.m., Gordon arrived at Ruben's suite with his briefcase and two sacks full of Chinese take-out. "Holly's on her way," he said, putting the sacks on the table and the briefcase on the floor.

Within a few minutes, Holly walked in carrying a folder, set it down on the coffee table, and joined them at the kitchen table. "Boy, did I have McIntyre wrong," she said, dishing up. "He might be arrogant and ruthless, but he's not a killer."

"That's the same conclusion we've all come to," Gordon said, twisting off a cap on a beer bottle.

During dinner, Holly talked about the commotion at Wilton over the offshore wells with faulty valves. Since that was the focus of everyone's attention there, it was easy for her to get into Pam's and McIntyre's computers without arousing any suspicion. "I'll call the temp agency in the morning and tell them I won't be able to return to Wilton due to a family emergency," she said between bites.

When they finished eating, Gordon opened his briefcase, took out a folder, glanced through it and began, "McIntyre's extremely upset over the Wyoming catastrophe. He even called his doctor to get a prescription to help calm his nerves. Before the disaster, he planned to attend a charity fundraiser in Galveston tomorrow night, but now he's leaving for Wyoming in the morning to see if he can help out.

"Sander called and tried to assure McIntyre that the software he created should have only been installed at one gas compression station on that pipeline. It was designed to damage the station and then automatically shut it down, stopping the flow of gas. It would have put the pipeline out of commission for a while, but that was all. Sander wondered if Jurovski had someone mess with the software. He mentioned the oil pipeline program worked as designed. McIntyre told him he already suspected Jurovski might've compromised the plan. He wanted Sander to stay away and not to call anyone else since he thought Sander could be in danger."

"Do you know why McIntyre thought that?" Ruben asked, jotting down some notes.

"Probably because Cromer works for Lemus, not McIntyre." Gordon took a swig of his beer and adjusted himself in his chair.

"In one of McIntyre's emails to Lemus, he wanted Cromer fired," Ruben said. "Since we know that didn't happen, I suspected there was a connection."

"From emails Lemus sent to Simmons," Gordon said, "he was upset that McIntyre had planned to have Fardown in the number two position at Trulin instead of him. At the same time, he wanted to cover McIntyre's back since he needed his know-how to get Trulin up and running. And he knew Trulin could make him a rich man. He was pleased that McIntyre was able to convince OSHA and EPA to allow Lark Refinery to start refining again and that McIntyre got the two agencies to shut down one of the other refineries."

"Yeah, I saw those emails," Holly said, leaning forward, resting her elbows on the table.

Gordon continued, "Lemus sent a lot of emails to Cromer. It appears he didn't want to take a chance on anyone interfering with McIntyre's plan, so he had any potential threats eliminated. He gave the order to terminate the two guys on the platform. He leased the abandoned warehouse and is responsible for Denton and Anders's disappearances."

"How about the guys who worked for the pipelines?" Gwynn asked.

"There weren't any emails about those guys," Gordon replied.

"I didn't see any emails about them either," Holly said, rising to her feet and getting another beer out of the fridge.

"The CT guys had the software installed," Ruben said, looking up from his notepad. "Their heads were on the line if an employee squealed on them. They were the ones who would financially gain from Starling. Ian Daniels and Josh Kessler planned on talking, so the CT guys probably took care of them." His eyes moved to Gwynn. "Remember, Karlee recognized Jurovski."

Gwynn nodded.

After gulping down his beer and shuffling through the papers in his folder, Gordon began again, "Simmons tried to see McIntyre at Trulin, but he kept putting her off. He went to see Fardown when he knew she was on her way to Trulin. She called him numerous times when she was at Wilton. He only talked to her once and cancelled their dinner date, saying he had a meeting he needed to attend. She was verbally upset. The way he kept avoiding her, I wonder if he suspects she's involved with altering the plan, especially since he turned around and asked Bev to have dinner with him. I don't think McIntyre invited her for anything but company. Dean agrees, but he's still going to keep track of her." He glanced down and picked up a document. "A couple of months ago Lemus sent McIntyre an email about Simmons that didn't make sense, probably because we're missing some of the facts and I couldn't retrieve his deleted emails."

"What did it say?" Ruben asked.

"Something about Simmons thinks Trulin needs more vice presidents, but he, Lemus, is going to take care of it. Maybe Carl Backman thought he'd become a vice president."

"No, that's not it, but it does make sense," Ruben said. "Simmons believes she's going to be a vice president at Trulin." He proceeded to tell them what he discovered from Simmons's emails. When he was through, he turned to Gordon, "I don't get the duffle bag. Was there anything in it besides a pair of workout clothes, a woman's undergarment, and a grocery list?"

A thought snapped into Gwynn's head. "Undergarment? A camisole?"

Gordon nodded, "Yes, that's what you ladies call it."

"Ruben, among Julie's clothing was there a camisole?"

Ruben raised his eyebrows as he flipped through his folder. He pulled out a sheet and studied it. "No."

"Julie and I went shopping often for lingerie. We both loved camisoles."

"You wear one all the time," Ruben commented.

"So did Julie."

"I know where you're going with this," Ruben said. "Gordon, can you describe it?"

"A light blue color, lacey."

Ruben glimpsed at the document. "Julie wore a blue blouse. Gwynn, would you know if it was hers?"

"Probably. Gordon, did it have a little blue flower in center of the top?"

"I didn't look at it that closely."

"I guess we'll be making another trip to Simmons's. Does anyone have any ideas about the fingerprints Simmons mentioned in the email?"

"The ones on the receiver," Gordon suggested. "Remember, we thought it was strange that Simmons's weren't on it since it was found in her drawer."

"You're probably right. Holly, did Simmons get all her drawers at Wilton emptied out?"

"I think so, but I doubt she would have taken that to Trulin. Maybe it's at her house?"

Staring at the floor, Ruben rubbed his chin with his knuckles. "After our visit to Simmons's house earlier, I suspect security will be increased there. This investigation needs to end. We'll go later tonight."

"What about Pam?" Gwynn asked, then took a drink of her Coke.

"Let me think about that." Ruben turned over a page in his notepad and picked up his pen. "Holly, besides what you told me on the phone, what else have you got?"

Holly stood, grabbed her folder from the coffee table, sat back down, and thumbed through it. "Lemus liked the way Simmons had handled Miss Morgan. He even gave her a thank-you gift for putting together the plan for the car accident. There were also some emails that implied Lemus had plans to eliminate McIntyre after Trulin became a solid company." She straightened the papers in her folder.

"Anything else?" Ruben asked.

"Nope. That covers it," Holly said.

"We're all going to Simmons's. Gordon, you and Holly will search her house for the receiver. Begin in her bedroom. If you find it, take it along with the camisole in the duffle bag. I'd like to have the additional evidence. However, I have enough information to close the case right now, so it won't matter if Simmons knows those items are missing."

"What will I do?" Gwynn asked.

"You'll distract Simmons if she is home."

"How?"

"We'll discuss it on the way."

CHAPTER 27

At 10:15 p.m., Ruben stopped Holly's Suburban in front of Pam's house. Holly and Gordon had gone in Gordon's car and were parked around the corner, waiting for instructions from Ruben.

Pam's front porch light was on. Outside that, the house appeared completely dark. Ruben pointed a directional mike and an infrared camera at it. "I'm not picking up anything. You head to the front door and I'll go to the side. If no one answers, get back in the car. Call if you notice anything out of the ordinary."

Gwynn rang the doorbell as Ruben crept to the side of the house. She heard the buzzing sound coming from inside so she knew the doorbell was working. After pushing the button three times, she headed back to the car. She held her breath every time she saw a car approaching, fearing it was Pam's.

Ten minutes later, Ruben climbed into the driver's seat. "They're inside."

"How long do you think it'll take them?"

"It depends if the duffle bag has been moved and if the receiver is in her bedroom. If we don't hear from them, they'll keep looking until I call."

"Did you reset the alarm after they got inside?"

"No. We don't want it going off if they have to leave in a hurry. We'll probably have company soon."

They both stared ahead as headlights came toward them. "It's not a van," Ruben said. "It might be Simmons's car. If it is, try to keep her outside as long as possible."

Gwynn bite her lower lip as a white Lexus, Pam's car, pulled into the driveway. She slipped out of the vehicle and hurried to the Lexus as Pam opened the driver's door.

Glaring at Gwynn, Pam's eyes narrowed and a furious expression flashed on her face. "What are you doing here?" she snapped.

"I wanted to talk to you. I went and saw Mr. Fardown in the hospital, and I feel awful about what I said to him," Gwynn said, attempting to look pathetic.

"So did Kent. How could you talk to him like that?"

"A man—one of Wilton's security guards named Luke—kidnapped me. He told me that Mr. Fardown ordered him to kill Julie."

"Gwynn, you need help," Pam said, stepping around her. "You're delusional."

Gwynn grabbed Pam's arm. "No. I'm not."

"Let go of me," she huffed, yanking Gwynn's hand away from her. "Why are you here? What do you want?"

"Luke told me he had given you one of Julie's rings. I want it. Please, let me have it."

"Why would he give me a ring?"

"You're not his girlfriend?"

"No! I know Wilton has a guard named Luke. I've never spoken to him."

Another set of headlights came toward them. Ruben rolled down the car window, poked his head out, and said loudly, "Gwynn, she's not going to give you the ring. Let's go."

Assuming the headlights belonged to a van, Gwynn rushed to the Suburban and climbed into the passenger seat. Ruben pushed on the accelerator before Gwynn could snap on her seat belt. They drove past a blue van. Gwynn expected it to turn around and follow them; instead the van proceeded to Pam's house.

"Did they get the stuff?" she asked.

"The camisole. They couldn't find the receiver. Simmons might not have been home since she cleaned out her desk. It could be in her car, but we won't look for it again."

****

Back in Ruben's suite, Gordon pulled a camisole out of a gray plastic bag. "Is this Miss Morgan's?"

Gwynn's eyes became moist as she touched the soft lace, held it up, and saw the delicate blue silk flower. She buried her face in it and smelled Julie's perfume. "It's hers," she murmured.

Ruben put his arm around her shoulder. "The investigation is over. You won't ever need to see Simmons again or anyone involved with Miss Morgan's death. I'll finish the report tonight and deliver it tomorrow with Gordon."

CHAPTER 28

The next morning, Ruben showered, shaved, and dressed while Gwynn slept. As she opened her eyes, he sat down on the bed beside her. "I'm looking forward to this evening," he said, his eyes glowing and a smile creasing his lips.

"So am I." Holding onto his arm, she pulled him closer and kissed his neck. "Have you decided if I can work for you yet?"

"I'll let you know tonight." He bent down and kissed her lips tenderly.

Gwynn felt hopeful he'd hire her since he had already given her two assignments and they had gone well.

After they finished eating breakfast, Ruben gave her a duffle bag to use for her things. He told her that Holly would drive them to his car that was still parked at the hospital. From there, he'd go with Gordon to deliver the report. Holly would take her to his place and stay with her until he arrived.

Even with Holly watching Gwynn, Ruben wanted her equipped to defend herself if a problem arose. "This is easy to use," he said, handing her a small pistol. "Just release the safety like this." He showed her how to do it. "One bullet from this gun will kill. There are six bullets in the magazine and they all contain a fast-acting poison, so be careful." He took an adhesive strip out of his suitcase. "This isn't a band-aid," he clarified. "It's an antidote in case you accidently get shot by one of the bullets."

She touched the padded strip.

"I want to attach this to your thigh." He waited while she lowered her sweatpants, and then he secured the strip to her leg. "If you get shot, all you need to do is hit this as hard as you can. That will disperse the antidote into your system, but you have to hit it within two minutes of being shot. Do you have any questions?"

"Do you think I might need to shoot someone?" she asked, scrunching her face in confusion as she pulled up her sweatpants.

"It's just a precaution," he said, getting a knife and a sheath out of his suitcase. "I want you to wear this. Sit." He nodded toward the bed. When she was seated, he raised one of her pant legs, secured the sheath to her calf, and slid in the knife.

"Why do you think I need this?" she asked, wondering if this was some kind of a test.

"It's only another precaution."

She smiled to herself thinking she might have to always wear something like this if she became his employee.

****

Since the spaces next to Ruben's Suburban in the hospital parking garage were occupied, Holly cut close to the back of the vehicle and stopped. Ruben and Gordon moved their suitcases to Ruben's car.

Gwynn slid out of the backseat, opened Holly's front passenger door and lifted her foot to the running board, preparing to climb in. Ruben slipped an arm around her waist, twirled her around, and pulled her against his chest. With his free hand, he cupped her chin, tilted her head and kissed her passionately, sending her pulse racing. Then he placed his hands firmly onto her shoulders and gazed intensely into her eyes.

The glum expression on his face sent an uneasy sensation vibrating through her body. "Is something wrong?" she asked as he gathered her into his arms again.

"No," he replied. "I'm just looking forward to later."

"I'll make sure she's okay," Holly said, leaning toward the passenger door.

Slowly, Ruben released his embrace and held Gwynn's arm while she eased into the car seat. Her mouth quivered as he closed the door, and she hoped the feeling of dread she felt was only her imagination.

Gwynn watched Ruben get in his car and longed to be next to him. "Do you think I could go with them if I stayed in the car?" she asked, fidgeting with her fingers.

"No," Holly answered. "If that were an option, Ruben would have already mentioned it to you."

Gordon waved his hand, gesturing Holly to drive away.

Gwynn's eyes remained fixed on Ruben's car while Holly proceeded toward the exit. Sadness crept through her when they drove around a bend and Ruben's car disappeared from her sight.

A loud explosion, crashing, and shattering of metal erupted behind them. A woman screaming echoed through the hospital parking garage.

"Stop ... stop the car!" Gwynn yelled, snapping off her seat belt and pushing open the door. She jumped out before the car came to complete stop and charged up the parking ramp.

Holly threw the transmission into park, pressed on the emergency brake, leapt out of the vehicle and ran after her.

Gwynn smelled and saw smoke as it stung her eyes. Flames shot up in front of her when she charged around the bend. Holly grabbed her arm, stopping her. Then she saw Ruben's Suburban smashed into the vehicle parked next to it and both cars were consumed in flames.

"No! No!" she screamed, tears pouring down her face. Attempting to get closer to the vehicles, Gwynn tried to yank her arm free from Holly's grip, but Holly held on tight. "Let me go!" she cried. "Let me go!"

"My car!" a woman shouted, pointing to the car burning by Ruben's.

Holly took Gwynn's other arm and swung her around. "We need to get out of here before any of them see you," she said, urgently.

"I can't leave!" Gwynn sobbed. "I can't leave! Ruben needs me!"

Holly continued clutching Gwynn's arm, preventing her from going to Ruben's car, and stared at the fire.

"Let go!" Gwynn yelled, squirming, still struggling to work her arm out of Holly's firm hold as tears ran down her cheeks.

A crowd began gathering when the throbbing sound of an ambulance drifted up the ramp.

Holly pulled Gwynn to the side so the ambulance could pass. After that, she couldn't get Gwynn to budge. She put her arm around her, and they watched a fire engine drive by them and stop ten feet from the burning wreckage. The firemen extinguished the blaze, removed a car door, and helped the paramedics get Gordon and Ruben out.

Gwynn was standing too far away to see their faces. Tears kept flowing as each man was placed on a gurney. She screamed and trembled when their bodies were covered with sheets. Then she stood silently and blankly stared ahead, not even seeing the ambulance drive past them without any lights blinking.

"Come on, Gwynn, we need to leave," Holly said gently, leading her down the ramp.

****

Lying in bed, Gwynn only had vague memories of what happened after Ruben and Gordon were put in the ambulance. She glanced around and saw Holly's jacket over the back of a chair, floppy hats on top of the bureau, and knew she was in Holly's suite.

"I couldn't get her to go to Ruben's place while we figure this out," Gwynn heard Holly say, her voice coming from the other room. "She wanted to go to her apartment, but that's too dangerous, so I brought her back here."

Someone closed the bedroom door. Gwynn could still hear voices, but could no longer make out what they were saying. Feeling groggy, she sat up and cupped her head in her hands, tears trickling down her cheeks. She wondered what Ruben would have done if she had been the one who died. *Would he want revenge?* Cromer had killed Julie, and she believed he had planted the car bomb that killed Ruben and Gordon. Even if he was following Lemus's or Pam's orders, she still held him responsible. She wanted Julie's and Ruben's murderer punished, but she knew she needed to pull herself together before she could make any plans. There'd be time for tears later. She summoned her strength, wiped her eyes and rose from the bed. With a pale and drawn face, she staggered into the adjoining room.

Holly and Dean sat at the table drinking bottled water. "How are you feeling?" Holly asked.

Gwynn couldn't understand why they didn't show any emotion. They both sat calmly — Dean leaning back in his chair and Holly resting her elbows on the table. "Don't either of you feel bad?"

"We feel bad," Dean said in a soft voice, sitting up straight. "We've worked for Ruben for almost ten years, and we've known Gordon all that time. This investigation isn't over. We need to stay focused. We'll mourn later."

"Ruben wanted you to go to his place," Holly said. "You'll be safe there until we know how to proceed. Won't you change your mind and let me take you there?"

"No," Gwynn replied firmly. "I want to help. What can I do?"

"Do you know the name of the client?" Dean asked.

"You don't know?" Gwynn asked, gazing at them in utter disbelief.

"No," Dean said. "Most clients like to remain anonymous, so Ruben only shares that information with the one in charge of the investigation. When Ruben leads an investigation, he shares that with the second person in line. For this investigation, that was Gordon. We've called Ralph. He's the number two guy in the organization. He doesn't know the name of the client."

"I know the client," Gwynn said without revealing the identity. "Do you have a copy of Ruben's report?"

They shook their heads.

Gwynn pursed her lips briefly and said, "Then I'll write a new one. It might not contain everything that was in Ruben's. I'll put in everything I know and deliver it."

"Ralph said he could be here late tomorrow," Holly said. "I think he should deliver the report."

Gwynn thought about Mrs. VanAusdell. "No, I'll deliver it. The client might want to be anonymous. Since Ruben's gone," she said, her eyes shining with unshed tears. "what will you and the other employees do after this investigation?"

Dean explained that Ruben didn't want the organization to fall apart if something happened to him, so he made arrangements for the lead investigators to follow in his footsteps. Ralph would carry on.

"Do you know the address of the abandoned warehouse where Luke took me?" Gwynn asked, looking at Dean.

"No. Why?"

"Taylor and Marilyn are buried behind that building. Ruben was going to anonymously give the police the address after he delivered the report. It's important that I know the address." Gwynn sat down at the table. "Dean, you attached a tracking device to the semi going toward the building. Holly, you tracked the device. Can you remember anything about it?"

"Let me check if I have anything on my computer." Holly pushed away from the table and headed to her working space.

"What needs to be done now to close the investigation?" Gwynn asked Dean.

"The report needs to be delivered, and we'll proceed with our current tasks until our scheduled departure."

"Holly, aren't you scheduled to leave now?" Gwynn asked, recalling the time frame Ruben had given her.

"I'm scheduled to leave tomorrow morning, but we're worried about your safety. My next assignment doesn't start until Monday, so Ralph wants me to stay with you until he arrives."

Gwynn thought, *they don't know I wanted to work for Ruben.* She decided not to say anything until Ralph got there. "What's Ralph like?"

"Business-like, like Ruben," Dean said. "He's very thorough and respected by everyone."

"He's in his early forties," Holly said, clicking through computer screens. "Tall, light brown hair, muscular, good-looking. I found the area where the semi turned around. I don't have the exact address."

"Can we drive out there?" Gwynn asked.

Holly and Dean exchanged glances. Dean shrugged his shoulders.

"It's not safe," Holly said. "I'll Google the area and you can see if any of the buildings look familiar. Maybe we can get the address that way."

Gwynn pulled her chair next to Holly and sat down.

"I need to get back to the Wilton Tower," Dean said, heading to the door. "Call me if you need me."

Holly nodded, and he left.

After searching for almost half an hour, they located the address and Gwynn wrote it down. Then she took a laptop into the bedroom to work on the report while Holly watched television for the latest updates on the fires in Wyoming.

About an hour later, Holly yelled, "You need to see this!"

"Has something else happened?" Gwynn asked, walking out of the bedroom.

"Yes," Holly replied, sitting on the sofa with her legs tucked up beside her.

The television screen showed a blazing fire consuming trees and shrubs. In the center of the screen was the tail of a small plane engulfed with flames. The reporter talked about the tragic accident that occurred when the plane flew to close to the fire, and its fuel tank exploded from the heat. The pilot, bruised and battered, attempted to rescue the passengers; the heat was too intense, so all he could do was stumble his way out of the burning forest. The pilot believed the passengers might have died on impact when the plane crashed into the trees. The reporter went on to say if they had survived the crash they couldn't have survived the fire. The pilot had been taken to the local hospital. The reporter announced that there were six-hundred-fifty-eight confirmed deaths from the pipeline accident and hundreds in campsites and the backcountry were still unaccounted for. CT was still trying to determine the cause of all the pipeline ruptures.

"You missed the first part of that news report," Holly said. "The reporter said the victims of the accident were new owners of another Wyoming pipeline. They were flying over it when they deviated from their course to survey the destruction caused by CT's Oxbow pipeline." She leaned on the arm of the sofa. "Besides the pilot, there were three passengers in the plane. The reporter didn't give any names of the victims, but how many people have just purchased a pipeline?"

"Could one be Lemus?" Gwynn asked.

"No. He's at Trulin. Bev saw him earlier."

"I wonder if he played a role in that," Gwynn said, mulling over the possibility. "Since that only leaves him in charge of Starling."

"It might just be an accident," Holly said. "Assuming it was the three CT guys, they got what they deserved. At any rate, we don't need to worry about it."

"I need to get back to the report," Gwynn said, moving toward the bedroom.

****

Gwynn had almost completed the report when Holly ordered a pizza.

Twenty minutes later, Holly shouted, "We need to get out of here!"

"Why?" Gwynn yelled from the bedroom.

"I recognize the guy walking down the hallway carrying a pizza, and he isn't alone," Holly said, anxiety audible in her voice. "I'm sending all my files and corrupting this computer's hard drive in case they seize it."

Gwynn opened the balcony door, looking for a way to escape. They were on the third floor and the balconies lined up. She ran into the other room, carrying the laptop. "Hurry, we can climb down the balconies."

A loud bang on the door sent a chill through Gwynn's body.

"Hide," Holly said, tapping rapidly on her keyboard. "I'll stall them."

"But ... but, you need ..." Gwynn stuttered.

"No," Holly interrupted. "Hide. I can take care of this."

Gwynn ran back to the bedroom as the knocking continued. She grabbed her gun and knife from the top of the nightstand and quickly scanned the room, searching for a place to hide. She looked out the balcony door again and saw a black Expedition parked right below. Sucking in air, she hustled into the bathroom, remembering the large cabinet under the sink. She climbed in it, curled her legs tight against her body, and slid the laptop in the space under the bank of drawers, hoping it wouldn't be discovered if they found her. From inside the cabinet she couldn't get the doors to snap shut, so she held them closed with her fingernails around the knob screws.

"Where is she?" a man with a rough voice asked in an angry tone.

"Who?" Holly asked.

"Gwynn Reznick," the man hissed.

Gwynn cringed when she heard commotion and a slapping sound, thinking Holly had been hit.

"She's not here!" Holly yelled.

"Check the bedroom," the rough-voiced man ordered.

Gwynn held her breath as she heard heavy footsteps coming toward her. To her surprise, someone walked right past the cabinet doors she held shut and stepped out of the bathroom.

"She's not here, but the balcony door is wide open," a man with a deep voice said. "I can't see her anywhere out there."

"Where did she go?" the rough-voiced man growled.

"I don't know who you're talking about," Holly insisted.

"You're coming with us."

Gwynn heard a thump followed by muffled voices, scraping and banging sounds, and shuffling of feet. A door slammed shut and silence descended over the suite. She didn't budge from the cabinet for fifteen minutes. Easing out of the confined space, she wished she could go to the police, though she doubted that was still an option. Gwynn suspected the police probably had been led to believe she was the one who had stolen trade secrets from Wilton. Knowing how those involved with Julie's murder operated, she assumed they had set up an elaborate plan if she went to the authorities. She'd either be turned over to them, or meet with an unfortunate accident.

She carried the laptop computer, her gun and knife as she made her way to the other room. The desktop computers and the printer were gone. The counter top and table had been cleared off. Wondering if the perpetrators had left anything behind, Gwynn began searching through the kitchen cabinets and drawers. Tucked in the back corner of the bottom drawer, she found a key ring holding two keys. Picking it up, she thought the keys looked familiar. Upon closer examination, she knew one belonged to a Suburban, like Ruben's. She pushed the "unlock" button on the other key and a light appeared, and realized it was a marker key.

Gwynn got her purse out of the bedroom, dumped out the contents on the table, and rummaged through them, searching for any bugs that might have been planted. Everything seemed in order. No bugs. Still, she ran her fingers over each item thoroughly as she put it back in her purse.

Next, she went through her things in the duffle bag Ruben had given her, pulling out one item at a time, shaking and examining it. Satisfied there weren't any bugs, she stuffed her clothing and toiletries in it. Then she rifled through Holly's clothing in the bedroom drawers and closet, hoping to find Dean's cell phone number or someone else's involved in the investigation. Nothing. Not one piece of paper.

Gwynn strapped the knife to her calf, put the gun in her purse, the laptop in the duffle bag, and went looking for Dean's room. She saw a "Do Not Disturb" sign hanging on room 326, pushed the unlock button on the marker key, shined the light on the doorknob and a red streak appeared. Convinced it was Dean's room, she knocked. No answer. Then she headed toward the parking lot.

From inside the hotel entrance, Gwynn's eyes scanned the cars parked next to the building and those she could see in the parking lot. She didn't spot any black Expeditions or vans that were blue or white vans, but she saw a Suburban in the second row. She made a hasty exit from the security of the lobby.

Reaching the Suburban, she pushed the unlock button on the key. She exhaled a long deep breath when she heard the click of the doors unlocking. She opened the back door and dropped her duffle bag and purse on the seat. Gwynn bent down and peered under the car. Everything looked normal to her. She pulled the hood release lever. Gazing at the motor, nothing appeared unusual, though she doubted she'd be able to recognize a small explosive device even if it was staring her in the face. She slammed the hood shut, climbed into the car, adjusted the seat and mirrors, and held her breath as she turned the key in the ignition.

CHAPTER 29

The engine roared, and she sighed with relief as she drove out of the parking lot. Her first stop was at Wal-Mart. There she purchased a memory stick, a notebook, envelopes, a bandana, a small metal suitcase, and a belt with a large, metal buckle.

Leaving the store, she noticed a white Chevy coupe with a circular emblem in a corner of the front windshield and a yellow, printed card hanging from the rearview mirror. She recalled seeing that car at the hotel. *Were they using a white Chevy now?* Just in case, she decided to drive around before going to her next destination.

She weaved in and out of traffic, maneuvered down several alleyways, and through neighborhoods but couldn't lose the Chevy. After Gwynn executed a left turn onto a busy road, the car was no longer behind her. She stopped for a red light at the intersection and saw the white Chevy approaching from the opposite direction.

Her eyes met the driver's as he whizzed past her. She didn't recognize him. She quickly made a sharp right turn, traveled up and down several streets, pulled into a parking garage, and waited for twenty minutes.

When Gwynn felt confident she had lost the tail, she drove to a public library. Once there, she finished the report, copied it onto the memory stick, printed it, and erased it from the computer. She folded the document and slipped it into a letter-sized envelope. Gwynn didn't know Mrs. VanAusdell's exact address, but she knew Julie's attorney's address. She sealed the envelope and wrote "To Julie Morgan's Grandmother" on it, not revealing her grandmother's name in case it was intercepted. She scribbled a note to Frank Young requesting him to deliver it. She put the envelope and the note in a larger envelope and addressed it. She placed the memory stick in her bra.

Before driving off, she checked in the glove compartment for the tool used to detect tracking devices. Smiling to herself, she pulled it out. After running it over the Suburban, she scooted into the driver's seat and went to her local grocery store; it had a mailbox inside. At the store, she purchased stamps and mailed the envelope.

As she drove away, she felt a crushing weight had been lifted from her shoulders knowing that Mrs. VanAusdell would receive the report even if something happened, and she couldn't deliver it personally. Now she could concentrate on Cromer — the man who killed Julie and most likely was responsible for Ruben's death. Her mind drifted to Holly. She stopped at a convenience store, called the Candlewood Suites from a pay phone, and asked for room 326. Dean answered.

"Where are you?" he asked in a demanding tone.

"Holly's been captured. They came to her room. I was hiding, so I didn't see their faces. There were at least two guys. Maybe more. Only two spoke."

"They didn't get far with her. She's staying at another hotel waiting for Ralph to arrive."

"But … how?" Gwynn asked, squinting, wondering how they knew Holly was in danger.

"I'll explain it after I pick you up."

"No. There's something I need to take care of first."

"Gwynn, it's not safe for you to be alone," Dean said, sounding worried.

"I've taken care of the report. It'll be delivered in the next couple of days." She hung up, thinking Dean might be tracing the call and she didn't want to be found.

Gwynn headed to her final destination for the evening, the YWCA. After parking the car, she secured the gun and knife under the lining of the metal suitcase and laid the laptop inside. She stepped out of the car, put on the belt, and picked up her purse and the suitcase, leaving the duffle bag on the backseat. At ten o'clock she entered the YWCA.

"May I help you?" the receptionist asked.

"Yes," Gwynn said, fidgeting with her hands, her lips quavering.

"Are you okay?" the receptionist asked.

"I'm afraid of my boyfriend," she said with moist eyes. "He hit me." She slightly lifted the bottom of her t-shirt, revealing part of her bandaged side, and rubbed it. "I don't dare go back to my apartment."

"Have you contacted the police?"

"No, not yet. I just need a safe place to stay for tonight so I can figure out what to do."

"We can take care of that," the receptionist said, giving her a comforting smile. "I'll put you in the secure, safe wing. It'll be forty dollars for the night."

As Gwynn reached in her wallet for the money, the receptionist picked up the registration book and placed it on the counter.

"Do I have to register?" Gwynn asked, giving the receptionist the forty dollars as her hand twitched and a few tears trickled down her cheek.

"No one will know you're here," the receptionist assured her.

"But," Gwynn sniffled, chewing nervously on her lower lip.

"Okay. Just register with an X."

"Thank you." She pulled a tissue out of her purse, wiped her eyes, and signed X.

"We don't allow weapons. Do you have any with you?"

"No." She held up the metal suitcase. "I only have my computer."

The receptionist gave her a plastic bag containing a toothbrush, toothpaste, small bottle of shampoo, and a comb. "You're in room 210. Take the left hallway." She raised her hand and pointed in that direction. "At the end is a metal detector manned by one of our guards. After you've been screened, take the elevator to the second floor." She handed her a pamphlet. "A social worker will be here tomorrow morning at nine. Let me know if you'd like an appointment."

"You're so kind. Thank you."

A twenty-five-year old, overweight male security guard with a buzz cut hair sat by the metal detector. He asked Gwynn what was in her suitcase.

"A computer."

"Take it out, place it along with the suitcase and your purse on the conveyor belt," he said.

She bent down, opened the metal suitcase, lifted out her computer, and laid it and her purse on the belt. The suitcase remained standing on the floor. When he finished scanning those items, she walked through the metal detector. It beeped.

"It must be this darn belt." Giving him a coy smile, she removed it and handed it to him, making sure to touch his hand in the process. "Thank you."

"Have you worked here long?" she asked in a flirty tone, her face only a few inches from his.

"I've been here for three years," he smiled.

"Have you ever had to arrest anyone?" she asked, gazing into his eyes.

He slightly backed away from her. "We don't do that," he said. "But I've often had to call the police."

"You certainly look like a person who's capable of handling any problem," she said, gently touching his biceps.

"Well ... aaah ... aaah ... I am," he stuttered.

She placed the suitcase on the moving conveyer belt right before she stepped through the detector, tripping, grabbing his arm. "Oh, I'm so sorry."

"No problem," he said, grinning.

She smiled at him while she eased the computer into the suitcase.

"Will you be staying with us long?" he asked.

"I don't know," she answered, pushing the elevator button. "Will you be here tomorrow morning?"

"My shift ends at four. I'll be back tomorrow night."

The elevator doors opened. "Maybe I'll see you then." Her smile widened as she headed into the elevator.

****

In the morning, Gwynn wrapped the memory stick in the bandana, tied it around her hair, and adjusted it to hide the lump. Her hands trembled as she strapped the knife to her calf again. She briefly closed her eyes and concentrated on her breathing, trying to calm down, knowing what she had planned would require steady nerves. If she survived the day, she'd have plenty of time to mourn and fall apart.

As she drove to her apartment, she worried Dean or Holly would be there waiting. In order to put her scheme in motion, she needed Cromer to find her first. Walking toward the entrance, she scanned the parking lot for other black Suburbans — there weren't any.

When she reached her apartment, she looked for something to wear so the bandana wouldn't look out of place. She found the perfect outfit in the bottom of her closet — a pair of paint-stained baggy sweatpants with a large hole covering one knee and an oversized white T-shirt speckled and smeared with dried paint. Her knife remained strapped to her calf. She stuck the gun in the pocket of the sweats with the T-shirt draping over it, keeping the pistol well hidden. Since she had never carried a weapon before, she hoped they wouldn't search her, and if they did, Cromer would be present.

Within half an hour, she heard a knock on the door and glanced out the peephole. There stood two men she had seen before at the Wilton Tower, and they were dressed in security guard uniforms. They both appeared to have muscular builds. One had a dark complexion with a thin face. The other one was shorter with beady eyes. She secured the chain and slowly opened the door. "Can I help you?"

The beady-eyed man put his foot between the door and the door frame, preventing Gwynn from closing it. "Yes," he said with a low, throaty voice, staring at her. "Luke wants to see you."

"What for?" she asked. "The investigation is over."

"Are you going to come peacefully or don't you care about your friends anymore?" he asked in a harsh tone.

"I care," she said, unhooking the chain.

The men stomped in and closed the door. "Check her," the beady-eyed man ordered the other man.

Fearing her plan was over before it even got started, she held her breath while the taller man frisked her.

He stopped when he touched the knife through her sweatpants. He raised her pant leg. "She has a knife," he said, pulling it out of the sheath.

Gwynn felt relieved he hadn't discovered the gun, but didn't show it.

"Okay, let's go," the beady-eyed man said.

Gwynn picked up her purse.

"Leave it!" the beady-eyed man snapped.

"But I need my apartment key," she said, doubting Cromer planned for her to return.

"You can take your key, but leave the fuckin' purse," he hissed.

CHAPTER 30

The taller man sat beside Gwynn in the backseat of the Expedition, and the beady-eyed man drove. No one said a word for the first twenty minutes.

"We've got a tail," the driver said. He glimpsed at Gwynn through the rear view mirror. "Who's driving the white Chevy?"

Gwynn's eyes opened wider, staring at the back of the man's head. "I don't know," she replied honestly, bewildered.

"I'm losing him," the beady-eyed man said, slamming on the accelerator. The vehicle darted in and out between the cars, almost clipping one. Horns erupted around them as he sped down five side streets.

While Gwynn was being tossed back and forth, she glanced out the back window at every opportunity and saw the Chevy keeping pace.

"That son of a bitch is still with us," the driver snarled, entering the freeway. "Omar, after we exit, shoot the fuckin' tires. That should slow the asshole down."

"Will do," Omar said, drawing his 9mm automatic from the holster under his jacket.

Gwynn held onto her injured side as the Expedition's tires squealed, weaving between lanes. The white Chevy managed to stay close behind them. She spotted another car, a blue Ford, with a circular emblem in the corner of the front windshield and a yellow, printed card hanging from the rearview mirror. Out of the corner of her eye, she kept track of the blue Ford without turning her head.

About ten minutes later, she noticed the blue Ford no longer displayed the yellow, printed card.

When they exited, the blue Ford drove past them, but the white Chevy remained close behind. The Expedition turned down a narrow, deserted road. Omar rolled down his window, aimed his gun, and shot the Chevy's front tires.

The Chevy swerved several times across the road and finally came to a stop next to a gully bordered by large trees and overgrown shrubs.

"We don't need to worry about that asshole anymore, unless he's a fast runner," the beady-eyed driver said, snickering.

No one said another word as Gwynn tried to memorize the route, anticipating driving this way again. Where she was going wouldn't be her final destination if she could successfully execute her scheme.

The Expedition turned down a graveled lane surrounded by woods. At the end of it stood a small house, badly in need of repair with a sagging porch, chipped white paint, and window panes cracked or missing. Two rocking chairs with broken slats were next to the front door.

Omar held onto Gwynn's arm as he led her into the house. The inside looked as dilapidated as the outside with peeling wallpaper, a heavy layer of dust, missing floor boards, and a blackened fireplace with a broken mirror hanging above it. The room was bare except for four chairs that stood in the center.

"Sit down," the beady-eyed man ordered Gwynn, pointing to a chair.

She moved to a different chair and sat down.

The man's face hardened as he glared at her. "Tie her up," he said to Omar, and then he strutted to the door. "I'm going to check on the Chevy. If the asshole is still there, Luke might want to ask him some questions."

Omar tied Gwynn's hands behind her back and securely bound her ankles together. From her prior captivity, she had expected the rope to almost cut off the circulation in her wrists and felt surprised when she realized the binding was rather loose. She thought that Omar might be inexperienced since he didn't seem like he knew what he was doing. She looked out a broken window and saw the tops of several bushes swaying and heard rustling of leaves without a breeze. She wondered who was out there.

Omar sank down in the chair opposite her. His face remained immobile as he stared at her in silence.

"When will Luke be here?" she asked.

"Shortly," he said, removing his pistol from the holster and ejecting the magazine. He loaded it with ammunition, inserted it back into the handgrip, and holstered the weapon.

A car bellowed down the driveway, sending a cloud of dust through the house.

Omar stepped to the door.

A minute later, the stairs creaked from footsteps pounding against them. Then Cromer's large frame appeared in the doorway. He entered followed by a tall, bald, gangly man in his late forties with dark, bulging eyes, carrying a medical bag.

"Where's Alwyn?" Cromer asked.

"He went to get the driver of a car that followed us."

"How far?"

"Just a little past the freeway exit. I shot out the front tires."

Cromer eyed Gwynn up and down. "Why's she dressed like that?"

Omar shrugged his shoulders.

Cromer bent down next to Gwynn and touched a stain on her T-shirt. "Did they make you paint?" he asked with a poker face.

"No. I was cleaning when your men wanted my company."

Cromer turned away from her. "Doc, wait outside until I need you. Omar, I don't want to be disturbed."

Omar nodded and left with Doc.

"You clean your apartment right after your boyfriend dies?" he asked, picking up a chair.

"Yes. It's the only way I can deal with the horror you've caused," she said, bitterly.

He placed a chair down in front of her and sat in it. "You shouldn't have gone to visit Fardown," he said with a trace of malice. "He's having a hard time recuperating because of you."

Gwynn sat silently, not showing any emotion, but she couldn't hide her glowing cheeks.

"Last time we met, your boyfriend and his buddy were across town when I left. How did you manage to get away from Todd?" His eyes riveted over her body. "Was it your charm?"

She peered up at him, meeting his eyes. "Yes," she replied, giving him a fake smile.

"Where is he?"

Did he think Todd could still be alive? "I had to overpower him. He left me no recourse. I took his gun and shot him."

"You know how to handle a Colt .45?"

"Well, of course."

After gazing at her for a moment, he spoke, "Last time we met, you were reluctant to answer my questions. Now you're going to tell me everything before ..."

"Before I join your other victims?" she said bitterly, interrupting him.

Cromer didn't respond as his brows drew together. He adjusted himself in the seat. "Let's see if you're capable of giving accurate answers before I resort to other methods of persuasion. The investigators aren't from Anderson's. I want names."

"First, I want to know what the meeting was about!" she said, raising her voice. "Last time you left before you finished telling me."

"I'm impressed that you're still feisty under the circumstances." He stretched out his legs in front of him. "It was about supply and demand, the cost of crude. A few pipelines just needed a little tweaking."

"Are you responsible for the disaster in Wyoming?" she asked, staring at him, knowing the truth, but wanting to hear his answer.

He scanned her face. "You seem to be under the misguided impression that you're in a position to ask questions. Let me set you straight—you're not," he said in an even tone. "What's the name of the firm?"

"Anderson," she insisted, as she wiggled her hands, trying to loosen the binding a little more. "But now it's over."

"No, it isn't," he said as he flung his hand across her face.

With moist eyes, she jerked her jaw from side to side and stared at the man sitting in front of her. The man she despised.

Cromer pulled a folded sheet of paper out of his blazer pocket. "Several times, including today, we've seen a black Suburban, like your boyfriend's, parked close to the Wilton Tower. We've attempted to trace the license plate, but that's a dead end. The car's always around at quitting time. So if you want your buddy, Cindy, to be safe, don't play games with me. We know a new employee works for the investigation firm. Who is it?" He unfolded the list and held it in front of her face.

She glanced over it and didn't see Bev's name. "I don't know any of those people," she replied, easing one hand out of the rope.

He grasped onto her thigh and squeezed. "Do you think I'm an idiot? Doc, it's time," he yelled.

Gripping the back of the chair and summoning all her strength, she raised her bound feet and kicked him hard in the groin, knocking him backwards. The force of her strike caused her chair to tip over and she landed with a thump five feet away from him. She rolled to her side, pulled the gun out of her pocket, raised the barrel and pointed it at Cromer.

"A pea shooter," he said, stumbling to his feet. His face held no indication he had suffered the slightest discomfort from her strategically placed blow to his body. "I thought you liked .45s." She saw Doc heading their direction, and Omar standing perched in the doorway, watching, and holding his hand under his jacket.

"Who gave you that gun?" Cromer asked. "Was it Alwyn or Omar?"

Without a second thought, she pulled the trigger.

Cromer flinched as the bullet lodged in his thigh and blood oozed through his pants. He yanked the gun away from her as he kicked her leg with his steel-toed boot.

She twitched and moaned and tears ran down her cheeks as the pain surged through her limp.

"Don't shoot her," Cromer yelled to Omar. "I want answers first."

Thinking he might kick her again, she pulled her legs tight against her chest.

Cromer sank down into his seat, laid her weapon on another chair, and tore his pant leg. Doc scurried over, bent down beside him, and examined the wound.

"How did she ..." Omar asked with his pistol drawn.

Cromer interrupted, "Who frisked her?"

"I did. She only had a knife. I took it."

Staring at Gwynn, Cromer's eyes narrowed. "Does Alwyn work for the investigation firm?"

She didn't answer as she lay on the floor wincing in pain, waiting for the poison to circulate through his system.

"It's not much more than a surface wound," Doc said, opening his medical bag.

"My leg can wait," Cromer said. "Work on her."

Doc's mouth curved up as he took a small towel out of his medical bag, spread it on the floor, and laid out medical supplies — tubing, syringes, clamps, surgical instruments, and small bottles containing clear liquid of varying opacity.

"Omar, tie her hands in front so Doc can get to work and make sure she doesn't have any more weapons."

Omar holstered his weapon, yanked Gwynn up, and sat her in a chair. She groaned and stroked her thigh. He frisked her and tied her hands.

Cromer staggered to his feet and fumbled for his gun as he fell to the floor. Blood drizzled from his mouth and nose. "What was in that bullet?" he mumbled, gasping for air.

Doc knelt next to Cromer again and ran his hand over the wound.

"I only wish I could share this moment with Julie," Gwynn hissed, glaring at Cromer and clenching her teeth having forgotten about the pain. "Die, you bastard, die!" Her eyes remained fixed on him as he took his last breath.

"You fuckin' bitch!" Doc yelled, his eyes darkened with rage. He picked up a syringe and filled it with serum from one of the small bottles.

"What the hell?" Omar said as he drew his pistol and shot the bald man called Doc. The man's body crashed to the floor, completely motionless, a puddle of blood forming under it.

Gwynn's eyes popped wide open as she stared at Omar. "Who are you?"

"Not one of Luke's men." He glanced at Doc. "I don't like shooting an unarmed man, but I need to get this place cleaned up before Alwyn returns." He cut the rope around Gwynn's wrists. "You okay?"

She rubbed her thigh. "Yes. Seeing Luke die was all the medicine I needed."

Omar gripped Cromer's legs and dragged him into the adjoining room. Next, he pulled Doc into that room. "Alwyn might be back any minute; I don't want to blow my cover yet," he said, wiping the blood off the floor with Cromer's blazer and Doc's towel. He stuffed the medical supplies back in the bag and threw it along with the blood-soaked blazer and towel into the other room, then went outside.

Gwynn heard the rumble of a car engine and assumed Omar was moving Cromer's car.

A few minutes later he came back in and loosely tied Gwynn's hands behind her back just as a car barreled down the driveway.

Footsteps echoed from the porch. "Luke's not here yet?" Alwyn asked, walking through the door with his slacks and shoes covered in dirt.

"No," Omar replied. "Is the guy in the car?"

"He wasn't there. Neither was the asshole's car. But some bastard driving a blue Ford forced me off the road onto some construction debris. I had to change a fuckin' flat tire. Then I got stuck in a mud hole getting back on the road." Alwyn glanced at Gwynn's face. "Did you slap her?"

"She got mouthy and I couldn't take it any longer," Omar answered. "She hasn't let out a peep since."

"I doubt Luke will mind." Alwyn ran his hand over Gwynn's T-shirt and lingered on her breast as she sat quietly, staring at him. "I'd have a little fun if I knew Luke wouldn't be here for a while." He pulled his cell out of his pocket. "I'll give him a call."

Gwynn held her breath, hoping Cromer's cell was turned off, as she kept her eyes on Alwyn.

"She's secure," he said into his cell.

Gwynn's eyebrows rose. *How could he be talking to Cromer?*

"What time are you going to be here? … Yes … Okay … I'll get back there." Alwyn put his cell back in his pocket. "Luke will be here in about fifteen minutes. He wants me to get back to Wilton and check on something for him." He looked at Gwynn and gave her a sinister smile. "It's too bad. We could've had a real good time."

Alwyn stopped at the door and turned toward Omar. "Luke might not like it if you get too rough with her before he's finished."

"I'm just hoping he gives me an opportunity when he's through," Omar said, staring at Gwynn.

Alwyn laughed as he left.

After Gwynn heard a car drive away, she removed the rope around her hands. "Who did Alwyn talk to?" she asked, rubbing her thigh.

"See for yourself."

An average-sized man in his early forties with ash brown hair and light blue eyes walked through the door.

"Sorry about the tires, Jack," Omar said, untying Gwynn's feet.

"I figured you had to do it," Jack replied.

"Are you one of Ruben's men?" Gwynn asked.

"No," Jack said. "I work for an organization that provides bodyguards. You're my current assignment."

Gwynn knew Ruben's report had recommended hiring a bodyguard for her, but that report was never delivered. "Did Ruben hire you?"

"Something like that," he answered.

Gwynn suspected Ralph had hired him after Ruben's death. "Instead of just following me, why didn't you tell me?"

"I didn't have an opportunity," he said.

"What about the other guy, the one who drives the blue Ford? Does he work with you?"

"Yes, but only when I need him," Jack replied.

"Who's going to drive me back to my apartment?" Gwynn asked as she picked up her gun, flipped on the safety, and put it in her pocket.

"Jack will," Omar replied. "No one will be watching your place. They searched it after we left. Did you leave anything there about the investigation?"

"No, she said, holding onto her thigh, limping toward them."

CHAPTER 31

As soon as Gwynn reached her apartment, she fell onto her bed and sobbed. Tears continued flowing as she showered and longed to be in Ruben's arm. Wanting to deliver the report, she managed to pull herself together. Though she knew Frank Young would deliver it within several days, she was anxious for Mrs. VanAusdell to receive it, ending the investigation. She sat down at her computer and revised the report to include a statement that Luke Cromer was dead without giving any details.

With puffy eyes, she drove to the nearest library with the white Chevy following right behind. Slightly limping, she went into the library and printed the report.

On the way to Mrs. VanAusdell's, she pulled over to the side of the road and stopped. The Chevy coupe did the same. She stepped out of the Suburban and Jack climbed out of his vehicle.

"Is there a problem?" he asked, moving toward her.

She leaned against the back of the Suburban, holding onto her thigh. "I'm planning to deliver a report to one of Ruben's clients. The client might want to be anonymous. I'll be driving on the freeway, but when I exit, could you not follow me?"

"No," he replied firmly. "But don't worry, I'll stay discreet. When you pull into someone's driveway or down a private lane, I'll find a place to stop where you won't be able to see me, and I won't be able to see the client."

"You'll know the client's address," she said in a frustrated tone, casting her eyes down to the ground.

"I won't reveal it."

"But ..."

He interrupted, "Trust me." A hint of a smile crossed his lips. "It won't be a problem."

She knew she'd have a hard time trying to lose him, especially with a blue Ford driving around somewhere close by. "Okay," she reluctantly agreed.

Jack took her arm and helped her get back in the car. "It will be okay," he assured her, closing the door.

Forty-five minutes later, she turned down the tree-lined lane leading to Mrs. VanAusdell's estate and stopped at the wrought iron gate. Whenever she went there with Julie, the gate automatically opened. Now she waited and watched a uniformed guard walk out of the gatehouse.

"May I help you?" he asked.

"I'm Gwynn Reznick, and I'm here to see Mrs. VanAusdell."

He looked at his clipboard. "I don't see your name. Do you have an appointment?"

Gwynn hadn't even thought about calling her first. "No. Can you call her and ask if she'll see me?"

"I'll check with her secretary." He turned around and went back into the gatehouse.

As she waited, Gwynn tapped her fingers on the steering wheel, shifted around in her seat, and stroked her sore leg. Her eyes lit up when she saw the gate opening and the guard emerging from the gatehouse.

"She'll see you," he declared.

"Thank you." She drove past the trees that shielded the house from curious onlookers.

The house was even more elegant than Gwynn remembered. It was a large Neo-Georgian red brick structure with white trim and a semi-circular portico surrounded by rose bushes. A blanket of grass started at the edge of the trees and ran to the rose bushes. Beds of flowers lined the walkways.

Gwynn got out of the car and looked up at the windows on the south corner of the second floor — Julie's room. She had the urge to cry again but held back the tears as she made her way to the front door. It opened before she had a chance to ring the bell.

"Please come in," said a tall, middle-aged butler, dressed in a black uniform.

Gwynn recognized him but couldn't recall his name. She stepped into the bright light-green foyer with a rosewood round table in the center. A large vase filled with long-stem roses sat on it. Against one wall stood a settee, covered in rose upholstery, flanked on each side by ornate small tables. She remembered sitting on the settee each time Julie said goodbye to her grandmother. She heard heavy footsteps quickly moving down the hall, coming her way.

A well-built, tall man wearing navy blue slacks and a sleeveless white undershirt entered the foyer with a holster loosely draped over his shoulder, the gun's handgrip protruding. Behind him was another man buckling up his belt, also carrying a gun. Both men appeared to be in the process of getting dressed.

"Please surrender your weapons," the butler said to Gwynn.

The armed men stared at her as she bent down, pulled the knife out of its sheath, removed the gun from her purse, and handed them to the butler.

"Do you have any other weapons?" the butler politely asked.

"No," Gwynn said, wondering how they knew.

"Would you mind entering the house again?" the butler said.

Gwynn shook her head. "No." She went out the door and walked in over the threshold again.

"All clear," the butler said to the two armed men. One retreated down the hall, but the other one remained fixed in the foyer.

Gwynn had often gone with Julie to her grandmother's. She had never seen any armed men inside the house, but at the same time she had never arrived there with weapons before.

The butler opened an interior door. "Mrs. VanAusdell will see you in the front parlor."

Gwynn went into the parlor and glanced around. It hadn't changed since the last time she was there. An oversized sofa, an ornate coffee table, and an upholstered, padded chair stood in front of the massive fireplace. On one wall, French doors opened to the terrace that ran around half of the house. On the opposite wall was a writing table and in the corner stood a grand piano that Julie had played.

"You're welcome to sit down," he said, gesturing toward the sofa.

She sat down and heard the door close. Her eyes locked on the painting of five-year-old Julie, her mother, and grandmother hanging above the fireplace. Gwynn had often wondered how Julie's mother died, but whenever she asked about her, Julie clammed up. She thought about how much Julie resembled her mother — long blonde hair, big blue eyes, and a warm smile.

Hearing the creaking sound of the door opening, she turned and stood up as she saw Mrs. VanAusdell coming toward her.

"Please sit down," Mrs. VanAusdell said, walking with her cane.

Gwynn eased back down.

Mrs. VanAusdell sat in the chair next to the sofa. "My dear, you don't look well. How are you feeling?"

"I'm not sick," Gwynn replied as she fought to maintain her composure.

Mrs. VanAusdell rose gingerly and moved to the sofa. She took Gwynn's hand. "Your face looks bruised. Have you been in an accident?"

Gwynn touched her cheek. "No. I just need to be careful when I'm cleaning out my closet. My bowling ball fell down."

"Oh, I'm so sorry," Mrs. VanAusdell said in a gentle voice. "Did you have a special reason for your visit today?"

With trembling hands, Gwynn pulled the report out of her purse. "Yes. I wanted to deliver the report of Ruben's investigation." She gave it to Mrs. VanAusdell.

Mrs. VanAusdell's forehead creased as she took the report and laid it down beside her. She lightly touched Gwynn's cheek and caressed her hands. "I've already received Ruben's report."

"But ... but ... how?" Gwynn stuttered.

"I thought you knew," Mrs. VanAusdell said. "Ruben prides himself on his theatrical exits."

Gwynn's eyes squinted as she tried to comprehend. "Ruben's car didn't explode?"

"It exploded," Mrs. VanAusdell confirmed. "But the bomb had been switched to one that was more compatible."

"Is Ruben alive?"

"Yes, my dear, but he did injure his ankle again. This time, Dimitri put his foot in traction, so it could heal properly."

"He's alive," Gwynn said softly with tears trickling down her cheeks.

Mrs. VanAusdell put her arms around Gwynn. "When you see Ruben, tell him I am not pleased that you hadn't been informed. He shouldn't have put you through that with everything else you've had to bear." She pulled a tissue out of a decorative, ceramic box standing on the coffee table and handed it to Gwynn.

Gwynn wiped her eyes, feeling overwhelming joy, knowing Ruben was alive. She inhaled and exhaled slowly, trying to control the excitement surging through her body.

"Ruben told me you were interested in working for his organization. He asked how I felt about that since part of his job had been to keep you safe." Mrs. VanAusdell took Gwynn's hand. "Ruben is a charming, pleasant-looking man, but do you really want to do that type of work or is this just a way to be close to him?"

"Being involved in this investigation has spurred something in me that I didn't know existed. Even when I was scared, I didn't want it to end. I planned on talking to the man who I thought was going to take Ruben's place in the organization about it. Ruben's accident didn't change my mind."

"You were going to talk to Ralph?"

Gwynn nodded and wondered how many of Ruben's guys Mrs. VanAusdell knew.

"During this investigation, Ruben lost a man," Mrs. VanAusdell said sadly. "Some of his investigations aren't very dangerous. There's no guarantee you'd be assigned to those."

"I know it'll be dangerous, but I want the excitement and challenge. I can't return to a regular accounting job." Gwynn knew she no longer needed to work, but a sedentary life without work wouldn't satisfy her, and she thought Mrs. VanAusdell felt the same way. Every time she went with Julie to see her grandmother, her grandmother was always involved with business meetings. She didn't live a life of leisure, even with the wealth she had amassed.

Suddenly, Gwynn recalled what Cromer had said the first time they snatched her. "Luke Cromer told me that before Julie's accident." Gwynn swallowed hard. "She asked him to give you a message. He's one of the ..."

"I know about him."

"She asked him to tell you she was sorry," Gwynn said in a strained voice.

Mrs. VanAusdell's eyes became cloudy, yet she maintained her composure. "Thank you for delivering the message."

Gwynn felt relieved that Mrs. VanAusdell didn't ask her how she obtained the message since she didn't want to tell her she had been kidnapped, and she hadn't mentioned it in the report. She heard a soft knock on the door, turned slightly, and saw Mrs. VanAusdell's secretary, Bradford, step into the room.

The elderly man stood by the door and nodded to Mrs. VanAusdell.

"Bradford, have them shown into the den."

He left, closing the door behind him.

"I have an appointment I need to attend to," Mrs. VanAusdell said as she rose from the sofa. "And I'm sure you're anxious to go to Dimitri's. Tell him to look at your cheek and let him know that I requested it."

Gwynn limped as she walked to the door with Mrs. VanAusdell.

"Is something wrong with your leg?"

"I bumped it on the corner of my nightstand."

Mrs. VanAusdell gave her a suspicious glance. "Have Dimitri look at that, too."

When they reached the foyer, Gwynn said, "You're going to be getting an envelope from Julie's attorney. In case something happened to me, I sent Ruben's report to him, sealed in an envelope, and asked him to deliver it to you."

"You don't need to worry about anything happening to you with Jack around," Mrs. VanAusdell assured her.

"Jack works for you?" Gwynn asked, surprised.

"Yes. Ruben recommended a bodyguard for you."

Bradford walked at a slow pace into the foyer. Mrs. VanAusdell glanced at him and hugged Gwynn again. Gwynn kissed her on the cheek.

"Bradford will call Dimitri's and let them know you're coming," Mrs. VanAusdell said. "I've enjoyed our brief visit. You'll always be welcome here, my dear. Please come and see me again."

"I will."

Mrs. VanAusdell turned and went with Bradford as the Butler opened the front door. He handed Gwynn her weapons while the armed man, now completely dressed in a suit, shirt, and tie, watched from the hallway.

Driving out of Mrs. VanAusdell's private lane, Gwynn saw the white Chevy and smiled. Then she wondered about Mrs. VanAusdell's business since the woman knew organizations like Ruben's, the bodyguards, and Dr. Kozlov's clinic, and she had a tight security system. Gwynn had never asked Julie about her grandmother's business, and Julie had never mentioned it. Now she suspected that business was not one hundred percent legal.

CHAPTER 32

As Gwynn drove on the freeway toward Dr. Kozlov's, she rolled down the windows, felt the wind swirling around her, and sang as loud as she could along with the songs on the radio. The sun was setting when she stopped next to the gate. After depositing her weapons and cell phone with the guard, she proceeded to the house.

Parking the car, she saw Matt standing on the porch. He walked down the stairs and opened her door. "Hello, Gwynn."

"Hello, Matt," she said, swinging her legs out of the car.

"Do you need any help?"

"No. Just got a few bruises. Nothing major. But I'd like to see Ruben before you give me any medical attention."

"He's been anxious to see you ever since he heard you were on your way." Holding onto her arm, Matt led her to the elevator. "Ruben is in room one. I'll be down shortly."

Her leg throbbed and her face ached as the elevator descended, but Ruben consumed all of her thoughts. When the door opened, Gwynn's heart beat faster and a tingling sensation swirled through the pit of her stomach. She took a quick steady breath and limped down the hall.

The door to Ruben's room stood ajar. Gwynn peeked in and saw him sitting up, supported by pillows, with a white sheet lying loosely over his body and his leg raised a foot above the bed in a traction device.

She opened the door wider, smelled the scent of fresh roses emanating from his room, and their eyes met. She couldn't hold back any longer and ran to him, threw her arms around his neck, and brought her lips to his.

His strong arms encircled her, and he pulled her on top of him as they continued kissing. "Have I missed you," he whispered, kissing her neck.

With her sore leg pressed against Ruben the pain intensified, but she refused to move as she felt the warmth of his body seeping through the sheet and his breath skimming her neck. "You're alive! I should be screaming at you for deceiving me like that, but I'm too happy to be mad."

"I'm glad you were able to find your way here," he said, brushing the side of her face with his lips.

"It was a long journey," she said, thinking of everything that had happened to bring her into Ruben's world.

His hand cupped the back of her head, he pushed her closer for easier access to her lips and kissed her passionately, sending her pulse racing and her desire for him soaring.

"I wish I could take off my clothes and climb in bed with you," she said shivering with excitement.

He gazed into her eyes. "So do I. When I heard you were coming, I had them move me to a double, so you'll be staying in here."

Gwynn glanced at the empty bed. "But it won't be the same."

"Maybe I can talk them into pushing the beds closer. That's probably the best I can do under the circumstances."

Matt entered the room. Gwynn quickly jumped off Ruben and stood on the floor. "I didn't mean to interrupt, but Gwynn needs medical attention," he said with an impish grin as he walked toward her.

Gwynn blushed and held Ruben's hand tightly.

Matt ran his fingers over her cheek. "How long ago did this happen?"

She looked at the clock on the wall. "Sometime around noon," she guessed.

"About nine hours ago?" Matt asked, wanting confirmation.

"Yes. Somewhere around then."

"Let me see your leg."

Gwynn pulled down her slacks. A large yellow, pink, black, and blue bump protruded from her thigh.

Matt softly touched it. "I'm going to have Dr. Kozlov look at this. Did it also occur around noon?"

Gwynn nodded.

After Matt took her temperature and blood pressure, he opened a cabinet and brought out a nightshirt. "Put this on," he said, handing it to her. "I'll be back shortly." He closed the door behind him.

"How did that happen?" Ruben asked with his eyes fixed on the injury.

"Luke kicked me after I shot him," she said with a sheepish grin on her face.

A faint smile creased his lips. "I heard you took care of him."

Gwynn changed into the nightshirt, and thought how much nicer it was than a hospital gown. Remembering the antidote, she asked, "Is it okay if I take this off?" pointing to the strip on her leg.

"Yes. It shouldn't be worn for more than a few days and you won't need it anymore."

She sat down on the chair beside Ruben's bed, removed the strip carefully, and laid it on the nightstand. "Why didn't you tell me about the car bomb?" she asked, lowering her eyes to the floor.

He raised her chin, took her hand, and kissed it. "It was hard not telling you, but I had to know how you would handle a situation like that. You came through like a trooper, even with the rough start." He gently squeezed her hand. "I'm proud of you and pleased that you were able to pull the trigger when you were in danger."

Gwynn froze for a minute as she pondered over the shooting. She wanted to tell him the truth—that she had planned to be captured so she could kill Luke, but decided to remain silent. *Since it was a killing for revenge, would Ruben approve?*

"Is something wrong?" he asked.

"No. I was just thinking about my leg."

He leaned over and felt the bump. "I'll have to talk to Omar about that. It was his job to make sure you were safe when Cromer questioned you."

"It wasn't his fault. Luke kicked me because I shot him. I didn't even know Omar worked for you until he shot a man called Doc."

"That was according to plan. Did Cromer slap you before or after he kicked you?"

"Before. But I'm glad Omar didn't interfere. Luke told me Fardown's having a hard time recovering from the surgery because of my visit, and I enjoyed hearing that. Also, if Omar had done anything before Luke was shot, he would've blown his cover."

Ruben rubbed her fingers. "You're right. I've had a hard time being in here and only receiving messages."

She stood and lightly kissed his lips. "I understand. You're used to being in constant contact with your people, and you were probably worried about me, but I've learned to take care of myself." Gwynn gazed at his handsome face. "It was easy with the gun you gave me."

"Where is it?"

"Dr. Kozlov's security guard has it, along with the knife."

"Good. I don't want the bullets falling into the wrong hands. I am curious how you were able to get away with signing an X in the YWCA check-in register. Did you tell them you didn't know how to write?"

"How did you know I was there?"

"I know everywhere you went after you left the Candlewood Suites — Wal-Mart, the library, a grocery store, and finally you ended up at the YWCA."

"How?" she asked, wondering if a tracking device was on the Suburban she hadn't detected.

"I have my ways," he said with a mischievous smile.

She looked into his brown penetrating eyes. "And I have my ways to be able to register with an X, but I didn't tell anyone that I couldn't write."

"Then it's probably pointless to ask how you got the gun and knife through their metal detector, since I know you didn't leave them in the car."

"Yes, it's pointless for you to ask," she said, playfully. "How long …" She abruptly stopped when the door opened.

Dr. Kozlov entered and strode over to Gwynn. "Let me see your leg." She raised the nightshirt, and he ran his hand over the bruised area. "Sit on the bed." He chatted with Ruben while she moved to the bed.

After she was situated on it with her legs dangling over the edge, Dr. Kozlov's attention returned to her. He rubbed and poked the bruised thigh. She clenched her teeth together as the throbbing pain in her leg increased with each movement of his hand.

"This needs to be drained," Dr. Kozlov said, lifting his hand from her leg.

Gwynn cringed, thinking about the pain of a needle being stuck in her sore leg; having it poked was bad enough.

Dr. Kozlov took her hand. "We'll deaden the area first. It won't be painful."

Gwynn sighed, hoping he was right.

"When was the last time you ate?"

"Around one," she replied.

"I want you to have something to eat first. I'll have a sandwich sent in," Dr. Kozlov said as he left.

****

Gwynn ate a sandwich while she watched the news with Ruben for updates about the Wyoming catastrophe. He told her he had been following the story since he arrived at Dimitri's, and he knew about the fate of the three CT guys. They both wondered if Lemus was responsible for their deaths.

The news reporter said that approximately twenty-five percent of the fire caused by CT's pipeline was now under control. The death toll had risen to over one thousand when firefighters were finally able to enter some prior inaccessible campgrounds only to find no survivors. It appeared all the campers had been asleep when the fire engulfed their tents and trailers, just like the victims from the earlier campgrounds. The reporter's voice cracked as he went on to say there were still missing campers. The news station broke for a commercial.

"Do you think the reporter has a loved one missing?" Gwynn asked.

"Maybe. I've seen that reporter all day covering this news story, and the rising death toll appears to be hitting him hard. A large number of the victims are children."

"I wonder what McIntyre thinks of this now."

"He's in Wyoming helping out," Ruben said. "I saw him earlier on the news giving blood and visiting some of the injured in the hospital."

Matt and Dr. Kozlov came into the room with a pushcart filled with medical supplies. Matt gave Gwynn a pill to take and had her stretch out on the bed.

Dr. Kozlov administered the anesthesia, carefully inserting the needle in her leg.

Gwynn was surprised and relieved that it wasn't very painful. She was instructed to close her eyes and felt Matt rubbing cream on her bruised cheek as she drifted off.

****

Opening her eyes, Gwynn saw Ruben with a tray in front of him, eating, and then she noticed their beds were only a foot apart.

He reached over and squeezed her arm. "How are you feeling?"

She trailed her hand over her injured leg and didn't feel any pain or a lump. "Good," she said, sitting up and glancing at the clock. "Is it really almost nine?"

"Yes. Dimitri didn't want anyone to wake you." His face lit up. "You need to see this morning's news report."

"Has something else happened?" she asked, turning toward the television, confused by his happy expression.

A reporter was giving an update about the disaster in Wyoming. The death toll had now increased to over twelve hundred.

"Is that what happened — more people are dead?"

"No," Ruben replied. "That's not it. Let me turn to the local news." He picked up the remote and flicked to another station.

Standing in front of a refinery, the reporter said, "...be missed. He made great strides in a short period of improving the Lark Refinery. The loss of Ethan Lemus is another tragic blow to the oil and gas industry."

Gwynn stared at the television, in shock from what she had just heard.

"It happened last night," Ruben informed her. "You missed the best part."

"What?"

"Pam Simmons perished with Lemus."

She twisted around and looked at him. "How?"

"On the earlier news, the reporter said it was a tragic accident," Ruben said with a sarcastic edge in his voice. "Lemus and Simmons were being chauffeured from Galveston after attending a fundraiser when an oil tanker truck was stopped over the crest of a hill on a sparsely traveled road with a broken axle. The truck driver was standing by the side of the road waiting for a tow truck. Their limousine plowed into the truck. The oil tank exploded, killing them instantly. The chauffeur wasn't wearing a seat belt. He survived by being ejected from the vehicle. He's in the hospital with a broken collarbone and a few burns on his arms from flying debris. The truck driver was unscathed."

Gwynn glowed and grinned. *Mrs. VanAusdell.* "Maybe if Pam had followed McIntyre's decision about Julie, she'd still be alive and so would Julie."

"I knew you'd be pleased that their lives ended abruptly, but their accident was an accident — nothing more." He took her hand and with a solemn expression on his face, winked at her.

Becky brought in a breakfast tray for Gwynn. They continued watching the news about the Wyoming catastrophe while she ate.

After she finished, she moved her tray and Ruben's and slowly eased into his bed. They kissed and held each other close. "I wish I could stay with you," she whispered. "But I need to get out of here so I can anonymously call the police and tell them the location of Taylor and Marilyn's bodies."

"Gordon's taking care of that today," he said, tucking a loose strand of her hair behind her ear.

"Then Cindy will call, and I need to be someplace she can reach me."

He felt heat radiating from her body and released his hold, knowing someone could walk in any minute. "Matt said you could leave after he checked your leg," Ruben said, controlling his breathing. He adjusted his body and hers so her head was lying on his shoulder. "I'll be out of here in a couple of days. My foot will be in a cast, but that won't stop us from celebrating."

Even with his foot in traction, she wanted him now as she leaned up and smothered his lips with another kiss. "Do we have to wait until then?"

He nodded. "This place isn't private, and Dimitri will be upset if I don't leave my foot in his contraption."

"I think we can manage with your foot raised," she said in a flirtatious tone.

"I'm sure we can, but I don't want to take a chance on anyone interrupting us."

She slid her hand under his nightshirt and ran her fingers down his bare chest. "I guess we'll have to wait."

"It won't be long."

"Will Jack be watching me?"

"It might take a few days for all of Cromer's men to realize they're no longer employed. Having Jack keep track of you is a safety precaution. How long will it take you to end your career at Wilton?"

She sat up straight and gave him a big smile. "My boss, Stan, has always treated me nicely, so I should give him a two-week notice. Maybe I could make it shorter. Let me see what he says."

"See what you can work out," Ruben said, pulling her down and kissing her forehead. "I'll make arrangements for your training."

She climbed out of bed, opened her purse, and took out the notepad.

"What are you doing?" he wanted to know.

"I need to send Karlee a note." She placed the notepad on the table. "I'll mail it when I leave."

"Let me see it when you're finished," Ruben said. "Before you mail it, you'll need to spray it to remove fingerprints. I'll have a can delivered to your apartment."

Gwynn wrote:

Dear Karlee,

Everyone responsible for Ian's death has been punished, but not in a court of law.

Ellen

ABOUT THE AUTHOR

Inge-Lise Goss was born in Denmark, raised in Utah and graduated Magna Cum Laude from the University of Utah. She is a Certified Public Accountant and audited oil and gas companies for over twenty years. She now lives in the foothills of Red Rock Canyon with her husband and their dog, Bran, where she spends most of her time in her den writing stories dictated by her muse. When she's not pounding away on the keyboard she can be found reading, rowing, or trying to perfect her golf game, which she fears is a lost cause.

www.Inge-LiseGoss.com

www.ingramcontent.com/pod-product-compliance
Lightning Source LLC
Chambersburg PA
CBHW071303170626
46809CB00001B/334